Toss

TOSS

A NOVEL

BOOMER ESIASON

AND
LOWELL CAUFFIEL

A DUTTON BOOK

DUTTON
Published by the Penguin Group
Penguin Putnam Inc., 375 Hudson Street, New York, New York 10014, U.S.A.
Penguin Books Ltd, 27 Wrights Lane, London W8 5TZ, England
Penguin Books Australia Ltd, Ringwood, Victoria, Australia
Penguin Books Canada Ltd, 10 Alcorn Avenue, Toronto, Ontario, Canada M4V 3B2
Penguin Books (N.Z.) Ltd, 182–190 Wairau Road, Auckland 10, New Zealand

Penguin Books Ltd, Registered Offices: Harmondsworth, Middlesex, England

First published by Dutton, an imprint of Dutton NAL,
a member of Penguin Putnam Inc.

First Printing, October, 1998
10 9 8 7 6 5 4 3 2 1

REGISTERED TRADEMARK—MARCA REGISTRADA

LIBRARY OF CONGRESS CATALOGING-IN-PUBLICATION DATA
Esiason, Boomer.
    Toss : a novel / Boomer Esiason and Lowell Cauffiel.
      p.   cm.
    ISBN 0-525-94429-X
    I. Cauffiel, Lowell.   II. Title.
PS3555.S513T67   1998
813' .54—dc21   98-19247
                                                                    CIP

Printed in the United States of America
Set in Transitional 521

PUBLISHER'S NOTE
This is a work of fiction. Names, characters, places, and incidents either are the products of the authors' imagination or are used fictitiously, and any resemblance to actual persons, living or dead, events, or locales is entirely coincidental.

For Michael Novak

CHAPTER

DeAndre said, "But what's yours is mine. What's mine is yours. We a team, baby. D&D."

He'd tiptoed across the searing sand on his way to the parking lot, but returned strolling, a regular fire walker. That's how Dianese knew he'd burnt her last rock, DeAndre all alone with the pipe in the car.

Dianese said, "You think I come out here just to carry your shit around?"

He grinned. "I'm down whichyou, baby. Day and night. Night and day. The man be on the corner after the sun goes down."

He switched on her Sony. They were at Sunken Meadow State Park, Long Island, DeAndre sprawling out on her blanket now, lighting a Newport. A family ten yards away. Parents telling their little girl to gather up her shovel and bucket, not liking the way DeAndre had cranked up the box, blasting Bobby Brown.

Dianese stood, swatted the sand from her thighs and started to leave.

He grabbed her ankle. "Baby, you walk, you better talk first."

She kicked sand in his face with her free foot, then pulled the other loose.

She said, "*Baby*, that pimp shit don't play with me."

In the parking lot, when she realized that he wasn't coming after her, she kept going. She walked nearly a mile to the ranger booth, then out to the main road, thinking: It was *her* money. Her score. She even bought gas, so DeAndre could use his brother's Escort. DeAndre paid for the park sticker, that's all.

A guy in a new Dodge Ram gave her a lift on the main road. A white guy, maybe sixty, fishing poles in the truck bed. It was five miles to I-495, he said, or eight to the train station in Huntington. He said he could take her only as far as Smith Park. A few miles down the road, she reached across and grabbed his dick, telling him what she could do for him if he took her all the way to the Bronx. He said, no, that was worth only a ride to the Long Island Railroad. She told him to go fuck himself. He pulled into a gas station and told her to get out of his new goddamn Dodge truck.

Walking to the curb, she checked her purse and realized DeAndre had taken her last twenty for Bacardi and two half liters of Coke. He owed her that, too. It was forty-five miles and a half dozen freeways back. She needed cab fare just to get to the trains.

D&D, DeAndre and Dianese. Coming at her with that same old lame line. She'd rather be locked up than go back to the beach. She pulled her spandex top an inch lower, then smoothed her grape beach shorts on her thighs. She was wearing sandals, but that didn't matter. The stroll was in the hips, not the feet.

The black-and-gold Grand Cherokee Limited Edition drove by, slowing, then came back around the block. It pulled up, the electric window humming down.

She leaned in.

"Aren't you a little far from your house?" the guy said. A brother. Shaved head, a pair of Oakleys riding low on his nose.

She glanced over her shoulder, checking out the swept streets, the little gift shops. "No more than you," she said.

The door lock clicked. She slid into the Grand.

Ten minutes later, he pulled up to a dorm building, the signs they passed all saying SUNY or the State University of New York at Stony Brook. She followed him in through a back entrance. The trick had a key for the door. The trick was wearing a gray T-shirt with some numbers across the chest, and black gym shorts that touched his knees. She watched his calf muscles flex into wedges as they climbed the stairs to the second floor. He seemed to be favoring one leg.

In the narrow room with one double bed he said, "I'm going to get some ice." He took a large Ziploc.

Dianese looked around. Perry Ellis slacks in the small closet and two pairs of Italian loafers, tassels with kilties. A half dozen silk shirts, all very GQ. She saw a 19-inch TV, a cable feed and a VCR underneath. A nice box, too, combo CD and tapes, surround speakers. Two shelves of videocassette tapes up high on the wall. On the top shelf, she saw a battered old football helmet, kid's size.

She'd already decided she'd double her rate when the trick came back with the freezer bag full. He plopped on the bed, punched up ESPN, then placed the ice pack under his right knee.

Dianese sat next to him, adjusting her top. "Okay, baby," she said. "Just what kind of party did you have in mind?"

He put a hand in his shorts, touching himself, but looking a little bored. He said, "What's the party store got on sale today?"

"A hundred for straight away. Two hundred for half and half. Anything beyond that, you're talking hourly."

"How much you just to hang?"

"Three hundred an hour," she said, pushing it. "In advance."

The trick reached over to a nightstand, grimacing a little. He peeled off three hundreds from a gold money clip, then his eyes went back to the TV, a beach volleyball game. She put the money away in her purse. Then, the trick got up, fumbled for a while at the shelves, his back to her.

"What's that helmet up there for?" she asked.

"Baby," he said, "that's my good luck charm."

Finally, he pulled a tape and slid it into the VCR. A fuck film, the video picking up right in the middle of a scene, a white chick taking it on her back, her plastic tits straight up, defying gravity.

Dianese pulled down her top. "Check it out, baby," she said. "That ho is skank, and these motherfuckers are real."

She looked him over as he stood over her, pulling off his T-shirt. Maybe thirty, she guessed. He was about six feet tall, but narrow at the waist, small boned, but his chest and shoulders went up like a yield sign, and his muscles were cut under his smooth skin like an anatomy overlay.

She said, "You shave your chest, or you just waitin' to shed your baby skin?"

He gave her another bored look, then sat, his long fingers reaching into the nightstand again. She gave him a half minute, then walked on her knees across the mattress. She reached around his back, putting her hand down his shorts.

"Slow down, girl," he said.

When he turned he had a Bible in his hands, four white lines laid out across the cover. He handed her a rolled-up hundred-dollar bill.

"You just run your clock," the trick said. "Leave the party to me."

She snorted two lines, thinking, and fuck DeAndre. She wished he could see her now.

"You look a little old for a schoolboy," she said, handing back the tubed hundred.

"Feel like one in this motherfucking box," he said. "I'm just here on business."

"Maybe the businessman got something to drink," she said.

The trick put the bill behind his ear and pointed to a small refrigerator. She walked over. She saw two bottles of Gatorade and a six pack of Pepsi. She returned to the bed with a Pepsi and cozied up next to him, lightly touching the sweating can to the bulge in his shorts.

She could feel the cocaine in the back of her throat, some serious shit, not all cut like they sold near her corner out at Hunts Point in the Bronx.

"You got some Bacardi?" she asked. "This kind of party, I need something to take off the edge."

The trick reached into the nightstand again, pulling out a brown plastic bottle. He tapped out four yellow pills into his palm, threw them into his mouth and took her Pepsi and washed them down.

He tapped out four more. "Try these," he said.

She hesitated, her eyes asking what they were.

"Just Percs, baby," he said. "Think of it as Bacardi with a script."

She hesitated, then pinched two from his open hand.

"*Two?*" He laughed. "Shit, girl. I take sixteen a day for my knee."

She swallowed the rest and chased them with Pepsi.

When she put her hand back on his shorts, he was erect, his eyes on the Triple-X flick. It took five minutes to get him off, Dianese giving him the big finish with her mouth.

Afterwards, the trick flipped the TV back to ESPN. She started to get up, but he drew out a couple more lines.

"Like I was saying, don't be in such a hurry. According to the clock, there's still another thirty minutes left to play."

"I've got to go to the bathroom," she said.

"Down the hall," he said.

She still felt amped. "You sure you can't find some rum?"

As she went out the door he was picking up the telephone.

She lingered in the women's room, the place looking like it wasn't being used. At the mirror, she teased her hair a little, then fixed her lipstick, thinking how DeAndre wasn't going to see one fucking dime.

When she came out, the trick was still on the bed. But another guy, a white dude, was slumped against the footboard, a bottle of Bacardi stuck between his legs, but a Bud in his hand. He was watching TV with that same bored look on his face. He was dressed in black, silver and teal balloon pants and a T-shirt like the trick's. He was blond and tanned, but wasn't as well built as the trick. Still, she could see him on the cover of one of those romance books.

"GB says you need some rum," he said. He looked up, smiling, holding up the bottle.

She took it, then heard the door behind her. More big men walking into the room now, two more brothers, and another white guy, stubble on his face. She could smell his sweat.

Dianese knew the rules: At the Point, you don't get into a car alone with more than one john. You don't let a bunch of guys talk you into going out.

The trick asked, "What's your name again?"

"I never told you."

"Everyone," the trick said, "I'd like you to meet '*I Never Told You.*' "

They all laughed. Hard.

"Bimbolina," the white dude at the bed said, pointing to the trick. "Just whack Glamour Boy here upside the head. I do it at least five days a week."

Dianese, still on her feet, looked them over. The others slumped on the floor now, their heads against walls and furniture, watching the beach volleyball. She adjusted her purse over her shoulder. She was feeling pretty fucked up now.

"This a company thing or something?" she asked.

"Yeah, a *thang*," one said. "You could call it that."

They all laughed again.

A brother on the floor turned from the TV, saying, "Hey, baby, be honest now. How much Glamour Boy paying you here to get next to his ugly black ass?"

The trick pointed at him, fire in his eyes. "You better hope you ain't goin' on the block. 'Cause I'm gonna come across the middle on you, my forearm nice and high."

The brother said, "Shit, I'll show you that white light, nigger, the one Irvin talks about. Remember, I put Mike asleep in *our* house. Difference is, Irvin hangs onto the fucking ball."

The trick said. "We will fucking see."

Dianese suddenly saw stars. STARS on the T-shirts. A pointed star on the ankle of the balloon pants. She remembered DeAndre in front of the TV the other night, and put it together.

"Hey, you guys play football," she said. "On TV."

The white guy was reading the *Post* now. He looked up and said, "They only think they do."

One voice in her head told her to book, another to stay, the same one that was saying, fuck DeAndre.

"Check out that bull," somebody said, pointing at the TV, a muscular girl spiking the volleyball over the net.

The trick said beach volleyball was no goddamn sport.

"Hey, she with my agent," another voice said. "I'm straight which-you, Glamour Boy. They ain't working for change on that beach ball tour."

The white dude at the bed handed her a drink, rum and Pepsi, already mixed.

"Sit down, baby," the trick said. "These boys won't bite."

Later, she was leaning back against the headboard, her eyes closed, when she heard a voice close. "You're fine, girl. How much would it cost to get a good long look at you without your top?"

Dianese looked up, the white dude standing over her. He had a roll of bills in his hand.

A brother on the floor said, "No man, a look at her stuff and a dance."

Dianese didn't say anything. She was feeling coy, and very high.

The white dude dropped a hundred on the bed, then another. Two hundred.

"I don't dance."

Three hundred.

"Damn, Glamour Boy," somebody said. "This ho should handle your deal."

Everybody laughed.

The bills started flying, from several directions, some hitting the bed, two landing between her thighs. Her eyes counted eight hundred at least, more than she could make blowing old cock in three nights at the Point.

She scanned their faces, all of them looking at her now, the white dude with a big innocent smile. She squared the bills into a stack, then folded them, stuffing the wad into her shorts.

Dianese popped up on the bed, almost losing her balance on the mushy mattress, then leaped onto a nearby dresser with the mirror.

Somebody shouted, "Sign her."

"I can't dance to volleyball," she said.

The TV switched back to the VCR, the volume louder, a bossa nova playing during an orgy scene.

Fuck it, she thought. She took off her top slowly, then her shorts. In her bikini bottom, they began coming up to her one by one, twenties rolled up in their mouths. She pulled up the elastic, letting them slide the money inside, giving them a peek and a sniff.

More than a thousand now, she figured, then she lost count.

The white dude got up from the floor, saying, "Let me show you motherfuckers how it's done."

He picked her up by the waist and walked her over to a chair. She kicked at the air a little, but was laughing. He sat down, setting her onto his lap, asking her to grind there for another hundred.

She felt like she was floating, not grinding, the Percs really kicking in now. She tried to grab his shoulders, but her hands went over his shoulders as his torso collapsed inwards. She felt his hand thrust into her, then twist.

Later, she would remember trying to kick at him, trying to say every foul word she knew, but her body not doing what her mind wanted.

The white dude picked her up again and tossed her facedown on the bed. The original trick, sitting cross-legged in front of her, bolted off the pillow. She saw hands grab her wrists.

She felt her bikini rip away, her hair pulled back, and then her head.

She would remember thinking about the money, the bills scattered across the floor.

She would remember thinking, D&D. She wouldn't want DeAndre to see her.

Not anymore. Not now.

CHAPTER

 **2**

They circled Manhattan, the pilot pointing out the bridges, the World Trade Center, the Statue of Liberty. Over Queens, the Bell Long Ranger dove five hundred feet and banked hard over the Stardome, the home of the New York Stars. Derek Brody braced himself against the window, looking down.

The pilot said, "See that roof? That roof's got problems. Part of it came down in the snow storm last year. City won't buy 'em a better one for six million. Stars were lucky no fans were in there."

"Must have been during a game," Brody said.

The pilot, about fifty, glanced back, his face framed by headphones and a wraparound mike. He grinned and said, "You know, I think you're going to fit in just fine here."

The chopper leveled, then sped toward the Manhattan skyline. Soon, they were racing low over the East River, the buildings going by like canyon walls. Brody saw balconies on some high rises.

"Those apartments?" he asked.

"That's the Upper East Side. The only place in the world where you can watch beautiful rich women scoop up dog shit on the street."

The pilot's accent, the pilot's attitude, reminded Brody of a couple of Martin Scorsese films.

Brody said, "That's supposed to be a good neighborhood."

"Broadway Joe's old stomping ground. They got a dog ordinance in New York, that's all I'm saying. Dog drops it. You gotta pick it up."

The pilot glanced back. "You got a dog?"

"I don't have time for a dog."

The pilot pulled back on the stick, climbing. "They got radio back in Michigan?"

"Sure," Brody said. "We're hoping to get television one day, too."

"I mean sports talk. People talking sports, twenty-four hours a day. WFAN. Number one in New York. Everybody listens."

"They have something like that in Detroit."

The pilot said, "You should have heard it yesterday afternoon. You know this guy, Franky Carcaterra?"

"Never heard of him."

"Well, he was working you over pretty good. But he's an asshole."

"If he's an asshole, why does everybody listen?"

"We specialize in assholes in New York," the pilot said.

Mike Scanlon, Brody's agent and attorney, was sitting directly across from Brody in the passenger cabin. "Derek, we need to talk," he said. Scanlon turned to the pilot. "Thanks for the tour." Then he swung the cockpit door shut.

His agent looked worried, a condition that appeared to worsen the closer they flew to Midtown. Scanlon, he guessed, would not relax until he saw Brody write his name on an official NFL contract's signature line.

"Derek, you're a good client," Scanlon began. He slapped his hands together and leaned forward. "Other players, I have to put them in harnesses. But you let me deal." Scanlon glanced around, as if to make sure no one was listening. There were only empty seats. "But it's over now, okay? You not only got the twelve million total, we bumped them two on the bonus. Six million just for signing. They already wired it this morning in good faith. You won, okay?"

Brody figured, six million becomes three after taxes. The rest averaged out to about a million a year in take-home pay. But he hadn't held out for the money per se. It was a tone he was trying to set. The more the Stars paid, the more they'd value him, and the sooner he'd be off the bench.

"You did good," Brody said. "I just want to meet with the owner before I sign anything."

Scanlon half smiled. "I'm not worried about formalities. I'm worried about the press conference afterwards. I think we should probably talk about that."

Brody turned to the window again. The skyline was below them now. It wasn't his first trip to New York, but it was his first trip into Manhattan this way. He felt a sense of vindication. This was the way you arrived in this town. The highest-paid rookie in Stars history. Earlier in the year, his Heisman Trophy votes spawned an invitation to the Athletic Club of New York for the trophy ceremony. He'd thrown the invitation out.

"Derek, look at me, okay?"

Brody turned.

"*Now* is where it begins. I'm talking first impressions. Make them good, it will go easier for you—and for me with potential endorsements."

"You heard from Nike?"

"These companies pay for impressions. That's exactly what I'm saying."

"So they gave you an answer."

Scanlon hesitated, then said, "When they don't return your calls, that's an answer."

"Good," Brody said.

"Good?"

"One less distraction," Brody said. "Give me the ball. I'll make all the impressions you need."

Scanlon nodded. "That's right. Get it out here, not at the press conference. Just keep saying that kind of shit to me."

Brody liked Mike Scanlon, though he wasn't what some might consider a classic sports agent. He represented bands, writers, radio personalities and a half dozen pro athletes. The big agencies, Proserve and IMG, had contacted Brody after the Rose Bowl. But Mike Scanlon was family, a cousin. And the bottom line was trust. Scanlon was a facilitator, a peacemaker. Brody had learned one lesson well in ten years of being approached by people trying to do things for him. You pick people carefully, usually ones with the better qualities you might not possess. Plus, Scanlon had a big network. He'd been schooled in New York, then returned to Michigan to launch a career in entertainment law. He was staff counsel for a large concert production company that booked major, international acts. In just a few years, he'd accumulated the kind of high-level contacts most attorneys took entire careers to attain.

Scanlon once explained it: "Most important people want three things. More money. More importance. And good concert seats." When contract negotiations stalled with the Stars, and Brody missed two mini camps, Scanlon used two hot Pearl Jam tickets to ply a Stars staffer for the closely guarded team playbook. Brody memorized it during the holdout and brought it along in his travel bag.

Brody tried to change the subject. "So, you were saying on the plane you had to get back? I was going to buy you dinner tonight."

"I'm closing a multi-show deal with Mr. Las Vegas. He's agreed to do four dates with us over the next two years. I've got to be there when he signs."

"Mr. Las Vegas?"

"Mr. Wayne Newton. He even brings his rain curtain."

Brody gave him a curious look.

"He makes it rain on stage," Scanlon explained. "Uses it when he does 'McArthur's Park.' "

"That was his song?"

Scanlon shook his head. "No, 'Dunkeshane.' That's his. But he covers a lot of tunes. Just parts of them, like he's dropping a record needle in and out of the grooves of famous hits."

"I don't get it," Brody said. "Wet or dry."

"The Wayniacs love it. In their eyes, the man can do no wrong."

Brody nodded. "Maybe I should have stayed in Detroit for the rain curtain. Made the Stars wait another day."

Scanlon shook his head. "No, we pushed the Stars to the limit. Plus, there's an equally important consideration here."

"Okay."

Scanlon held up three fingers. "There's only three kinds of people in the world. People who've seen Wayne Newton and love him. People who've seen Wayne Newton and hate him. And people who've never seen him and don't know what he's like. The last category is your safest bet."

They both laughed.

Scanlon had told him a lot of strange stories about performers and their demanding contracts: A pop singer you couldn't make eye contact with. A Motown diva who had to be furnished with one hundred and fifty paper toilet seat covers for her dressing room john before she went on. The memory got Brody thinking about his own deal. Football had no nonsense like that. It was all performance. He liked the incentive bonuses. Make twenty-five TD passes in a season, and every one after that was worth thirty grand. Improve the New York Stars 3–13 record, and every win over six was another fifty thou. Go to the Super Bowl, pick up a quarter million. And, there was the attendance schedule. The Stars averaged only 33,000 fans in the seats last year. Get the gate up past fifty, get another ten thousand. Sixty to seventy thousand fans, get twenty-five. Sell it out and sock away fifty thousand dollars. *Per game.*

What he didn't like was the boilerplate, the standard language negotiated by the Players Association and the NFL. Section 4b, particularly: "Player will cooperate with the news media . . ." He understood the need to promote and sell tickets. But *cooperate* meant smile as you bent over. He'd never forget the way the Detroit columnists first trashed him at Michigan, then dispensed forgiveness with each victory, saying he'd "matured."

Shit, he thought, he didn't change. They did.

Brody turned to Scanlon again. "Speaking of contracts, maybe I should tell the reporters I have a special clause. Any sportscaster who comes within fifteen feet of me has to wear a condom over his head."

Scanlon blinked rapidly, his face expressionless. "That's it. Get it out. That's exactly what I was talking about. You start out like that in this town, it's not Ann Arbor. Here, the media fucks with people for sport."

"I wore a coat, didn't I?" Brody said. He wore a gray linen jacket, black jeans and a black T-shirt underneath. On his feet, a pair of Airwalks, skateboarder's shoes.

Brody said, "Any other suggestions?"

"You don't go into *any* contract details. They'll ask you, but you stick with generalities: How you're happy to be here and the usual good-time-rock-and-roll crap. You get into the details, you'll distance yourself from fans."

Scanlon paused, then asked, "What do you plan to say about the car crash? You know you're going to get questions."

"I didn't answer them in Michigan. I'm not going to answer them here."

"They're going to be more persistent."

"I don't talk about it. They'll learn."

Scanlon leaned back, sighing. "You seem awfully confident about that."

"That's my system. It's worked so far."

Scanlon looked at him curiously. "You've got a system for reporters?"

Brody pointed to Scanlon's briefcase, saying, "Give me some paper. I'll show you."

A couple seconds later, Brody was drawing a circle. "Okay, this is me," he explained. Around it, he drew six more circles, connecting them all to the one in the middle, like the spokes of a wheel. He labeled the others: COACH. TEAM. FANS. MEDIA. FRONT OFFICE. And finally, WIFE/GIRLFRIEND/FRIENDS.

"That's how it's different for a quarterback," Brody said. "All these circles can threaten your game. 'Don't let the gifts of football take you away from football.' That's how my old man used to put it. That's why I don't really give a shit about the Nike deal. Or the news conference. You focus only on winning. Winning will keep all these other circles in line."

"And if you don't?"

"You become the third most criticized person in town."

"Who's first and second?"

"The head coach or the mayor—depending on who's having a better year."

The chopper hovered over Midtown now, bumping with the turbulence, heat coming off the granite and concrete below. Scanlon's fingers wrapped around each armrest. Brody went with it. He liked the way the city looked, the sun turning windows into glaring mirrors, like it was sending him signals.

Brody said, "You did tell them I wanted to meet with the owner *and* the coach, didn't you?"

Scanlon nodded.

"*Together,*" Brody added.

"They said it was no problem," Scanlon said slowly. The attorney appeared to forget about the bumpy ride. "Derek, we do have a deal with these people, don't we?"

"I just want to talk to the man," Brody said.

"The owner or the coach?"

"The owner. But I want the coach hearing it."

Scanlon laughed nervously. "Talk what, that you're not happy about playing with the Stars?"

"I never said that."

"Your words: 'The Stars are the most fucked up team in the NFL.' "

"You're telling me they're not?"

"They've had a lot of injuries."

"And coaches. Offensive systems. Picks that didn't work out. That's okay. I can deal with that. I kind of like it, in fact."

"So what's the problem?" Scanlon asked, his voice rising. "Derek, we got their money. What the fuck are you doing to me here?"

Brody glanced out the window. The chopper was descending. Brody saw a white circle on top of the building below.

"The Stars already have a starting quarterback," Brody said.

Scanlon strained against his seat belt, looking at him with intense eyes. "Bobby Loeb is not a franchise player. *You* will be a franchise player. *They* believe you will be a franchise player. That's why we got the kind of deal."

Brody didn't respond.

Scanlon read his mind. "Don't tell me you're going to demand you start this year?"

"Demand may be a bit strong," Brody said.

Scanlon blinked three or four times. "Derek, name me a rookie quarterback who's started in this league."

"Rodney Pete when he signed with the Detroit Lions, right out of USC," Brody said. "But, I'm better than Pete."

"But Pete was in training camp, if I recall."

"He missed a few days."

"But not the first preseason game."

"So that makes us about even, doesn't it?" Brody said.

Scanlon leaned back. He took off a pair of small Gucci frames, set them in his lap and rubbed his eyes, a good twenty or thirty seconds. When he put the glasses back on, he folded his hands in his lap and looked at him with that practiced, dispassionate look some attorneys got when they were miffed.

"So what's the owner supposed to say, Derek?" he asked calmly.

"The right words."

"And if he doesn't say the right words?"

Brody said, "Then the Stars will be able to get a new roof."

"What does that have to do with anything?"

"You know," Brody said. "Buy one with the six million we'll have to give back."

CHAPTER

 **3**

Parnell "Papa" Goldman, the owner of the New York Stars, pointed his smoldering bulldog down the long table. "You're saying I've just wired this kid six million dollars," he shouted. "And he still couldn't gct on a goddamn airplane?"

Goldman stuck the pipe back between his teeth, its sterling band glistening on its stem, its smoke wafting over his silver hair. A spectacular view up Park Avenue sprawled behind him. In front sat three team executives and twenty-five feet of rare Brazilian mahogany, the table the centerpiece of the football club's conference room.

Jack Petrus, president and general manager, looked down at a yellow legal pad, his neck turning red. Dominique Goldman, the owner's daughter and vice president of communications, crossed her long legs and gave out a dramatic sigh.

Carl Montan, vice president and director of team personnel, was farther out on the Brazilian plank, but comfortable. He liked watching Dominique push the old man's buttons. He enjoyed seeing the overweight Petrus perspire. Both so predictable. Dominique always playing the future, Petrus hopelessly mired in the past.

The subject of discussion was the Stars number one draft pick, a quarterback, a potential franchise player and training camp holdout.

Petrus finally said, "Papa, his agent assured me that once we wired the bonus, he'd be here."

"Maybe the agent is the goddamn problem," Goldman said. "You dealt with him before?"

Petrus shook his head. "He's new, but competent. In fact, I'd say he's more than competent. It takes guts to hold a player out half the summer."

"And it takes a greedy player," Dominique said.

"Or a confident one," Carl Montan said. "Right, Jack?"

Montan looked over at Petrus. The GM was wearing a narrow clip-on tie and short sleeve dress shirt, the man dated in more ways than one.

Petrus said, "All I can tell you is the agent gets a call from the pick this morning. The pick says he's taking a later flight and wants a one-on-one with the owner before he reports."

Goldman looked at his watch. "Three hours later? Didn't someone explain the drill?"

Dominique said, "I called the agent about the news conference, Papa." She sounded bored.

"So the agent's coming?"

"Landed in LaGuardia a half hour ago," Petrus said.

"Christ, I hope somebody sent a car. They hit the streets with my six million we might not see them for days."

Montan decided to rescue all of them from themselves. "No reason to be alarmed, Papa," he said. He glanced over at Petrus again. "The pick's aware of the news conference. The pick just chose to ignore it. That's the way players are these days."

Montan looked back at the owner. "I've sent the chopper over, Papa. I told the pilot to give them the circle tour."

Goldman puffed a little on the bulldog, then said, "Good. Now maybe we can end this circle jerk."

Montan leaked the story the night before. After four months of negotiation, the Stars and their top draft pick ostensibly had come to terms. The news prompted both new orders and cancellations at the Stars ticket office. Fans were calling the team opinion line, one of Dominique's innovations, with praise or profanity. A press conference was set for the afternoon, called off, then rescheduled. Now, beat reporters were arriving at a nearby briefing room, wiring the lectern for sound. Adding to the day's anxiety were two CPAs. They'd been roaming the front office complex, two floors from the top of the MetLife tower, the forty-first floor. They were conducting an audit of the team's books.

Goldman said, "Well then, goddamnit, I suppose we ought to get V.R. in here. Make him feel involved."

Montan said, "Let me see if he's outside."

He stopped at the glass door to the lobby, momentarily looking at his transparent reflection in the glass. He'd been at camp earlier, and it was Friday, so he'd worn Perry Ellis khakis, Bruno Magli's, and the Stars golf shirt, the colors black and teal with a silver star on the breast. For more formal days, he preferred Italian designers. Jackets and suits by Armani, Corneliaui or Canali. Bulgari watches, he had three. He liked full trousers, tapered and cuffed at the ankle with that Armani break. Going for that Pat Riley look. In his mid fifties, but with it. Ahead of it, in fact.

Vincent Read, or V.R., was in the lobby, waiting as if he were a visitor. It was his first year as head coach, just named in the spring. He hadn't had time to claim an office in the team's headquarters. V.R.'s stomach was pushing the limits of his team shirt, his Docker's wrinkled. His black hair was swept back haphazardly and streaked with gray. He'd been around the league as an assistant as long as turf shoes, two years as the Stars defensive coordinator. Papa Goldman was the first owner to give Vincent Read a shot at the top coaching spot.

V.R. followed Montan inside the conference room and hesitated ten feet from the table, looking as if he didn't know where to sit. He held copies of a scouting summary in both hands.

Goldman said, "V.R., tell me, what do I need to know about this pick? Maybe if I feed the media people first, the rookie won't make trouble for himself out there."

V.R. handed out copies of the summary, the last one going to Dominique Goldman, and V.R. saying, "Here you go, my dear."

She glared as he sat.

"Just give me the goddamn talking points," Papa Goldman continued. "And go easy on that stopwatch crap."

V.R. glanced at his copy, the pick's name set in black bold type across the teal cover. "Okay, Derek Brody, quarterback," he said. "The University of Michigan."

Everyone but Montan opened to the two color photos: Derek Brody head-to-toe in maize and blue gym shorts, one view from the front, another from the back. He was clean shaven, his dark brown hair a half inch from a buzz cut. A barely perceptible scar descended from his hairline, past his right eyebrow, continuing to his jaw. The face expressionless. Stats and summaries made up the rest of the report.

V.R. said, "We took the photos at Michigan. The numbers come from our workout there. As some of you know, he refused to go to the Combine." The Combine was the league rookie camp in Indianapolis where hundreds of potential draftees were probed, tested and timed.

Dominique asked, "Carl, when you talked to him, did he say why? We didn't address that in the press release."

Montan smiled, eyeing her black Zappa jacket and skirt. At twenty-eight, she was the highest-ranking female executive in football, a graduate of Harvard Business School.

Montan said, "He said he didn't go to 'cattle calls.' "

Dominique said, "I don't think we'll quote him on that."

V.R. resumed, "As you already know, Brody was runner-up for the Heisman. By every standard, he should have had the trophy. He did take the Davey O'Brien National Quarterback Award."

"Did Michigan send out promo tapes?" Petrus asked.

"Talent was never the issue," Montan said.

"I thought people go for his sort of story," Goldman said. "Phoenix from the ashes. All that happy crap."

Montan said, "There are also some things people won't forgive."

V.R. said, "Particularly the Mormons. Brody took all those Brigham Young records. He took McMahon's single season efficiency. He took Detmer's season total." Read tapped the scouting report with his finger. "He can throw the football, Papa. He *can* throw the football down the field."

"That's reassuring," Goldman said. "For twelve million total, it's goddamn good to know we've signed a quarterback who will be throwing *down* the goddamn field."

Montan added, "More than three and a half miles down the field, Papa—in a single season."

V.R. continued, "Two hundred. Six-two. That's two inches short of ideal. But the forty in 4.5. Great speed and maneuverability, though he does prefer the pocket. And injury free. Michigan had the biggest offensive line in college football."

Goldman relit his pipe. "That school's awfully goddamn liberal. I know. My socially conscious neighbors, their daughters all want to go there."

"Some call it the People's Republic of Ann Arbor," Montan said. "But the football program is a cash cow."

"I thought there were protests," Dominique said.

Montan said, "You've got to hand it to the Michigan program. When Brody started his sophomore year, the MADD crowd brought in people from all over. They marched in front of the athletic department every Friday. Then the wackos showed up. PETA saying football exploited animals with red meat and leather. Green types saying stadiums squandered earth space. Then he starts winning."

"They stopped?" Goldman asked.

Montan said, "When they couldn't get on the news anymore."

Petrus raised a hand. "Led the school to its second national championship in fifty years, Papa."

Goldman waved his pipe at the GM and turned to Montan. "Carl, tell me something I don't know."

The scouting summary was only a fragment of a larger dossier Montan maintained. He'd accumulated some two hundred pages on Derek Brody. Medical reports. Psychological testing. News clippings. Notes from NFL Security files. Notes from his own sources. Reports from a private investigator. Standard research for most teams, though Montan believed his data exceeded any other personnel department in the league. Montan had computerized every potential rookie and free agent over the last five years. With the average playing career lasting only three, Montan was only a couple of key strokes away from profiles on most of the athletes in the NFL. The software tracked categories: Combine workout. Medical. Character. Stats. Positives. Negatives. Projected Pro Potential. All were considered to produce scores for character, health and physical stature. Those were averaged into another number. The perfect player scored 1.5, the lowest a 1.0. Derek Brody was a 1.5, a score that surprised some when Montan began pushing Brody before the draft.

Montan said, "Well, Papa, as you know, I'm very big on character."

Goldman said, "That's why I've always found it a little curious you've been so high on this young man."

"He got a raw deal."

"And I'm not sure I understand why police charged him."

Montan nodded. "Michigan law. He's in the car with his father, who's also his high school coach. His father's drunk, showing off the kid on a bar crawl the night after they win the state high school championship. Young Brody admits to police he knew that, but he lets his old man drive."

"But he's the goddamn passenger."

"The old man crosses the center line. Plows his pickup into this scholarship student. Smart black kid from Detroit heading up to a college in Marquette, way up there in the Upper Peninsula. Brody's home town is just across the Mackinac Bridge, but the accident is in the adjacent county. Prosecutor there goes after him. Good attorney, Brody might have skated, but he pleads out."

"Some crawl," Dominique said.

"Serious indiscretion by the father," Montan said. "But there's not a whole hell of a lot to do up there but fish, shoot deer and drink. It's a lot like upstate."

He looked back at Papa Goldman. "You can be charged with vehicular manslaughter if you're a passenger. The old man dies of internal injuries. Brody survives." Montan held up the photo. "He didn't get that scar playing ball. The pickup rolled. They were both thrown from the truck."

Dominique interjected. "I did a Nexus search. The subject remains strictly off limits in interviews. We're going to have to work on that."

"So how does he end up at the University of Michigan?" Goldman asked.

"Thirty colleges scout him at the state final. They hold that at the Pontiac Silverdome, where the Lions play. After Brody's charged, nobody's interested. The official story is he got into Michigan academically. He walked on, which took the university's athletic director off the hook."

Goldman said, "Tell me more about the family."

Montan opened his own summary. "The old man was the starting quarterback at Eastern Michigan, decent football team, but largely a teachers school. Mother was a teacher. They met working in a Detroit suburb, then she dies when Brody's six. Lupus. So the old man and the kid head three hundred miles north and he takes a phys ed job at this small high school. Builds his own little football dynasty there."

"Don't tell me he hung a tire in his backyard for practice," Dominique said, looking bored again.

Montan smiled. "He put the kid in front of a TV. The old man worshiped Y.A. Tittle, but he didn't have any Giants game films. So he starts the kid off with Namath videos. And every Sunday, he's getting feeds from all over the league on a big satellite dish. Marino, Elway, Kelly, Young, Montana, the father making a study out of it. When Brody gets to high school, his old man is twice as hard on him as his teammates. He doesn't start him until his junior year. The team played out of a pro set."

"They have a good relationship?" Goldman asked.

"Depends on how you define it."

"What I'm asking, is how about Brody's head?"

V.R. chimed in. "Neck measures only seventeen and a half."

"That's not what I goddamned meant," Goldman snapped.

Montan said, "IQ, 135. Top one percent of his high school class. At Michigan he majored in sports administration and kinesiology. That's what they call the study of athletics, phys ed."

Dominique interrupted. "I think what my father is asking, Carl, concerns his emotional stability. God knows he's always been concerned with that."

Goldman closed his eyes, Dominique pushing buttons again.

Montan continued, businesslike, "Brody took a Millon Multiaxial Inventory as well as the Activity Vector Analysis, the one we use with all the players."

"We're giving two tests now?" Goldman asked.

"Just Brody. I wanted to be thorough. The Millon identifies various personality disorders. The AVA measures various attitudes, insecurities. The AVA takes the guesswork out of coaching. The Millon lets us know if we've got a certified psychopath."

"And?"

"Brody did show slight antisocial tendencies. Made a pretty good bump on the aggressive/sadistic chart. Somewhat compulsive, but not excessively so."

"In English, Carl," Goldman said.

"Your basic slightly maladjusted player who needs to prove something."

"Prove what?"

V.R. said, "It doesn't matter what. We supply that."

Goldman relit his pipe, puffing the bulldog for a few moments. "Very good," he finally said. "But what does NFL Security have to say?"

Montan opened his own file and found the notes he'd jotted at the NFL office on Park Avenue, where NFL Security kept background investigations on college players expected to be taken in the draft. Sometimes, Goldman stopped by Montan's office to leaf through the secret dossiers. The owner seemed to enjoy reading about players' private sins.

Montan said, "No drugs, high school or college. Hasn't drunk since the accident. No babies. No sexual assaults. A couple of minor scrapes at Michigan. One with another player at practice. The other two, strangers, but justified. Single-handedly wasted two guys who'd ripped off a girl's top at a frat party. That's it. Very clean."

"How chivalrous," Dominique said.

"How's he with The Posse?" Goldman asked.

She turned, saying, "God, I hate when you say that."

It was one of Goldman's favorites. The Posse meant not only blacks, but all the ramifications. Lawsuits. Quotas. The EEOC. Unfair labor practices. The Rev. Jesse Jackson's mission to promote black executives in sports.

Montan said, "He likes to play dominoes with the black players. No problems at Michigan."

Goldman asked, "What about women?"

"The league doesn't have anything more than what I've told you."

"Do you?" Dominique asked.

"A few girlfriends. Nothing serious."

"He's starting to sound pretty boring," Dominique said.

Montan tapped his finger on his report. "This kid is pure football. His coaches at Michigan say he plays like a natural and prepares like a coach. He studies game films, scouting reports, offense and defense schemes. He holds off-practice meetings with his receivers and offensive line."

Goldman eyed Brody's photos again, then looked down the table at V.R. "Coach, what kind of promises can I make?"

"Bobby Loeb looked sharp last night," V.R. said. "It's preseason, but it's still a win."

Everyone at the table knew Loeb was the presumed starting quarterback. He'd labored five years as the backup to Eric Smith, the Stars' longtime starter, who'd left football last year after a crippling hit against Detroit.

V.R. gave the league litany anyway. Brody was stepping up to a new level. Brody probably thought he was capable of starting, but that would change when the offensive coordinator dropped the five-inch-thick playbook in his lap. Loeb's time had come, V.R. said.

"Bobby's doing *that* well?" Goldman asked.

"Good enough to put Brody under his wing."

"You think Loeb will work with him?" Petrus asked.

Montan said, "Bobby will be no problem."

Papa Goldman looked at the photo again, then held it up, showing it to everybody. "What you're telling me is that this young man has no problems. With a face like that?"

"Not since his release from prison," Carl Montan said.

CHAPTER

 **4**

There was another New York skyline, the lit city at night. A mural sprawled across the wall behind the receptionist's desk. Underneath: DO YOU WANT TO OWN THIS TOWN? JUST WIN.

They waited for a half hour, a tape playing on the office sound system, radio play-by-play sound bites from past Stars games.

Scanlon said, "We made them wait. Now it's their turn."

In his first few moments after he entered the conference room, Brody got that feeling he had at the start of the Rose Bowl. He was acutely aware of details—the finish on the table, the smell of a pipe, the view up Park Avenue—but he had trouble with the big picture. He felt like he was watching himself, rather than just being there.

Head coach Vincent Read smiled only briefly as they shook hands, then resumed a semi-pissed-off look. Trying to get inside his head already, Brody figured. Coaches did that.

Brody addressed the owner as "Mr. Goldman," but the owner said, "Call me Papa. All the players do."

The owner's silver hair gave him a certain glow, accentuated by bright accessories. The pipe band, a silver tie tack, which was the team's star. Brody noticed a stainless Timex on his wrist when he shook his hand. A multimillionaire with a thirty-dollar watch. Brody thought, okay, what the hell.

After he sat down, Goldman asked, "Where are you staying?"

"Camp," Brody said.

Goldman folded his hands in front of him, resting his arms on the table. "It's going to be awfully quiet out there this weekend." The owner looked at coach Read. "Players don't have to return until when, V.R.?"

"Sunday," he said.

"The league is tampering with the schedule this year," Goldman said. "A preseason game on Thursday. It's already hard enough to get a good crowd." Goldman paused, then asked, "Did you see the game last night?"

Brody said, "It wasn't on Michigan cable."

That was a half truth. He saw it on a DSS dish. Stars 17, Miami 10. Brody watched it after his second practice session in Ann Arbor. Wind sprints. Intervals. Power training. He'd worked out all summer with Michigan players also taken in the draft. Then, in August, the Michigan coaches let him join in the brutal two-a-days in the punishing heat. He'd asked Scanlon not to tell the Stars that. He wanted everyone thinking he was clueless, out of shape. That way, he figured, he'd look twice as good.

Goldman said, "But now you're finally here."

"Yes I am."

Goldman asked, "Have you considered taking a couple of days to see the city?"

"I'm here to play football."

"But you have to give some thought to where you're going to live."

"I figure I'd think about that in camp."

V.R. said, "In my camp, you'll hardly have time to think about taking a shit."

Brody liked what he was hearing. First the stick. If V.R. remained true to form, next he'd offer a carrot.

Goldman smiled, ignoring the coach. "All the more reason to stay in the city this weekend."

The owner picked up the phone and told somebody, "Book Mr. Brody for two nights at the Plaza. Put it on our account."

He hung up and said, "I'm going to have Carl Montan, our director of player personnel, have someone show you around the city."

Brody asked where the hotel was.

V.R. looked at Goldman and said, "Let me handle it." He looked at Brody. "I'll have a car outside."

The carrot, Brody guessed.

They got around to the reason Brody wanted the meeting. He threw the questions out to both men, but Goldman gave the answers. Brody said there was a lot of inaccurate information about him in past news stories, mainly the accident and his short prison term, and that if New York was anything like his early days at Michigan, he didn't want that kind of coverage costing him his shot.

"You'll find we reward players based on what they do, not what they've done," Goldman said.

Brody said, "How about the practice field? I can make an impact right away."

Goldman turned to the head coach. "V.R. is a fair man. We don't play politics here, do we, coach?"

V.R. said, "You'll get your reps."

That's all. But that's all Brody needed. Reps meant he'd run plays in practice with the other quarterbacks. The important thing was, he'd get his hands on the ball.

"So, you think you're ready to contribute?" V.R. asked.

"I plan on dominating," Brody said. He added, "Right away."

"The average rookie thinks that," V.R. said. "But you're the first I've heard come right out and say it. What makes you so damn sure?"

"I'm not your average rookie," Brody said.

★   ★   ★

After he signed the contract, Brody was waiting again, near the door into the news conference, Scanlon, standing next to him. Papa Goldman inside under the lights, making a long introduction, microphones sprouting on top of the lectern.

Goldman called him to the lights.

"Remember what I told you," Scanlon whispered.

Goldman put a Stars cap on his head, the camera motor drives rattling all at once. Office staff, lined up around the back of the room, applauded. In the chairs, hands remained on notebooks and around pens.

Brody told himself he'd say just a few words, take only ten minutes of questions, then get the hell off. He'd learned the drill in college ball. Use the language of color commentators. Stating things so obvious they would be comical in any other setting. Statements like: "I'm here to play football." "I like to throw the football." And, "The Stars can play football." You get *football* in there somewhere, and you were home free.

"I guess the only thing I have to say is that I'm anxious to start football practice," he said. "And I can't think of a better place to play football than in New York."

He paused momentarily. Hands suddenly shot up.

He tried to go around the room for the questions.

What did he think of the Stars?

"They have people who can play football here."

Did he think the holdout would hurt him in camp?

"I've been doing a few pushups."

What about the pro game?

"I've been throwing from a pro formation since high school."

Somebody asked, "What was the holdout about?"

"Money," Brody said.

He pointed quickly to another hand.

"You're coming to a team that hasn't had a winning season in seven years. How do you feel about that?"

"How should I know? I've always been with winners."

"So you're saying the Stars are losers?"

"No, you said it."

After that, he felt the room turn.

"Do you think New York fans will be able to overlook your past?"

"You'll have to ask them."

"Do you expect the MADD people to protest?"

"What I expect has nothing to do with it. They'll do what they want. I'm here to play football. Besides, I don't talk about that."

"Why not?"

Brody quickly located another hand, one in the back row, half curled. He saw a cap pulled down over the guy's eyes.

Brody pointed.

His chin came up. The guy had a Don Johnson stubble.

"You're arguably one of the best passers to ever come out of the college game." The voice was deep and hoarse.

Brody thinking, radio.

"Yet, they did not give you the Heisman. And you didn't even attend the dinner. Talk about that."

Brody thought, talk? Like I'm what, Chatty Fucking Cathy?

"Talk about what?" Brody asked back.

"How you'll probably never be able to live down your past."

"Sounds like you've come up with your own answer," Brody said. He looked the guy over again, his body slumped in a chair, his elbows resting on the top of vacant chairs on both sides. No notebook. A pony tail under the cap.

"So, you're saying you aren't bitter about the Heisman?"

The guy not backing off.

"My goal has always been the National Football League," Brody said. "The Heisman people picked someone who deserved it."

"Disappointed, perhaps?"

"No."

"So you don't feel you deserve it?"

"I didn't say that."

"Dummy me. Then what are you saying?"

The room was quiet now, no hands up. Brody kept his eyes on the guy, thinking for a couple seconds, thinking about what Scanlon had said. Then he thought, fuck it. It came to him, so he went with it.

"If I want a trophy, I can always buy OJ's."

That's when Papa Goldman stepped in front of him, gently pushing him aside.

★   ★   ★

Carl Montan closed the door to his office and took the phone call. It was the team's head trainer, Johnny Josaitus.

"We've got a situation out here," he said.

"At Stony Brook?"

"The dorm," Josaitus said.

Montan listened to the details, his eyes scanning the depth chart on his wall: More than three dozen magnetic cards, lined up in offensive and defensive formations on a large green panel, a line of scrimmage between the two. The names of players were on the cards, and their intensity scores, the cards color coded. Blue meant they were signed, red unsigned, or in the option year.

"I'll be coming in the chopper," Montan said. "Thirty minutes, max."

Montan made a phone call, then took the fire stairs up to the roof.

Ten minutes later, the pilot was flying over Long Island Sound, hugging the northern coast.

They landed at the practice facility, on one of the practice fields at SUNY. A navy blue Crown Vic was parked under the goal post, two men, his most trusted scouts, leaning against the hood, one of them smoking a cigarette. Montan told the pilot to wait.

Montan sat in the back of the Vic, saying nothing as they drove to the dorm. He picked his people as carefully as his players. The scouts were subcontractors, not listed on the team's salaried payroll. The driver was hardly thirty, his Nordic blond hair waxed into a precise flat top. He called him Surfer because when he wasn't working he was riding waves at Montauk Point or the Jersey north shore.

The other was a few years older. Everyone called him the Turk, a name players bestowed on the staff underling who delivered the bad news to players who were cut from the team. "The Turk gonna come see you tomorrow morning, ask you for your playbook." Or, "The Turk gonna catch up to you if you don't get off your ass." The scout hadn't done that since Montan brought him from the expansion team where Montan worked before the Stars. But the name stuck, even though the Turk rarely dealt with roster players anymore. The Turk was from LA. He had olive skin and black, wiry hair. He could pass for a foreign graduate student at universities, not drawing attention, alerting other pro teams. He'd impersonated Greeks, Italians, Mexicans, Puerto Ricans, Albanians, Armenians, Arabs, Israelis. He'd passed for a light-skinned black at the old negro universities. And, the Turk claimed, he could go Pakistani in a pinch.

When they reached the dorm, Montan touched Surfer on the shoulder. "Just drop us off at the back," he said. "Then wait at the loading dock."

The dorm hallway was deserted, the players off to see wives and girlfriends for the long weekend. Montan knocked once on the room door. It opened. He walked past the head trainer, and stopped a foot away from the black girl on the floor.

She was facedown on the carpet, a white sheet pulled up to her shoulders. Her cheek was stained with dried caramel-colored vomit, her mouth slightly open. Her eyes were closed.

Montan tapped her temple with his toe. She didn't move.

"She's gone?" he asked.

"Just messed up," the trainer said.

Johnny Josaitus was sitting on the dresser now, his belly poking out between his belt and shirt, his hand in a bag of Doritos. The players called him Squat.

"Messed up on what?" Montan asked.

"Percs, plus whatever she had before. She's no local."

"That's observant," Montan said.

Squat took one more chip, then closed the Doritos, the bag crackling. He pulled out a capsule of smelling ammonia from his shirt pocket. Still chewing, he said, "You want me to try bringing her around?"

Montan put out a cupped hand. Squat slid off the dresser and dropped it in Montan's palm. Montan slid it into his pants pocket, then pointed toward the door.

"I'll be in my room if you need me," Squat said.

The Turk took the trainer's spot on the dresser, lit a cigarette and reached for an empty Bud can for an ashtray. He looked at the girl, leaning left, then right, studying her from a couple angles.

"Nice fucking tits," the Turk said.

Carl Montan turned toward the room's window, where Reginald Thompson, the team's highest-paid receiver, stood with his arms folded, staring at the parking lot. They called him Reggie, or Glamour Boy, or GB. Everybody had nicknames.

"Glamour Boy," Montan said.

Thompson turned around.

Montan's eyes locked onto his.

"She's just a ho, Carl," Thompson said, shrugging. Trying to look casual about it. "Shit just got out of hand."

Montan asked, "How many of you?"

"A few."

"How few?"

"Three, four, maybe. Maybe more. I don't know. I booked."

"All players?"

Thompson nodded. "It was just a little party, Carl. Like I said, shit just got out of hand."

"I want names."

"*Shit,*" Thompson said, punctuated it with a jerk of his head. He looked back out the window, not so casual now.

Montan walked over, putting both of his hands on his shoulders, turning him around.

"GB," he said. "Have I ever fucked you?"

Thompson's head lowered, his eyes on his feet.

"Look at me." When he had his eyes, he said, "You think about who was here, and when you're done thinking, I'll expect a list."

Thompson nodded.

Montan walked back over to the whore, tapping her head again with his toe. "It's not very smart to bring city people like this out here, Reggie. In fact, it's plain fucking stupid."

"I didn't bring her. She was just walking, man. Near that town up the road."

"Anybody see you?"

"You think I'd have stopped if they did?"

"Who is she?"

"Like I was saying, just a ho. I think she said the Bronx."

"Out here?"

"She said she was at some beach with her boyfriend. She told me they had a fight."

"So where's the pimp?"

"Shit, Carl," Thompson said, whining now. "How the fuck should I know?"

Montan reached down and lifted up the sheet. A spandex top, beach shorts and torn bathing suit were piled next to her. She still had her sandals on. He lifted one of her arms and saw needle tracks.

Montan stood and looked at the Turk. "Call Squat. Tell him I'm sending GB over to his room."

The Turk dropped his cigarette into the Bud can, listening to it sizzle for a moment, then walked toward a cellular phone lying on the dorm room desk. Thompson brushed against him as they passed, the Turk giving no ground.

Thompson stopping a couple feet from Montan. "Carl," he said, "what the fuck we going to do, man?" Whining again.

Montan said, "We are going to do nothing. You are going to go to see Squat. Tell him I said to rub you down."

"What about this ho?"

"She'll be given what she needs and she'll forget all about it. We're all going to forget about it, in fact."

Thompson's eyes looked away. Montan reached out and steered his head back, saying, "I won't be able to do a goddamn thing for you, Glamour Boy, unless this stays between you and me."

"I didn't say anything last time, did I?"

Montan saw a flash of anger in his eyes. He steered him toward the door, then closed it quietly behind him as Glamour Boy walked away.

Montan surveyed the room for a few moments, then said to the Turk, "Get trash bags out of the waste baskets and clean this place up."

He walked over to the nightstand and opened the drawer. He saw a rolled bill, the Bible with white residue and an empty snow seal.

"Dumb fucks," he said.

He picked up the paraphernalia and the Gideon and handed them to the Turk. "Get rid of this shit, too."

They cleaned the entire room. When they were done, Montan kneeled over the whore again. He broke the cap and waved it under her nose. She hardly stirred, a hand coming up, then falling back.

The Turk said, "I better get the Surfer."

Montan looked up, "No, get one of the equipment lockers from the supply room, and a dolly. You can wheel her out."

He stood up, brushing carpet fibers from his trousers.

"You're leaving?" the Turk asked.

"I need to get back to Midtown and prepare for a cap meeting."

The Turk said, "So what you want us to do with the whore?"

"Take care of it."

"Take it where?"

Montan cracked a half smile, a little pleased with himself at the thought. "She brought her bathing suit, didn't she?" he said. "I think it's time she took her swim."

CHAPTER

 **5**

They walked from NYU to the small park on Fourth and Sixth, talking the whole way. He was naming names she didn't know, detailing bad boy stuff he and his former teammates had pulled. Athletes in trouble. Jocks getting favors.

"I guess people suspect things like that go on," Shay Falan said.

"I go public," Eric Smith said, "they'll *know.*"

They found an empty seat in the shadows, the other filled with Village types who congregated in the park on warm nights.

Shay Falan pulled her shoulder-length red hair into a pony tail. "So what's that the program says? Balance, moderation, self-management. All that is behind you now."

"I'm thinking the other one," Eric Smith said.

He twisted off a childproof top on a script bottle with the same fingers that held it, then tossed two small yellow pills into his mouth. He washed it down with a coffee he'd brought from the meeting.

"What other one?" she asked.

"Personal fucking responsibility," he said.

They talked every Friday in the park after their Moderation Management meeting at the university. He'd approached her after group sharing a couple months earlier, told her he liked what she had to say, then asked her to coffee. At the time she was auditioning for a part in a new off-Broadway drama. Young woman plays confidante and confessor to a troubled male lead. She'd considered her chats with Eric character research at first. She didn't get the part, but Eric Smith still sought her advice.

The guy was lonely, that's all. A guy nearly thirty and on a pension, without a single good friend. The night he'd complained about that at a meeting, a couple of the Moderation Management malcontents told him he was full of shit and self-pity. But Shay had seen the same syndrome in theater. It was hard to get close to people outside a celebrated business. Inside, jealousy and arrogance ruled.

Smith took another sip from his foam cup and said, "The way I read it, that's what the program means by making a positive fucking lifestyle change. That's what the fuck it's all about."

He liked the word fuck and its conjugations.

"I'm not sure I can see anything positive about putting your sordid past on every newsstand in the city," Shay said. "In fact, it's destructive."

"I'm thinking one of the networks," Smith said. "They have this new NFL magazine show that's done a lot of investigations."

She thought about what he was saying, the pressure of that kind of scandal. "Isn't there some official you could talk to first?"

"You're talking about NFL security."

"I guess." She didn't know anything about pro football, the game or the league. "Don't they investigate?"

"They prepared the case that threw me out."

"I thought you told me it was an injury."

"I went into the hospital with the compound fracture. The cocaine showed up in the blood screen. Some fucking resident who didn't like the way I played faxed it directly to the commissioner. Hell, I beat league drug screens all year."

"All the more reason."

"For?"

"I'd think if you want people to believe you, you're going to have to come clean with those people first. Otherwise, it's just going to look like sour grapes."

Smith nodded. "You may have a point."

"Have you talked to anybody else about this?" she asked.

Smith shook his head. He pulled out a cigarette and lit it, drawing hard, then flicking an ash that was hardly there.

"You don't put stuff I've got to say on the street," he said. "Not without a little protection."

"Another good reason," she said. She laughed a little. "And you're telling me because you trust me. That's a big leap, especially after what I pulled this week."

He picked up the coffee again. "I just want to be able to kick back and have a few beers, like college. But this shit's been eating at me night and day."

She sighed, looking him over. He had a full beard, badly trimmed. A white T-shirt, a pair of faded balloon pants, scuffed Nikes. She knew he was halfway through his first abstinence period. That was the MM drill. You abstained for thirty days. Worked on the reasons you drank excessively. After that, you were allowed no more than four drinks a day, a maximum of fourteen a week. For women the limit was three and nine, a metabolic adjustment. Neither sex was supposed to drink every day.

Shay Falan never drank every day. Her problem was quantity, not consistency. She'd easily handled three 30-day dry outs in the last year, after which she promptly made up for lost time. Her last little bender had cost her a small, but good, role in an off-Broadway show, a dark comedy. She'd been cast late Tuesday, tried to celebrate with three glasses on Wednesday, but slept until nearly noon Thursday, when the director called her and told her she was fired for missing the first read through. Before the first glass on Wednesday, she'd written down her priorities and examined the reasons why she drank too much, as the MM program instructed. She'd theorized that she binged because she had too much time between voice-overs, trade shows and modeling jobs. She wrote that she drank excessively because, at twenty-eight, she'd gone two years without a decent theater role. If she could stay busy, she'd be okay. On Thursday, she'd found the paper under a drained half gallon of Carlo Rossi red.

"I'm beginning to think it's like trying to convince myself I'm just a little bit pregnant," she said. "Either you are or you aren't."

He asked, "What are you saying?"

"I'm saying I go overboard on everything I like. Maybe this MM thing is not for me."

Smith looked a little shocked. "But they say you can either cut back or go on the wagon entirely. It's your fucking choice."

"Somehow, sitting around a meeting while someone talks about how great it is to drink a glass of wine with dinner doesn't strike me as support. My brain hears that and starts making deals. It says how about we drink nothing for seven days, then drink all seven glasses at once on the eighth day."

Smith hit the cigarette again. "Two more weeks," he said. "I'm buying a six of ice cold Bud. That's what I'm going to do."

"That's four, remember?"

"I'll save two for a couple days later."

He reached into his pocket and produced the script bottle again, tapping out one more pill.

She asked, "What are those for anyway?"

"I'm in fucking pain," he said.

"They don't look like aspirin."

"Percodans."

"Aren't you worried about those?"

"They're ordered by a doctor."

"So is an autopsy," she said.

He downed the Perc, flicked away the smoke and set down the coffee cup. He reached for one of her hands, squeezing it. He looked desperate.

He asked, "So you think I should do this quietly?"

"You've got to ask yourself, am I just doing this to become the center of attention again, or am I really trying to clear my conscience." She was a little surprised at her own insight.

"I'm just trying not to get wasted anymore," he said.

She thought, eating those Percs like Sweet Tarts, how could he even tell?

★   ★   ★

Derek Brody scanned the playbook the head coach handed him after the news conference. Five inches thick, divided into headings: Pass Protections. Running Game. Passing Game. Nickel Offense. Two-minute Offense. Short yardage and Goal Line. Defensive Formations. Defensive Coverages. A couple hundred plays and formations he'd already committed to memory. In the back he saw two sections that weren't in his bootleg copy: Club Policy and Rules. NFL Policy and Rules, including prohibition from nefarious associations.

Brody tossed the book onto the seat and extended his arms across the top of the leather back seat of the car. It was a Cadillac, but not a traditional limo. The traffic was stop and go, the driver listening to the radio, the volume low on the speakers in front.

His eyes watched the Madison Avenue storefronts and the streams of people on the sidewalks. He saw a fire truck ahead, trying to nose its way into Madison as the cars ignored its bellowing siren and horn. He liked the way New York felt. He guessed that when the cameras weren't on, the city would offer anonymity and distance.

Brody said, "My man, the radio."

"Kill it?" the driver asked.

"Is that the local sports rap?"

"Franky Carcaterra in a couple minutes. I'll pipe it back there."

Speaker crackled behind Brody's ears.

"Who is this Carcaterra guy, anyway?" Brody asked. "The Rush Limbaugh of sports?"

"More like what you'd get thirty years after Howard Stern did Roseanne." The driver's eyes smiled in the mirror.

He wheeled the car through a turn. "Hey, if I knew I was picking you up, I'd have brought a big car. Give you some privacy back there."

"I'll get plenty of that tonight," Brody said.

The driver turned, giving him a quick profile. He had heavily moussed black hair, swept straight back. Maybe thirty-five and possibly Italian, or Greek. The nose looked as if it had been broken once.

"First time in New York?"

"More or less. I drove here one summer in high school with friends, but we didn't do much but get caught in a lot of traffic jams."

"You got business tonight?"

"I'm just going to look around. But I'm not sure where to start."

"You say the word, anything you want."

Their eyes met in the rear-view mirror.

"Want as in?"

"Card games. Craps. Dog fight. All very upscale. Very nice places. Very discreet. First class. No rip offs."

"I don't gamble."

"Smart man. Nobody beats the house over the long haul." The driver paused. "How about an escort?"

"You mean a girl?"

"No, a Ford." The driver paused. "I'm talking very high quality."

Brody had seen *Screw* and other sex papers in boxes outside the buildings. He couldn't believe the way they sold it out there on the street, like it was *USA Today.*

Brody said, "I think I'll pass on that, too."

The Caddy's speakers started pumping out power chords and a metal beat. Brody recognized AC/DC's "Ball Breaker."

The bumper music lowered, then a voice shouted, *"Break 'em, baby!"*

The music back up, then down.

"Yeah, baby. Break 'em down."

Brody recognized the voice. "That's him, Carcaterra?" Brody said, leaning forward.

"Like I was saying, number one show in New York."

"Breaking their balls, baby!"

It was the voice from the back row of the news conference.

Within seconds, Carcaterra was playing the sound bite. The question about the Heisman, then his answer: "If I wanted a trophy, I'd buy OJ's."

"Listen to him, will ya?"

He looped it, "I'd buy OJ's" running a half dozen times.

"I guess he's saying he and The Juice have a lot in common. Hey, they both should have done more time."

"Ball Breaker" kicked back in, Carcaterra booming it.

"They dredged up another one, New York. Only the sorry-ass Stars could come up with this guy."

More music.

"We'll be right back with your calls. Don't dummy up on me now."

The driver turned down the volume and said, "I'd like twenty minutes alone in a room with that man. Twenty minutes with a chair, some tape and a drain snake."

He turned around, saying, "Can you believe that fucking guy?"

Brody wondered if the driver even knew who he was. He was thinking about introducing himself when the car swerved to the curb. Brody looked out. He saw horse-drawn carriages across the street and a large fountain. Central Park, he guessed, judging by the street sign. On the other side, a doorman approached.

"This is the Plaza," the driver said. "Years ago, the Stones threw television sets out the windows here."

They got out. Brody looked up at the statuesque hotel, then around, people walking by at a fast clip on the sidewalk. Men in tailored suits with carved-handle umbrellas. Stylish older women. He saw a younger one in platform boots and crisply pressed slacks walking alone. He smiled at her as she passed. He remained in her peripheral vision. She looked preoccupied with something, and pissed off.

The doorman took Brody's bag out of the trunk and disappeared inside.

"You sure I can't interest you in something?" the driver said.

Brody pulled out a five.

"No tip necessary. I'm doing this as a favor for V.R."

"You know Coach Read?" Brody was thinking about those NFL rules in the back of the playbook.

"I know a few players, too."

Brody shoved the bill into his hand anyway and started walking.

The driver shouted, "Hey, so what you gonna do, toss a couple Sonys out the window?"

Halfway up the steps Brody pivoted and said, "Not unless that guy on the radio has a TV show."

★ ★ ★

Carl Montan listened to the thumping blades of the departing chopper as he poured himself a drink, Remy Martin Louis XIII, a hundred a bottle, glowing under the tiny light from his credenza's foldout bar. The only other illumination in the office came through the window, the office's ceiling painted with light from the buildings and streets below.

"Carl," Jack Petrus said.

He was standing at the threshold, documents between his fingers, the hand hanging at his side.

Montan swirled the snifter of cognac twice, took a sip then walked to his large pecan desk and sat down. Montan said, "I was just thinking of you, Jack. I have a case of Beaujolais Nouveau coming over from Georges DuBoeuf on the Concorde. Third Thursday in November, the very day it's released by the French. Can I put you down for a bottle?"

Petrus walked in. "I thought we could talk about Reggie Thompson and the cap," Petrus said. "We can give him the extra million he and his agent want and still not go over."

Montan smiled. "I'd rather talk about the wine."

Petrus stopped at his desk. "Look, we can do it, even with the Brody deal. We know a couple of the older veterans won't make the cut. We replace them with lower-paid rookies." Petrus dropped the paperwork on Montan's desk, next to a small black iron sculpture of a Stars helmet, the star inlaid in sterling. "The figures are all here. I thought you'd be interested in looking them over before we meet formally tomorrow with V.R."

Montan sighed. He knew the drill. The NFL limited total player salaries per team to two-thirds of the league-wide average gross revenue. Thompson was in his third year of his contract. After four, he'd be eligible to negotiate with anyone as a free agent. Thompson's sports agent was trying to renegotiate his current contract for another million a year, starting this season. In return, Thompson would sign a two-year extension and prevent a bidding war for his services with other teams after next year. But Thompson wasn't the game threat he used to be when they acquired him from the San Francisco 49ers, Montan reasoned. He saw the agent's ploy as a desperate attempt to cash in by Thompson in the twilight of his career.

Montan didn't reach for the paperwork. "You know, Jack, you spend way too much time running your ass off on matters that simply could be delegated. You should concentrate on the big picture. I know you've been doing this job for nearly twenty years. But this is a different league. In case you haven't checked, players don't take summer jobs anymore. They're too busy meeting with their CPAs."

He reached inside a humidor and produced a Hoyo de Monterrey double corona, a fifty-dollar Cuban. He bit the cigar gingerly, then removed the severed end from his teeth and placed it in a black iron ashtray, doing it with a certain reverence.

Montan faced the humidor toward Petrus. "Go ahead, Jack," he said. "Help yourself."

Petrus shook his head.

Montan scanned Petrus's bulbous body, letting him know he was looking. A recent physical had revealed two constricted arteries clinging to the GM's heart. Montan knew it, but Petrus didn't know he did. Montan had access to all the medical files of the front office staff.

"Watching your diet I can accept, Jack," he said. "But now you're turning down the best goddamn cigar in the world."

Petrus reached for the humidor, saying, "I'll smoke it later."

Montan closed the lid just in front of his fingers. "A fine cigar should be shared with associates and friends." Montan lit his, then added, "Wouldn't you agree?"

Petrus snapped, "Look, I didn't hang around all fucking night to play games."

Montan liked riling the GM. On the table of organization, Petrus was his superior. But that was only a technicality. He smiled with the Hoyo in his teeth. "Everything's a game, Jack. Everything requires strategy. Football. Managing the men who play it. Finances. League relations. Even the guys who sweep the Stardome after games have a strategy. Would you want any less when it comes to spending Papa's hard-earned receipts?"

Petrus rolled his eyes. "Christ, Carl, it's Saturday night. I should be home with the little woman."

"Which one?"

Petrus glared.

"Sorry," Montan said. "I thought you were talking about one of your whores."

Montan took another draw on the Hoyo, blowing it out slowly, making Petrus wait. Petrus sat down in a leather chair near the wall, shaking his head.

Montan said, "So you'd give our Glamour Boy the million, just like that?"

"He can make trouble for us."

"Only at his own peril. In fact, his career here seems to be getting more perilous by the day."

"I wasn't talking about football."

"Neither was I," Montan said.

Petrus snapped, "Maybe you could say something directly for once."

Montan pulled the cigar from his mouth, examining its ring. "There will be no renegotiation, no extension, for Reginald 'Glamour Boy' Thompson."

"Whose decision was that?"

"Papa's," Montan said.

"Why wasn't I told?"

Montan didn't answer.

Petrus rose from the chair, approaching Montan's desk again. Asking, "That's final from Papa?"

Montan's eyes remained on the Hoyo. "Not even on the table anymore."

"But a lot of players listen to Thompson."

He felt the big man standing over him now. Montan blew on the glowing ash.

"You piss off Glamour Boy now, he could infect the entire team," Petrus said.

Montan faced the humidor toward Petrus again. He opened it and looked up, renewing the cigar offer.

"Now you're concentrating on the big picture," he said.

CHAPTER

6

Brody woke Saturday morning with a headache. No hangover, just a late night among strobes and lasers and smoke. He sat up in Suite 317's king size bed, the first thing on his mind, the same as the last before he fell asleep. Maybe he ought to apologize.

The night turned bizarre not long after he checked in to the Plaza. He asked the desk clerk how much the room was. The clerk said $3,000.

"A week?"

The clerk handed him a stack of phone messages and said, "A night."

The slips were stockbrokers, accountants, insurance salesmen, financial advisors, realtors and just names, none he recognized. He pitched all of them in the trash, thinking, everybody looking for a piece of his six million. He also wondered, how did they all know which hotel to call?

He'd walked around the hotel for a while. Curiosity drew him into a small lingerie store off the lobby called Bellissima, the place hardly bigger than a walk-in closet. Only a half dozen items were hanging behind the clerk, the rest of the merchandise in uniform white boxes tucked into built-in shelves.

The saleswoman smiled. "Sir, we feature Lisi Charmel from France and La Perla from Italy." She was about fifty, her fingers covered with rings.

He asked for the price of a white lace corset hanging behind her. She said it was hand embroidered, and $1,100.

He bought it, just to do it. See how spending that kind of money felt. Afterward, he felt foolish. It felt like nothing, and he was down more than a grand.

Across from the shop, he saw an open area, a restaurant called the Palm Court. Crystal chandeliers and palms in big urns. White chairs and tables. Red carpeting with floral patterns. People eating very quietly while a violinist played classical on a small stage.

The gift-wrapped lingerie in his hand, he walked to the hostess station between two marble pillars and asked to see a menu. He recognized a "Seared Black Angus New York Steak," but wanted to know about a salad with the entree, something called "haricot vert."

The hostess called a waiter over to explain it, the guy sounding like he was from Spain, or maybe Portugal. "It's a type of green," he said. "It's like string beans."

The hostess asked, "Would you like a table, sir?"

Brody looked at the people digging into their dishes in slow, measured movements.

"No thanks," he said.

Back in his room, he called room service and had them send the steak up. The salad tasted pretty good. He ate while he watched a ten o'clock newscast, the sports. They used a couple of the football-talk sound bites, but nothing about OJ. Brody had already decided: He'd simply never answer a question from the radio asshole again.

There was a knock at the door. That's when the night began to turn bizarre. He thought it was room service coming for the empty trays, but he opened to a tall blonde. She walked right past him, going directly to the window, and looked out.

"Not bad," she said. "In the winter, you can see people skating on the Wollman rink from here."

She walked back toward him, stopping three feet away on a Persian rug. She put out her hand. "Hi, I'm Nicky."

Brody shook her hand, but didn't answer.

She laughed, apologetically. "I'm sorry," she said. "I'm here on behalf of the Stars."

She was tall and slender, in her late twenties. Her hair was cut at her jaw line, parted on one side, the other tucked behind her ear. She was entirely in black. Black platform boots with clasps and laces. Black tights. A black skirt, six inches above the knee. A black spandex top. She had cobalt eyes. The black made her skin and hair radiate.

Brody asked, "You're from *where?*"

"Long Island," she said. "But don't hold it against me."

She took his hand, pulling him over to the window, pointing down. "I've got a car down there waiting for us."

Brody saw a long black limo, maybe the other one the driver was talking about earlier. Maybe the driver had recognized him and sent somebody.

Brody pointed at the car. "You work for that guy?"

She looked at him curiously. "I left a message with the hotel service. You didn't get it? I guess I am running a little late."

She sounded businesslike.

"I must have missed it," Brody said.

"But you didn't miss *me*. I'm here to give you the night tour."

He remembered what the owner said, about having someone show him the city, but this couldn't be that. Now he wasn't thinking about New York. He was thinking about that corset he'd bought, seeing her in it.

He looked at his watch. It was after eleven. "Won't places be closing soon?"

This girl Nicky said, "Not the place *I* have in mind."

She talked nonstop on the way over to a place called Club USA, pointing out buildings and museums and stores. He'd tried to talk *with* her at the club. He tried to talk about football, but the deafening volume turned him into a mime. She probably didn't give a shit about football anyway, he figured, especially when she insisted he see the USA's VIP room. The VIP room had a bondage and fetish theme, Nicky pointing out the accessories in that same tone she had while showing him the sights. He asked her to dance. She danced with her eyes closed, like she had a special connection with herself and the music.

The way he was now remembering it, he'd decided to skip the talking stage in the limo on the way back to the hotel. He'd kissed her, and she went with it. Then, in front of the Plaza, he said, "You're coming in, right?"

And that's when she said, "What, you think I'm some kind of whore?"

"Aren't you?"

And then this Nicky reaching into her small black purse and slapping her business card on his leg. DOMINIQUE GOLDMAN. VICE PRESIDENT OF COMMUNICATIONS. An address in MetLife, car and office phone, and a page number.

"You related to the owner?"

"Call me when you get up," she said.

Then she pushed him out of the car.

★   ★   ★

First thing, Brody rolled over and picked up the telephone. He called the Stars switchboard. He identified himself and chatted with one of the season ticket sales people, the saleswoman thanking him for twenty hours of overtime.

"A lot of new customers and a lot of old ones," she said.

"You mean I'm selling tickets?"

"And causing cancellations," she said. "Right now it's running about half and half."

He got it out of her in a roundabout way, the saleswoman saying, sure, Dominique Goldman was the owner's daughter.

"But she goes by Nicky."

"No, Dominique. She insists."

He decided to call her after he stepped out of the shower, but she came in right behind the room service with the black coffee and a bagel. Not in black, but tan shorts and a Stars golf shirt, bobby socks and Nikes.

"You need to get dressed," she said. "You have a schedule today."

He cinched the towel tighter. "I was going to look for an apartment."

She glanced at her watch. "The realtor is expecting us in fifteen minutes."

He asked, "What exactly do you do for the Stars?"

She looked bored. "I set up your press conference. I was there, but you were apparently occupied. I'm doing this as a favor for Carl. You've met Carl, haven't you? You want to know more, read the media guide."

He'd met Carl Montan in Ann Arbor, after he decided not to show at the Combine.

"First the realtor, then a Mercedes dealership on Long Island," she continued. "Carl's arranged a free car for you for the season."

"What do I have to do?" he said.

"Shake a few hands," she said. "Drive it away."

He reached for his coffee. He was used to people whose main duty seemed to be making his life comfortable. There must have been three or four dozen in school, young women, mostly, some sent by athletic directors, others volunteering on their own. They brought meals, tutored him for classes and washed his laundry. Dominique Goldman was quite a step up. But what the hell, he figured. This was the NFL.

She said, "You should thank Carl personally. He's very good to the players, but he gets a little offended when they don't respond in kind."

He offered her coffee.

She declined, saying, "The realtor, Mr. Brody."

Mr. Brody, now. "Call me Derek. I won't call you Nicky."

She said nothing, bored again. He poured a second cup anyway, carrying both of them over to the window. He motioned with one cup to the northeast. At a high rise in the distance, well above the tree line of Central Park.

"See that building," he said. "Those apartments?"

She lingered near the door momentarily, then walked over and looked out.

"I see a hundred buildings," she said.

"That tall one," he said. "I know it's near the river. I saw it from the helicopter."

"That's the Lucerne," she said. "Seventy-ninth and First. Maybe fifteen thousand a month. That's the Upper East Side."

"That's the one I like," Brody said.

"That's exactly where we're going," she said. "I've got a car waiting outside."

"The same one you brought last night," he said, grinning.

Her eyes were dead.

Fuck her, he decided. She'd sandbagged him. No apology required.

★   ★   ★

The priest wiped the gold chalice at the main altar, the host already served. At the 51st Street entrance, a bridal party was arriving. The first of five weddings that day, the usher said. St. Patrick's Cathedral,

Saturday morning. Carl Montan was halfway back, row sixty of 128 pews, trying to ignore dozens of noisy tourists meandering in the side aisles.

The man in the creased khakis and royal-blue golf shirt entered at the 50th Street entrance. He had a flat stomach and well-tanned arms, his highlighted brown hair swept back in a pompadour and sprayed.

Montan waited for the man to locate him, his eyes returning to the Mass, but not looking directly at the altar. That was too far away. He watched on a TV monitor bolted to a pillar. A half dozen people sat several rows ahead of him, Catholics waiting for confession behind the door near the Holy Face of Our Lord shrine, the parish priest doing brisk business inside.

When Raymond Bullard crossed the main aisle, he dropped to one knee and blessed himself. A few seconds later he slid into Montan's pew.

Montan said, "That's the first time I've seen you on your knees." Montan had a hymnal in his lap.

"I'm not Catholic, but I know the moves," Bullard whispered. "Jesus fucking Christ, Carl, couldn't you have picked someplace less public?"

Montan's eyes remained straight ahead. "Raymond, nobody in here cares who you are or what you do. But they soon may. This is my parish. Show a little respect, please."

Montan was still observing the Mass's protocol. He stood as the priest gave his final blessing, his voice echoing, "Go in peace."

Bullard said, "I'll meet you outside."

Montan sat back down, shelved the hymnal in the back of the pew and looked up. "Raymond," he said. "Sit down."

Bullard turned around, looking at the cathedral's main entrance. An usher was opening the doors, preparing for the wedding. A hot breeze blew in off Fifth Avenue. The Mass over, the chatter of tourists rose.

Bullard sat.

Montan said, "Tell me, when you were with the strike force were you this agitated when you were under?"

"Undercover wasn't my line."

"I thought NFL Security was one of those retirement jobs," Montan said. "A way to augment that fat federal pension."

"With the Stars it isn't, and that pension isn't that fat. Not with what you spend in this town to eat, sleep and shit."

"Apparently not," Montan said, turning now, giving the NFL security rep his eyes.

"Let's get this over with," Bullard said. "It's a blast furnace in here." Sweat had cracked a fissure in the sweep of hair over his forehead.

Montan said, "You'd think you could deal with it, ten years in the desert."

"Only five in Vegas, Carl."

"But I'd think you'd have to maintain your composure with Tony the Ant and all his goons running around on The Strip."

"Like I said, I was never under."

Montan looked directly at him. "You know, I knew some people in that town in the Seventies. Everybody knew Spilotro was the muscle behind the outlaw line. But I never heard your name."

"Tony knew I was there," Bullard said. "Before he got fucking whacked, he was doing the surveillance—on us."

Montan put his finger to his lips.

Bullard continued, quieter. "We hit the Ant's house with a warrant in '78. We find copies of our own fricking reports. The guy has *our* list of snitches. He has grand jury transcripts. Turns out Spilotro has somebody in the Vegas PD, a cop feeding him the whole ball of wax."

Montan squared his body toward Bullard, resting his elbow on the top of the pew. "So tell me, Raymond. Just what kind of wax are you peddling today?"

The pipe organ roared into Mendelssohn's "Bridal March." Bullard glanced over his shoulder, a bride starting a fifty-yard walk up the center aisle. When he looked back, Montan hadn't moved his eyes.

"This isn't nickel and dime," Bullard said. He glanced at the bride again.

"Let me be the judge of that."

Bullard leaned closer. "Eric Smith called me last night."

"How's our former starting quarterback doing? Has he learned to walk yet?"

"Like I said, it was a phone call. But he says he's on the wagon. A couple of weeks."

"That's some accomplishment."

"That's where it gets a little waxy."

Montan said, "Eric's marginal football career is over. He'll be steering one of those walkers with wheels down Eighth Avenue at our age."

"He wants to talk," Bullard said. "Officially."

"So he's ready to officially acknowledge all the shit he put up his nose? Or does he want to talk about some of his associations off the field?"

"Not exactly."

Montan waited.

"He's in some kind of group. They teach people to drink in moderation."

"Eric has never done anything in moderation."

"He was using all these buzz words, that happy self help crap you hear on *Oprah*. He says he has to take responsibility for all his actions. Purge his conscience. All that."

Montan pointed at the small door in the Holy Face shrine. "Bring him next Saturday. They do that here, too."

Bullard looked at him blankly.

Montan said, "I'd like to see it. Player files a complaint against himself."

"He wants to file one against the front office," Bullard said.

"For what? Against who?"

"You," Bullard said. He paused. "He says he's making positive steps toward a lifestyle change."

Montan looked back at the altar, shaking his head. He put his fingertips together, touching them to his lips.

"Has he talked to anybody else?"

"I don't think so"

"*Think* isn't good enough, Raymond."

"I told him these matters were best handled by the league. I told him I thought we should talk it over face to face. In the meantime, keep his mouth shut."

Montan said, "Three drug suspensions in seven years. Nobody would believe him anyway. He's a fiend, and a drunk. Even *Sixty Minutes* wouldn't touch him."

Bullard said, "That's the problem. He said he'd thought of that first. He may not stop with the league."

Montan heard something in the outer aisle, ten feet away. A Korean family at the Holy Face of Jesus, the dad in dress shoes and shorts igniting the splints used to light holy candles. Montan watched the slant give the burning splints to his two kids, the kids waving them around now, like sparklers.

He stood and walked over, snatched the splints from the kids and carefully lit two candles, the old man just watching.

"You speak English?"

The slant shook his head.

"When you learn, maybe you'll understand that I've just lit two sacred candles for you in *my* church. In the meantime, you can find that fat Zen fuck with the lotus flower in the junk stores up on Seventh."

The slant grabbed the children's hands and walked, not liking what he was seeing.

Montan sat back down, exhaled and turned to Bullard. "Raymond, you need to have a good talk with Eric."

Bullard said nothing.

Montan reached into the lapel pocket of his linen *Vestimenta* and set an envelope between them on the varnished pew.

"Placate him," Montan said.

Bullard glanced at the envelope, saying, "I don't do drops."

Montan looked. "Like I said, I take care of *my* people. Eric Smith is no longer among them. But you are."

Bullard slid the envelope into his trouser pocket.

The wedding party was at the altar now, the couple exchanging vows.

"You know those kids up there?" Bullard asked.

Montan shook his head.

Bullard stood up. "You're sticking around?"

Montan remained seated.

"I'm waiting for confession," he said. "I haven't been a very good Catholic this week."

★   ★   ★

Brody expected to see a sign out front of the Mercedes dealership announcing he'd be signing autographs. There was nothing, and only a few people in the lobby.

Inside, the dealer shook his hand, asked him a few general football questions, then said, "Things go well for you, Derek, you remember me. That's all I ask."

"Count on it," Brody said.

Scanlon had been telling him for weeks that there would be little advertising interest. Not only the shoe and deodorant people, a gig extended to only a handful of superstars, but the regional companies, where emerging or journeyman players made decent money selling tires and cell phones on local TV.

"It's not just the prison thing," Scanlon had said. "They're looking for a certain type of personality, and, frankly, if you want it, you're going to have to work on that."

Scanlon suggested he hire a personal media rep in New York, someone who could turn his past in his favor, like Ron LeFlore did with the Detroit Tigers. LeFlore signed with the Tigers in the 1970s after playing prison ball. Scanlon said Brody needed a handler to spin that story. Top high school prospect involved in fatal, learns his lesson and turns his life around.

"That's bullshit," Brody said. "I'll do all my spinning on the ball."

The car was a Mercedes-Benz 600 SL, the color red. Brody sat in the two-seat roadster, feeling the leather steering wheel while the owner of the dealership went over the goods. Built-in cellular. Bose sound. Six CD changer. Climate control. V–12 engine, forty-eight valves, 389 horsepower. Zero to sixty in 5.2. Top speed, 155. The convertible top disappeared behind the seat.

"And it's safe," the dealer said. "Side airbags and more."

Brody wondered about the more.

"It's got ESP. Electronic Stability Program. It will automatically apply a brake to one wheel, correct itself, if you start to lose control."

The dealer stepped back. "We installed LoJack. It gets stolen, we can locate and recover it anywhere within three hundred miles." He pointed to a gas pump at the back of the dealership. "I'm throwing in a full tank, too."

Brody looked up at Dominique, who was standing with arms folded outside the car, looking bored again. He wondered if she practiced it in the mirror.

"C'mon," he said. "Let me give you a ride back."

She dismissed her driver and slid into the seat. Brody put the Benz 600 in gear and darted to the pump, Dominique still strapping herself in. A guy in a mechanic's uniform shuffled out and stuck the nozzle in the tank, a Camel dangling from his lips.

While the pump ran he walked up.

"So, you're Brody," he said.

Brody nodded.

"You think you can help the Stars?"

Brody said, "I've been in New York two days and I haven't touched a football yet."

The guy stepped back, the smoke dangling. "Nice car. Nice color."

Brody didn't like the color. Base price: $123,000. But what the hell, it was free.

The guy continued, "You know, I don't get it. I've been trying to beat the spread on the Stars for ten fucking years. I take them with ten, they don't cover. I bet them to go in the tank, they go the other way. Worst team on the board."

"Not the kind of team you want to take your kids to see," Brody said. "You could get arrested for child abuse."

The guy didn't laugh.

"That's what I don't get," he said. "Stars do nothing but cost me fucking money. You don't even touch the football, and you get a Mercedes 600."

When they drove away, Dominique said, "You should have that asshole bounced. I've seen players go nuclear for far less."

Brody looked at her, her hair straight back in the wind, her face as emotionless as a hood ornament.

"But the guy was right," he said.

★   ★   ★

On the drive back, he talked her into having dinner with him at the Plaza. He didn't know why. Just something to do. He led her to the Oyster Bar, a restaurant on the lower level he saw earlier. Dark wood everywhere, aging seascapes.

They sat.

"God," she said. "This place reminds me of my father. Everything so . . . *heavy*."

"Derek Brody?"

He looked up and saw the man in the pompadour and cleanly pressed slacks standing inches from the table, his hand out.

"I'm Raymond Bullard. From NFL Security."

Brody looked at Dominique, then back at the guy. She got up, just like that, saying, "Maybe I'll see you at camp."

And she was gone.

Bullard sat down before he was invited, called the waiter over and ordered a Maker's Mark on the rocks, taking his time doing it. Brody ordered nothing. He wasn't thirsty, or hungry. Not now.

Brody said, "What's this about?"

"So, tell me," Bullard said. "What did you do last night?"

"What the fuck business is that of yours?"

"Don't get so testy." He picked up a menu, glancing at it. "I think I'm going to order some oysters. Want some?"

Brody shook his head.

Bullard called the waiter back over and added the oysters to the order. He reached across the table for a wine carafe filled with party mix, pouring a mound of little fish crackers and tiny pretzels in his hand.

Chewing, he said, "Look, I'm just trying to break the ice. I heard you got in last night."

"You don't call first?"

"My line of work, you don't leave a lot of paper around."

"I don't like people parachuting into my life."

"Better get used to it," Bullard said.

The bourbon came. Bullard took a healthy gulp and asked, "You sure I can't buy you a beer?"

Brody shook his head again.

"I'm here because the league requires it. The league requires that every NFL rookie hear what I'm about to tell you—before you start camp. It's for your protection, really."

Brody said, "You must have worked for the government at one time."

"Justice Department, actually. How did you know?"

"People in Michigan say that," Brody said. "They say their troubles usually start when some guy shows up with a version of that line."

Bullard drank again. "And what line is that?"

"I'm from the government and I'm here to help."

Bullard leaned forward, putting both elbows on the table. "Look, son, you can listen and do yourself some good. You've been, shall I say, *inside*. So I'm banking that wised you up. Or, you can choose to blow me off like other players have. I'd like to tell you how to reach them, but some of them can't afford a telephone anymore."

Law enforcement, Brody thought. The deputy warden of the Huron Valley Men's Correctional Facility used to talk that way, always pre-

senting choices. Making you think you really had one in a place everyone called The Valley.

Brody said, "You buy me a Coke, maybe we can start over."

After a mug arrived, Bullard began, sounding like he was giving a
speech he'd made a hundred times. "The National Football League
is the parent organization of what remains the most popular game
in America today. But because of that popularity and the 2.1 billion
dollars generated annually by teams—that's only the legit money—
football attracts an array of dark forces, most of them motivated by
greed."

Brody said, "I know about gambling. I've heard the rules."

"That's only one aspect. Gambling has many faces. Tossing a game
is virtually nonexistent in the NFL. Even the outlaw operations have
to preserve the integrity of the line. The influence is far more subtle.
People will seek you out not only because of your status, but because
of what you know. There's always a risk of players and personnel passing team information to known gamblers, oddsmakers, bookies, shy-
locks, sharks. You name it. And this town is the world capital of that
crowd."

Brody asked, "So what do you expect from me?"

"We expect you not to associate with people involved in sports betting. We expect you to steer clear of any suspicious individuals. We
expect you to report any contacts or attempted contacts to my office.
Specifically, me. The Stars are mine. There's a rep assigned to every
team."

Bullard took another sip of Bourbon. "As for yourself, you, of course,
are prohibited from gambling on professional football. Even at the Vegas sports books. In fact, we *suggest* you avoid gambling of any sort.
These people are always looking for an angle. Running up a debt is one
sure way to end up in somebody's pocket. You don't want any markers
with the mob."

"How about dominoes?" Brody asked.

"Dominoes with players are fine, as well as Pick Up Sticks."

Brody laughed. The guy just doing his job, he thought. Probably
messed up his Saturday night, too.

"Look," Bullard said, "I'm not going to get into the specifics. You
should have received the league policies and rules with your playbook."

Brody nodded.

"Everything is covered. Pay close attention to the section on illegal substances, prescription drug abuse and alcoholism. The guidelines are based not only on health concerns for players, but it goes back to my original point. You don't want your name in somebody's book. Buy drugs, they not only get your money, they get leverage. That includes steroids. We test for those now, as well."

"I'm aware of that," Brody said.

The oysters came. A dozen on the half shell over ice, horseradish, Tabasco, Worcestershire, cocktail sauce on the side.

"You want another Coke?" Bullard asked.

"Camp tomorrow," Brody said. "I'm hitting the sack early."

Bullard loaded an oyster with all the condiments, then slid the shell past his lips and slurped the meat and juices, doing it in a way that didn't seem to fit his meticulous appearance.

"Son, I *know* players." He was still chewing. "The only athletes who get to this level are the very best. And the very best are used to getting everything they want. I don't have to ask you to know that you sat back and sucked soda in your high school coach's office, watching game films, while your phys ed class did push-ups on the fucking gym floor."

"I'm not sure I understand what you're telling me."

"It's like I heard the Juice say the other night. They were running his old interviews, clips before they wheeled his old lady away. Juice was saying he didn't play football for the money. He said he played so he didn't have to wait in a goddamn restaurant line."

Brody said, "The Juice is before my time."

"What I'm saying is there's going to be a lot of people trying to do a lot of things for you. Business ventures. Franchises. Partnerships. Investments. Especially a guy who just picked up six mill."

"I just tossed a stack in the trash."

"And I'm here to help on that front, too. If you want, NFL Security will investigate potential offers, and the people who make them. Unfortunately, many players don't and get burned. Like I said, I know players."

"I'm not your average player."

"I know quite more than you think. The NFL is an association of team owners, who are, in fact, employers. For the money they dish out, they want to know all about their potential hires. Think of it like a credit report."

"Do I get to read it and correct mistakes?" Brody asked.

Bullard went for another oyster.

Brody added, "And who knows? Maybe I could also add a few fuck-ups that you might have missed."

Bullard laughed. He took a drink, studying him for a second. "I like your sense of humor, son," he said. "You sure your old man wasn't a cop?"

"A teacher," Brody said. He paused, then asked, "Since you brought it up, what's to prevent some of this information of yours from getting in the wrong hands?"

"Teams cannot physically possess our files. They are kept at NFL Security. For a period of ten days before the draft, one representative from each team is permitted to come to the Park Avenue office and look at any prospect's file. They may not copy anything, but they can take notes. We also give them a private access code so they can call up to the last minute and have files read to them on the phone."

Brody asked. "What if I want to know about a teammate, or maybe one of the coaches?"

Bullard shook his head. "Prohibited." He sucked the last drops of the bourbon clinging to the melting ice. "Look, I probably shouldn't be telling you some of this. But most players know the drill. The union doesn't like it. But there's not a goddamn thing they can do about it. Plus, it's good for the integrity of the game."

"So you're telling me you mainly work for the owners."

"*And* you, with some limitations. I'm not here to bust your balls."

Bullard handed him his business card. "You certainly don't seem intimidated like most rookies. Like I said, I'm banking you're a little older and wiser."

Bullard stood up. "You see trouble, call me. Before, not after. That's not a get-out-of-jail card."

It wasn't until after he walked away that Brody realized he'd stuck him with the tab.

★   ★   ★

Five minutes later, Brody walked into his room to a ringing telephone. He answered it, plopping down on the bed.

"This the rook?" a voice asked. A low voice, very laid back, like Barry White in a ballad.

"This is Brody. Who's this?"

"This Reggie Thompson."

Wide receiver, Brody thought. The leading receiver on the team, even with a less than stellar performance last year.

"Some people call me G.B.," Thompson said, saying the initials staccato, and louder. "That short for Glamour Boy."

Brody said, "What do you want me to call you?"

"Anything you want, 'cept one."

"Which is?"

"That bad-ass nigger you just cost a million bucks."

Later, on the steps of St. Patrick's, Raymond Bullard told Carl Montan what happened on Sunday morning. "So Smith is waiting in the dog run near Washington Square, no canine with him, just a cup of coffee. And it's pretty noisy, 'cause somebody's Doberman is in there raising hell."

He said Eric Smith was wearing a nylon jogging suit and Nikes, but he didn't quite look like a quarterback who passed for nearly four hundred yards in his NFL debut. Thick beard. Dishwater blond hair pulled into a stubby pony tail.

"So, I'm asking him about those meetings he said he was attending, what he talked about at those."

"Smith says, 'responsibility.' "

"I ask him if he ever talks about the game. You know, the business?"

" 'Fuck no,' he says, 'That's why I go.' "

Bullard said, "I tell him, Eric, I'm quite willing to investigate. You know how the commissioner feels about the integrity of the game. But you have to let me do my job. And that means you keep your fucking mouth shut. Then I ask him straight up, had he told *anybody*.

"Then he says, get this, 'That's why I wanted to meet there.' He didn't want to be seen with NFL security anywhere near Midtown.

"I say, 'Who?'

"He looks into his coffee cup and says: 'Nobody. Everybody. Montan.

One of his fucking flunkies. It wouldn't matter. It's a fucking cesspool with the Stars.'

"Then Smith asks me, 'You talk to this new fucking kid yet?'

"I say, 'Derek Brody? Saw him last night, in fact.'

"Smith asks, 'Is he clean?'

" 'You know I can't share that information,' I tell him.

"He says, it doesn't matter. The Stars will get a piece of him. 'In the future. In the present. In the past.'

"I tell him, 'Shit, man, you're talking in riddles here.'

"And he says, 'One word: Montan.' Then, 'Montan, that's the way he fucking works it.'

" 'Works it?'

" 'Works the fucking players. I wasn't the only fucking one.'

" 'Doing what?'

" 'Doing what the fuck they wanted.'

"I ask him if he was shaving points.

"No, he says, just 'doing what came naturally.'

"I tell him I have a hard time believing that. I never met a player at this level who liked to lose.

"He says, 'Who said anything about fucking liking it?' "

Bullard paused, thinking about the next part, then continued. "So, it went on like this for another five or ten minutes, Smith just giving me tidbits. I'm starting to think he's seriously paranoid. And with this fucking Doberman barking, I've about had enough.'

"So finally I say, look, Eric. You're not telling me a fucking thing here. I need details. I need games and scores. I need basic facts.'

" 'The facts tell you nothing,' he says. He tells me I have to look at 'the overall picture.' Only then does it start to make sense.

" 'It?'

" 'The way Montan fucking works it.'

"I get up off the bench and start to make like I'm leaving. I'm saying, I've come all the way down here to listen. Even rode the goddamn subway, which I avoid at all costs. But I didn't come down here to hold his hand and guess.

"He says, 'There's just a lot fucking to it.'

"I ask him if he knows any other words besides fuck, fucking and fucked. I'm walking away now."

Bullard paused, Montan figuring he was going for the big finish, earning the $5,000 Montan had brought along.

Then Bullard said, "So, that's when I say to Smith then how about you just *fucking* get to it? And you know what he says? He takes a sip of his coffee and says:

" 'Okay, where do you want me to start? The dope. The bookies. Or, maybe I should start with the whores.' "

★   ★   ★

A banner hung above the door to the Stars locker room in the Indoor Sports Complex at Stony Brook:

THE FINAL FORMING OF A PERSON'S CHARACTER
LIES IN THEIR OWN HANDS—A. FRANK.

Brody read it as he walked under. He'd been seeing slogans, hearing slogans and dreaming slogans for ten years. This one he didn't recognize.

He was in a hurry. He'd left the Plaza by seven a.m., but hit construction on I–495. It was nearly eight-thirty when he took the turn hard into the main campus, the tires not even squealing because of the Benz's ESP. It was a sprawling, grassy campus. He figured he'd found the right building when he saw the parking lot. A couple dozen four wheelers. Grands. Suburbans. Range Rovers. He'd seen a black Dodge Ram four-by-four and a Lexus, then a group of a half dozen black players lingering outside the complex doors, half of them with cellulars out, all of them looking at him. When he'd walked toward them, they'd all turned and gone inside.

The locker room sounded like all the others. Players standing around talking trash. Others complaining. Big men working out of little cages. But when he walked in, the room stilled. Then they began leaving, presumably headed for the practice field. Those who remained turned their backs, busying themselves with their shorts, jerseys and shoes.

"You must be Brody."

Brody turned and saw a short guy with a beer gut, about thirty. He was standing in the doorway to the training room. Had a tool belt with tape and scissors. A trainer.

"What's up?" Brody said.

The guy picked up a bag just inside the big equipment cage and tossed it to him. Brody looked inside. Shorts, jersey, a pair of shoes.

"Size eleven, right?"

Brody nodded, then pulled out the jersey. Number 14.

"That okay? Carl assigns the numbers, but he's good about changing it if you want."

Fourteen was Y.A. Tittle's number with the Giants. "That's fine," Brody said.

"After morning practice, see the equipment manager," the trainer said. "He's out on the field now. He'll get you fitted. No pads today. Take an open locker, if you can find one. *Do not* put your clothes in anybody else's. It will probably be a veteran's. You will find them burned, if you live through the day."

Brody started to look around, hardly any players left now.

"Oh," the guy said. "I'm Johnny Josaitus. But everybody calls me Squat. Anything you need to know?"

About a hundred things, Brody thought. He asked, "How did you get stuck with 'Squat'?"

"That's how you'll see me when I bring you around on the field." He added, "You need anything, see me, if you know what I'm saying. Pain management has come a long way in this league."

Brody had never taken anything more than Advil.

"Get dressed, I'll tape you," Squat said. "Get here on time, there'll be a taping line. First come, first serve. You'll see a half dozen strips of tape on the wall. You write your number on the tape to reserve your place. You cross it off when you come out."

All the players had left now. The downside of a holdout, Brody thought. Missed all the orientation. Knew nobody, standing there holding that pile of stuff.

"Where's the coach?" Brody asked.

"Which one?"

"The head coach."

Josaitus pointed to a doorway beyond an equipment cage. "V.R.'s office is in there. But nobody goes in there unless he invites you in. No players. Reporters. *Nobody*."

Brody nodded.

Josaitus glanced at his watch, saying, "Hey, you gotta piss? I need you to drop some urine."

"Now?" Brody said.

"Are you clean?"

Yeah, Brody said, he was fucking clean.

Josaitus ducked into a small room and came out with two plastic beakers, milliliter marks in raised plastic on the side.

"I guess the league doesn't screw around," Brody said.

"It's not for the league. It's for us. You may need it later."

Brody clasped the container, looking at it, thinking what did that mean? Need it later.

Squat said, "You better get your ass moving."

"One question," Brody said.

"Shoot."

"Which way to the field?"

★   ★   ★

Position practice in ten, somebody said, when the air horn blows. The defense counted out cals in one end zone, everybody in unison. On the other end of the field the offense loosened in clusters. Some receivers and running backs sat on the grass, doing butterflies and hurdling stretches. Others ran off ten-yard jaunts, jogging at first, then slowly working their way up to a half sprint. A few offensive linemen lay on their backs, loosening up their abs with crunches. Others stood rotating at the waist, trying to limber up iron spines.

A light rain was falling.

Brody saw four footballs on a pedestal in the center of the field, at the fifty-yard line. Three players stretched at the forty, a couple of blue medicine balls nearby. The numbers and equipment told him they were the quarterbacks: The starter, his backup and an arena football player paid a hundred bucks a day to handoff and throw for the defensive play drills.

As Brody jogged toward them, the backup and the arena player got up and began a lap.

"Hey!"

Brody turned in time to take ten pounds of medicine ball in his chest in mid stride. It almost knocked him off his feet, but he held on.

Bobby Loeb was standing at the fifty on Brody's blind side, grinning big time. He looked like what fans expected a quarterback to look like. Six-foot-four, about two hundred and ten. Golden hair, thick on top, shaved on the sides, a front wave cascading over his square forehead. Chiseled chin and high cheekbones. Brody had seen him model Tommy Hilfiger in a *GQ* spread once. He had everything. Height. Strength. Experience and a tight spiral. But in the game films, Brody noticed Loeb had a happy right heel. It tapped like a hoofer as he set up. A heel like that was wired, Brody believed, to a part of Loeb's brain he'd not been able to shut off, the part that anticipated pain. Brody had shown it to Mike Scanlon back in Detroit one night on tape, saying, "That heel is why I'm going to take his job."

"Nice catch," Loeb said.

Brody lowered the medicine ball to his waist. Loeb came over and shook his hand. "I'm Bobby. But I want you to call me 'Teach' in camp. And don't complain, you're getting off easy. I'm not into all that cretin shit. All I want is the *Post* and *Newsday* in my locker every morning. A paper for the teacher. The rest of the time, I don't give a fuck what you say or do."

Brody had expected rookie hazing. But he'd already decided, there were limits. The papers, he could live with that.

Loeb backpedaled ten yards and stopped. "You gonna just stand there? Or you gonna toss me that fucking ball?"

Brody one-handed it from his chest. The game of catch began.

"What they call you in college?" Loeb asked.

Shit, Brody thought. Everybody was pretty fixated on what they were called.

Brody said, "Just my name."

"I'll be calling you 'rook' in front of the team. Lot of guys take this rookie shit real serious. Me, I could give a fuck. But you know what I'm saying. I need every one of these guys. And just about the time you get used to all the bullshit, the season begins and it stops."

"I can handle it," Brody said.

"You sure they didn't call you something at Michigan?" Loeb said. "Shit, it wouldn't be football if they called you by your regular name."

"Some called me Bro," Brody said.

"The brothers?"

"I guess that's who started it."

Loeb laughed. "I can tell you right now, *Bro*. They ain't going to be calling you that here."

He lowered his voice, telling Brody he needed to be clued in on a few things from the get-go. Somebody was going around complaining that Brody's signing bonus had sabotaged his contract negotiation.

"I heard from him last night," Brody said.

"Glamour Boy called you?" Loeb said. He looked surprised.

"Yeah, Reggie Thompson."

"No shit," Loeb said. "You got to watch that Negro. He's NWA."

"NWA?"

Loeb whispered, "Nigger With an Attitude."

Loeb tossed the medicine ball away, picked up a football and dropped back twenty yards. They threw thirty passes, each one picking up velocity. Brody's fingertips started to sting. He figured Loeb was sending him a message, saying, I'll talk to you, help you here and there, but that doesn't mean I'm going to give you my job.

"You loose?" Loeb asked.

Brody nodded.

Loeb walked over, palming the ball.

"So what you tell the boy, anyway?" he asked.

"I said I didn't create the world, I only live in it."

"Not bad," Loeb said. "But it's a definite problem here."

"Money?"

"Not exactly. It's gotten worse in the last few years. OJ seemed to get everybody fucking worked up. Guilty. Not guilty. All that kind of shit. We had a goddamn full-blown brawl between the lines in the weight room."

"Over OJ?"

"Over some fucking music. White men wanted Metallica. Homies wanted that gangsta shit. Now, there is no fucking music. Front office even banned Walkmans."

A whistle blew, the offensive coordinator calling them to the sidelines. Brody started to jog, but Loeb grabbed a fistful of his jersey.

"Quarterbacks don't run for no fucking whistle."

Brody said, "You're saying Reggie Thompson can make this money thing into a race thing."

"I'm saying Glamour Boy has his posse. If I was you, I'd stick close. GB and I get along okay. He needs me to get him the ball. See, I know these motherfuckers. If you were starting, he'd blow your little white dick if it meant you'd always be looking for him up the right sideline."

Loeb put his arm around his shoulders. "Point is, rook, you do not want that Negro fucking with you. I mean, I'd say you're vulnerable, man."

Brody didn't get it. "I didn't set the salary cap. I told him that, too."

Bobby Loeb stuffed the football lightly into Brody's gut. "That's not what I meant."

Brody asked what the fuck he did mean.

"Correct me if I'm wrong, but wasn't that a Negro kid your old man took out back in the Michigan boonies?"

The whistle blew again. Brody ran this time.

CHAPTER

 **8**

He had no roommate at the dorm, the equipment manager explaining that with his holdout, it just worked out that way. Brody bought newspapers from boxes outside early Tuesday morning. He delivered them to Bobby Loeb's locker, taking a moment to scan a *Newsday* story. A body part washed up on a Long Island beach, the shark-chewed torso of an unidentified black woman in shredded Spandex, cocaine in her system. Later, Brody thought he should have taken it as an omen. It was going to be that kind of day.

Second day now, and he still felt detached, like the Rose Bowl and Papa Goldman's conference room. After drills that morning, lunch was served in catered boxes at tables in the Sports Complex. Bobby Loeb had told him it would probably happen at dinner.

"They're going to want you to sing. But you want to make a statement, get the team's respect. In other words, you refuse."

They came at lunch, walking over from a freezer full of Drumsticks, Klondike and Dove bars. Reggie Thompson and the posse Loeb had talked about, Brody thought, half of them licking ice cream. Loeb and the two other quarterbacks were sitting with Brody.

Glamour Boy stopped five feet from the table. "Show time, rookie," he said.

Brody looked up from a half-eaten chicken breast. Reggie Thompson was six-two and had pecs that looked like they'd been chiseled by

Michelangelo. He'd been a Pro Bowler two years with San Francisco, but hadn't been back to that show as a Star.

Thompson took a bite of the Dove bar. "C'mon, rook. Everybody here wants to hear that fucked-up Michigan fight song."

Brody said, "You want a singer, check the classifieds. I'm here to play football."

Thompson looked around at his posse, laughing a little, sucking on the Dove. "You believe this shit?" He looked back at Brody. "Maybe I didn't make myself clear, motherfucker. That's tradition here."

Brody glanced up again from the lunch box. "You want to see a good show?"

"Yeah, that's right."

"Then look for me on the field."

Thompson tossed the Dove off to the side, the ice cream landing on the floor. Nearby tables quieted.

Bobby Loeb looked up and said calmly, "Reggie, back off. Nobody's sung all year."

"Six-million-dollar man going to sing. Like a fucking snitch sittin' on a wire."

Brody was thinking about Thompson's call at the hotel. He was thinking about fear. He felt fear in every football game. Fear was the whole point. Facing it, inflicting it.

Brody said, "You seem pretty sure about that."

Thompson glared, a vein above his eyebrow throbbing. "We got ways to make fucking sure."

Brody buried his fork in the breast and stood up, going with it now, letting some of that fear flow. The two other quarterbacks picked up their trays and scampered off, but Bobby Loeb stayed.

"Who's fucking first?" Brody bellowed.

He jerked the lunch table aside, the food staying put, but Loeb sitting there holding a fork, nothing underneath it. He looked at them all. Made sure they saw him looking at their ice cream, the way they were holding it, like school kids.

He added, "Or all you motherfuckers all want to try at once?"

He saw it in Thompson's eyes first, the receiver doubting himself a little now, maybe doubting what he'd got all his pals into. Five seconds passed. Brody wanted to hit somebody now.

When nobody moved, he jerked the table back and sat.

Loeb, still holding the fork, said, "Glamour Boy, why don't you go get yourself another Dove Bar."

★   ★   ★

Just before the afternoon session began, the owner's chopper veered in low over the treetops. Whistles blew and players converged from both end zones. The Long Ranger set down at the fifty. A chant started, fists pumping: "Pa-pa. Pa-pa. Pa-pa."

Brody asked Loeb, "What's that all about?"

Loeb said, "Never too early to angle for a raise."

Goldman waved as he stepped onto the turf. Carl Montan and Dominique stepped out behind him. They walked to the sidelines where Goldman settled into a director's chair. PAPA in black letters printed along the back. As the chopper took off, Dominique stood next to her father, some kind of conversation under way. Montan walked twenty yards up the sidelines. He was alone, surveying the field, his arms crossed.

Brody jogged over to Montan. "Hey, appreciate the car," he said.

It was a gentle handshake. People who knew players gripped gently. Outsiders tried to make statements with their grips and ended up crushing hands that were broken, sprained and bruised.

"Nothing but the best—for the best," Montan said.

Brody remembered meeting with Montan in Michigan. The Stars had sent Montan to evaluate him, not the head coach. V.R. hadn't been picked yet for the top job. After the workout and psychological tests, Montan insisted they drive fifty miles into Detroit to eat at a restaurant called the Rattlesnake Club, saying he'd read it was four stars and they had something called white chocolate ravioli he had to try. Montan spent two hours sampling hors d'oeuvres and asking questions. Questions about Brody's family and where he saw himself in five years. Did it casually, in a relaxed, self-assured tone. Almost too casual, Brody remembered thinking, for a football man. When dessert came, Brody asked his own questions. Montan told him he'd joined the Stars three seasons back, coming over from the same job at an expansion franchise. Before that, he'd been at the University of Nevada.

Montan glanced toward the bench, then put his hand on his shoulder. "Getting along okay?"

Brody nodded.

He handed him a card. "You have problems, you call me. Those numbers, I'm available night and day."

An air horn blew. Brody stuck the card in his shoe and jogged back to the team. That morning, the team had split for positions practice. Kickers practiced at one goal post. The offensive and defensive lines squared off on the opposite end, Brody and the arena quarterback running plays. At the fifty, receivers and defensive backs worked with the two more experienced quarterbacks. They threw to the flankers as backfield coaches shouted instructions to defenders. Everyone was in helmets, shorts and jerseys. Light contact. All the quarterbacks wore red jerseys, stop signs that told pumped-up players: Do not hit this man.

Now, the horn was signaling team scrimmage. Brody saw V.R. pull to the sideline in a golf cart. He'd spent the entire practice the day before under its canvas canopy, V.R. driving with a smoldering El Producto in his mouth, a microphone in his hand. The cart had a PA, the bullhorn on the roof. A guy sat next to V.R. The guy was maybe forty. Short black hair, creased dress slacks and well-shined oxfords. The guy was riding with V.R. again today.

Brody asked Loeb about the passenger.

Loeb said, "He takes care of Vince's cable."

"What, like that movie, *Cable Guy?*"

"The cable for V.R.'s earphones during games. Makes sure it doesn't get all tangled up and shit."

"So, he's with the team."

"Not exactly. He's V.R.'s bud. Name's Molito. He owns a pretty nice tit bar in Queens. Old V.R. spends a lot of time there."

Brody watched the scrimmage for a good fifteen minutes, Loeb and the backup getting all the reps. The backup was a sixteen-year veteran named Clinton Lisle. He'd started in the Canadian Football League and spent another ten years riding the NFL bench. Lisle had accuracy, consistency, but no zip left in his arm.

Dominique Goldman was fifteen yards away on the sidelines. Brody walked in her direction, but stopped when he reached Hadley Henderson, the offensive coordinator.

"What do I have to do to get some of this?" Brody asked.

Henderson kept his eyes on the field. "Memorize the playbook."

"Done," Brody said.

Henderson watched a play unfold, but slammed his clipboard to the turf halfway through it. Exploding, "Jesus Christ, Cobb, you fucking pull! Pull! *PULL!*" He glanced at Brody. "Fucking idiot's trapping on Jersey. He's supposed to trap on Queens in that formation."

V.R. and Henderson had designed a system quite unlike anything Brody had ever seen. Normally, teams used colors to denote formations, left and right to locate where players line up and code words and numbers to indicate plays and receiver's routes. A quarterback might say, "Red right 24 trap on two" for a running play. Red meant the splitback formation. Right would signify the strong-side formation where the tight end would line up. Expected holes in the line are numbered. The "24" sent the right halfback through the hole between right guard and right tackle, the ball snapped on the second "hut."

V.R.'s code followed a crime theme. He had names for four different huddles. A regular field huddle was a "Mug."—"C'mon, mug-up, now." He called a sideline huddle a "Bail." A hurry-up huddle was called "Bopper." No huddle was called "Dirty Dozen." The split back formation was "Black." The single back formation was "White." Right was "Queens," east of Midtown. Left was "Jersey," west of the city. There were personnel designations. The regular formation of two runners, two wide receivers and one tight end was "Crew." "Hitman" was three wide receivers, one tight and one running back. Types of running plays had names. "Pimp" was a trap. "Snitch" was a draw. "Zip" was a direct hand-off. "Mule" was a toss. "Bleeder" was a screen. "Felon" was a sweep. A common blocking scheme, back on strong safety, or BOSS, became "Gotti." Receiver formations were famous serial killers' names. A split was "Ripper." A slot was "Bundy." A simple running play could become a racial slam. The right halfback trap play was "Black jersey 24 pimp on one." Read predicted the lingo not only would keep defenders guessing, it would disrupt their concentration when the quarterback shouted audibles just before the snap.

Coach Henderson called Eddie "Homer" Cobb to the sidelines, chewing on him for failing in his duties as a pulling guard. There was something surreal about seeing a man who stood six-six and weighed 320 on the edge of tears.

"But Darius fucking with me, coach," Cobb said, anguish flushing in his pink face. "He's after my fucking balls."

Left tackle, Darius Wallace, 285 pounds, six-year veteran from Colorado.

"Then knock Darius on his fucking black ass."

Henderson turned to Brody. "How about hitman? White Jersey ripper 629?"

Brody started to explain the play.

"Don't tell me. Fucking show me." He turned back to the field, yelling, "Bobby, come in."

As Brody jogged out, he mulled over the play. The halfback would line up on the right, helping form the pocket. The left flanker would fly down the sidelines. The slot man would be in motion to the left, then head out on a curl. The right flanker, Reggie Thompson, would sprint fifteen yards up the right side and post, where the quarterback would hit him in the seam. If Thompson wasn't open, he'd be looking for secondary receivers.

That's how it looked on paper. But plays were a theoretical result based on the presumption everything went as planned. Over the years, Brody tuned in to a different schematic, one that he trusted to come instantly after the ball was snapped. He didn't see individual players or patterns. He saw the entire field—a picture cluttered with missed assignments, unanticipated defense and very big men trying to knock him on his ass. He'd learned to go with it. Let it produce its own form, and new opportunities. Brody believed *this* was his talent, finding form in chaos. He valued that more than his arm.

Brody called the play in the "mug" huddle.

Nobody responded but Reggie Thompson. "Now we see if we can get down with you, rook," Glamour Boy said.

The center snapped the ball with the laces on the wrong side. The halfback sprinted into the line, a missed assignment. Brody dropped back, turning the ball for a grip, an almost unconscious reflex. He was looking left all the way, first at the motion receiver, then the receiver on the left fly, selling it. The left tackle, the halfback's man, almost ran Brody over, but he sidestepped him. His arm was already back when he looked over the middle, Thompson's back still facing him as he ran the post.

He fired the ball to a point in space just to the left of Thompson's shoulder.

Glamour Boy turned. The ball right there.

He held his hands out, his head cocked to the right, a smile showing through his face mask.

The ball bounced off his numbers to the turf.

Henderson screamed, "GB what the fuck you doing? We're playing football! Take that faggot shit to a soccer field!"

As everyone jogged back, Brody could see a couple players in Thompson's posse laughing. In the golf cart, Molito was saying something to V.R. Brody glanced at the owner and his daughter. They were talking, too.

The offensive coordinator did not call him back to the sidelines.

They huddled again.

Thompson was out of breath, bent over, his hands resting on his knees. He looked up. "Nice throw, White Boy Rick. But that's not where I like it."

Brody looked at him and said, "It's Derek."

Thompson grinned. "Rick part of Derek, ain't it? *Dare Rick.*" He looked at the other players around the huddle. "Fits. I'm going with it."

"Rick dares you to fucking catch it," Brody said.

"I catch on Sundays, Rick," Thompson said. "When it counts."

V.R.'s voice crackled through the bullhorn. He called the next play himself, but added, "With Conlin this time."

"Shit," Thompson said, punctuating it with a snap of his head. He jogged away to the bench.

A mouthy rookie receiver named Jedi Conlin joined the huddle.

Brody said, "Defense knows what's coming now."

Conlin said, "Fuck those motherfuckers. Those motherfuckers can't understand their own fucking shit, let alone figure out our fucking shit."

The play: Both wide receivers on a double fly. A play action would give them a step. Then it was the QB's choice.

"I'll be fucking there," Conlin said.

Brody said, "On three."

Brody faked the hand-off, then dropped the ball lazily to his side as he backpedaled, holding it by its nose, the stitches up his wrist. He sold the fake with his body, relaxing his shoulders as his eyes watched the runner with no ball hit the line. When the pocket formed, he rolled right, looking left. In his peripheral view he picked up the right flanker with two steps. He waited one more second, then looked right, seeing the flanker running at full speed. He launched the bomb, knowing it would come down between the five and the end zone. He saw his right fingers extended in the follow-through, a momentary snap-shot, his hand against a cumulus cloud, the ball sailing away.

That was the last picture. That and a little white light surrounded by darkness, like a blown out picture tube.

Sometime later, ammonia vapors punched his sinuses. But it was the shouting that opened Brody's eyes.

"You fucking color blind!"

He focused five yards away, above him. Homer Cobb's dirty white fists flailing at Darius Wallace's face mask. The black defensive tackle just standing there, letting the right guard break up his hands.

"C'mon, Homer, show me what the fuck you got!"

Two assistants pulled them apart. Later, Brody learned it was Wallace who'd nailed him after the release. He thought they were fighting over a quarterback hit, until somebody theorized, "I think they're still trying to work out the weight room music thing."

"You okay," Squat said, the trainer over him.

Brody sat up, his eyes looking for Jedi Conlin now. The receiver was holding the football, a couple yards away. He could tell by his eyes he'd caught it.

Brody stood up, slightly wobbly. Clinton Lisle, the aging backup, passed him, taking his place on the field.

When Brody reached the sideline, he was still dizzy. Loeb was smiling, the corner of his mouth stained with Skoal.

He spit. "Not bad."

"What the fuck happened?"

"Seventy yards in the air."

"No, with the tackle."

"He tripped over the guard. He took you with him when he went down. If you ask me, though, I'd say it was intentional."

Loeb spit again. "The tackle's one of Reggie's boys."

Brody pulled his helmet off and looked to his right toward the owner's chair. Dominique was no longer with Goldman. She was walking toward the end zone on the sidelines.

Loeb said, "Like that?"

Brody said nothing.

Loeb said, "Like it or don't like it, you want to stay away from it."

Brody turned. "*It?*"

"It likes to spend the old man's money. Spent a half million last year just redecorating the front office. It got him to go with these new uniforms. Some say it's even got a hand in player selection. Got both eyes on the franchise when the old man checks out. For now, she just runs the old man ragged, pulling that daddy's-little-girl shit."

"She doesn't look very little to me."

"That's what I'm saying. She's got a thing for quarterbacks. Chew you right up, then spit you out, rookie. Ask Eric Smith."

Brody said, "I thought Smith left New York."

"He's still around." Loeb looked over at Dominique again. "Way I figure, she starts doin' Smith, that's when all his trouble began."

"So they're still together?"

Loeb shook his head, then turned. "Don't tell me you fucked her already."

"She helped me find an apartment, that's all," Brody said.

The offensive coordinator barked, "Loeb, get out there."

Bobby Loeb put on his helmet and said, "Or she's planning to cut another one out of the herd."

★   ★   ★

An hour later, the lights dimmed and a projection TV fired up with a snowy screen, Tuesday's practice scheduled to conclude with film and comments from V.R.

They were spaced around a lecture hall that smelled of sweat, sod and analgesic balm. Some eyes were on playbooks. And concealed inside were sports sections, *Football Weekly*, comic books, publications on hunting, fishing, off-road, rap, hip-hop and the Nation of Islam, not to mention letters from mothers, Bible tracts and a few suspiciously stained copies of *Hustler* magazine. Other players slumped. Half closed eyes fought sleep, while overhead a thunderstorm pelted the roof in waves.

A free safety named Antoine Lense was sitting two chairs from Brody on his left, Loeb on his right. All three of them were halfway up the small auditorium, concealed in the shadows.

Lense muttered, "One day I gonna slip Vanessa Del Rio into that tape machine when nobody lookin'."

Loeb chuckled.

Lense continued, "Or one of Glamour Boy's tapes. You seen them

Bobby. Triple fucking X. Or those ones he got of the bims he's did. Wake *every* motherfucker up in here. V.R., too."

Brody had a headache.

V.R. walked through the video beam to the lectern, clutching a remote in his hand. He looked up. "All right, listen up, men. Pittsburgh. Game two, preseason. If you're worried about being cut, I'd say you're looking at crunch time. Why anyone in your situation would dog it is way beyond me. But if you are, you've got Pittsburgh, Houston, Arizona, before we take your jocks away."

The rookies straightened in their chairs. Most of the veterans remained slumped.

Lense muttered, "Fucking Calvins, man. Nobody wear a strap no more."

V.R. continued, "Now, I thought we'd just take a quick look at the Steelers. They've made some adjustments on both sides of the ball. The following is from last week's game against the Lions."

Thirty select plays flashed across the screen, V.R. mapping formations and blocking schemes with a laser pointer. A couple of impressive catches and hard hits stirred comments, but Brody still saw a lot of eyes in playbooks. He saw some eyes closed.

Brody devoured the film. You learned from film, saw tendencies and individual player quirks, his old man always said. But Brody also liked to study film alone, undistracted by a coach's commentary.

When he saw Los Angeles Coliseum flash on the screen, he thought he was imagining things. Then he saw Michigan's maize and blue, USC's red and gold.

"Hey, coach," somebody yelled. "That don't look like Pittsburgh fucking PA to me."

Brody recognized it as his Rose Bowl.

V.R. let the tape run, saying, "I want you all to see this new quarterback. We're going to be dealing with him somewhere down the road."

Brody felt players looking at him. He felt awkward.

When he focused on the screen again, the laser pointer was behind the USC center, the USC quarterback taking the snap, the USC quarterback throwing long, forty-five yards over the middle.

V.R. said, "Pittsburgh picked up this boy. Look at the cannon on that kid."

Brody's anger built as V.R. showed ten USC passing plays. He did not show Brody racking up 522 yards in total offense for Michigan. He did not show Brody bootlegging the ball with eight seconds left, running through the linebacker at the one-yard line to win the game. Shit, Brody thought, the USC passer went in the fourth fucking round.

The lights went up.

Antoine Lense leaned over. "V.R. fuckin' with you, rook," he said, chuckling. "Man, he fuckin' with you *bad.*"

CHAPTER

★ ★ ★ **9** ★ ★ ★

The way it usually worked, Shay Falan would walk into a small room at the casting agency with her accompanist. Walk right to the X on the floor near the piano. You don't say hello to the director or the casting agent or the producer. They sat behind a small table. You don't speak until you're spoken to. You don't look at the floor, either. You just smile and begin.

The show was a musical stage adaptation of a popular feature cartoon, an all-animal cast, most of them hairy primates. On the questionnaire, she'd put down she was auditioning for the mother orangutan's part. The ape belted two songs and one ballad in the newly written show. The part called for heavy face makeup and a stifling body costume. Her dancer's build would not be a casting factor, only the athletic ability to perform in fifty pounds of rubber and red hair.

Auditions came down to two chances at the X. First you sang an entire tune, nothing directly from the show, but material similar to the sought part. Shay had picked "Miss Marmelstein," a big, fat belting number with a lot of high Es, the song from an old, obscure musical. Directors were impressed by musical theater knowledge, at least the good ones were. Then, Shay planned to do a sixteen-bar, a quote from another song, ten seconds to display her best vocal and dramatic skills.

Juilliard had taught her the moves. When she left Albany ten years ago, she was the town's Irish darling, riding into the prestigious New

York music college with three forensic state championships, a dozen high school leads and a full scholarship. Juilliard professors not only tuned her pipes and stage skills, they passed on Broadway trade secrets, such as performing to a metaphor. You took a song like *Oklahoma*'s "I'm Just a Girl Who Can't Say No" but acted it to a completely unrelated situation. You sang about getting laid, but you acted as if you were scolding a dog for chewing a shoe. The effect was bigger than life. That's how the best reached the cheap seats. In the past five years, she'd reached a dozen chorus parts, a handful of leads in off-Broadway roles in shows that closed and a principal role in the revival of Sondheim's *Company*. But lately, her career seemed to be one of those metaphors. On the outside, actress looks like a stone pro. Inside, actress is losing her stamina and poise. Actress gets call from her agent, saying he's managed to get her a shot at this orangutan part.

She tried to imagine her persona filling the room as she walked through the door. Spine erect, her breasts riding high. She could feel the producer scanning her butt and legs. Her sixteen-bar was going to be "If I Loved You" from *Carousel*, which she always nailed. But she was worried about the big "Miss Marmelstein" number, belting those high Es hardly a week from her last binge.

There was no X, but a red line, just to the right of a black upright, its top stained with beverage rings. Her accompanist, a Juilliard student, sat down and opened his sheet music. Shay smiled, turned briefly to the student pianist, and nodded her head.

The high Es would not be a problem. She hit the first, but then they stopped her.

"Thank you," said the director, a guy imported from Burbank, his face stretched with that disingenuous L.A. smile.

The producer looked down at her audition sheet. "Miss *Felon*," he said. "Tell me . . ."

"It's Falan. Long A, like Fay."

He smiled again. "Miss Falan, tell me, what are your favorite Broadway shows these days?"

A dangerous question. The answer could decide a walk or a call back. She took a good look at him now. He was maybe fifty-five, but aiming for ten years younger in a ribbon shirt and a well-crafted, and nicely highlighted, toupee. She thought, he's either looking for kudos about other shows he had running or he's going to offer her some tickets. She'd have to pick them up from him personally at his office, of course, and that's when he'd make his move.

"You don't have a favorite?" he asked again. His eyes made the round trip between her breasts and ankles in less than a second.

She smiled. "My favorite show is any one in which I'm cast."

Five minutes later, she was standing outside on 49th and Broadway, handing her accompanist two twenties.

"You're much too lovely to be an ape," the student said.

She stood there a while after he walked off, surveying the marquees and show billboards around Times Square. What she really wanted to tell the producer was, "What Broadway?" There was hardly any *Broadway* left. She wanted to tell him she worshiped Sondheim, honored Rodgers and Hammerstein and credited Maltby and Shire. She used to loathe Andrew Lloyd Webber, his big productions that pushed aside the more cerebral musicals. But now even Webber looked good. Conglomerates, like the Mecca Entertainment Group, dominated Broadway now. It produced unoriginal adaptations and other silly shows that cast sitcom, movie and rock stars with marginal pipes at the expense of real stage talent. Mecca had even developed a new show district on 34th Street, replacing a sin strip near the Garden with theaters and virtual reality arcades. Hell, she wanted to say, "Pretty soon your theater lobbies are going to offer carnival games and dunking booths."

Shay's eyes came to a stop at the All Star Sports Cafe, the large, illuminated pictures of Jordan and Gretzky over the doors. Only the sports theme stopped her. She'd buy the wine when she got back to the Village, she told herself.

The compulsion passed on the B train.

A half block from her East Village apartment, she saw a figure hunched on her front steps. At first she thought he was a vagrant.

It was Eric Smith.

He was smoking a cigarette and clutching a manila envelope to his chest.

★   ★   ★

Montan said, "I swear to God, Jack, one day you're going to just burst into fucking flames."

Petrus was in the leather chair across from Montan's desk. He was moving his head in a circular motion, trying to loosen the muscles at the base of his neck.

"You sure Bullard's not shaking us down?" the GM said. "That just doesn't sound like Eric."

Montan looked at his fingernails. "My people checked with his slinger. Dealer hasn't heard from him in a month. He's either straight or has found a better source."

Petrus stilled. "I told you. You pamper these players enough, pretty soon they forget who signs their checks."

"That's an interesting notion. I wonder if we put him back on the payroll, would that make a difference? I never really intended for him to leave the way he did."

Petrus leaned forward. "Christ, we don't have room for another assistant coach."

Montan nodded. "We're beyond that now anyway."

Petrus said, "You sure he named me?"

"You. Me. Squat. A number of players."

There was a light rap on the door. A pool secretary came in with a large tray. Montan had ordered an antipasto from a nearby Italian deli. A secretary had transferred the meal to china bearing the Stars logo, an amenity provided by Dominique Goldman when she recently contracted for $5,000 in custom-designed tableware.

The secretary closed the door behind her.

Montan ripped off a piece of bread. "Have some prosciutto, Jack. It's very good."

Petrus stood up, only to begin pacing.

Montan stuck his fork into the prosciutto, carefully twirling it around his fork. He savored the salty taste, then swallowed. He enjoyed food, from the process of finding a good restaurant to the deliberate way he consumed. At fifty-two, his stomach remained flat. He could eat what he wanted, where he wanted, and never gained. One time, he asked the team doctor about it.

"Maybe you have some kind of digestive parasite," the physician said. "We could run some tests."

Montan said, "Let's just leave it where it is."

That was his guiding philosophy. Everyone possessed certain attributes. Most people divided them up, like a decision-making exercise, writing down the pros and cons on both sides of a line. He saw no line.

Character was not split. He'd come to this conclusion by studying players and their psychological reports. Assets and liabilities were one and the same. A receiver's blinding speed got him open, but also made him overrun the ball. A safety's rage jarred balls loose on tackles, but also prompted him to beat his wife. That's why authoritative coaches produced. Players needed to be channeled. Football makes men out of boys, the saying went. The way Montan saw it, pro football suspended men in boyhood. Take care of their basic needs and give them a father figure. All they were required to do was play.

Petrus was still pacing.

Montan snapped, "Jesus Christ, sit down."

Petrus stopped, but didn't sit.

Montan said, "It's simple, really. Eric believed he inspired the team all those years. Now he's only trying to do it in a different way, only off the field."

Petrus blinked a couple of times. "That's a reason, not a solution."

Montan looked at his deli plate. "Raymond will work him for a while. See if he's got any more surprises. Look at it this way. This is an internal matter. We've got the league covered."

"What if he goes elsewhere?"

"Where? The feds? They haven't taken a serious look at professional football in years. And when they did, football wasn't the focus. The mob was."

"Eric knew gamblers."

"Look, they start with the Stars, they better keep right on going. They better start rounding up every tipster in every camp in the league." Montan paused. "No," he said. "There's only one concern here. That's the media. But, without corroboration, Eric is not exactly a reliable source."

Petrus said, "He can still go on camera. Make a charge."

"Not without us having some lead time."

Montan reached for a slice of provolone, saying, "We extend Eric's career by a good three years, and this is how he shows us his gratitude. Such betrayal."

He looked up, saying, "Some provolone, Jack?"

Petrus said, "You created this situation."

"Thank you," Montan said. He placed the cheese on a crust of bread, but decided it needed something.

"You created it, Carl," Petrus said. "Now it's up to you to get it under control." The GM reached for the door.

"Only if you do me a favor."

"And just what the Christ is that?" Petrus mumbled.

Montan said, "Tell my girl to bring some olive oil and balsamic in here."

CHAPTER

☆ ☆ ☆ **10** ☆ ☆ ☆

For two weeks Brody thought, they want to play mind games, he can do that. Forty-yard conditioning sprints. They ran in groups, quarterbacks and receivers in one, linebackers and the defensive backfield in the other. Ten sprints, thirty seconds rest in between. Few players ran them full-out. They practiced painful facial expressions, making it look good. Brody turned on the burner and won them all by yards.

One day, Bobby Loeb said, "Slow down, rook. You're making a lot of veterans look bad out there."

Brody said, "Some don't need my help."

The next morning, coaches put Brody with the defensive group. As they lined up, Aubrey Johnson, an eight-year strong safety who hung with Glamour Boy, said, "You pull that road runner shit here, Rick, your dick is going in the dirt."

Johnson, six-three and 220, had a vicious temper. Brody had seen him smack an equipment intern in the head for inadvertently handing him a used towel.

At the whistle, Johnson bolted into the lead. Brody caught him, only to have Johnson cut in front of him with another player. Brody laid a forearm into Johnson's kidney, then drove his shoulder into the other runner, crashing to the turf with him. Johnson finished first, shouting profanities. But nobody boxed in Brody again.

When they couldn't slow him, they tried to humiliate him. He found his clothes tied in knots, pages missing from his playbook. They crossed his number off the tape list. One day, a helmet was passed around the locker room, everyone signing it for a charity auction item. Brody was the last to autograph it, then he realized it was his. The number had been peeled off. He practiced the rest of the week with their signatures around his head. The next week, he found it filled with piss.

Bobby Loeb was the only veteran who'd talk. Some days they sat together at team breakfast, team lunch and team dinner. Some days Brody sat alone. There were meetings with assistant coaches after evening meals and a curfew at eleven. Many players ignored it. Loeb asked him if he wanted to hit this local bar late one night.

"What if the coaches see us slip out?" Brody asked.

"Won't happen," he said. "They're waiting for us to buy them rounds, up at the bar."

Brody passed.

He spent most of the first week throwing balls against the defense with the arena quarterback. He sat on the bench during the second preseason game against the Steelers, which the Stars lost 45–0. After the game, Dominique Goldman approached him on the sidelines.

"I was hoping we could have dinner on your day off," she said. "Maybe talk about getting you involved with a charity."

"After camp," he said, and jogged off.

He did what worked in The Valley. Stuck to himself. Say little and let them wonder where he was coming from. In prison, mystery generated more fear than boasts. In camp, he rose two hours earlier than everyone else. He'd jog over to the field at twilight and drill himself on fundamentals, without the ball, like a mime. The Stars had no quarterback coach, so he became his own. He did two dozen three-, five- and seven-step drop backs, with a hitch throw and without. He worked on arm movement and release, the balance in the balls of his feet. Over the years, his movements had become machinelike. His father had always preached consistency, drilling body movements so they perked up from the unconscious in a game. Enough unpredictable things happened in football, he used to say. But your body, that you could control.

Mostly, Brody stayed in his room. He bought a VCR and a small TV to study game films. He invited the offensive line to study film with him in his room on Wednesdays, the receivers on Thursday. Nobody came, except a rookie named Toby Headly. He was a tight end from the University of Florida. He had a bad stutter, for which he was harassed constantly. Brody figured he was more interested in quiet company than film.

One night Brody went looking for Bobby Loeb to copy a page from his playbook. He found Reggie Thompson in his room, the two of them sucking on Miller Ice, Glamour Boy showing one of his X-rated videos.

He asked Loeb the next morning at the lockers. "You tell me the guy's trouble, but there you are partying in the same room."

"I'd let him fuck me, too," Loeb said. "If it meant another five catches a game."

In meetings, V.R. reminded the team not to read the daily sports pages, listen to sports radio or watch TV coverage about the team. Brody presumed V.R. meant current news. He found a library in Smithtown and read every clipping he could find on the Stars in the past five seasons.

Media coverage was more extensive than anything he'd read in Michigan. There were stories about the team's solvency. Papa Goldman had been meeting with the city, trying to negotiate a new lease. The city built the Stardome for the Stars six years ago, but in zeal to get a free stadium, Goldman had signed an agreement inadequate for the higher player salaries of today. The Stars received the gate and $42 million in TV broadcast payments from the NFL. That was the bulk of the team's income. The city received all the stadium's other revenues: Parking, concessions, advertising and a hefty $10 million for 100 sky suites. Even Goldman had to pay $110,000 in rent for the owner's suite. Goldman was rumored to be running out of money. A *Times* story quoted an NFL source who said Goldman was under pressure from the commissioner to sell "to preserve the stability of the league."

Brody had to admire Goldman's response. "Last I checked, the commissioner is employed by the owners," he'd told the paper. "I'd sooner run the Stars into the ground first." Brody wondered about the accuracy of the report. Goldman had coughed up six million to bring him aboard.

Brody wanted to know more about his teammates, but he found the coverage shallow. And that thought gave him an idea. He'd been over-looking his greatest resource. He had a lot of money. He could get things with that. He bribed the equipment manager with a grand to make copies of every game film in the past three seasons. He watched two games a night, isolating players still with the squad. The way Brody saw it, the Stars had talent, but tripped up on the details. Bad snaps. Lazy pass routes. Linemen out of position. Defenders missed tackles, players trying to make highlight films with big hits when a straight tackle would do. He saw no gang mentality. The defense didn't swarm. Players walked to the sidelines before the whistle blew. They celebrated sacks and tackles when they were hopelessly behind.

Reggie "Glamour Boy" Thompson was a case in point. He frequently got open and made spectacular catches. But he often dropped dead-on throws on crucial third downs. His touchdown celebration resembled a police sobriety test. He spiked the ball, then walked a straight line, heel-to-toe, alternately touching his index fingers to his nose.

In camp, he saw other things. Situations, mainly. He walked into a narrow hallway outside the locker room one afternoon and found himself between Homer Cobb and Darius Wallace, the two linemen who'd fought on his second day of camp. They were standing, five yards to his left and right, pointing at each other, shouting at full volume, but not moving forward.

"I'm gonna mess you up," Wallace was screaming, foam glistening in the corners of his mouth. "I'm gonna mess you up and then I'm gonna shit in your mouth."

Cobb inched closer. "Go for it. Go for it so I can show you something your momma never taught you about white boys."

Brody ducked back through the door.

When some players weren't arguing, he heard them comparing: Who had the best cellular phone. Who had digital. Who had the smallest. "But mine, motherfucker, got a built-in pager, too."

Brody would nap on the locker room floor after lunch, a towel under his head, his eyes closed, listening. Who had the best car, the best tires, the best stereo, the best wardrobe, the best agent, the best-looking girlfriend. "I'll give you that, man, but mine put out more."

By his second week, Derek Brody decided the New York Stars were not a football team. They were a third-world country of warring tribes.

Blacks against whites. Offense against defense. Rookies against veterans. Glamour Boy's posse against the Fellowship of Christian Athletes, nicknamed the God Squad. Blacks bitched whites got more commercials and appearances. Whites complained the blacks had a chip on their shoulders. The defense complained the offense didn't give them enough rest during games. The offense complained the defense never turned over the ball. The posse snuck off to the city in GQ fashions, returning well after midnight. The God Squad broke practice with a prayer circle at the fifty, conducted Bible study after dinner and patrolled the dorm in T-shirts that read: JESUS—WE'RE ON HIS TEAM.

Two days before the third preseason game, GB's posse coated a God Squader's cup with Atomic Balm liniment, sending the player screaming to the showers as soon as he broke a sweat. Leonard Toysy, a six-eight defensive tackle and six-time Pro Bowler, was the head of the FCA jocks, himself an ordained minister. At the end of practice, Toysy stood in the dressing room, holding the cup up high over his head and demanded the perpetrator identify himself.

Reggie Thompson said, "What you gonna do, Toy, if the fool steps forward? I thought you supposed to turn the other cheek."

Toysy hurled the cup, Thompson ducking. It hit another player in the face. Seconds later, players were squaring off, clutching one another's jersey, pushing each other around like a hockey brawl. It took three God Squaders to hold back Toysy, Glamour Boy just laughing.

A whistle blew.

Everyone's eyes went to the sound. It was Squat. Next to him stood Carl Montan, leaning against the door frame of the training room. He had a cotton sweater tied around his shoulders, hands bunched in his pockets. The exec shooting a pose.

"Gentlemen," Montan said calmly. "Now what would Papa say?"

And just like that it was over.

Montan, in fact, seemed to conjure a special chemistry. He visited camp daily, usually in his golf shirt and tan slacks. He chatted with beat reporters, often promoting the lesser-known players for interviews. He spent a lot of time talking to players individually on the sidelines. He sat with groups at the lunch tables and fetched refills for parched throats.

"So what's his story?" Brody asked Loeb one hot afternoon.

"You got a problem," Loeb said, "Carl's the man to see."

Brody kept waiting for V.R. to address the flaws. Instead, he drummed the same mantra at team meetings: "I don't give a shit about nothing but three hours on Sunday. Sundays you come to fight. Sundays you come to brawl."

Brody remembered how his Michigan coach corrected bad fundamentals. An assistant carried a golfbag full of wooden yard sticks on sidelines during practice. If players lined up out of position, the coach would freeze everybody, go out on the field and measure. If you were off a couple inches, he'd break the stick over your helmet or shoulders. Later, you'd find the pieces in your locker. Few missed their marks again.

V.R. never left the golf cart. He smoked cheap cigars, sounded his air horn and talked to Molito, his cable guy. Other than the slam at Brody with the Rose Bowl film, he never criticized players publicly. He did meet individually with athletes every day. Players disappeared into his office, then came out a few minutes later. He walked them to the edge of the locker room, embraced them, then returned to his inner sanctum. The Stars assistant coaches tried to drill the players on fundamentals, but lacked the clout to put unresponsive veterans in the coach's doghouse. When an assistant rode a player too hard, the player would request a meeting with V.R. and get his hug instead.

Brody started getting reps with the first-string offense the second week. In the preseason game against Houston, V.R. gave him nine downs at the end of the contest, the game out of reach in an Oilers rout. He made straight hand-offs and fired two short passes which were dropped.

The next week, the dorm grew more rowdy, the team sensing the end of camp was near. Only tight end Toby Headly was showing for his private film study. Brody started finishing off his evenings with the 600 SL, driving along Ocean Parkway, through the state beaches and reserves. He liked smelling the salt air and exploring South Bay. Or, heading north, finding back roads along the Long Island Sound.

All the bullshit, he kept telling himself, was just the pro game. Everyone said the NFL was unique. He told himself Reggie Thompson and Dominique Goldman had done him a favor. Woke him up and made him focus. His passing was sharper than ever and he had a firm grasp on the Stars system. It would be only a matter of time before the coaches noticed. He could wait.

He was there to play football, not to fuck or fight.

★   ★   ★

Brody was removing the laces from a pair of turf shoes the morning before the final preseason game when Johnny Josaitus walked up.

"V.R. wants to see you."

"In a minute." He was only halfway done.

"Now," Squat said.

Brody walked into the office behind the equipment cage, the laces flopping on the concrete floor. The guy Molito was slumped in a chair next to V.R.'s desk. He was suited up for business, or a funeral. Charcoal, double-breasted suit, a burgundy tie with matching handkerchief poking out of the pocket. He smelled of cologne.

V.R. said, "Brody, say hello to Tommy. He's a good friend of the New York Stars."

Molito's grip was soft.

Molito said, "My driver tells me you don't take shit from nobody. I like that."

"Your driver?"

"Yeah, he took you over to the Plaza, the day you hit Midtown."

"That driver," Brody said.

"Tommy runs a real nice place in Queens," V.R. said. "Very beautiful girls. Of course, I go there for the food."

V.R. laughed hard at his own joke.

Molito slid a card into Brody's hand. "Friends of Vincent, they never pay. Come down any night. I'll introduce you around. And nobody will bother you there. No autographs. Nobody moonlighting."

Brody looked at the card: TOMMY'S PLACE—GENTLEMANLY ENTERTAINMENT. "Moonlighting?" Brody asked.

"Snitches for the tabs, like downtown. A man of your stature goes out to have a little fun. What the fuck, next thing you know, you're seeing red dots and your picture the next day in the *Post*."

Brody looked at V.R.

The coach nodded. "You've got to be careful. You want to stay away from the high profile tit clubs like Scores."

A cellular phone rang, Molito pulling it from his breast pocket, using a quick wrist move to flip it open.

"Yeah . . . Okay . . . Okay." Molito's eyes stayed on Brody, but his mind was somewhere else. "Okay, lay it off downtown." He flipped the phone shut and slid it into his pocket.

His hand out again. "I gotta go." He shrugged. "Problems. But like I was saying, stop by sometime, shooter."

Brody thought, *shooter*? He turned to V.R., the door clicking shut behind him.

"Sit the fuck down, Brody," V.R. said.

The head coach looked tired. No, Brody decided, he looked hung over, and he needed a shave. Vincent Read, the third coach in three years for the Stars. He'd kicked around the National Football League for twenty years. Defensive back coach at Tampa, then assistant coaching stints in Atlanta, San Diego and LA. The Stars hired him three years ago as defensive coordinator.

Brody remembered reading an old, scathing *New York* magazine piece in the library about Papa Goldman and his coaches. In twenty years, the owner had never hired a proven NFL head man, and often hung on to his failures too long. The last three years were different. Read replaced Lou Smythe, who resigned late last season after he nearly dismantled a midtown steakhouse during a fight with cops, following a fight with his wife. Before Smythe, the Stars had a first-year college coach from Colorado. He'd abruptly quit at season's end, saying the pro game wasn't for him.

Everyone had their theories. But the *New York* story applied pop psychology to Goldman's hiring trends. It speculated that because Goldman had been fired as a young engineer from a major can manufacturer when he was young, his choices reflected a psychological need to mirror his own entrepreneurial success through the surrogates he employed. Goldman had earned his first fortune by patenting a new injection molding machine that spit out beer cans with tab tops, then doubled it building malls in New Jersey and Connecticut. The magazine writer interviewed Goldman's ex-wife, who now lived in Grosse Pointe, a posh suburb near Detroit. She bitterly told the magazine that Goldman's main interest had never been football. The team was only a vehicle to cut and paste him from the business sections to the front pages. She said, "I told Papa when he bought the team, this is nothing more than a vanity buy."

But mostly, it was GM Jack Petrus who took the heat. Most sports columnists saw him as incompetent, perhaps because Petrus worked for Goldman in manufacturing before he bought the team. "The Stars will never get to the playoffs as long as Jack Petrus is GM," the mantra went. Or, "There's nothing wrong with the Stars that firing Jack Petrus won't cure."

Critics blamed Petrus for the string of top draft choices who'd failed in the last five seasons. Three never lived up to their potential. A lineman fell over dead with a heart attack during an icy Packers game on Lambeau Field. Another, a defensive back, was decapitated after rear ending a semi, driving home drunk after a home game.

Two years ago, Petrus himself found trouble. He solicited a vice decoy near Grand Central. Police booked and printed him in time to make the morning tabs. But the owner stuck by him. That was another criticism Brody read. Papa Goldman, a few columnists wrote, was loyal—to a fault.

V.R. said, "Brody, I've been watching you, and I've decided you're fucking strange."

Brody said nothing.

V.R. leaned back and sipped coffee out of a foam cup. "In fact, you're about the strangest fucking rookie I've ever seen."

Brody shifted a little.

"I've been watching kids come into this league for twenty years. Most rookies, sure, they have trouble with the new system, the way things are done. But they make an effort to get to know the other players. You, you already know the offense better than most of the veterans, but you're walking around like a fucking postal employee. You got weapons stashed in your dorm room?"

"I donated them to the militia when I left Michigan."

V.R. shook his head, chuckling a little now. "You don't have a clue, do you?"

"About what?"

"What some of the players are saying. Part of my job is to know what's going on in the heads of my players. And you've crawled into quite a few."

"Tell me."

"Some mention the salary. Others talk about the car."

"The team gave me both."

"Myself, I'd have picked out something a little more low key."

"I—"

"Don't give me excuses. Besides, there's not a damn thing you can do about that now. What concerns me now is this story going around about you and that kid."

Brody asked, "What kid?"

"The kid your old man wasted back in Michigan. He was a jig, wasn't he?"

Glamour Boy, Brody thought. Loeb was right.

Brody said, "It could have been anybody. It could have happened to anybody."

"But it happened to you. And now you're here. And *you* have a problem."

V.R. pointed to a small boom box on his shelf, saying, "Don't you listen to the radio?"

"What does the radio have to do with it?"

"That asshole on FAN. He's been milking it all week. Yesterday, I'm told, he did a phone interview with the prosecutor who locked you up."

"I took a plea. And you said don't listen to the radio."

"But other players do."

V.R. studied him a couple seconds. "I could like you, Brody. Twenty years I've been telling players to ignore media. Twenty fucking years, I actually believe you're the first player who's taken my advice."

V.R. leaned forward, lowering his voice. "In case you haven't noticed, you're gonna have to learn to deal with it here. This football team is no different than the rest of the country. It's there. And it's here. And it will continue until the fucking media stops drilling this race shit into our head every day."

V.R. paused, then said, "You been talking to Dominique?"

"Trying not to."

"Between you and me, I'd be more worried about her than that asshole Carcaterra."

"I've heard."

"The girl's in a hurry. Funny thing, she also loves the game. Told me once there was a *purity* to it. One side beating the shit out the other side, no complications like her own life. Or at least that's what she said."

"That's good, isn't it?"

"As long as you fit into some of her other schemes."

"How does jumping quarterbacks fit in?"

"Just to fuck with the old man, run up his pressure. She won't slow down until she's sitting in his chair in the box upstairs."

Shit, Brody thought. He was smart keeping his distance.

V.R. took another sip of coffee. "You talk to Carl much?"

"Just briefly. I've talked more with Dominique."

"You talk to Dominique, you're probably talking with Carl."

Brody blinked.

V.R. added, "Some say she's fucking Carl."

"He's almost twice her age."

"Like I said, girl's in a hurry. She's worried the old man will sink the team before she can get it. And she may have a point. The old man's out of the old school. He thinks he can make a living doing this."

"It's an NFL franchise."

"If you're the fucking '49ers. Fill the dome, maybe get the city to turn over those suites. That's why he brought Montan aboard, Carl and all this shit about a three-year plan. You know he's got a personal contract with the old man, don't you?"

"I hadn't heard."

"He guarantees a winning season by the third year, that's this season. And the playoffs by five. He doesn't produce, he's gone."

"Sounds more like a coach's deal."

"He has final say in draft choices, trades, all personnel matters. I've never seen anything like it."

"He's had some bad luck."

"Carl snagged Reggie from the Niners. I tell Carl what I need, Carl makes the picks. We don't always see eye to eye. That goes for you, too. I have a fucking quarterback. I was against you coming here. But now that I've taken a good look at you, I'm starting to come around."

"I thought you only cared about Sundays."

"That's exactly what I'm saying. I've already got enough bullshit on the team. Glamour Boy's a fine receiver, if we can keep his head in the game. One way or another, you're gonna have to nip this, or it's going to be an awfully long goddamn year."

Brody had about a half dozen questions he wanted to ask on other matters. What was V.R. doing hanging with a guy like Molito? The guy right in camp. And his driver? What about the league rules?

He held his tongue.

V.R. thought for a couple seconds, then said, "Maybe you ought to look up Eric Smith. He knew how to handle Reggie and his posse."

"I've been talking to Bobby."

"Bobby looks out for Bobby. Smith, yeah, he was a fuckup. But Glamour Boy would do anything for him."

Brody wanted to say, except win. Still, it wasn't a bad suggestion.

V.R. said, "Like I was saying, you fire that fucking ball like a bazooka. So, I'm also going to give you a little help. Just don't make an asshole out of me."

V.R. rubbed his whiskers, then stretched. "Now, get the fuck out of here."

Brody rose, saying, "I'd be grateful for anything you could say."

V.R. said, "I'm not going to *say* a fucking thing."

"Then how are you going to help me?"

"I'm going to give you something they all want."

Brody asked with his eyes.

V.R. crushed the empty coffee cup in one hand and tossed it into the trash. "The fucking *football*, Brody. You're starting the second half tomorrow night."

Vincent Read didn't follow him out for a hug.

CHAPTER

★ ★ ★ **11** ★ ★ ★

Montan waited in Nat Sherman's on 42nd and Fifth late Friday afternoon, sitting upstairs at the tobacco shop in one of two stuffed leather chairs. A black grand piano, a digital player, filled the room with Gershwin selections, the keys going up and down like Ira's ghost had dropped by for a tune and a smoke.

A German tourist, a tall man in his late forties, sank into the chair next to Montan and lit a Cuban he'd brought into the shop. He said he was from Hamburg, saying the first syllable "*ahh*," like a doctor was checking his throat.

"Ahhmburg vus nise. Now, the vawl is down, and it's overrun by commie fuckers from ze east. I liked the vawl. The vawl kept zem out."

Montan decided the tourist needed work on "fuckers," stop saying it like it was the German airplane. Montan was smoking a Nat Sherman Dakota. He figured, you sit in one of Nat's two smoking chairs, you ought to be burning one of Nat's cigars.

The kraut kept talking, saying he was an internist. "Me, I'm sick of practicing in Europe. I vant to move to zis place you call Montana. I vant to get a motor home." He looked at Montan. "Do you know much about Montana?"

"Underestimated," Montan said. "Eighty-second player picked in the '79 draft." He sent a stream of smoke at the kraut, then glared.

The tourist left. Montan checked his Bulgari. He had three hours to kickoff, Arizona at the dome. A minute later, Raymond Bullard arrived and sat down. He began briefing Montan on several meetings he'd had with Eric Smith.

"Names. Dates. Incidents. Violations of the standard contract agreement and league policy, not to mention several felonies, too. He also gave up a made guy who worked him all last year for an edge."

"Did he tell you he put down money as well as provided inside information?" Montan asked.

Bullard nodded.

"Who's the dino?"

Bullard said, "Guy named Tommy Molito out of Queens. Smith says he introduced him last year to one of the coaches."

Montan took a long pull on the Dakota.

"He also lists incidents and front office coverups with other players. Apparently they talk among themselves more than you think."

"Character attracts character," Montan said. "How many?"

"About a dozen."

"About?"

"Thirteen, to be exact."

"He's sure of the dates."

Bullard nodded. "And locations. Get this, he's kept a log for three years. You and a couple of your scouts make quite a few appearances."

He pulled out an envelope from his pocket and handed it to Montan. "He's got the original," Bullard added.

Montan slipped the envelope into his coat. "What, he thinks he's breaking a lease?"

"He's concerned nobody will believe him."

"He ought to be concerned this doesn't find its way to Molito."

Bullard leaned closer. "And I'm not sure he trusts league security."

"Eric's not an idiot," Montan said. "Sooner or later, it will dawn on him NFL Security has never busted an owner." Montan paused. "Has he mentioned the Players Association?"

"There's bad blood there. Apparently he's not happy about the way they handled his drug cases."

"So you're saying?"

"He's demanding to talk to the commissioner. By next week, he says. Or, he's going the media route."

Montan drew again on the Dakota, asking with his eyes.

Bullard said, "The commissioner will not take a call from a player on something like this. Security gets the referral. I'd have to set any meeting up."

Montan thought about it a while, then said, "You don't smoke, do you, Raymond?"

"Two packs a day in Vegas," Bullard said. "But what does that have to do with anything?"

Montan looked at the Dakota between his fingers. "These are different. You savor. You're not reaching for one every time you eat or fuck or the wheels come off."

Bullard touched the edge of his well-sprayed hair line with his fingertips, still wondering where Montan was going.

Montan continued, "And unlike a cigarette, a cigar can be unpredictable. You get a flaw in the binder, the fire begins to run up a side. You can pay thirty or forty dollars, but it still happens. They're rolled by people, not machines. And people are human. They make mistakes. It's the risk you take, but also a part of the adventure."

"That's fascinating, Carl," Bullard said.

Montan looked at the Dakota again. "Some people try to finish them anyway. But you know what I do when I get a cigar like that? No matter how much I paid, I snuff it out. Then I find something else to smoke."

Montan set the Dakota in the ashtray, turning, his voice low and controlled. "Tell Eric Come-to-Jesus Smith he's got his meeting. Set it for Tuesday. That ought to hold him."

"I'm booked Tuesday," said Bullard.

Montan said, "So is the commissioner, no doubt."

★   ★   ★

Shay Falan picked up the ringing telephone on her rolltop, the desk just under her rare poster of Ethel Merman from *Annie Get Your Gun*. Bookcases with more than five hundred vintage videos, noir classics and musicals lined the nearby walls.

"I'm thinking you may be right," Eric Smith said.

She pushed her hair behind her ear, putting the earpiece tight. "Right about what?"

"This fucking MM thing."

She heard traffic in the background, street sounds.

"Where are you?"

"Third Avenue. I just came from a travel agent. I booked a flight to Palm Springs. I'm leaving tomorrow and wouldn't you know it. I'm coming down with a fucking cold."

"I'd sniffle in Palm Springs."

"No, Betty Ford. I'm going to check it out. If I like it, I'm going in."

"You can just do that? Show up at the door?"

"They took Brett Favre."

"Who's he?"

"Green Bay quarterback. One year he's strung out on Percs. Goes to Betty Ford the next year and he's the fucking MVP."

She was glad to hear some bravado. She'd been thinking about Eric Smith a lot lately, thinking Smith had been uncomfortably similar to a lot of men she'd befriended and dated in New York. A string of whiny actors. A tyrant director who suffered from angst. A stockbroker who made guests take their shoes off on his polished hardwood floors.

"That's a bold step," she said. "I guess you won't be getting those four beers."

"I plan on drinking them on the plane," he said. He paused, street noise crackled in the earpiece. "You got what I gave you safe?"

"My safety deposit box," she said. "Right next to all my diamonds and black pearls." She was happy for him.

Smith said, "Look, something happens to me. The plane goes down, you know, or I fucking die in detox, you got to promise me something."

"Now you're talking silly."

"No, promise me. This is fucking important. That's why I gave it to you." She heard anger in his voice.

"Okay."

"I can't fucking trust anybody. I don't know if I'm paranoid or just thinking better without the booze. But this guy I told you I was talking to from the league, I think he's in on it."

"You've never told me what *it* is."

"You don't need to know. Just listen."

Be a good listener, she told herself.

"Something happens, you make two copies of what I gave you and you take it directly to the commissioner of the National Football League.

They're in the book, an office on Park Avenue. You put it directly in his hand. You don't give it to a secretary, or an assistant. If they try to send you to league security, you demand the commissioner."

"Okay."

"Other copy, you take to *NFL Magazine*. It's on that new network, MEC. Ask to see a producer."

"You talked to them?"

"Not yet. It'll be my first call after Betty Ford."

Shay thought about what he was saying, all this top-secret intrigue. She hadn't even looked at the paperwork he'd given her. "Eric, why don't we get together tonight and you can try to explain to me what all this is about."

"I'm going to a meeting."

"I thought you said you were done with that."

"No, NA. I went to one a couple nights ago after I saw this story about Favre. That's where I started thinking maybe I belonged in Palm Springs."

"You're off those pills?"

"I've cut back. The NA people said I might go into a seizure if I stopped."

"So we get together after the meeting."

"Can't. This guy is coming over."

"I thought you said you didn't trust him."

"No, this player who wants some advice. Derek Brody. Maybe you seen him on TV."

"You know I don't follow football."

"He wanted to buy me dinner Sunday. Seemed liked a decent kid. I told him it would have to be tonight. He's coming by after the game."

"You said you didn't trust anybody."

"He's a rookie. They're clueless. Besides, I'm curious to know what's going on with the fucking team."

She heard him break into a side conversation, someone on the street bitching he'd been too long on the pay phone.

"Look, I got to go," he said.

"So, I'll call you at Betty Ford, huh?"

"No, this guy at NA says you can only call out, but not until the second week. They have all kinds of security there, confidentiality. All this shit, that's another reason I'm going."

"So you can get some rest," she said.

Smith said, "No, so I can disappear."

★ ★ ★

Brody did not make his passing debut in the second half. V.R. sent him into the game in the second quarter after a 262-pound rookie linebacker trying to make the Cards drilled Bobby Loeb, crushing his ribs between his shoulder pads and the turf. Loeb lay on the field for ten minutes, Squat and a couple of coaches hunched over him. The score was 29–0, Arizona.

Hardly twenty thousand people were scattered around the Stardome, but they were vocal. Loeb had told him to expect a mix of diehards and friends and clients of season ticket holders who didn't want to waste their time on a preseason game.

"It's slap dick football," Loeb said. Most of the starters would ride the bench in favor of the marginal camp players who coaches wanted to evaluate one more time before the roster cut. You saved the starters for the regular season, avoiding injury in a meaningless game. But Loeb had thrown a sideline fit with V.R. at the end of the first quarter, saying he wasn't going to sit on the bench until he scored. He paid the price, finally walking off the field unassisted, holding his right side. The crowd didn't applaud, the traditional salute to an injured player. They booed.

V.R. asked Brody to stand next to him in the first quarter, the coach with a laminated sheet of plays, Tommy Molito behind him, minding his cord. V.R. had a necklace mike with one-way radio communication to the quarterback's helmet. He wore a button on his belt he needed to push when he talked. Sometimes he'd call upon Brody to make hand signals, the radio sometimes cutting out.

With the crowd small, Brody had a difficult time tuning out hecklers. By the second Arizona score, a fan wearing Reggie Thompson's jersey and a New York Department of Sanitation cap started mouthing off from the front row, just behind the bench.

Brody was signaling.

"Hey, *Brodeeee*! This is football. Not a school for the fucking deaf."

Then, later, "Hey, *Brodeeee*! What's your *problem*? You both deaf and dumb? Why won't you talk to us on FAN?"

And, "Hey, *Brodeeee*! Your parole officer is sittin' right here. He don't like what he sees."

As Brody ran in to replace Loeb, he conjured up a mental image for himself. He did that in games, visualizing something simple, just working with that. He'd learned it from a vocal major at Michigan, a girl who helped him study. He imagined the Stardome was empty. No fans, except one. The sanitation guy. Play for him, like a vocalist singing to a single seat.

Jedi Conlin was in for Glamour Boy. They'd moved him over from left flanker to the right side, his college position. V.R. called a long fly up the right side for his first play, Brody figuring the coach was going to let him get the idea of passing out of his system. But Conlin got open, Brody's first NFL pass a sixty-yard touchdown, the small crowd exploding, silenced only by the gun.

For two weeks in camp Loeb had been telling Brody how much faster and bigger the pro game was. But it didn't strike him as that much quicker, and he'd played against plenty of behemoths in the Big Ten. When the second half started, the biggest challenge was the helmet radio. V.R.'s voice kept cutting in and out, Brody not hearing the entire play. He signaled to the bench, pointing to his helmet.

Over the earpiece, Brody heard arguing among the coaches upstairs and V.R.:

"This fucking thing ain't working."

"You gotta hold the button down, V.R."

"I'm holding the fucking button."

"You gotta hold it for a second before and after you call the play."

The Stars defense shut down the Cards. The slap dicks were pumped up by the TD before the half, all of them trying to hit their way into a roster spot.

The Stars offense ground out fifty yards rushing in the third quarter, V.R. calling mostly running plays. When he did pass, V.R. had him throwing to the left side for short gains and first downs. Jedi Conlin kept coming back to the huddle, saying he was open up the right side.

"Rick, throw the ball to me. I fucking own this guy."

The drive stalled.

At the start of the fourth quarter, when they got the ball again, Brody rested on one knee in the middle of the huddle. "Some of you guys are going home," he said. "You want to go home slapping your dicks, or you want something to remember?"

"We down seventeen, Rick," somebody said.

A lineman ran into the huddle announcing a play Brody had already heard in the helmet.

"Shit," Conlin said. "Rick, I'm telling you, all day long. Throw me the fucking ball."

Brody had seen it, too.

"What's the play, Rick?" somebody said.

Brody saw something in their eyes. "From now on, nobody fucking talks in the huddle but me. That's the way it works. You want to talk, you fucking sit on the bench. You want to win, you listen to me."

Brody paused. "Okay, Queens White Hitman. Fake Zip. Two. Six. Eight. On two."

It was a passing play. V.R. had ordered a run.

What Brody saw was that feeling. He'd tried to explain it to a date at Michigan once, the girl asking him a bunch of questions, trying to fix psychological reasons to why he played. So he put on NFL films, video of bombs, smash mouth, and hits over the middle. He turned up the volume, the rock soundtrack.

"That's what it's about," he told her. "Feel it."

"That's awfully *esoteric*." She added the definition, saying the word indicated the matter was understood by, or meant for, only the select few who have special knowledge or interest.

"You're goddamn right it is," Brody said.

He called fourteen plays in a twenty-three-play drive, his helmet crackling with V.R.'s profanity on every play he changed. Brody just pointed at both his ears with both fingers, as if the radio wasn't working.

He bootlegged the ball himself into the end zone.

When he jogged off the field, V.R. was screaming at the equipment manager. Brody ran to the bench and threw a towel over his head. The equipment manager took the helmet, checking the wires.

Four minutes later, he went back and did it again, hitting Toby Headly in the flats, Conlin in the zones. Arizona sent in a couple defensive backfield starters to try to cool him down.

They got the ball back on the eighteen and drove again. The little crowd raising hell now. But they stalled on the Cards' 13-yard line with less than ten seconds to go. V.R. called for a time-out and Brody walked slowly to the sidelines. The PA was pumping out Dick Dale's "Nitrous." Manic guitar riffs ricocheting off the empty seats and concrete walls. Brody had the feeling, too. He was going to get the ball into the end zone, even if he had to carry it in himself.

The equipment manager pulled off Brody's helmet. He looked inside and said, "I'm fucking telling you, there ain't a thing wrong with that radio, V.R."

V.R. spat and turned to Brody. "I gotta say this, asshole. You got fucking balls."

Brody wiped his face, then put the helmet back on.

V.R. said, "You're lucky I enjoy a good show."

Brody nodded, still catching his breath.

V.R. gripped both sides of his face mask, stiffening his arms, letting him know he had his head. "Presuming you ever get the chance, you pull shit like this in the regular season, I'll personally pack a line dummy up your ass."

When he let go, he smacked his helmet.

"Hey, *Brodeeee!*"

Brody tuned the heckler out.

"What you want to do, coach?"

"It's your game. You fucking win it now."

"I'm thinking right corner, Hitman Jack."

"Jack?"

"That's what I've been calling it. Defense was getting hip to Ripper. If Conlin is covered, I'll run it in."

V.R. said, "Reggie will get open. I'm moving Conlin back to the left."

The idea infuriated Brody. "Reggie's been on the bench the whole fucking game. The dicks have been out there kicking ass."

"They'll be in the nickel," V.R. said. "Some day you're going to need Reggie." He turned toward the bench and shouted, "Glamour Boy."

At the snap, Brody dropped seven steps and set. He saw Thompson on his route to the corner, Glamour Boy already getting his step. Brody also saw thirteen yards of turf to the end zone, one linebacker to outrun, or knock down.

V.R.'s words brought his arm back.

The pass floated in a high arc to the back corner. Later, he'd study the throw on the game film, confirming his first impression: Thompson leaping and catching it just above his helmet with both hands, then in one continuous motion, palming and spiking it with one hand.

The official signaling, *incomplete*.

Brody sprinted over to the line judge, almost on him before Glamour Boy restrained him.

The official shouting, "Did not have control. Did not have control."

The line judge walked off, his eyes on his feet, the crowd booing at first, then falling into a murmur.

Thompson let go, saying "Chill, White Boy Rick."

Brody spun around, saying, "What the fuck you call that?"

Glamour Boy took off his helmet. "Six-million-dollar throw," he said, his eyes dead. "Two-million-dollar catch."

Brody said, "You cost us the game."

"That was slap dick," Thompson said. "And slap dick don't mean shit."

Thompson jogged toward the tunnel, Brody's eyes following. Beyond the receiver, Brody could see Dominique Goldman at the entrance. She was talking with a TV crew.

"Hey, *Brodeeee!*"

Brody turned to the heckler in the sanitation hat. He was leaning over the railing behind the bench, a beer sloshing out of his cup. Brody walked straight toward him. When he crossed the sideline, the rail bird backed up a couple rows on the stairway.

"Nice throw, Brody," he said, polite now.

Brody stopped and spit. "I'll be talking the same shit to you on Monday. Out my window."

"What's Monday?" the guy said.

"The day you pick up my fucking trash."

CHAPTER

★★★ **12** ★★★

Behind him, the empty Stardome droned with the sound of a turf sweeper, a groundskeeper sucking up paper airplanes, tape and plugs of chewed snuff. Montan held out both hands, palms up, his pose framed by the window in the owner's suite.

"I told you, Papa," he said. "He's another Broadway Joe."

Goldman looked up from an overstuffed leather chair, Petrus from the corner of a long leather couch. The suite was dimly lit, the accent lighting on the bar.

Petrus said, "I hear he's having problems with players."

"Give him time," Montan said.

He walked over to the bar, poured himself a Johnnie Walker black and explained that Brody's Activity Vector Analysis revealed an initial tendency to withdraw in a new social environment, but a strong ability to adapt in time.

Petrus said, "That's an opinion. There's a lot of opinions in those head reports."

"When I first saw him in Ann Arbor, I could have swore he was a kicker," Montan said. "He was a real loner his sophomore year."

"You spotted Brody that long ago?" Goldman asked.

"I was making a character check on a tight end. I spotted Brody throwing in a scrimmage."

"I just saw the tight end on the waiver wire," Petrus said. "I guess Miami let him go."

"That kid they took in the first round?" Goldman asked.

"The one picked up with a concealed weapon," Petrus said.

Montan said, "Remember, Papa, campus police found a .357 Smith in his car during a routine traffic stop. They buried the report. The team was playing Ohio State that week."

"But Miami took him," Goldman said.

Montan sipped the scotch and nodded. "That's why you can't rely on NFL Security checks. They're just not as good as our PI. He also had parking tickets."

Petrus said, "I never saw a problem with that."

"A thousand dollars worth?" Montan said.

"There's no place to park at most colleges."

"That's no excuse," Montan said.

Goldman held out his hand, stopping the bickering. "Carl, so you've been after Brody all these years?"

"I had scouts watching him. Let's just say he's been one of my pet projects since I took the job."

The door to the suite opened. Dominique Goldman walked in, saying hello to Petrus and Montan, but ignoring her father. She slid onto a stool at the bar.

She flung a lock of hair out of her eyes with a jerk of her head. "Buy me a drink, Carl."

He held up the Johnnie Walker for her approval.

She nodded. "Lots of ice."

Papa Goldman asked, "Were you in the press box, darling?"

She nodded, reaching for the drink.

"Anything interesting?" Montan asked.

"I left near the end of the fourth quarter, but already they all were talking about next week. A TV crew also grabbed Brody as he ran into the tunnel."

"I hope he stopped to talk," Goldman said.

"They asked him if Bobby couldn't play next week, did that mean the team had a quarterback controversy. He had a pretty good answer. *'Not unless you make it one.'* That's what he said. Then he headed to the locker room."

"That's our boy," said Montan.

Dominique's eyes went to her father. "We need to talk," she said.

Goldman sighed. "The last time you said that it cost me a half million dollars."

Petrus, sensing an argument brewing, stood up. He complained it had been a long day, then lumbered out the door. Montan finished his drink, then rubbed his hands together, saying, "I better go too."

"Stay, Carl," she said. "You need to hear this as well."

She turned to her father. "I'm firing the entire press office. Get new people in."

Goldman rolled his eyes. "My God, why?"

"I make a simple request Monday. Tell them to look into booking Brody on the Carcaterra show. Five days later, and nobody has even made a phone call. All these guys know how to do is pass out credentials and make sure the reporters are watered and fed."

"And just who would you replace them with?"

"People who know how to spin. Like they do in Washington. People who can sit right there with a straight face and lie."

"That's goddamn ridiculous. This is football."

"And you're going to need people like that, if we're ever going to get these stadium concessions."

Goldman rose to his feet, struggling a little. "I will not lie to our fans."

She remained coldly analytical. "You wouldn't be lying to them. You're lying *through* them. They're the ones who'll put pressure on the city. You got to make people think you're ready to pull up stakes. Make people think of the Dodgers and the Browns and the Colts."

Goldman walked to the window, then pivoted, his face bright red. "Those men in the press office have worked for me for years. You want to book somebody on the show, you goddamn do it yourself."

Montan looked at Dominique and said quietly, "What makes you think either one is interested? Carcaterra has been hammering Brody for weeks."

"Brody owes me one," she said coldly.

"What's that supposed to mean?" Goldman said.

She ignored the question. "And everybody will want to talk to Brody after tonight, even Carcaterra."

Montan set down his empty glass and put up his hands in mock surrender. "I really must go. I've made some plans."

Dominique turned, her eyes full of mischief. "Sounds like a woman to me, Carl."

She eyed the length of his body. He'd worn one of his favorite power suits, a Hugo Boss, black with gray pinstripes.

"Is she right, Carl?" Goldman asked, enthusiastic about the notion. "Don't spare us the details."

Montan pushed his glass away and said, "Let's just call it another pet project—the personal kind."

★   ★   ★

Brody saw only a couple pedestrians on the sidewalk when he made his first pass in the Mercedes. Soho, Smith had called it. Warehouses transformed into residential, but few groceries or other businesses on the street. He found a private garage three blocks away on Greene Street. LoJack or no LoJack, he wasn't parking a $130,000 car at the curb. The words of a car thief he'd met in The Valley came back to him. The color red, the con said, shouted steal me, please.

He was still fuming about Glamour Boy. He'd slipped out of the locker room before it was opened to reporters. He'd figured he might take some heat for that, but still would be better off than saying something he might regret. He wished he'd grabbed an ice pack on the way out. His elbow was throbbing, the one he'd placed just under the line-backer's chin when he ran for the second TD.

The entrance was a metal door. It looked like it once was used by warehouse workers, but now had an intercom bolted to the side of the jamb. Brody pushed the button to Smith's loft. Waited about thirty seconds, then pushed it again.

"Yeah," a voice crackled.

"It's Derek Brody."

The lock buzzed.

Inside, there was a freight elevator. He lifted up the wooden gate, closed it and pushed the button to the fourth floor. It jerked up-ward, its motor grumbling. As it passed each floor something under-neath, something that sounded loose or broken, made a noise like a cracking whip.

Smith's loft was at the end of a white hall added when the building was converted. There was a laundry and storage room in the corridor, but no other apartments.

Brody knocked.

He heard a muffled voice say, "Yeah."

"Derek Brody," he said. Shit, he'd told him twice now.

He heard dead bolts clicking. Three of them, then a couple of them clinking again, as if Smith was struggling inside to figure out when they were all open.

The door finally swung inward.

"Fuck," Smith said, hardly glancing at him. "The fucking super finally gives me locks today, but forgets the fucking peephole. The super here is a motherfucking lame."

Smith didn't look anything like the quarterback he'd watched in the game films. Sandals. A plain white T-shirt. And balloon pants, a squiggly pattern in Stars colors, but badly faded from too many washes and spins.

Smith said, "Saw the fucking game on cable. You did some serious shit out there."

"You sure it's not too late?" Brody asked.

"I'm not the motherfucker who has to look at game film in the morning. Get your ass in here so I can lock the fucking door."

Brody walked in, hearing the locks click shut behind him. The loft had fifteen-foot ceilings, bright ash woodwork and blond hardwood floors. He saw a modern steel sculpture near a tall arched window. It was a passing quarterback, life-sized. The body was shaped from twisted reinforcement bar, the head, a large rusted machine gear.

Smith walked slowly to the kitchen area. Toddled, really, from his leg injuries. Brody went to the window. The World Trade Center, speckled with lights, rose in the distance outside.

Smith asked if he wanted something to drink, but added he didn't have any beer. He'd quit drinking, he said.

"Heard a good line about that at a meeting I went to tonight."

"What kind of meeting?"

"NA, it's like AA. They say you keep shit in the house, it's like dropping by to chat at a whore house while you're trying not to fuck around on your wife."

Brody had this momentary thought about his father. His old man didn't have a problem, and neither did he. But he'd stopped after the accident. He vowed he'd never lose control again.

Smith held up a Coke, saying "This okay?"

Brody nodded.

Smith toddled over, handed him the sweating can, then plopped down in a low-slung chair, a leather bean bag with arms on it. He groaned when he extended his legs. A pile of magazines were stacked on the floor, on top of it a box of Kleenex, used ones next to it in another pile. A phone and an ashtray balanced on one armrest, a hair dryer on the other, a long extension cord plugged into a nearby wall.

The guy lives in the chair, Brody thought.

Smith lit a cigarette, exhaled, then doubled into a cough. When it subsided he said, "Late summer fucking cold. The worst. But I'm treating the motherfucker." Smith looked at his watch. "So, what's up? What kind of fucking shit have you gotten yourself into already?"

Brody sat down on a futon. "What makes you say that?"

"Because if you weren't swimming in shit you wouldn't fucking be here at goddamn midnight. Big debut like tonight, shit, you should be out getting fucking basted, like I did when I was your age."

"I'm not that young."

"I fucking heard," Smith said. He checked his watch again.

The way Smith kept swearing and looking at the time, Brody wondered if the visit had pissed Smith off. "Maybe I better go," he said.

Smith leaned back into the chair. "Relax. I need to keep an eye on the clock for my fucking treatment." He popped the top on his own Coke. "Hey, you want some fucking pizza? I'll have it delivered."

Brody said he could probably eat a slice or two. He listened to Smith order, the clerk on the other end apparently saying it would be at least an hour, Smith saying he'd make it worth their while if they "hurry it the fuck up."

Brody thought about where to start. Glamour Boy and his posse. The divisions on the team. Or, maybe this guy Carcaterra on the radio. Maybe Smith dealt with him. Another part of him wanted to bring up Dominique Goldman. Do it casually. See where Smith went with it.

Brody said, "I've got a problem with the black players."

"Reggie Thompson," Smith said.

"Yeah, and his people. How'd you know?"

"Reggie told me you might be looking me up. Heard from him before you called."

"I didn't tell Reggie." He'd told only Loeb.

"Reggie gets around," Smith said. He paused, then asked, "How do you like the people in player personnel?"

"Montan? What's he got to do with it?"

"He been helping you?"

"Arranged a car. But as far as I'm concerned, players are my problem, not Montan's."

Smith drew on the cigarette deeply, looking him over, then exhaled.

Smith said, "I saw that circus mazurkas shit Reggie pulled in the end zone. He tanked that."

"I know," Brody said. "He does a tightrope thing, not a spike."

"That's Glamour Boy. Shit, man, you're catching on."

"Coach says you might be able to help me sort it out."

"What coach? Fucking V.R.?"

Brody nodded.

Smith laughed, then blew his nose. "What the fuck else V.R. say?"

"He said something about a blocking dummy, but that's an unrelated story."

"Shit," Smith said, chuckling. "V.R. is a fucking bum."

"He's got a strange system, but it's creative."

Smith laughed again. "Fuck his system. You met Molito yet? The guy with the tittie bar?"

Brody nodded.

"Yeah, his friends call him the Mole. Molito's a fucking bookie. I'll bet you didn't fucking know that, did you?"

"Actually, I suspected," Brody said. "You telling me the coach bets."

"I'm in the car with the man once and he wants to wager a hundred on whether the next guy who pulls up to us at the traffic light has a fucking smoke in his mouth. I go to Vegas with him once, he gets a half a dozen of us to bet on the exact time of the landing. We write our times on hundred-dollar bills. We land, I'm looking at the bills to determine the winner. You know what V.R. wrote? *Fucking crash landing.*"

Smith laughed, hard.

"So he's laying action on games?"

The laughter turned to a cough. Smith butted the smoke, then became serious. "V.R.'s a fucking bum, but he ain't fucking stupid. Not football. Not even college. Horses, golf games, mainly. Molito keeps him supplied with booze and pussy."

"For what?"

"Injury reports. Starting assignments. Team preparation. Shit like that. I mean, it's nothing direct. There's no paper. V.R. just runs his mouth. And Molito's got good ears."

"How do you know this?"

"I introduced him to Molito." Smith looked around, then said, "Look, I shouldn't even be telling you this shit. But you ought to know what you're dealing with here. It's pretty fucking complicated."

Brody said, "If you know, the front office must. I mean, this Molito hangs with the coach. He doesn't look like a rep from the United Way."

Smith said, "The question you've got to ask yourself, is how the fuck did V.R. ever get a head coaching job in the first place?"

Brody shrugged.

Smith leaned forward a little. "The fucking Stars, that's how. And that's where it all gets complicated."

Smith checked his watch again, then reached over for the hair dryer, switching it on to high. "You gotta let me do something here," he said.

Smith opened his mouth and aimed the dryer at his face, the nozzle three inches from his lips, his mouth open like a fish, his beard fluttering in the hot breeze.

Brody asked, "What are you doing?"

He pulled the dryer away. "Fucking treatment, man. Give me five minutes. Make yourself at home."

Smith aimed the barrel at the back of his throat again and closed his eyes.

Whatever, Brody thought. He walked over to the window and stood next to the sculpture, staring at the World Trade Center again. Then he worked his way over to a wall of mementos. Photographs, action shots, some magazine covers. Smith passing. Smith running. Smith looking down the field. There were plaques from high school and college, one of them, All-American, hanging crooked. You had to pull some serious grades for that, Brody thought. He looked back to Smith again. That old anti-drug commercial about frying an egg crossed his mind.

Brody straightened the All-American citation. A sharp pain shot through his elbow.

"You wouldn't happen to have a cool pack?" he asked.

Smith opened his eyes and pointed to the bathroom.

In the john, Brody searched through three drawers in the vanity. He found a chemical ice pack in the bottom.

The dryer stopped as he came out. Brody twisted the pack to activate it, then wrapped it around his elbow as he sat back down.

Smith held up the blow dryer, like it was something precious. "Northwest pilot I met hipped me to it," he said. "On the onset of fucking symptoms, you blow hot air into your windpipe for five minutes. Four times a day. Germs live at 98.6. Hair dryer blows at 120. Fucking germs can't handle it. Fucking germs die."

"Or have nice hair styles," Brody said.

"Pilot says he hasn't had a major cold in fifteen fucking years."

Brody said, "I was asking you about the players."

Smith lit another cigarette, not coughing this time. He contemplated the question a few moments. "There's a lot of shit I could tell you," he finally said.

Brody stared at him.

Smith leaned forward. "Your problem isn't Glamour Boy. It isn't his fucking posse. It isn't V.R. Your problem is the fucking Stars."

Brody was getting impatient. "You said that earlier. And it still doesn't tell me a thing."

Smith took another drag on the smoke, but kept his eyes on him, looking like he was trying to decide just how to explain it, or whether to explain it at all.

"What the fuck," he finally said. "You're going to hear about it all soon enough."

"Hear what?"

"Your problem is the organization," Smith said.

"The front office?"

"No, the organization within the front office, the organization within the team."

"Every team has front office problems," Brody said.

Smith reacted angrily, his voice rising. "I'm not talking about shit you read in *SI*. I'm talking about born fucking losers. Look around you in the huddle, man. Open your eyes. You understand what I'm saying?"

Brody said he didn't understand a thing.

Smith said, "They come for your urine yet?"

"They took a sample," Brody said. "Said it was for reference."

"Squat?"

Brody nodded.

"That's bullshit. They use that if you get dirty. That's your free pass when the league shows up with a cup."

Brody wanted to know how that worked.

"Get fucked up," Smith said. "You'll find out."

Smith lowered his voice, leaning back in the chair. "The last three years the back of my mind was saying something's fucked up here. But I had my own problems, you know what I'm saying? That's the way they do it. Keep you fucked up. Let you have your party. Shit keeps building up. Pretty soon football's the last thing on your fucking mind."

Brody said, "I still don't understand." Smith was talking a circle around something.

Smith hit the cigarette hard. "Carl Montan," he said. "He's the guy you watch. Squat reports to him. And Squat might as well have been Elvis's fucking trainer. The GM, I think he might be in on it, too. He never challenges Montan."

"Why would the director of player personnel waste the team?"

"Because he can. I think he's connected. Maybe to that Vegas crowd."

"Maybe?"

"Tommy Molito was telling me one night. The Mole had a few drinks in him, and was saying some of his people remember Montan in Vegas years ago. They said he worked at the hotels."

"Doing what?"

"The Mole didn't say."

"I read his press bio," Brody said. "He did a good job with that expansion franchise. Before that, University of Nevada. There was nothing about Las Vegas."

Smith looked at him like he was an idiot. "You think Montan's going to advertise, maybe put it up on the big screen at the dome? I'm saying Tommy said it. And the shit Tommy knows you ain't gonna find in no fucking bio. In fact, you're never going to find it written down."

"So you're telling me Montan is connected with the mob?"

Smith said, "I didn't say that. Tommy would have never said anything if Montan was a made guy. I'm just saying there's some slippery motherfuckers working for the Stars."

"Hired by who, the owner?"

Smith raised his eyebrows. "I do feel bad about that, what this could do to the old man. Papa's clueless. But shit knows, I'm going to look pretty fucked up myself when this whole fucking mess comes out."

"When *what* comes out?" Brody demanded.

"Stay tuned," Smith said. "Like I said, losers."

"Gambling?"

"Seven fucking years in the league. And never approached to do that. Not once. League's too sophisticated now."

"Then *why*?"

Smith pulled his legs close to the chair, helping them a little with his hands. He leaned forward. "I don't fucking know." His tone suddenly deflated, his voice low. "That's the fuck of it. I need some help to figure it out."

Smith reached into a pocket and pulled out a script bottle, twisting the cap off, popping a couple pills. Doing it with one fluid motion. Brody looked at the pile of butts in the ashtray, the hair dryer, the pile of tissues. He was thinking of that egg again.

Brody stood. Visiting Smith, the way the NFL rules were written, he figured, was as bad as hitting Molito's tit bar.

Smith looked up. "Fucking pizza ought to be here soon, man."

Brody held out the ice pack. "Can I take this? I've got a long drive back to Stony Brook."

Smith nodded, then struggled to get up.

Brody walked over, extending a hand. Smith grabbed on. Brody pulled him to his feet.

At the door, Smith unlocked the dead bolts.

He sounded apologetic. "Look, I wish I could tell you more. There's a lot of nuances, a lot of details. I get into the whole thing, and that just puts you at risk. And that's the way they like it, always watching your back."

Brody started for the door, but Smith grabbed him by the shoulder. "That's how it starts," he said. "You'll get into some kind of squeeze and then you'll be dealing with Carl. He'll ride in like the white fucking knight. And then you're part of *his* team."

Brody said, "So what do you suggest? I came here to play football." Brody humoring him now.

"Walk out. Call your agent. Get traded. Take a pay cut. Sit out a year if you have to. You've got no future here."

Brody stared at him a couple seconds, then reached for the door handle. "Good luck with that treatment," he said. "Maybe I'll try it myself sometime."

★   ★   ★

The Surfer dropped Montan and the Turk off, then sped off to park two blocks away. Montan pushed the button. About thirty seconds passed. He pushed it again.

"Pizza?" the voice crackled.

Montan looked at the Turk, smiling.

"Man's going to make it easy," the Turk said. The Turk leaned close to the intercom and said in a clipped accent, "Yeah, pizza here."

Eric Smith was reaching for a twenty in his billfold when the apartment door opened. Montan walked right past him, the Turk behind him, the Turk closing the door and flipping one of the dead bolts.

Montan stopped in the center of the room, looked around and said, "I see you're managing on your pension."

Smith, still at the door, started to say something, but Montan turned around.

"Sit down, Eric."

Smith hesitated.

Montan put out his hand, making a motion. "Down, Eric. You were always very good at that."

Smith limped over to the bean bag chair, then lowered himself slowly, supporting himself with his arms. The twenty was still between his fingers.

The intercom buzzed. The Turk walked over to the panel.

"I've got a pizza coming," Smith said. He blinked a couple of times. "Jesus Christ, Carl, what the fuck you doing here?"

Montan ignored the question, looking at the former starting quarterback, shaking his head. Just standing there, letting him wonder.

"Eric, I hate to say this, but your appearance has seriously deteriorated. You look like shit, in fact."

"It's past midnight," he said, his voice trying to sound normal. "Why didn't you call?"

Montan said, "I'm making a character check."

There was a knock at the door. The Turk opened, a Korean in his early twenties holding a white pizza box in front of him, HOT AND DELICIOUS! printed in red across the top.

The Korean stutter-stepped inside, the Surfer with a handful of his back collar, directing the Korean, like his fist was a rudder.

The Surfer said, "He buzzed the fucking apartment. I was right behind him."

Montan turned to Smith and said, "Your pizza's here."

Smith unconsciously held up the twenty, the pizza guy looking confused, trying to figure out what he'd walked into.

"Our treat," Montan said.

The Turk walked up to the delivery man, as if to take it, then stepped behind him, reaching for his back pocket.

Montan nodded.

The Turk's .22 Llama semiautomatic touched the back of the Korean's head and made a quiet pop. The Korean fell forward, the pizza sliding across the hardwood floor, stopping a couple feet from Smith's feet.

The Korean's body twitched, then stilled.

Montan looked at the pizza, then Smith. He was frozen now, looking sick.

Montan said, "Drugs will do that to you, Eric. You know your appetite is always the first to go."

The Surfer stepped over the Korean and came around behind Smith.

Montan saw the hair dryer, the extension cord snaked across the hardwood floor. "Doesn't that belong in the bathroom?" he said.

Smith's eyes were on the Turk now, the Turk walking to the kitchen breakfast bar, the Turk putting on surgical gloves.

Montan said, "Eric, look at me."

Smith had a pleading look.

"Seriously, you need a housekeeper. I mean, bathroom shit out here in your living room. I'm figuring, I go for a piss, I'm probably going to find a couch."

Smith started talking, stammering detail about a lot of nothing. Montan thinking, he figures if he just keeps jabbering he'll get time to make some kind of move. Talking about some airline pilot and temperatures, talking about germs.

Montan let him go. Listening to the story.

"It's a treatment," Smith said. "That's all."

Then, running out of words.

Montan said, "As I recall, you always needed a lot of treatment."

Montan folded his arms. He still hadn't moved from the spot he'd staked out after his entrance.

"Where's the log?"

"*Log?*" Smith said, looking right at him, trying to sell it.

Montan nodded to the Surfer. The Surfer crouched behind Smith, grabbed a handful of hair and jerked his head back. Smith's eyes drifted over to the Turk, who now was pulling out paraphernalia from a freezer-size Ziploc.

Montan pulled out his copy from his liner pocket, waving it like a hand fan. "Don't fuck with me, Eric. You'll only make it more painful for yourself."

Smith pointed to the stack of magazines. The Surfer let go of his hair and scattered the magazines with a swipe of his hand, a manila envelope falling out.

Montan picked it up, looking inside.

Smith said, "Carl, can't we work this out?"

Montan looked up from the paper. "Where's the original?"

Montan glanced at the Turk. He was burning a lighter under a spoon. Items were lined up on the breakfast bar. A syringe. A small crack pipe. A bag of rock. A packet of heroin, opened.

Smith said, "I destroyed it."

Montan laughed.

Montan walked over to the bean bag, reached down and picked up the hair dryer. He turned it on high, aiming the hot flow at his cupped hand.

"Carl," Smith said, looking up. "Carl, I'll do fucking anything, man. Just say the word, and I'm fucking there."

Montan dropped the hair dryer into Smith's lap, still running.

"Let's start with a little demonstration," he said. "Maybe you can show me how to get through the cold season this year."

CHAPTER

★ ★ ★ **13** ★ ★ ★

Brody overslept. He bolted out of bed, slipped on a T-shirt, jeans and sandals and jogged to the Sports Complex. He didn't stop for Bobby Loeb's newspapers. As far as he was concerned, the paper route ended with the last preseason game.

The offensive coordinator had called for a game review among the quarterbacks at ten o'clock. He arrived in the locker room at 9:50. Through the glass windows of the training room he could see Bobby Loeb lying on his back on a training table, Squat over him with a syringe. Squat slid the needle into Loeb's middle rib cage, then looked up, eyeing Brody.

Aubrey Johnson, the strong safety, was the only other player in the locker room. He was in street clothes.

Brody walked over, saying, "Nice game."

Johnson pulled a handful of underwear from his locker and fired it into the duffel bag on his stool. "Motherfuckers started early. Five guys already. Fucking Squat playing the Turk, banging on our doors this morning, telling us to get over here."

Brody winced. "Roster cuts? You?"

He had a hard time believing it. Johnson still looked sharp. Then he remembered how the coaches had kept the eight-year veteran in the backfield the entire slap dick game.

Brody said, "The coaches must have worked all last night."

Johnson said, "I don't think the coaches did shit."

He grabbed his duffel bag and stormed out.

Brody went to his locker, slipped off his clothes and reached for a pair of team shorts.

"Carl wants to see you."

Brody turned. Squat was two feet away, twirling a roll of tape around his fingers. Brody glanced back at the training room, Loeb still flat on the table, his eyes closed.

Brody pulled up his shorts. "Tell Carl I've got a meeting."

Squat kept twirling, chewing gum, too. "The meeting was canceled. I'm taking Bobby into the city. See our orthopedic man." Squat pointed. "Third office down the hall."

Brody glanced at the dressing room door, and it dawned on him. That's the way they did it at the Stars, Bobby Loeb warned. They send Squat to say the director of player personnel wants to see you. Carl Montan tells you about the great contribution you made in camp. Then he tells you you're gone. After that, you turn your playbook in to V.R. He gives you a big hug and you're out of football. Just like that.

No way, Brody thought.

Brody walked to the office in his shorts, no shirt, no shoes. He stopped at the open door.

"Sit down, Derek," Carl Montan said.

He saw a folding chair against the cinder block wall on the right.

"And close the door."

Inside, Brody said, "What's this about?"

Montan said, "Derek, say hello to Detective Randolph. He works with the New York City police."

Brody turned around and saw a man sitting in a folding chair in the corner on the opposite wall. Mid-fifties. Mustache. White short sleeve shirt and clip-on tie. Wrinkle-free polyester slacks.

The detective looked up from a small notebook, his face expressionless. Brody sat down in the chair, not walking ten feet to shake his hand. He thought, guy wants to look at him like a statue, fuck him. He can come over if he wants to shake.

"Saw you in the Rose Bowl. That was good," Randolph said, saying it like he was talking about the weather. "Saw the second half at the precinct last night, too. Everybody was saying, it's only preseason. I was saying, hey, who cares?"

Brody looked at Montan. "So, am I being cut—or arrested?"

Montan didn't smile. "Detective Randolph would like to ask you some questions, Derek."

The office felt chilly, that concrete floor and cinder block everywhere. "Maybe I should put on some clothes."

Randolph told him it wouldn't take long. "I worked a double last night," he added. "I'm about out of gas."

Brody remembered the way the detectives questioned him after the auto accident. That's the way they did it. Make you think they're tired or disinterested or incompetent, just before the squeeze began.

Montan said, "Detective Randolph has agreed to let me sit in on this. Presuming that's okay with you."

Brody sat down, rested his elbows on his knees and looked up. He asked, exactly what was *this*?

The detective only said, "What did you do after the game last night?"

Brody looked in his eyes, hesitated, then answered.

"I left right after I showered, why?"

"And?"

"I drove into the city."

"Where in the city?"

"I think you call it Soho."

"Why?"

"I wanted to see somebody."

"And who is *somebody*?"

"Eric Smith, and I'll say it again. Why?"

"Don't you read the papers? Listen to the radio?"

Brody looked over at Carl Montan. Montan, with his hands folded in front of him, his eyes telling him nothing.

Brody said, "Coach says don't read the papers in camp."

Montan nodded. "That is correct, detective. Some coaches believe news coverage distracts players."

The detective said, "Eric Smith was discovered dead in Soho very early this morning."

Brody wasn't sure he'd heard it right. "Found dead at his place?"

The detective said, "If you don't read the papers, how did you know we found him there?"

"I didn't."

"Then why did you mention it?"

Brody sat back, took a deep breath and blew all the air out of his lungs. "I just assumed."

"On what basis?"

"He was waiting for a delivery when I left."

"Drugs?"

"No, not drugs," Brody said. He heard his own voice get an edge.

The detective waited.

"He ordered a pizza."

The detective nodded, scrawling something. "So, what were you doing there?"

"What was I doing there?"

The detective looked up. "That's the question."

"I was having some problems with a few players. The head coach suggested Smith would be a good man to contact. Help me sort it out."

"What kind of problems?"

Brody said, "Just camp shit. Rookie hazing."

"Are you aware of Eric Smith's problems over the years?" the detective asked.

"Only what I've read."

"I thought you said you didn't read the papers."

"In camp," Brody added.

Brody looked back at Montan again, Montan nodding a little now, giving him a half smile, like Brody was doing well.

Brody looked back at the detective. "What the fuck is this? Something happens to a guy I meet once, and you drag me in here in front of people I work for like a crack head off the street?"

The detective held up both hands. "Relax now, son. Or this may take a lot longer than you'd like."

Montan interjected calmly, "You can blame that on me, Derek. Detective Randolph called me, wondering where he could find you. I asked him before you came in if I could sit in. I'm just here to protect our interests. Your interests, and the team's."

Montan stood up. "I'll leave if you wish."

Brody looked up, looking for something in Montan's eyes again.

They were gray, almost silver, the black pupils pinpoints under the fluorescent light. They reminded Brody of surveillance mirrors they had in The Valley. He could see you, but you couldn't see in to him.

Brody said, "You know, you're right. Stay. Maybe I should also call my lawyer."

"You need one?" the detective asked.

Montan sat back down.

Brody put his elbow on the back of the chair. "Let's just get this over with. I've got nothing to hide."

Detective Randolph said, "Okay, so you were saying you wanted to talk to Smith. At *midnight?*"

"He said he was leaving town on Saturday."

"Did he say where he was going?"

"No." Brody paused. "How did you know what time? For that matter, how did you know I was even there?"

Montan said, "Detective Randolph is with homicide, Derek."

Christ, Brody thought. He flexed his feet. His toes felt numb from the cold concrete.

The detective explained. "We dusted; you appeared."

The questions came quickly.

"Was he using drugs?"

"He popped a pill. I didn't know what it was. I was only there a few minutes."

The detective made him pin down the time. It wasn't a few minutes. It was nearly an hour.

"It seemed like a few minutes," Brody said.

"How about his behavior?"

"He was talking a lot of nonsense."

"What kind of nonsense?"

Brody's eyes stayed on the detective, but he could feel Montan staring.

"He had this hair dryer, some whacked-out cold treatment he kept talking about."

"You saw the blow dryer?"

Brody nodded, then explained Smith's cure for the common cold. He concluded, "I'd call that whacked out, wouldn't you?"

The detective studied him for a few moments, then said, "The pizza place called the precinct when their guy didn't return. We sent a patrol car to check it out. They found him—and the dryer." He paused. "How about you?"

"Like I said, it sounded like a bunch of bullshit."

"No, drugs," the detective said. "What kind were you doing?"

Brody glared. "Show me a cup and I'll piss in it."

The cop said, "Then maybe you can explain to me why we found your fingerprints are all over the bathroom vanity."

"I asked him for an ice pack for my elbow."

"So, you saw his works?"

"I'm not sure what you mean."

"You know *works*, syringes, spoons."

Brody paused. Something told him to go carefully now. "I wouldn't know what I was looking at if I did," he said.

"I thought you did time."

"I didn't go to prison to party. And I've never used drugs."

"That's how we got your prints. Convicted felon, new FBI computer spits them out pretty quick." The cop paused. "So you're saying syringes wouldn't get your attention?"

Brody remembered seeing disposable razors, clippers, over-the-counter meds, stuff people accumulate in bathrooms. But he didn't want to go there.

"I'm saying I wasn't looking for needles," he said. "I was looking for an ice pack."

"You'd overlook needles?"

"Some players need injections."

The cop glanced at Montan.

"There's a drug called Toradol," Montan said. "An anti-inflammatory that acts like a pain killer. Non-addictive, non-narcotic. It's widely used in the National Football League."

"But Smith was no longer in the league," Detective Randolph said.

"If you check with our orthopedic man, you'll probably find Eric had a prescription. It comes in a pre-loaded syringe."

Brody thought, Montan, helping him a little now.

The detective said, "These weren't scripts." He looked over at Brody. "See them?"

"I don't know," Brody said, shrugging.

"How about a small crack pipe on the kitchen counter?"

"I didn't look at the counter, not closely, anyway."

The detective consulted his notebook. "See anybody? Anything suspicious?"

Brody shook his head.

"Phone calls?"

"Just the pizza."

"Which was exactly?"

"About 12:10."

"How do you know?"

"I looked at my watch."

"How about the street? Cars out front?"

"The street was dead."

"Did Smith mention he was expecting anyone?"

Brody shook his head. "We talked about football. That's all."

"So what did he say? I'm curious—as a fan, I mean."

Brody told himself, don't go near it. Not here. Not now. "He told me every rookie goes through it. He told me everything would change once the regular season began."

Thirty seconds of silence passed, the detective waiting for Brody to say something, trying to shake something loose.

Brody finally said, "Is that it? You done now?"

Detective Randolph said, "So, it's your statement that Smith *was* loaded."

Brody had been thinking between the questions, ever since the detective mentioned the vanity drawer. He thought about the NA meeting Smith mentioned. He thought about the cans of Coke, no beer. He thought about what Smith had said about Molito and V.R. and Montan. One wrong answer, he thought, and he blows the entire season out his ass.

"I said he was talking crazy," Brody said. "If that's being loaded, yes."

"You own a gun?" Randolph asked.

"No, I do not own a gun," Brody said.

There was another long pause, the cop studying him again.

"So that's it?" Brody asked.

"That's it." He turned to Montan and said, "I'm satisfied."

The detective stood up.

Brody said, "Wait a minute. Now, I've got a few questions. You going to tell me what happened, or do I go out and buy a newspaper?"

The cop half smiled, closing his notebook, sliding it into his shirt pocket. "Heroin and cocaine. Speed ball, they call it. That's the medical examiner's opinion, but we won't know the dosage for a couple weeks. I'd appreciate it if that information didn't leave this room."

"So he overdosed," Brody said.

"Not exactly."

Montan interjected, "Speaking of information, detective, is there any reason Derek's involvement—or, should I say, lack of it—needs to be made public? This young man has enough pressure on him as it is."

The cop looked at Brody, then back at Montan. "I'll see what I can do. But I do have a partner who tends to talk too much."

The detective walked over and put out his hand. "Sorry, about the third degree. But I need to eliminate people. Actually, I've been a Stars fan for years. My partner and I bring some kids to the dome each year. Little cop program we've got that tries to keep kids from going juvie."

That's very nice, Brody thought. "You mentioned the hair dryer. You asked about a gun."

"Just part of the crime scene. Please keep that in confidence as well."

"You didn't tell me how he died."

Randolph looked at Montan, then back to Brody. "Small-caliber bullet to the head. Never leaves ballistics. Very professional. We think Smith might have owed money, or crossed somebody. Somebody took out the pizza boy, too. We figure he stumbled into the situation. I guess that makes you lucky, doesn't it?"

"I don't follow you."

"Lucky you weren't hungry."

Brody slumped a little. He hadn't thought about that. "Where does the hair dryer come in?"

"It was still running—halfway down his throat."

Brody said, "He didn't put it *in* his mouth."

"Somebody sending a message, I figure."

"To whom?"

"Anybody else who owes," the cop said.

Montan shook his head. "Tragic. Eric's sad history is one of the reasons we put so much emphasis on character." Montan paused, then asked, "Are you a season ticket holder, detective?"

The detective shook his head, no. "The team comps us the tickets. They're in the upper level."

Montan stood and came around the desk, talking. "You know, we set aside a block of some prime seats on the forty-five. Section 222, just under the press box, the lower fifteen rows. We comp them out to friends of the team, guests of the visitors. I'd like to put you there. I could give you a block of, let's say, a half dozen for the first two games, and, depending on the box office, you might be able to sit there the entire year."

Randolph said, "That would be generous."

Montan smiled, adding, "For you and your partner, and those kids, of course."

★   ★   ★

Brody leaned over, resting his elbows on his knees again, staying in the room as Montan had asked while the personnel director escorted the detective to the parking lot. He ran through the entire visit with Smith again. He kept getting stuck on what Eric Smith said about Montan, the white knight riding in.

"You're lucky they like football. I've just managed to save you a hell of a lot of grief."

Montan was leaning against the door frame, his arms folded. Brody took a good look at him now, Montan really happy with himself. Not worried at all.

Brody didn't say anything.

Montan walked over, stopping only a couple feet away. He held a business card out between two long fingers. "I thought I gave you one of these, but apparently you lost it. You have problems with team-mates, next time you call me."

"Where I come from, you solve your own problems. You don't snitch on teammates."

Brody looked into those silver eyes again.

Montan said, "You're in a profession now, not prison. This is the National Football League, not college. This is the world's greatest city. This is *not* fly-over land." He paused. "My dealings with players are strictly confidential, as is this situation. It's in your best interest to keep this whole matter between us. Do you understand me, Derek?"

Brody took the card, saying, "It was just rookie shit."

"Shit draws flies," Montan said. "And in this game, they're very big."

Two minutes later, Derek Brody found a pay phone in a distant hallway of the Sports Complex and called his attorney in Detroit.

CHAPTER

★★★ **14** ★★★

Shay Falan saw the *Post* front page at the table next to her in the Cornelia Street Cafe, a pair of hands holding the tabloid open, the headline facing her: FADED STAR SNUFFED IN DRUG DEN. And a picture. A night shot. Two New York police standing in Soho. A body bag on a stretcher, the medical examiner's van at the curb.

She leaned over. "Excuse me."

The paper didn't move.

"Sir, excuse me."

The paper lowered. The man was in his sixties, an aloof look on his face. NYU professor, she guessed.

"Excuse what?"

"Could I see your paper for a moment?"

He looked at her a couple of seconds, then held the paper back up, showing her both sides. "There," he said. "You've seen it. If you intended to say, you want to *read* it, there's a newsstand two blocks down."

She left a coffee, two blueberry waffles and a grapefruit juice. A couple minutes later on Sixth Avenue she had the *Post* open in her hands, and the *Times* and the *Daily News* under her arm. She was still reading as she began to walk.

She collided with a pedestrian. A dark-haired man, Italian-looking, kind of young. The other papers flew out from her arm. She stooped to pick them up, the guy bending over to help.

"You all right?"

She nodded.

"You sure? You don't look so good."

"I'll be fine."

The man handing her the sections he'd picked up. "I'm sorry," he said.

"No, it was my fault."

"Let me buy you a coffee," he said. A grin on his face. "I insist."

He was in jeans, Reebok's and a *Weekly World News* T-shirt, the front with a silk screen of the tab's front page, a picture of a bald kid with pointy ears and the headline: BAT BOY FOUND IN CAVE!

She thought, what did he think she was, nuts? She said, "Thanks for the offer, but I've got to be going."

A half block later, she found a place to stand away from the foot traffic, under a market's awning, just next to the fruit display.

The *Post* story lived up to its headline, a police source quoted as saying Eric Smith appeared to have taken street drugs prior to his death. The Soho loft had been ransacked. He'd been murdered "execution style." The source said, "Everything points to drugs, business with the wrong people."

She read quickly through the background material about Eric's football career, his drug suspensions, his injury and ejection from the league. She saw nothing about Eric Smith's plans to go to Betty Ford.

"You buy something now?"

A Korean grocer in a white apron, both hands in his pocket, standing close.

"You buy something now, or you move."

She looked up over the paper, and there he was again, a hundred feet down Sixth. The Bat Boy guy, sucking on a cigarette, his head quickly turning away. He looked into a store window, an adult video store. Then he dropped his smoke and crushed it with his heel.

Shay crossed Sixth Avenue and walked along Fourth Street to Washington Square. She didn't look for the guy again until she found an empty bench near a bronze statue of Alexander Lyman Holley. She saw a couple of guys playing chess at the park table. She put the Sunday papers on her lap. It took her a couple seconds to catch her breath.

The guy was a creep, she thought. That's all.

And then it hit her, really hit her. She opened another paper and began to read every detail she could find.

★   ★   ★

Brody remembered when he and Dominique first looked at the Lucerne apartment. Two bedrooms. Nine-foot ceilings. Marble bathroom with a whirlpool tub. Indoor pool. Attended garage and a twenty-four-hour doorman. An Italian market around the corner, Agata & Valentina, featuring gourmet carry-out. There was a little bistro on First Avenue called The Cowboy Bar, a bison head on the wall. But it was the balcony view that sold him, about as far as you could get from the eighteen months he'd spent in The Valley. He'd never forget the prison. Outside it looked like a community college with razor wire. Inside, you slept in a ten-by-twenty and watched the sun rise through a window the size of two postcards. On the balcony, Dominique Goldman kept telling him that was the Queensboro Bridge to the south and a stretch of the East River called Hell's Gate to the north. He remembered planning to call Mike Scanlon from the perch the day he moved in, saying, "I'm standing here, looking right at the gates of hell."

It didn't seem so funny now.

The decorator Dominique had recommended the day he signed the lease met him outside the Lucerne Sunday morning, helping him carry cardboard boxes he'd brought from camp. The decorator was maybe thirty, wearing tight black jeans and a leather Stetson. Brody had turned the whole job over to him from Stony. No time to pick out themes and colors. He'd had only one request. He had this picture he and his father once found in a Time-Life book on news photography. Quarterback Y.A. Tittle on the field for the Giants in 1964. A classic. Brody sent the Pulitzer prize image to the decorator, saying, find a way to work it in somewhere.

The apartment reminded Brody of the Ponderosa living room in *Bonanza* re-runs. *Nouveau* western, the decorator said. The overall result *was* inviting. Lakota rugs in earth colors. Cowhide couch and chairs. A large, primitive cabinet that opened to a surround sound stereo and a 35-inch TV. In the bedroom, a king-size bed, the frame made of hand shaped timbers. The kitchen cupboards were stocked with plates, silverware, glasses, all western designs. Pewter utensils. Copper cookware. In the refrigerator was a case of beer, Lonestar tall necks.

The western look stopped with the art, Brody figuring that's where the *nouveau* came in. Most of the moderns were unrecognizable, except with one large painting dominating the living room wall. It was a hand-tinted blowup of the Y.A. Tittle photo, but the image still intact. The Giants' quarterback sitting on his heels in the end zone grass. Number 14, his helmet discarded behind him, drops of blood running down from his balding head.

Brody stood in front of it, looking a while.

"I thought you'd like it," the decorator said.

He wrote the decorator a check for $52,000.

The decorator tipping his hat at the door and saying, "Enjoy."

Brody walked to the balcony. The air was hot and still, the view of the bridges and the midtown skyline looked as if his eyes had diffusion filters, the kind they used on old movie stars to mask blemishes in close-ups. He plopped down at the patio table and sat there for a while.

He'd been entertaining the idea of bailing. Tell Scanlon face to face that he was walking out, taking his losses. Not necessarily believing Eric Smith, but simply because the team was so entirely fucked up. And what about this Molito? Maybe he was behind the homicide. The Mole, V.R., Montan. Maybe Dominique. All of them hooked up in something. Maybe Reggie, too. Shit, he'd called Smith. Maybe Glamour Boy had set him up, put him in the middle of something.

He imagined himself saying he was quitting, and Scanlon saying, okay, but are you fucking out of your mind? Give back the six million. Move back to Ann Arbor. Maybe get a little three-room campus apartment and work in a record store. Brody told himself, shit, the money didn't matter, not really. Playing mattered, not just playing, but making some noise. It had taken six years to regain his momentum after the accident. Bail, it would take six more, stuck with that "problem player" tag.

Brody got up and walked into the apartment. He found himself looking at the Y.A. Tittle painting again. Tittle looked dazed, the photo taken after he'd been wasted by a 270-pound Pittsburgh Steeler. But he got back up. The record books proved that. And that's how you did it, he thought. In football you had to look like that sometimes. Not just look like that, but be able to get back up.

There *is* that, he thought. And a hell of a lot of money, too.

★　★　★

Scanlon arrived by cab in the late afternoon, the security desk calling, then sending him up. The attorney made a beeline from the apartment door to the balcony. He ran his hands over the railing, then gripped it, looking up and down the East River.

Scanlon turned around, grinning. "Dude, you have seriously arrived."

The smile left. "That said, maybe now you can tell me what surprise is so important you couldn't tell me about it on the phone."

Brody wanted to get his thoughts together, say it just right. "After dinner, it's pretty involved."

Agata and Valentina delivered the food. Brody transferred the meals to the new dinnerware. They ate at the iron table on the balcony. Spare ribs and sesame chicken fingers. Sides of potato gratin and grilled corn on the cob.

Brody told him about camp, the problems he'd had with some of the players. The factions on the team. He told him about Reggie Thompson. The dropped pass.

"Sounds like a typical rookie camp," Scanlon said. "At least from everything I've heard." He paused. "That's what you wanted to talk about."

Brody shook his head.

Scanlon smirked. "No, I'm not buying it. This is some kind of ruse. You're into the bims already, and you've got one with this very hot roommate. We're all going to cut this wide swath tonight through the Apple. Your way of saying thanks. I appreciate it. And I accept."

Brody said, "It's a surprise, all right."

The wind picked up a little, sending a couple of paper napkins on a long trip to the street below.

"Want another beer?" Brody asked.

Scanlon nodded. "Only if you tell me what she looks like."

Brody went to the kitchen and returned with a Lonestar, and a copy of the Sunday *Post*. He pushed the *Post* across the table.

Scanlon glanced and said, "I saw the headline at the airport. I was meaning to ask you what you've heard."

Brody said, "I was there."

Scanlon blinked a couple of times. "What do you mean, you were *there*?"

Brody asked him to read the entire story. Scanlon wiped barbecue sauce from his fingers and picked it up. The tab's angle was that the homicide was the inevitable conclusion to Smith's drug tainted career.

Scanlon tossed the paper back on the table. "There's nothing about you in there."

"And there won't be," Brody said.

He told Scanlon everything he could remember, visiting Smith, everything the former quarterback had said. V.R.'s bookmaker friend. Getting the ice pack. He told him about Carl Montan, how he'd reached out during the police interview. Brody adding, "That's the part that's got me a little worried, not to mention the Mole."

"The *Mole?*"

"Tommy Molito, that's what Smith called the coach's buddy."

"Christ," Scanlon said. He leaned back, his eyes going back and forth between the paper and Brody. "I'm not sure what you're trying to tell me here, Derek."

"Smith was murdered."

Scanlon tapped the paper. "That's what it says here, buddy."

"Maybe Smith was taken out by these people he was talking about. He sounded like he was going to go public."

Scanlon laughed. "Based on what evidence?"

"Christ, he'd just come from one of those meetings."

"That's not evidence."

Brody leaned forward. "Smith was *clean*."

"Opinions don't make good evidence, either. Unless, of course, you pay an expert."

"It's more than an opinion. You read in the story about the paraphernalia police found?"

Scanlon nodded.

"Like I told you, I was in that bathroom. I'm telling you, it wasn't there."

"You just told me a few minutes ago that you told the cop you might have seen something."

Brody said, "I lied."

"To the cop or to me?"

"To the cop. To Montan."

"Ouch," Scanlon said. He sipped the beer. "I can't think of a single good reason for that in a police statement, but go ahead, take your shot."

Brody rose and went to the railing. "I came here to play football," he said.

"You tell what you know. So what?"

Brody turned around. "Maybe not," he said.

"I'm listening."

"Suppose what Smith said was true. Suppose Smith was set up."

"Okay."

"So I put myself in the middle of this. The next thing I know I'm spending all my time talking to cops and prosecutors. Wasting time in some attorney's office with one of those girls punching keys on that little machine. Talking to reporters. People hassling me. Or, maybe they come after me. Find a way to discredit me. Next thing you know I'm out of the game."

"Anything else?"

"I don't like this guy Montan."

"He likes you, that's all that counts. They don't spend that kind of money on people they don't like. Way I see it, he helped you with the cop, didn't he?"

When he didn't answer, Scanlon asked for specifics.

Brody couldn't give him any. It was just an impression, something about the guy. Montan all dressed up, but with a look he'd seen in The Valley. Seen on cons who were too friendly, usually setting you up to shoot some kind of move.

Scanlon took a deep breath and exhaled. "Can I be blunt?"

Brody said, "That's one reason I asked you to come."

"You've been under a lot of pressure, a good part of it probably of your own making. That's fine. You jam yourself up so you can respond to it, even if it's not there. I have no problem with that. And, yeah, dead people are nothing to dismiss lightly. But Eric Smith was the Keith Richards of the NFL. I think you're getting paranoid."

Brody asked, "What about Molito?"

Scanlon shrugged. "Gamblers have been tapping the league for info for years. You got owners who've owned horse and dog tracks. Others with friends in Vegas. It's nothing new. They say $25 billion is bet a year on the pro game. Everyone's just trying to get an edge."

Brody turned back to the street. He could see the dinner napkins still riding the thermal currents between the buildings, a good ten stories from the ground.

Scanlon said, "So, what do you want to do?"

Brody turned around. "Four years, I've been trying to put this kind of shit behind me. Not bring it back."

Scanlon picked up his beer and joined him at the railing. "I agree," he said, making a toasting motion. "I think you should concentrate on football."

"Concentration might be a little hard to come by."

"There are some things we can do to make you feel a little more secure."

Brody said, "You'll check out this guy Montan?"

"I was thinking more along the lines of drug screens. You say Smith told you the team could clean up dirty players. If that's true, they could go the other way, too. I know an independent lab here in New York. I want you to drop urine once a week so we can build a record."

"What about Montan?"

"If he's connected, that kind of information is not exactly easy to come by. But I can do your basic background check. Criminal record. Credit report. I've got a PI who can handle it."

Brody reached into his back pocket for the list he'd been working on all afternoon. "I've got something else." He handed the sheet to Scanlon. "These are the Stars' top draft choices for the last five years. Names, their colleges. Plus, there's some trades there. Not only Reggie Thompson, but a couple of his buds."

Scanlon, "You want background checks on all these players?"

"Yeah, but I don't much care whether or not they can get a Visa card. Drugs, alumni payments, that kind of thing."

"That's a lot of work."

"Money's not a problem."

"This could take weeks. But let me see what I can do."

Scanlon looked at the list. "All these players were very hot in college."

"But they didn't work out as pros. My theory is that if somebody was trying to sabotage the team, they'd start with the draft choices."

"And Montan is in charge of the draft."

"And trades. The head coach told me that."

A troubled smile spread across Scanlon's face. "But Derek, *you* are the top draft choice. You're worried the Stars signed you for twelve million total, because they expected you to wash out?"

"That's the big surprise."

"Why?"

Brody said, "That, I don't know."

Scanlon looked back out at the river, taking a deep pull on the beer. He wiped his mouth.

"I guess this means there's no roommate, huh?"

"Not even a girl," Brody said.

CHAPTER

☆ ☆ ☆ **15** ☆ ☆ ☆

By noon Pacific, Sunday, Carl Montan was standing inside The Oz, his eyes climbing the ten-story atrium of Las Vegas's grandest new casino hotel. The lobby was designed to mirror the great hall of the 1939 movie classic, after the hotel's owner, Mecca Entertainment Corporation, acquired the film as part of a multibillion-dollar purchase of MGM. Original blueprints called for a wizard as well, until David Harvey, Mecca's chairman, learned the details. Yes, they were in the business of smoke and mirrors, he told shareholders, but that didn't mean that they should rub it in.

Most people knew Mecca's story. In less than twenty years, David Harvey and junk bonds had transformed Mecca from a small film and amusement company to a conglomerate of subsidiaries aimed straight at the contemporary American family: newspapers, magazines, books, radio, multimedia, music and movie rights, broadcast satellites, and entertainment product development. The member firms had names, but most insiders just called them all *Mecca*.

"Mecca bought it."

"Mecca's doing the film."

Every subsidiary struck wholesome chords. Mecca Studios put out two animated features a year, usually featuring environmental and multi-cultural themes. Mecca sitcoms pushed family values. Mecca newspapers refused to advertise strip clubs and massage parlors. Mecca records refused to sign gangsta rap, Harvey himself making a rare public appearance before Congress to condemn the music. Mecca's new TV network, MEC, brought back the prime time family period: Two hours, sex-and-violence free.

Then David Harvey went after football—$300 million a year for the rights to broadcast half the NFL's schedule, a lion's share of the $800 million a year broadcasters paid the league in rights each season. MEC's coverage was the talk of the league. Producers offered more than play-by-play and back-slapping half time shows. MEC's *NFL Magazine* investigated questionable associations by NFL owners with organized crime figures. Commentators hammered away at high ticket prices, sweetheart stadium deals, free agency, player drug use, sports agents and the NFL Player's Association.

After the spring NFL owners' meeting, Papa Goldman told Carl Montan, "A good number hate that sonovabitch Harvey."

"What about the others?" Montan asked.

"They're happy as long as his checks don't bounce."

Media critics said Mecca was biting the hand that fed it. But Mecca had a five-year broadcast contract and fans loved the populist approach. *NFL Magazine* was a hit with both cynical X-ers and older viewers who clamored for a return to simpler times.

After Las Vegas changed from a mob town to a "family-friendly" destination, David Harvey was not only destined to do business in the desert, many believed he brought social responsibility to the gambling town. Mecca companies made all the politically correct moves: An aggressive affirmative action program. Company child care. Environmental activism. A public service campaign against tobacco.

And then there was The Oz. David Harvey and Mecca came to Las Vegas, quite literally, with a bang. After the MGM acquisition, Harvey ordered the MGM Grand raised by a spectacular implosion for his new hotel and theme park. The hundred-acre site was hardly five years old. "We wanted to devote more space to the children," a Mecca spokesman said.

Montan checked the time on his Bulgari, then approached the concierge's desk, asking for the location of the sports book.

A young valet in a palace guard's uniform pointed to a set of double-wide escalators. "All gaming is located on the second floor. You'll find the sports book at the end of the west wing."

Gaming. The word "gambling" was forbidden at The Oz, another Harvey dictate.

Montan walked past a series of the tunnels leading to children attractions: Virtual reality rooms and interactive amusement rides. Sports clinics in football, baseball, basketball and soccer, taught by retired pros. Computer and special effects workshops. Adults sent their children into the tunnels, then rode up the double-wide escalators to the tables and slot machines.

The entrance of the sports book looked like a stadium tunnel. Astroturf covered the floor, yard markers spanning the room. Inside, a couple dozen gamblers eyed walls covered with lit displays of hundreds of potential betting situations on professional and college teams. Another dozen people were lined up at the betting stations, wagering on everything from the afternoon's baseball games to the winner of next year's World Cup.

Montan walked over to the National Football League display. He studied the long-range odds first, the probability Stars would win the Super Bowl. When he first joined the team, it was a hundred-to-one. Now it was triple that.

A man in a dark suit walked up, stopping next to him. He had a ledger in his hand and silver name plate, ASSISTANT ODDSMAKER.

"You look like you might need some help," he said.

Montan pointed to next Sunday's games. "What's going on with the Stars opener?"

"Stars-Packers in New York," the oddsmaker said. "Looks like the Pack will get off to a good start."

"When I left New York this morning Green Bay was favored by nine," Montan said. "Now it's seventeen."

"The outlaw line moved overnight. The smart money must know something." The outlaw line, set in Las Vegas, was a private line set for select high rollers.

Yes, they did, Montan thought. V.R. had an awfully big mouth.

The oddsmaker checked something on his ledger, then asked, "You bet the Stars often?"

Montan said, "Do I look like I'm out of my mind?"

He called up on the house phone, then took the elevator to the penthouse level. Suites there were reserved for the high rollers, special guests that received complimentary rooms, meals and gambling chips.

Movie stars. Politicians. CEOs from around the world. Montan re-membered what it was like when he worked the upper floors, taking care of guests called the "whales." The whales—smart and sophisti-cated people—thinking they were getting some kind of deal, then los-ing three times the money at the tables than the hotels comped in daily perks.

An assistant greeted Montan inside a vestibule a hundred yards from the elevator. He led him through a pair of double doors, through a short hallway, then across a sunken living room. The assistant rapped lightly on a mirror-like stainless steel door, then pushed it open, mo-tioning for Montan to go first.

The suite's office had windows from floor to ceiling, a panoramic view of the strip. The midday sun bathed the man sitting behind a large black walnut desk in light. He had charcoal hair, but exception-ally few lines in his face for a man of sixty. He was casually dressed, a pair of black full-cut linen pants, a black T-shirt under a tan two-button, double-vent Givenchy, Montan guessed. Going for that Holly-wood look.

The assistant lingered behind Montan.

"Good afternoon, sir," Montan said. He'd known him for many years, but he still addressed him as sir.

"Carl, sit down. Would you like a non-alcoholic beverage?"

"I'm fine," Montan said. He sat in a wingback chair two feet from the desk.

The assistant was dismissed.

"Good flight?"

"Good flight."

"You going back tonight?"

"The red eye."

The office door closed. A copy of the Sunday *Times* slid across the desk. The paper was opened to the story about Eric Smith.

David Harvey said, "So, Carl, tell me, what other surprises are you planning in New York?"

★   ★   ★

First thing Monday, Brody dropped urine at the downtown lab Scanlon set up, then sped to the Stardome. In the new locker room he saw a hand-painted version of the camp slogan across the wall: THE FI-

NAL FORMING OF A PERSON'S CHARACTER LIES IN THEIR OWN HANDS—
A. FRANK.

He asked Bobby Loeb, "Who is A. Frank?"

Loeb was unbuttoning a long-sleeve shirt, having a hard time with it. "Anne Frank. No wonder the team can't fucking win. We're following a twelve-year-old girl."

Brody looked at his name above his locker, next to Loeb's. All their names were painted in black, a teal background, a silver star with their number over the top. They didn't do that in college. Other than that, the locker room wasn't much more elaborate than Michigan's. The lockers were wire mesh, no door. Front office sales clerks got cubicles. Players making a half million a year prepared for business from three-by-five cages. Inspire a team mentality, the thinking went.

Everyone was trying to personalize their space. The playbook prohibited certain items: Alcohol, drugs, nude photos and firearms, it read. They hung pictures of mothers and girlfriends and kids and cars and boats and motorcycles. Crucifixes. Bumper stickers. News clippings. In Reggie Thompson's, Brody saw a picture of Malcolm X. Brody taped an old photo of his father and mother, their arms around each other in their college days.

Clinton Lisle, Loeb's presumed backup, had been assigned a locker toward the back. Odd, Brody thought, because the assignments tended to group certain positions together. Everyone called Lisle the Old Man behind his back. He hardly spoke during practice. After the roster cut, Loeb told Brody the Old Man had made his two season goals: Draw a check and sit one more year in the league.

Loeb saw him looking. Loeb's shirt was off now, his rib cage in an elastic brace.

"Looks like the U.S.-of-fucking-A is finally gonna get a look at the Old Man," Loeb said. "They don't want me serving these ribs up to Green Bay."

Brody pulled his shirt over his head, saying, "Especially with a name like the Packers."

Loeb didn't laugh. He was sitting on his stool now, his eyes looking a little glazed.

"So what did the doctors say?" Brody asked.

"Two fractured, and bruised. Three weeks. I plan on being back in two."

Hadley Henderson, the offensive coordinator, walked in and handed Brody and Loeb new playbook inserts, then walked over to Lisle. Brody sat down and read. Two pages of logistics and practice schedules, broken down by positions. The quarterbacks schedule was severely cut back from the pace in camp. Monday mornings they reported at seven-thirty to go over the Sunday game. Tuesday was a day off. In the evening, the quarterbacks were faxed new plays. Two-a-day sessions were held midweek. Wednesday they practiced first and second down plays, Thursday, third down offense. Friday was a half day devoted to nickel, red zone, two-minute offense, short yardage and goal line. The morning before the game, everyone checked into a hotel, both home and away.

They would practice at the dome through the regular season, except for the coming Saturday. The city had booked the dome for a tractor pull. Several thousand yards of dirt had to be trucked in that day, then removed in the middle of the night. Practice would be held at Downing Stadium, across the Triborough Bridge on Randalls Island, the equipment manager had announced.

Brody asked Loeb about it.

He was looking at his feet. "World Football League used to play there," he mumbled. "It's fucked up."

"Crappy locker room?"

"The entire situation."

A lot of the logistics didn't make sense, Brody decided. Even the lowly Arizona Cardinals had a separate practice facility with several football fields, the team offices attached. Stars players were always complaining. You had front office business, you couldn't handle it at the dome. You had to go all the way to MetLife. Fight the traffic. The team physicians were uptown, the rehabilitation therapists in Queens. Team media reps had to cart press releases and stat sheets out to the dome in cardboard boxes every day. The reporters had a small room in the dome where they could file their stories. But they couldn't set up shop there. The city owned the stadium. The city set the regs.

The second playbook insert detailed rules for the regular season. No cigar smoking. No family members, girlfriends or agents, even after games. A team robe had to be worn in deference to female sports reporters. Outside interviews had to be cleared with the media office.

No entrance into the training room without a trainer's permission. No pissing in the whirlpools. The ban on music was continued.

Brody asked, "Bobby, whose idea is this music bullshit?"

Loeb didn't answer. His eyes were closed, his head leaning back against the locker's edge.

"Bobby?"

Loeb kept his eyes shut. "Carl sets the rules."

Squat walked up, saying to Loeb, "You all right, Bobby?"

Loeb opened one eye. "Cruisin'," he said.

Squat reached into his tool bag and pulled out a small nose spray dispenser, handing it to Loeb. He said, "If the Demerol's too much, try this later."

Loeb reached for it, still looking with one eye.

"It's Stadol," Squat said. "Couple of blasts, no pain."

"My nose is fine," Loeb said.

"It's just absorbed there. It's opiate based, like the Percs and Dems, but chemically it won't show up. Saves you answering a lot of questions you get pulled in for a screen."

Brody said, "Advanced pain management?"

Squat turned to him. "Speaking of screens, expect the league lab this week. Every player has to be tested before the season, and you weren't here for the big drop."

Squat looked away, then said, "V.R. wants you in his office."

Loeb opened his eyes and struggled to sit up.

"No, Bobby, I mean Brody," Squat said. He looked back at Brody and said, "Now."

The little fat fuck likes to bark orders, Brody thought.

He took his time.

It was like the camp setup, the head coach's office behind the equipment room. V.R. had the phone cradled under his ear. He pointed to a seat, then covered the phone with his hand, saying, "Hang loose, Brody. Sit."

Brody looked around. Hardly anything inside but a desk and couple chairs. Nothing on V.R.'s desk but a calendar and a pile of video-cassettes. On the wall, another rendition of the Anne Frank line.

Brody was seeing V.R. differently now. Puffy eyes. His tongue swollen. He needed a shave. What he first thought was just a crusty football character, now looked like the early warning signs of somebody about to go on their ass.

V.R. had a pained look on his face, doing a lot of listening. Then he exploded. "You know what kind of fucking problems I've got here, and the fucking season hasn't even started yet."

He pulled the phone away from his ear, like he wanted to bark, "Fuck you." Instead he took a deep breath and said, "Fine. I understand."

Then he slammed it down.

V.R. put his face in his palms, then dropped his hands. He looked at Brody. Looking at him like he was his next problem.

"*You* need to have a good week in practice," he said.

"I'll do my best," Brody said.

V.R.'s bloodshot eyes glared. "Your best isn't fucking good enough, Brody. You've got a lot to learn about this goddamn league."

V.R. eyed him for a couple moments. Finally, he said, "Well, I guess you're not going to be getting any help from Eric Smith."

Brody didn't say anything. He thought, V.R. doesn't know he was there. And he couldn't think of a single good reason to tell him.

V.R. cocked his head. "What the fuck did you do in prison, anyway?"

"I was a trusty."

"And what was that?"

"You don't get locked down as much like the others. You have low-security jobs. Like landscaping. They even let you outside."

"You what, grew fucking flowers?"

"I eventually worked in the records room. Word processing. Maintained files."

"You ever get fucked in the ass?"

Brody hesitated. "A couple tried—once."

V.R. grinned. "Were they rolling dice for your asshole? You get some protection?"

Brody nodded. "It had nothing to do with football. Some cons wanted favors from the record room. They watched my back."

V.R. shook his head approvingly, loosening up a little now. "I was a company clerk in the Army. They drafted my ass in sixty-four, but I didn't get sent to Nam. They sent me to Germany because I could fucking type. Everybody wanted to be friends with the clerk. So, I understand."

The coach lit an El Producto, then waved the smoke from his face with a lazy gesture. "I'm going to simplify the offense. We're going to be working out of Black, get some increased blocking from the backfield. No razzle dazzle bullshit. No Hitman. A lot of Pimp and Snitch."

"That's a pretty limited passing game," Brody said. "If the Old Man gets hurt, I'd like to have the opportunity to air it out."

"The Old Man isn't going to get hurt," V.R. said. He laid the cigar in an ashtray and stood up. He walked to the door.

"C'mon, Brody."

Walking behind him, Brody said, "It's football, isn't it. Anybody can get hurt."

V.R. stopped at the edge of the locker room, most of the players still in front of their lockers. A few looked up.

"You don't fucking get it, do you?" V.R. said.

V.R. reached out, grasped Brody by the shoulders and pulled him to his chest. He squeezed hard. Brody could smell liquor as well as cigars.

"Get what?" Brody said.

Everybody watching now.

V.R. said, "You're starting against the Pack."

★   ★   ★

Monday, Montan met the Turk in the empty lot at Shea Stadium, the two of them parking their cars side by side, Montan in a Mercedes 600 sedan, the Turk in the Crown Vic. The cars idled, facing in opposite directions. The Turk lowered his window, cigarette smoke wafting out.

"Well?" Montan said.

"The bim hangs in the Village," he said. "Coffee shops, restaurants, mainly. Always taking stuff to read. I got a look at something she had on the table. Looked like a play or a movie. I figure she's an actress, so this morning I call Actors' Equity and she's listed. I think we're wasting our time."

"You sound awfully sure."

"Guy leaves a bim's name and phone number on a matchbook next to his phone. That tells me he got her number in a bar. Smith probably just wanted to fuck her."

"And today?"

"Surfer says Bimbolina hasn't left the apartment."

Montan thought for a few moments, then switched subjects. "Everything set at the Lucerne?"

"We've got a good view of his balcony, living room and bedroom from our apartment window across the street. I told you giving the decorator those portable phones might come in handy. Rigged to stay on one radio frequency. All you need is Radio Shack, a scanner. No bugs, shit people can find. He calls or goes anywhere, we're on him. Plus, we got the LoJack."

"The rental office ask any questions?"

"Rental office went for the Surfer's story." The Turk laughed. "Surfer told 'em he was in town on *protracted* business. Guy's got the words when he wants to use them, drop all that *dude* bullshit. I guess they were saying no three-month leases, until Surfer pulls out the twenty-five K in cash, saying he wants to pay in advance."

Montan said, "You won't be there that long."

"What about furniture? Place is bare ass."

"Take care of it. Nothing extravagant, though."

"Can't move in until tomorrow. They're still painting."

"Brody's not going to do anything right away. Today, he's got football on his mind."

The Turk hit the smoke and exhaled. "You think Smith told Brody something?"

"You'd think Eric would've given that up, the girl, too, after I put the dryer on high. But you don't risk three years of work because some dumb kid might have stumbled onto something."

The Turk shrugged. "So, how long you want us to stay on the girl? Can't be uptown and downtown at the same time."

Montan said, "First chance you get, take a look around her apartment. You handle it. Alone. See if the log is there. In and out. Make it look like a break-in, but be sure to take something. If there's nothing there, forget about her. Concentrate on Brody."

The Turk flicked the cigarette away between his thumb and middle finger, the butt sailing to the pavement. "What if the log *is* there?"

Montan slid his 600 into drive and said, "Then you don't come out right away."

Fifteen minutes later, Montan was sitting in a booth in a Denny's near the Stardome, blue hairs all around, coming in for the senior specials.

Jack Petrus walked in, sat down and said, "I'm done, Carl."

"The food hasn't even arrived. I ordered for you."

"I'm talking about the entire goddamn thing," Petrus said. Montan noticed a little tremor in his hand.

Montan said, "Jack, I'd say you passed that threshold some time ago."

"I never signed on for this kind of shit."

"But the important part is: you did sign on. And you will be compensated. If I were you, I'd be looking for a nice retirement home near Vegas. They have an awful lot of nice looking girls on the street out there."

The waitress arrived, putting two Grand Slams in front of them. Montan began cutting up his sausage. "So, tell me. Did Dominique suggest a memorial service for Eric at the morning meeting?"

"I couldn't believe it," Petrus said.

"Well, it would have to be a memorial. They've shipped the body back to Montana already. Of course, team only. But I suggested Saint Patrick's when she talked to me about it. That way TV could get some good bites."

"That's what she was saying. Team honors fallen comrade. All that nonsense. Talking about spinning it, making the team look good."

"It would." Montan took a bite of the sausage. "So, what did Papa say?"

"Maybe you should have been there. Seen him blow for yourself."

"He didn't like the idea of the church?"

"Cut the bullshit, Carl," Petrus said. "He said, no way."

"You know, I never could figure the attraction," Montan said. "Beautiful, bright girl like that with a piece of shit like Smith." He thought about it. "Maybe it's genetic. Wasn't her mother hospitalized for depression?"

"It has more to do with Papa," Petrus said. "She's never forgiven him for using that to win custody when they divorced."

"Dominique was what, fifteen or sixteen?"

"She was twelve. She's been making him pay for it ever since."

Montan said, "Papa say anything else about Smith?"

"Papa called it predictable."

"That's an appropriate word."

Petrus looked up. "So was it?"

Montan sipped his orange juice and said, "Eat, Jack."

Petrus picked up a fork.

Montan asked, "You bring me a copy of the audit?"

Petrus nodded. "It's in the car."

"And it says."

Petrus looked up. "Papa's busted. What, you expected something else?"

"Specifics," Montan said.

"He's got the 42 million from the league in broadcast royalties. You know, NFL collects from the networks and cable, then splits it up evenly."

"I know how it works," Montan said.

"TV's paying the league a billion a year," the GM continued. "But they're losing a hundred million a season. Networks keep telling themselves it's worth it. They push their regular show schedules during the games, hoping to make it up in prime time ratings."

"That won't last," Montan said.

"That was the consensus at the league meeting. A lot of owners out there looking for new ways to raise money. Goddamn agents. Nobody can afford these salaries."

Montan emptied his glass of juice. "So, Papa gets the forty-two mill. That won't cover payroll. What else?"

"League's take on the licensed merchandise is projected at $200 million this year. All the teams will get about five. Papa's got the radio deal, but that's hardly worth counting. That leaves the attendance, which of course, has to be split sixty-forty with the visiting team."

"The numbers," Montan said.

"We're looking at seven million there, depending on how the away dates go. Fill the dome, that'll jump to fifteen million. Of course, that's not going to happen. Not with this team."

Montan said, "So, the bottom line?"

"He'll be looking at Chapter Eleven before the bye, unless he can refinance and get the stadium lease. The CPA offered to start drawing up the papers."

"Papa look worried?"

"He was more upset about the suggestions of a Smith memorial."

"What did the old man say about the numbers?"

"He talked a lot about getting the new dome lease. With this low attendance, the sky suites do almost as well as the regular gate. Seven million there. The city's got all of them leased. They get a pretty good crowd up there."

Montan said, "The city's aggressive. You want help from the mayor's office to do business in the city, first thing they do is show you a Stardome suite."

"Papa figures, he picks up the suites and, let's say parking, or concessions, he's out of trouble."

"The CPA talk about refinancing?"

"We're already carrying thirty-two million. Everyone saw that *Business Week* rating us last year as the NFL's 'least sound' franchise. I don't think there's a bank in town that would touch Papa."

"What about Papa's friends?"

"What friends?" Petrus asked. "Not in this town."

"Other owners. Remember when Billy Ford loaned Tose ten million so he could keep the Eagles?"

"And Lenny Tose still lost the team. The old owners remember that. The new ones want him out."

Petrus pushed his plate away, suddenly looking a little nauseated.

"You okay?" Montan asked.

Petrus leaned close. "So what we going to do if this happens again?"

"If what happens?"

Petrus said. "There's a lot of potential exposure with these players of yours."

"Smith was your draft choice, not mine."

"What's that supposed to mean?" Petrus said. He put his arm back on the seat behind him, showing a little bravado. He bumped the senior in the booth behind him, his elbow hitting her short, sprayed hair. She turned around and glared, Petrus oblivious.

Montan leaned forward. "I build loyalty, Jack," he said quietly. "*My* players are family."

"Yeah, one big dysfunctional family," Petrus said.

CHAPTER

☆ ☆ ☆ **16** ☆ ☆ ☆

Being named the starter helped push Eric Smith out of his mind. Brody kept going back to that diagram of circles, everything in manageable units. Avoid Tommy Molito. Deal with V.R. only on a player-to-coach level. Watch your back with Reggie Thompson. Be civil to Carl Montan. He'd considered contacting Raymond Bullard at NFL Security. But snitching out the coach and teammates wasn't his idea of leadership. He'd turned the matter over to Scanlon. He decided, let Scanlon handle it all for now.

He embraced the same routines he'd used in college. Practice during the day. Relax after dinner with mindless TV shows, no news. News only worked him up. Save that for the game. After TV, study. First an hour of game films, then an hour or two studying coverages and plays. He'd continue to invite the offensive line and receivers to watch films. But so far he still had no takers, save Toby Headly. The stuttering tight end credited their sessions as the reason he'd made the cut.

Brody also got to thinking, maybe he needed to lighten up. He remembered this hill where they played sandlot as youngsters, level ground hard to come by in his sub. They found new speed sprinting downslope, and churned in slow motion going up. They rolled down after tackles, laughing. Maybe he needed to interject some humor. Maybe he'd let his intensity follow him off the field. He had to find ways to get them to join him, not fight him.

That was the challenge now.

When he walked into the locker room Tuesday morning he found another team mood swing. It was quieter than usual. Players were talking in small groups and hushed tones. As he wrote his number down for the taping line he could feel eyes burning holes in his back.

At the locker, he asked Bobby Loeb what was going on. Loeb said the players union had released the team salary list. Loeb was the players association rep.

Loeb reached into his locker. "Here's your copy."

Brody sat and scanned the list. The numbers were the way Scanlon once explained, typical of the league. A few players were pulling down seven figures. Loeb, 1.8 million. Glamour Boy, 1.2. Homer Cobb, the nose guard, 1.1. Pro Bowler Toysy topped all players at 2.6. Brody looked at the offensive line. Toby Headly, the rookie tight end, had signed for only $180,000. Headly had negotiated his own contract, not a wise move, particularly with his stutter. Most of the other players were averaging about $300,000 a year. There was no middle class in the NFL. Players lasted an average of three and a half years on the field. Half went to taxes. So, amortize the half million take-home against an average guy's forty-five years in the workforce, that came to an extra $10,000 a year, presuming a player didn't blow it. Considering the cars and toys, Brody thought, that was a big presumption to make.

Brody asked Loeb, "So this is about the money?"

"Happens every year. It'll blow over." Loeb looked up. "You're not going to dinner tonight with the offensive line, are you? I wouldn't recommend it."

"What dinner?"

"Didn't anybody tell you?"

Brody shook his head.

"Rookie linemen take the veterans out to dinner before the first game. It's tradition. Quarterbacks are always invited."

"You're not going?"

Loeb shook his head, adding the Old Man wasn't going either. The rookies would get hammered by the bill, he added. "They don't know what's coming. The Old Man and I figure, why add to their pain?"

Brody wanted to know how much the dinner cost last year.

"More than six grand."

"In a restaurant?"

"They're farm animals. Farm animals eat."

When Loeb disappeared into the training room for treatment, Brody walked over to Headly's locker. The tight end's hands were gripping rails of the locker cage, his body leaning into it with an isotonic push. Jimmie Smothers, a rookie left offensive tackle, was sitting next to Headly on his stool.

Brody said, "Headly, I just found out we're going to dinner tonight."

"Y-y-y-yeah."

Smothers glanced up.

"Maybe next time you can give me a little notice," Brody added.

Headly looked at Smothers, then back at Brody. Smothers said, "We told Bobby to tell you last week."

Loeb wasted on pain killers, Brody thought.

"Bobby's not coming," Brody said. "But I am. What time?"

"S-s-s-seven," Headly said. He released the cage and turned, pulling his shoulder blades back.

Brody asked them both, what restaurant?

Smothers answered. "Last year they ate at a place called Spark's, where that gangster was killed outside a few years back. But it's our choice. That's the tradition. It just can't be no burger joint."

"You make reservations?" Brody asked.

Headly nodded. "S-s-s-sparks."

"Cancel 'em," Brody said. "I've got another suggestion if you guys are game."

★   ★   ★

Four hours later, after a long shower, Brody stood naked in front of his locker, massaging his hair with a towel.

"Congratulations. I'm told you're starting."

Brody turned. It was Dominique Goldman, holding a black leather notepad to her chest. Brody checked the clock over the equipment room. They had another five minutes before the dressing room opened. But who was going to throw her out? Not him.

He glanced at his team robe, but then figured, she's already gotten a good look if she wanted it. He reached for his full-length briefs, JOCKEY across the waist band.

Dominique half smiled, all eye contact. "Sorry to surprise you. I wanted to talk to you before the press came in."

He slipped on the shorts. He saw her eyes glance down.

"You know Calvin Klein is looking for endorsements for their new sports underwear line," she said. "I could put in a good word."

"I don't have much luck with endorsements," Brody said. He swiped deodorant under one of his arms. "And realistically, I've got a lot more important things on my mind."

She smiled. "Maybe you need a better agent."

"I'm satisfied," he said. "But if you can line up a panty hose ad like Namath did, I might reconsider."

She sat down on Loeb's stool and opened the notebook. The top of her golf shirt was open. He caught a glimpse beyond the black buttons. Her breasts were small and firm, no bra, her nipples pressing against the teal cotton.

She closed the notebook. He looked away.

"I'd like to buy you dinner tonight," she said. "We have a lot of things to talk about."

He said, "Tonight's no good."

He didn't want to get that internal debate going. He'd already done that, thinking about Dominique Goldman as he lay alone in bed the night before. Part of him wanted to continue what they started in the limo, the same part that became only more excited about the risk of the proposition: Dominique being who she was, Dominique probably hooked up with Carl Montan. But football, starting against the Pack, forced better judgment.

"How about later in the week?" Dominique asked.

"I do a lot of game preparation," he said. He didn't want to be rude. But he was trying not to encourage her either.

Behind her, Brody saw Bobby Loeb come out of the training room. He was wrapped in a towel around the waist, sweat dripping from his face. His right rib cage was discolored, shades of blue and red. Closer, Loeb undid the towel. He threw it over his shoulder as he stopped a foot or two from Dominique Goldman's back.

"Excuse me," he said.

Dominique turned around, his dick not a foot from her face. Loeb looked down at her, his eyes bloodshot from the whirlpool. She calmly rose, not letting him have the satisfaction of a reaction, and moved to the other side of Brody's locker. Loeb watched her, then sat on his stool.

Dominique put her back to him and looked at Brody again. "Well, I've got something else you might want to prepare for. The Carcaterra show wants you later tonight. That's the number one radio show in town."

Brody said, "You mean the number one asshole."

"You let him push your buttons at the news conference. Now you can push a few of his."

His eyes asked how.

"He'll be on your turf. He's doing a live feed at the All Star Sports Cafe. It's right in Times Square. The place will be packed. It's a great opportunity for you to turn his listeners around."

"I've got plans."

"It's not until ten. That's why I was going to buy you dinner first."

Brody remembered what V.R. had said, that a lot of players listened to the show.

"So I get to hit him?" Brody asked, half serious.

She smiled, but it quickly disappeared. "Look, I'll book a couple of other players, so you'll have some help. I can make sure we have plenty of supportive fans in the audience. And Carcaterra has already agreed to my—I mean, your—ground rules. No questions about your father's accident or your prison term."

Brody said, "From what I hear, he's already covered that pretty well."

She lowered her head, watching him through a lock of hair, her eyes resolute. "This is a win-win, Derek. If you don't take care of this now, he'll ride you not only for the season, but as long as both of you're working in New York. You have to trust me on this. It's what I do."

Brody looked over at Loeb. He was still naked. He had the Stadol spray nozzle up his nose. Brody said, "Bobby, talk to me. Should I do the Carcaterra show tonight?"

Loeb nodded, pumping the inhaler.

Brody looked back at Dominique, adding, "Can you book Bobby, too?"

She asked, "Interested, Bobby? But you'll have to wear clothes."

Loeb sniffed loudly and said, "I'm good to fucking go."

The equipment manager opened the doors to the locker room. Two TV crews and other sports reporters walked inside.

Dominique said softly, "They're going to want to talk to you. So be nice. They're just beat reporters. They're harmless, until they start to follow Carcaterra's lead."

Brody sat on the stool and pulled a shirt over his head. "If I do the show, I'm not going to take any shit from Carcaterra."

Dominique stood up and smiled coyly. "That's exactly what I had in mind."

★   ★   ★

Shay Falan chucked the empty bottle of Carlo Rossi into the trash, then shuffled to her bedroom, a cup of coffee in her hand. Late Tuesday morning. She wished she could have slept in and avoided hating herself before noon.

Shay sipped while she surveyed more than four dozen dresses, slacks and blouses. She paid little attention to a colorful collection of swimwear, shorts and flimsy tops, the entire working wardrobe dangling from a rod that stretched across her entire bedroom.

The show executive for the steel company had said, "Sexy, but sophisticated. Our sales reps are not animals, but they are still men." She'd be standing next to a monstrous punch press for six hours in Javits Convention Center, handing out brochures.

Shay stood on her bed to get some distance, bouncing a little, the coffee sloshing to the rim. The East Village apartment was tiny, even by New York standards. The living room was just large enough to hold a futon, one chair, her stereo. She'd lined the walls with bookcases holding more videos, sheet music and show sound tracks. Two people could squeeze into the kitchen, as long as the refrigerator was closed. The bedroom, she'd pretty much cut in half with her wardrobe.

She reached for black slacks and a satin top, low cut, then stepped down from the bed and hung the ensemble in her travel valise. She'd put on her makeup at home, but dress at Javits, sparing the outfit wrinkles and A train grime.

She found what she expected in the mirror, little pillows under both eyes. Her high cheekbones were gaunt, her golden freckles anemic. A half gallon of wine could do that. And for what? Eric was still dead, she thought, and she hadn't accomplished a goddamn thing.

Shay Falan considered going to the precinct first thing Monday, sitting down and having a talk with a detective. Then she played it out, imagining it like something off Broadway in two acts, one scene lead-ing to another. The first scene: You go in and talk and pretty soon a cop's asking you questions about where they met. Her saying, oh yeah, we'd go to these meetings together to learn how to drink and drug in moderation. The next scene: Her story finding its way into the news-papers. And a bunch of scenes to follow: The ramifications on her floundering acting career. The possibilities had kept her drinking all day Monday. She'd woken with a pillow tucked between her legs and the feeling that what had happened to Eric was her fault. She should have taken a real interest, not used him like a script stand-in. The guy really was in trouble. She tried to tell herself, but what if she was wrong? What if Eric had relapsed? He certainly was capable of it. She puts herself out there on the line in the papers and . . . He was just somebody she'd met at a meeting, she kept telling herself. They weren't emotionally involved.

She applied just enough base to generate some color and mask her freckles, adding a little more under her eyes. Checking the results in the mirror, she told herself, do what you promised and be done with it.

That's all.

She poured another cup of coffee and sat down on the futon with the phone and the Manhattan directory. The National Football League was on Park Avenue, just as Eric had said.

She spent five minutes trying to negotiate the automated answer-ing system, finally punching zero in frustration.

The voice on the line: "National Football League. Can I help you?"

"I'd like to speak with the commissioner."

"May I ask who's calling?"

"Actually, I'd like to set up an appointment with the commissioner."

"Who's calling?"

"I have a delivery."

"You can leave a delivery at the receptionist's desk."

"I'm supposed to deliver it personally."

"One moment."

Another secretary. "Good morning. This is the commissioner's office."

She went through it again, the second secretary wanting a name, too. She said, "The delivery is from a former player."

"What is this concerning?"

"I'm not sure. I just know it's important."

"I still have to have a name," the voice said. "And, the commissioner is not available this week."

"When will he be available?"

"If you give me your name, and the player's, you can leave it with the receptionist. I'll see she delivers it to me personally."

"I think this is sensitive material."

"Let me connect you to league security."

Shay hung up, remembering what Eric had said about that.

Maybe she was jumping the gun, she thought. She reached for the remote and turned on the television. Maybe there would be more information on Eric on the noon news.

The time display appeared on the screen with the picture. It was 12:20. She'd missed the lead stories, the sportscast was on now. Her finger touched the power button, but she hesitated when she saw a player in a Stars T-shirt sitting on a stool. He was looking up, lockers behind him, a Channel 7 microphone about six inches from his jaw.

It was his eyes that held her there, something in them. You worked on looks like that doing film. No dramatic gestures like on stage, but doing it with the eyes. This player's eyes had a certain cockiness, but there was also anger.

DEREK BRODY, STARS STARTING QUARTERBACK.

It was under his image. That's when she remembered Eric Smith saying something about a meeting with a rookie the night he died, and telling her that name.

★   ★   ★

The two rookie linemen met Brody in front of the Plaza Hotel ten minutes before seven. He'd wanted it that way. Brody wore a sports jacket, tie and black jeans. Smothers and Headly were appropriately dressed. Smothers was GQ, wearing dress slacks, a linen jacket and a silk shirt, the top button fastened. Headly had squeezed into his college sports jacket, which was stretched tight across his back from three months of pro strength conditioning. A winch couldn't have buttoned the coat.

"What gives, Rick?" Smothers asked. "Why all the fucking mystery?"

Brody reached into his coat pocket and handed both of them bank envelopes. "Barry Sanders buys his line Rolexes," he said. "But from what I'm told, you're going to need this more than a watch."

They started to look inside the envelopes.

"There's four thousand each. But that's just where the fun begins."

He took a couple minutes to lay out the plan.

"That o-o-o-ld gag will n-n-n-never work," Headly stuttered.

Brody said, "It worked at Michigan. Just do what I say."

That's why he'd chosen the Plaza, specifically, the Palm Court. The classical music, the palms, the dainty decorations and the white tables. The uptight patrons. All that was going to make it work.

When the other players came they all walked to the court together from the lobby. A dozen of them, none except Brody under two fifty and six-four, most six-seven to six-eleven, most pushing three hundred pounds or more.

The hostess looked up from the reception station smiling, then her eyes flared and her fingertips touched her mouth. She exhaled and said, "Perhaps you gentlemen would prefer the Oak Room. It's a little more—masculine."

Homer Cobb's eyes were riveted on the string quartet. He blurted, "Yeah, what the fuck is this shit?"

Smothers said, "Our call, remember?"

Brody grabbed a menu and opened it, saying, "Hey, they got Black Angus steak here."

The hostess showed them three tables on the left side, laying out menus. As she walked off, the players pulled the chairs back and pushed the tables together. Brody could feel the eyes of the entire court on the group.

The show was about to begin.

Three waiters served them. The veterans ordered three bottles of Dom Perignon while they looked at entrees. After Cobb had drained two glasses, he bellowed to the quartet, "Hey, you guys know any fucking Stones?"

The entire table burst into laughter, the clanking of sterling ceasing at nearby tables. An older couple rose and left. A young teenage girl at a nearby table giggled.

Cobb nodded in approval. "I like this place," he said.

They ordered the entire menu, and more. If they didn't have it, they special ordered, had it brought over from the Oak Room and the Oyster Bar, the waiters accommodating, expecting a generous tip. The wait staff slid another table over to hold all the dishes. Beluga Caviar at $65 an ounce. Give us twenty ounces, somebody said. Shrimp cocktail, raw oysters, oysters Rockefeller, broiled shrimp in lemon butter, prosciutto with melons. Then, the salads: The salad with Haricot Vert, spinach salad, mixed greens with tomato wedges, sliced tomato and onion, spinach salad. They brought the entrees. Grilled Long Island duck, veal loins and rib lamb chops. A lot of steak. Sliced steak. Sliced steak with sauteed onions. Prime sirloin. Filet mignons. Steak fromage. Beef scaloppini. They special ordered side vegetables. Hash browns. Baked potato. Spinach. Broccoli. A couple added fish dishes. Swordfish. Halibut steak. Four lobsters were added to the dinner mix, jumbos. They were loud and obnoxious as they ate, washing it all down with hundred-dollar bottles of Sauvignon Blanc and Cabernet Sauvignon.

One customer, a woman in her forties, her hair in a french twist, stopped at the table on her way to the bathroom.

"What do you gentlemen call what you're doing?" she asked.

"Surf and turf, baby," somebody said.

"And what's for dessert?" she asked politely.

Cobb said, "You, girl, if you're serving."

She walked off in a huff.

Brody rose. "I gotta take a piss," he said.

When he returned five minutes later, they were ordering dessert, names such as Plaza Cheese Cake, Lemon Custard Tart, Australian Pavola, Valhrona Chocolate and Caramel Marquise, Vanilla Creme Brulee and California Raspberry Napoleon. They ordered sundaes and peach melba and something called Coupe Romanoff, strawberries over vanilla ice cream, topped with Grand Marnier and whipped cream.

A couple linemen washed it down with Heineken.

They kept pushing the desserts on Brody, but he waved them off. They were getting louder. Half the patrons had left, but the other patrons had remained. The string quartet took a break.

The bill came quickly. Homer Cobb snatched it from the waiter, examined it and smiled. He slid it across the table between the two rookie linemen and burped loudly.

"Hope you two rooks applied for gold cards."

They slowly counted it out, a pile of hundreds smothering the check. The total, just over $7,000. Some of the other big men were looking nauseous now, their guts packed with pounds of food. Others continued catcalls to the stage, asking for more music.

The restaurant manager came over.

"Gentlemen," he said politely. "I'm going to have to ask you to keep it down. Our other patrons are complaining."

The entire restaurant was silent now, watching.

"Hey, look at Rick," Cobb said. "He don't look too fucking well."

Through the entire dinner, Brody had been swiping entree samples, sealing them in a Ziploc he'd brought. In the bathroom, he'd poured a dozen little coffee creamers into the bag.

He had the bag in his lap now, his back to the wall. He dropped his head, reaching down, then came up with the hands, making a retching sound, squeezing the baggie. The mixture exploded onto the pile of money.

Brody dropped his hands, letting his chest convulse.

"Motherfucker!" somebody yelled.

The big men scattered. A big nose guard knocked over a large plant vase. He fell with it, crushing its palm tree. People at nearby tables stood up. The manager was shouting for waiters.

Cobb, sitting there, a contorted look on his face.

Headly and Smothers made their move. They picked up the bills and began licking them.

Cobb sprang to his feet, shouting, "What the fuck?"

The teenager at the nearby table threw up.

And Toby Headly looked up in perfect innocence, his stutter gone. Saying, "Hey, we're still hungry, man."

CHAPTER

★ ★ ★ **17** ★ ★ ★

half hour later, Brody stood waiting for the crossing light in the triangle of pavement formed by Broadway and Seventh, all the signs in Times Square competing for his attention: Kodak, Hertz, AT&T, Coke, Panasonic and Mecca, plus the new network's outdoor screen five stories up, an anchor delivering headlines, subtitles overhead.

A street vendor paced in front of the All Star Sports Cafe. Hardly five feet, in his seventies, the vendor's grungy tweed sports jacket was covered with souvenir buttons. When he approached, Brody saw one he liked, black and white, a lot of words packed under a three-inch circle of laminate:

I LIVE IN NEW YORK
FOR THE SAME REASON EVERYBODY ELSE DOES—
TO BE READY TO RULE THE WORLD,
SHOULD THE OPPORTUNITY ARISE.

He handed the vendor ten, tipping him five. He pinned the button onto his lapel, and went inside. He felt good. The linemen discovered the plastic bag and the practical joke as they were asked to leave the Plaza. Everyone lingered outside for a while, reliving it, laughing. The fake vomit was Brody's idea, the other rookies confessed. Brody covering the tab remained secret, and he wanted it that way.

Dominique Goldman was waiting in the lobby. She reached for his hand, saying, "We need to hurry. I was just about to write you off."

They took an elevator up one floor. The main lounge featured a large, elevated round bar. It was surrounded with tables and a dozen big screens built into the walls, all showing different sporting events.

Dominique pulled him up a set of stairs to another level overlooking the bar below. He saw memorabilia in glass cases. Patrick Ewing's shoes. DiMaggio's jersey. Damn, he thought, the pair of panty hose Joe Namath wore for Leggs.

Ahead he saw a couple hundred people packed around oak tables with pitchers of beer and bowls of popcorn. Others stood along the walls, nursing drinks. Cigar and cigarette smoke hung like layered fog. Frank Carcaterra was facing the crowd behind a round table against the wall. Reggie Thompson was on the other side, a pair of Oakley sunglasses eclipsing his eyes. Both men were behind microphones. A small PA system piped out the interview to the crowd, but it hardly cut through the music blasting in the main bar below.

Dominique stopped at the edge of the tables. "You're up next."

He saw her looking at his button.

She touched it with her fingertips. "A man after my heart," she said.

Brody searched for familiar faces. He saw a producer with a boom mike for audience questions. He saw an engineer with a mixing board. He didn't see any other players.

"Where's Bobby?" he asked.

Dominique kept her eyes on Carcaterra. "He wasn't feeling well."

Glamour Boy was talking into the mike. "The bottom line, I think we can turn it around."

Carcaterra said, "But you're starting a rookie. Talk about that."

Thompson lowered his head, glancing at Brody over his shades. He looked back at Carcaterra and grinned. "Yeah, Bobby's hurtin'. But my boy out there, Rick, he can throw the ball."

"Rick?" Carcaterra said.

"Yeah, that's what we call him. White Boy Rick."

The audience laughed.

"Ball Breaker," the bumper music, came up as the station went to a spot. Reggie got up and strutted into the crowd, his shoulders back, his fingers flexing like they did when he lined up at the line of scrimmage, just before the snap.

Carcaterra motioned with his fingers at Dominique, saying, "Okay, send *Rick* up here."

Brody hesitated. He saw two photographers moving toward the front. They stopped at the front edge of the crowd, crouching down on opposite sides of the interview table. They had motor drives and strobes. Dominique said they were from the tabs.

Brody turned to her. "What are they doing here?"

"I guess they expect trouble," she said.

★   ★   ★

Shay Falan swiveled on her chair, spotting the young quarterback talking with a blonde in a black jacket and slacks. Then the fan from Brooklyn put his arm around the back of her chair and said, "I'll tell you whose balls I'd like to break."

Shay ignored him, thinking, that's an endearing pick-up line. She'd already taken a good look at the fan's bloodshot eyes when he'd staggered into the seat next to her, clutching a pitcher and two shots of peppermint schnapps. Faded Stars jersey and yellowed jeans. His hair short above the temples, but long over the collar. Maybe thirty-five. For the last fifteen minutes he'd been trying to impress her with football statistics while he stripped her clothes off with his eyes. Shay thought, the way she's dressed, what else should she expect?

She'd come up with the outfit after hearing about Derek Brody's appearance at the sports bar from a couple of sales reps at the Javits show. Black shorts, not trashy, but snug at the top of her rear. A teal halter top with an inch of cleavage. Smart black sandals. All team colors. In Times Square she'd bought a Stars cap she'd spotted in a store window.

Shay Falan, super fan.

The way she had it planned, she'd check out this Derek Brody first from a front table seat. Maybe give a few seductive smiles. Wait until the interview was over, then make her first move. Chat the guy up and see what he was all about. If he was okay, she'd improvise the rest. Find a way to get him alone for the tricky questions. See if he'd visited Eric. Find out if Eric was using. Then decide where she was going from there.

But now she had this problem, the fan who couldn't take a hint. He leaned into her, talking nonsense and blowing fumes in her face. She kept her eyes on Derek Brody as he wound his way through the crowd and took a seat behind the microphone. She watched him lean back in the chair, one arm over the back. He stared at the show host for a good fifteen seconds. The host never looked up, his eyes on some notes.

When the quarterback finally turned away he looked right at her. He smiled. She smiled back. There was no hint of the anger she'd seen on TV.

The drunk shut up as the bumper music started.

Finally, she thought.

Until she felt his callused hand scrape across her shorts, then grapple for her skin just under the inside seam.

★   ★   ★

Carcaterra said, "Let's all welcome Derek Brody, who will be starting the home opener for the Stars."

Brody heard the applause, but he was watching the girl and the guy in the jersey, the two of them about thirty feet out, the girl with long dancer's legs and engaging red hair cascading from under her cap. The girl was having some kind of trouble. She pushed the guy with the jersey away twice, almost sending him to the floor.

Brody looked back at Carcaterra.

"Can I call you Rick?" Carcaterra asked.

"You seem comfortable calling me anything you want," Brody said. "It's your show."

Carcaterra said, "Well, Rick, my listeners know where I'm coming from. But they don't know you. So let's start with questions from the audience here at the All Star Sports Cafe."

Brody's eyes went back to the front table. The guy in the jersey was standing now, but he had a tight grip around the redhead's wrist. She was trying to jerk it away.

"Yeah, I got a question," he shouted.

The producer swung the boom. The guy let go of the girl and wrapped both of his hands around the barrel of the mike, steadying himself. He's drunk, Brody thought.

"This is a question for Franky." The drunk paused. "Franky, why are you such a fucking asshole?"

Carcaterra covered his microphone. "Sit down, nitwit." He quickly turned to the engineer and said, "Dummy that on the delay."

Franky Carcaterra didn't see the drunk snatch the boom from the producer, but Brody did. He also saw the redhead leap to her feet and backpedal. Carcaterra turned in time only to see the drunk charging, the boom over his head like a war club.

The angle later reminded Brody of the time he took out the left linebacker in an Ohio State game. He sprang from his chair and hit the drunk in the air.

Cross body style, just above the knees.

The drunk going airborne and horizontal.

The motion had a stop action look when it happened. Later, Brody realized, that had to be the camera strobes.

★   ★   ★

He was surprised Carcaterra resumed the interview five minutes later, after the producer ran two sets of spots. The drunk was out cold through half the interview. He lay in front of them until the paramedics came. They put him in a neck brace, boarded him and carried him out. Everybody went on with business as usual, even the audience, back into the pretzels and beer. Carcaterra didn't say thanks. Later, he said, "I guess I owe you one." Off the air.

The interview skirted his past, as promised. But Carcaterra seemed to have a scout's eye for his current challenges on the field.

Carcaterra said at one point, "Early on, you had trouble throwing right on the three step drop in practice."

"Only when I don't set my foot," Brody said. He wondered to himself how Carcaterra knew that. Shit, he'd never seen him in camp.

"But you favor the left on the three, and you've got a Pro Bowler on the right in Reggie Thompson."

Brody wanted to say *former* Pro Bowler, but he bit his lip. Glamour Boy must have fed Carcaterra the expertise, he decided, probably before the show. Telling him what questions to ask. Fucking with him again, he thought.

Anywhere he could.

After the interview, he signed autographs on programs, beer napkins, menus and the jersey over the top of one girl's breasts. The redhead didn't approach for an autograph. But he spotted her leaning against the wall near Namath's panty hose, looking at him. She smiled when their eyes met.

Dominique Goldman walked up after he signed the last autograph. "That was very good," she said. "Saving his butt. The interview. Everything. The town's going to eat it up."

She touched his arm. "Look, I know a good place on the Upper East Side. They serve great cannoli. It's not far from your place."

"I've already had enough excitement for one night," he said. "I've really got to go."

"Where?" She said it in a demanding way.

"I thought I'd sign that drunk's body cast in the hospital."

"You're funny." She wasn't smiling.

Brody looked over at the redhead. She was still standing there, as if she were waiting for him.

Dominique's eyes followed his. "A new friend?" she asked.

"Something like that," he said.

★   ★   ★

Shay watched Derek Brody walk away from the woman in the black outfit, then approach, in no hurry, but smiling. He stopped only a foot away.

He said, "Sorry about your boyfriend. I didn't mean to hit him that hard." He paused. "No, that's a lie. Actually, I was trying to hit him as hard as I could. He'll probably sue."

Shay put out her hand and said, "He wasn't my boyfriend, and I should be thanking you."

She liked the way he shook her hand, giving her a bit of a grip, not limp the way most men did.

"My name's Shay."

"Derek."

She could have said, "I know," but she didn't. She liked the way he said it, not assuming everyone should know his name, like prominent actors often did.

"That jerk had his hands all over me," she said.

"I saw. You didn't know him?"

"I came alone. He happened to sit next to me. Everything went downhill from there."

"You must be pretty committed, to come here by yourself."

"I wanted to see you," she said. She hoped he didn't start talking football. He did that, she'd have to switch to full bimbo mode.

He glanced over his shoulder at the blonde again. She was talking to the producer now.

"Friend of yours?" she asked.

"She's with the team." He looked back at her. "You doing anything?"

"I'm talking to you."

"Why don't we get out of here?" he asked.

"What's wrong with here?" Shay asked back. She didn't want to look easy, but something also gave her the feeling he was trying to ditch the blonde.

"I don't really like these kind of places," he said. "I'm always worried somebody is going to frame me and hang me on the wall."

She laughed. "Where did you have in mind?"

"You name it. I promise, I won't lay a hand on you."

Shay thought about it, then said, "And why should I believe you?"

"Because I limit myself to only one lawsuit a night," he said.

They hailed a cab, the girl Shay giving directions to somewhere in the Village. She took off her Stars cap and shook her hair out. The citrus-like smell of her shampoo filled the back seat.

She said, "Wasn't that horrible what happened to Eric Smith? I'm surprised there was no service or team tribute."

Just like that, out of nowhere. Brody looked at her face. In the dim cab, passing lights made her eyes flash several shades of green.

"A lot of players leave the game and disappear," he said. He added, "From the public, I mean."

She pulled an elastic band out of her small purse and wrapped her hair into a pony tail. "Did you know him?"

Brody hesitated. "Met him once."

She'd been a convenient excuse to ditch Dominique. Now, she was looking like a lot more than that.

"You just bought that, didn't you?" he said.

"Bought what?"

"The Stars hat."

She had a surprised smile. "How did you know?"

"Most people bend the brim, or wear them backwards."

"That looks stupid. I mean, wearing them backwards, especially with the plastic bands. You look like you're strapped in an electric chair." She smiled. "People have no sense of style anymore. The old movies, now those people knew how to wear hats."

"Women with fish nets over their faces."

"And the men. Lizbeth Scott and Bogart in *Dead Reckoning*. Bogart is in this trench coat and fedora. There's this great scene where Bogie gets a guy to confess by pouring napalm on the floor. Lighting it and it's burning toward him. They called it creeping jelly back then."

Brody chuckled. "From hats to napalm. That's pretty good."

"What I was meaning to say, is, did you ever notice, when guys in those movies take their hats off, they never have a hat ring?"

"I'm not sure I follow you."

"Hats in the movies, you don't get this." She pointed to her own head, a ridge in her hair just above her ears.

She leaned back, "You like Lizbeth Scott?"

"Never heard of her."

"She was the queen of noir, as far as I'm concerned."

"I'm not sure what that is, either."

"A lot of dark, high contrast scenes. The hero is always painted into a corner. Blackmail or double crosses, usually. Often from women. They're all black and white, unless you get the Turner colorized version of *Out of the Past*, or *The Maltese Falcon*. Ruined the movies. But, Turner also makes a fresh print in black and white and saves them before the originals disintegrate in the can. So, I guess he's okay."

She took a breath.

"You study film, or something?" he asked.

"I went to Juilliard."

"I thought that was a music school."

"I was in musical theater, and drama."

"So you're a dancer?"

"What makes you say that?"

"The legs."

She blushed slightly. "I do a little of everything. That's my problem. Musical theater is the only place where you can do it all. But those parts are hard to come by. Lately, I've been doing a lot of conventions and jingles to pay the bills."

The cab pulled up to a small restaurant on Broadway and Fourth. Brody paid the fare. As the cab drove off, he noticed she'd left the Stars cap in the back seat. He didn't say anything.

Inside, there was a small bar and small tables, and an antique espresso machine. He ordered a club soda and lime. She asked for coffee.

She asked, "You nervous about the game Sunday?"

"I get nervous when I run out onto the field for the first series. But that goes away after the first contact, the first hit."

She said, "You like hitting people?"

"I'm usually the one getting hit."

"But when you do it."

"You have to like it, or you don't last very long out there."

"It looks awfully brutal. I'm not sure I understand how you do it."

"I'm not sure I do either. It's just something that's there."

"And when did you first realize?"

Brody thought about it. "Johnny Cheeseman," he finally said. "He used to sit behind me in fifth grade."

"You got into a fight?"

Brody shook, no. "I couldn't do that. My father was a teacher in the school district."

"So?"

"This Cheeseman was one of those kids, you know the type. Always messing with you. Used to take a pencil and flick it into the back of my ear. Shove me in the hall. Little stuff that really didn't matter when you look back at it later. But it mattered then."

Brody swigged the soda and continued, "Anyway, my dad said I was finally ready."

"For what?"

"Football. End of the first week of practice, we put on pads and the coach lines us up in two columns for a blocking drill. And guess who's right across from me?"

"That kid," she said.

Brody grinned at the memory. "After I got his attention, we actually became good friends. He was the halfback on my high school team. Scored the winning touchdown at state."

"But you became a quarterback," she said.

"I had a good arm. I'd been practicing. My father was a quarterback. Plus, it's better."

"Why's that?"

"You're the chief, the man. Every quarterback I know wants that. He wants to be the man."

"That sounds tribal."

The girl was no bim, Brody thought. "I had this men's studies class at Michigan," he continued. "You know, cultures for centuries had these rituals for boys. Certain age, puberty usually, the boy is taken from his mother. Some tribes, kidnaped, to live for a time only with the men. He's taught the ways of war, or hunting, given his own identity—apart from women. He's not allowed to go back among the women until he gets that. Then he's ready for a wife, his own family."

"How do they know he's ready?" she asked, leaning forward.

"The elders circumcise him or cut off a finger. Some tribes, he gets to wear a shield across his groin."

"Kind of like a jockstrap," she said.

"I'm serious," Brody said. "Think about it. Where else you going to get that? The closest thing is sports. Trouble is, for a lot of jocks, it's just another way to get laid. Find 'em, fool 'em, feel 'em, fuck 'em and forget 'em. I've been hearing that in locker rooms for years."

"But you're different."

"What makes you say that?"

"Just a hunch," she said.

★   ★   ★

He told her about his mother dying, the town where he grew up. His father's influence. She told him about growing up in Albany, her high school years. A drama teacher who inspired her. A father, a carpenter with a drinking problem, who still maintained that acting and the arts in general were pursuits reserved for the chosen rich.

Shay liked Derek Brody. "You know, you don't sound like a football player," she eventually said.

The smile suddenly left his eyes. "That's the difference between you and me," he said.

She gave him a curious look. His entire demeanor changed.

"See, I do it," he snapped. "You pretend. My guess is, you've never been to a football game."

"What makes you say that?"

"You forgot your hat."

Shit, she thought.

He added, "And you haven't asked me a single question about Vince Lombardi."

She tried to stay with it. "I like Vince Lombardi."

"You think he'll do okay with the Pack?"

She shrugged. "Probably."

He finished the club soda, eyeing her over the rim. He smacked the glass down on the table and said, "That could be a *real* problem."

"What makes you say so?"

"Lombardi's been dead for twenty years."

He stood up, pulled a twenty from his pocket and flung it on the table.

"Wait," she said.

He walked out of the bar. But she caught him before he crossed Broadway. He was waiting for the traffic, his hands in his pockets.

"That guy Molito send you?" he said, his eyes on the street.

She told him she had no idea what he was talking about.

He turned and grabbed her arm, not hard, but firm. "What do you want?"

Now or never, she thought.

Shay said, "Some answers about Eric Smith."

CHAPTER

★ ★ ★ **18** ★ ★ ★

He was shaving at the mirror when she said, "Carl, damn you, come in here."

Montan cut the last swipe of cream from his left cheek with the gold-handled razor, then doused his face with water. He stepped back from the mirror to use the towel, then massaged his face with shaving balm. He lifted his chin, then lowered it, checking for loose skin on the neck.

"Carl, goddamnit."

He walked into the bedroom, a towel over his shoulder, his lower body in Tommy Hilfiger boxers. Dominique Goldman was leaning against his headboard, the sheet only to her waist, her breasts like her ambition, Montan thought. Easy to spot and always pointed up.

She'd shown up the night before at his apartment. Walked right in without an invitation and headed straight for his single malt scotch. He'd pretty much detected a pattern. She came to him for sex when she was frustrated or wanted to enlist him in a scheme, usually aimed at changing her father's mind.

Dominique gestured at his bedroom TV with a remote. It was the local news cut-in for *Good Morning America*.

"Christ, Carl, you almost missed it."

"Missed what?"

She held up a hand. "Just watch and listen."

The TV had a shot of the front page of the *Post*, a picture of Derek Brody in midair. The headline: DOUBLE TROUBLE. Underneath a smaller headline with the guy claiming he was assaulted. The anchor was making a segue now, saying, Brody's display wasn't the only team problem. The *Post* was also reporting in a copyrighted story that the Stars were facing bankruptcy, the newspaper quoting from an audit it had obtained. Montan guessed that's where the *double* came in.

Dominique tugged the sheet over her chest, her mouth open. "My god," she said. "Where did they get that?"

"You said you invited photographers."

"Not the fight," she said. "The audit."

Montan sat next to her on the bed. "You frighten me, Nicky," he said. "I know you have a certain animosity for your father, but I never thought you'd publicly humiliate the man."

"You're only half right," she said. "I didn't leak the report."

She looked worried. He rested the palm of his hand on her leg. "Sometimes it colors your thinking, you know," he said. "Sometimes it works against your self interest."

Her eyes never left the TV. "Carl," she said, "why don't you finish getting dressed."

They went to breakfast together at the old Russell, now a Sheraton on Park Avenue. Montan invited her, offering to buy, then to drop her off at MetLife before he headed to the dome.

When they sat down Montan said, "You know, the lounge across the hall is pretty famous."

She said, "Do I look like I care?"

Dominique was staring into her coffee cup and stewing. She'd bitched the entire ride from the apartment. The Brody story would have been good coverage, quarterback saves airwave enemy, she kept saying. But the audit gave it an entirely different spin.

Montan continued his story anyway. Making the breakfast casual, and the conversation. The way it had to be. "That movie, *The Verdict*. Paul Newman as the drunken lawyer trying to turn himself around by winning a big malpractice case. They shot this big scene in the hotel lounge. Near the end, Newman meets Charlotte Rampling there and finds out she's a mole. They've been sleeping together through most of the movie, but it turns out she's spying for the defense team."

Montan took a sip of coffee. "So, you know what he does?"

She looked up at him, blinking twice.

"He slugs her. A nice right cross. Right in the jaw. Then he walks out."

"That's precious," she said.

"Only Newman gets away with that. Most other actors, that would have been it for their careers."

Dominique said, "Carl, did you leak that audit?"

"How can I leak something I haven't even seen," he said. Montan hesitated, then said, "Maybe Jack did, probably with Papa's blessing."

"That's crazy. Why?"

"Maybe to put more pressure on the city. The stadium negotiations. But I'm only guessing. Other than the cap, I try to steer clear of anything that requires a CPA." Montan paused. "Did Papa say anything to you?"

"The city isn't budging."

"Maybe he needs to threaten to move," Montan said. "That's how it's usually done."

"He won't do that. He's got city water for blood."

"Did he say why? The city, I mean."

"Papa met with the Mayor last week at Gracie, going over the numbers. The Mayor says the city has to retain control of the dome. You're familiar with the deal. The stadium revenues are used to pay the bonds. The Mayor said, maybe after the next election."

"The team goes under, how are they going to retire bonds with empty seats?"

"That's what Papa suggested."

"And?"

"The Mayor said tractor pulls."

Montan laughed. "The Mayor actually said that?"

She nodded.

"I don't believe it."

"I heard it," Dominique said. "I was there."

"So what do you think Papa's going to do?"

"He keeps saying it will turn around. That the team will finally go over five hundred. And we'll squeak through." She looked him in the eyes. "Carl, be honest with me. How close are we?"

"If Reggie Thompson hadn't spiked the ball, we'd be at five hundred for the preseason. That's acceptable. But Bobby's down, hurt bad. We'll have to see what Brody does Sunday."

She tapped the table with her finger. "That's why I've been putting in the effort. He's a good story. I'm figuring he could put people into the seats."

Montan said, "That's a long shot. I mean, he is a rookie."

"But there are other ways. Contests. Giveaways at half time. I'd worked out a deal with Pizza Hut. Spent a month on it. We were going to do this animated feature at half time. Three pizzas dressed as football players, each one representing the three different levels of the stadium. The one that wins, all those people with those tickets, get a free pizza at any Pizza Hut after the game. Of course, each level wins through the season."

"That starts Sunday?" Montan asked.

She shook her head. "I take it to Papa and Jack, and Papa says, 'I won't resort to gimmicks.' Papa's just not in touch. No wonder the new owners want him out."

"What did Jack say?"

"Jack just sits there, agreeing. Sometimes I think Jack is trying to tank the team."

Montan said, "Maybe Jack is your problem, not Papa."

He wanted to proceed carefully now. He motioned the waitress over first, telling her they were ready to order. He ordered the poached eggs over corned beef hash. She wanted grapefruit and a croissant.

When the waitress left, Montan said, "Think about it. Jack also handled that overture from the West Coast."

"Overture?"

"Jack didn't tell you?"

She didn't answer.

"That's strange," Montan said. "He didn't seem reluctant to share the information with me."

He could see her getting angry. He wanted her that way.

Montan continued, "The way Jack was telling it, the overture came from a major player. From one of the conglomerates that has a real interest in the team."

"League rules prohibit corporate ownership," she said. "Only individuals can own teams."

"That's what Jack was saying. But I believe this guy wants it for himself. Jack says he's worth a bundle."

"Who is it?"

"He didn't give me a name."

"Why didn't you ask?"

"Like I was saying, it's not my territory."

Dominique shook her head. "Papa would never sell. He'll self destruct first. That's what worries me."

"The way Jack was telling it, the guy was looking for some kind of limited partnership, a minority interest. Offered to build a practice facility, use his clout to get a better stadium deal. He even talked about throwing a team plane in the deal."

"So what does he get?"

"He likes the fact the team is in New York, the national exposure. Kind of platform for his other efforts, like Victor Kiam did for a while with the Pats. Football sells razors, all that."

Dominique's eyes lit up. Exposure. He knew she'd like that.

"I'm surprised Papa didn't tell you," Montan said.

She ignored the statement. "So what else did Jack say?"

"Jack was dead against it. He said bringing somebody else aboard, the drawbacks outweigh the benefits."

"Christ," Dominique said.

"Jack was saying he reminded Papa of Tose and the Eagles. The way the minority partners mounted a takeover. That kind of thing."

"What do you think?"

"I think Jack is just being Jack. You know how Papa trusts him. Don't get me wrong, Jack is earnest, but he's a little like your father."

"Antiquated."

Montan didn't respond directly. "Those are your words, not mine," he said. "I do work for both men."

Montan let her mull over the story. Let those resentments, a character trait working both for her and against her, fester against her father. She was as predictable as his players, he thought. But with Dominique, he didn't need a psychological report.

He'd let her suggest it. It might take a day or two. Maybe a week. It took far less than that.

She leaned close. "Carl, I want you to find out who this buyer is."

He didn't say anything.

"Can you do it?" He felt her hand touch his leg under the table.

"You're asking a lot. I get the name from Jack, he finds out I told you. My job's on the line."

He knew she really didn't give a damn about that.

She said, "Look, maybe I can set up a meeting with this guy. Feel it out, then take the deal to Papa, without Jack. Try that different approach you were talking about earlier."

The breakfast arrived, the waitress distributing the dishes. Montan reached for his fork and knife.

"Carl?" she asked.

"You with me or against me?"

Montan cut the poached egg and hash in half, then said, "I don't know, Nicky. You know how I hate to get in the middle of things."

★   ★   ★

An hour later, he was parked in the Shea Stadium lot again, the Turk explaining what happened the night before. The Turk was slouched in Montan's sedan, deep in the seat, enjoying telling it, dragging on his second cigarette.

"So, I wait for Bimbolina to leave the apartment and she finally goes, dressed in team colors, no less. Looking hot, too. I get into the apartment and spend an hour in there, taking apart every fucking thing. You should see the clothes, and the fucking CDs. A lot of old shit, too. And sheet music. Like I was saying, she's into some kind of stage thing."

Montan said, "I don't care what she does. You find the log?"

The Turk pulled hard on the smoke. "I'm getting to that." He flicked the ash out the window. "So I trash the music all over the goddamn apartment. Did the B&E thing, like you said. Took her CD player. Wanted the TV, but that was too big. Took a couple of CDs, too. She had *Annie Get Your Gun*. Did I ever tell you I played Curly in that show in high school?"

"Turk, I'm not interested in your acting career, either."

The Turk held up his hands. "No log. Nothing."

"You checked inside books?"

"A bunch of self-help crap."

Montan turned to him. "Let me get this straight. You asked me to drive over here, to tell me you didn't find a fucking thing?"

The Turk started to say something, but Montan cut him off. "You talk to the slinger lately? Is he still taking care of Glamour Boy?"

The Turk scratched the stubble under his sideburns. "The slinger says business has dropped off a little. But, shit, Carl, Sunday's the opener."

"I guess that's to be expected," Montan said.

The Turk leaned a little into the passenger door and said, "Now, you going to let me finish my story?"

"There's more?"

The Turk nodded. "Yeah, the good shit is yet to come." He lit another smoke, then exhaled out the window.

"So, I leave the apartment and head over to Times Square. Figure I should get on Brody. Surfer says he's at the All Star. Earlier, I guess he and the line made quite a little scene over at the Plaza. But that's another story. So I get to the All Star, and who the fuck is there, sitting at the front table? Fucking Bimbolina. Wearing a Stars cap, taking in the whole show. She's sitting with the guy Brody nailed in the *Post* picture, guy with his hands all over her. That's why I figure Brody did it."

"Did *what*?" Montan asked.

"Laid the guy out. He was watching it. Shit, he wasn't trying to save Carcaterra. Carcaterra is an asshole."

"You're saying Brody made a move on her?"

The Turk drew on the smoke again. "After the show. And they leave together. I follow them to the Village, the two of them getting all intense in this place on Broadway. Next thing I see, they're jumping in a cab. That's when I lost them. But Surfer tells me they both showed up later at the Lucerne."

The Turk sharpened the ash on his smoke in the ashtray. "I think that proves it."

"Proves what?"

"With Smith gone, she's trading up. Bimbolina's a tunnel lizard, man."

Montan had heard players called them that, eager women who talked their way past security, hanging out in the tunnel after games, trying to snag players. The name lizard had stuck because the older ones had reptilian skin from too many salon tans.

Montan said, "You see them in bed?"

"Not exactly. He's got the bedroom blinds closed all the time. But she got that rookie's fucking attention. Surfer's, too."

"That doesn't take much."

The Turk grinned. "You're not listening to what I'm saying. I follow Brody over to the dome this morning. There's no sign of Bimbolina. I'm figuring she left in the middle of the night."

Montan was growing weary of the story, and the Turk thinking with his dick, but probably right. "Keep an eye on both of them for the next couple of days," he said. "See if they call each other, make some kind of move together. It seems awfully coincidental."

"Brody's already made his move," the Turk said, confident about it. "And she liked it. A *lot*."

"That's not the kind of move I meant," Montan said.

"And she won't be calling him—not today, anyway."

"She'll be picking up," Montan said. "Filing a B&E report in the Village."

The Turk shook his head, dragging a last hit on the smoke and pitching it out the window. "No she won't. I just talked to the Surfer. She's out on the balcony in a pair of his shorts. Fucking topless."

"At the Lucerne?"

"That's what I'm saying, Carl, she's still at Brody's place."

CHAPTER

★ ★ ★ **19** ★ ★ ★

A second practice session was scheduled for Wednesday afternoon, first and second down formations and plays. Practice in pads. Brody liked the way the offensive line was hitting. He liked the way some of the players were talking to him now. The Plaza gag had spread around the locker room, then to the coaches.

"Legendary," the offensive coordinator said.

Now he had this other problem. On Wednesday morning, he'd found the girl sitting on his balcony, reading the *Village Voice*. Shay had a decanter of coffee and a cup waiting for him. She had a notebook and a pen. The small overnight bag she'd taken from her apartment sat near her feet.

He'd sat down, traffic droning below. "Any luck?"

"This is no place to look," she said, her eyes still in the paper. "I'm going to call a realtor." She tossed the *Voice* onto the table. "Maybe I should just take a train to Albany. Make it easy on myself."

"You really are scared to go back," he said.

She looked at the river. "Maybe I just don't want to give up this great view." She reached out and touched his hand. "You've been so sweet."

"Sweet. I haven't been called that in years."

"This is a big week for you, and here I am, creating problems. It would be like my father moving in with me a couple days before I opened."

"I remind you of your father?"

She laughed.

He'd told her to make herself at home. Take her time to figure out what she was going to do.

Her being there wasn't the problem, he was thinking now. What she told him was a problem. He'd walked her home to her apartment, Shay shooting questions at him. Saying she was Eric Smith's girlfriend and that Smith was planning on going into Betty Ford. Was he using when he saw him? If he wasn't, why didn't he tell the police or the newspapers that? He gave her half-ass answers, like he did with the cop. Then, arriving at her apartment, finding it trashed, the girl became hysterical, saying she had nowhere to go. He'd told her she could spend the night.

Now one night was turning into two.

She had dinner made for him when he returned from practice. Veal marsala, pasta and a nice salad, Shay saying it was the least she could do. They talked about Eric Smith again at dinner, Shay saying she guessed it was the town that did him in, or the game. She wasn't sure. He had this feeling she was holding back. And he was holding back, too, part of him thinking this was more New York insanity, the other part thinking, maybe someone was just looking for information, this girl Shay sent to find out exactly what he knew.

The plates empty, she said, "Eric really didn't tell me that much about playing. I have no idea what your life is like. I just know a quarterback throws the ball."

He found himself drawing that diagram with the circles on a napkin. Coach, team, fans, media, front office, then wife/girlfriend/friends.

"They're all looking to you for something," he said.

"What about 'self'?" she asked.

She had a point. "I should add that, shouldn't I?" he asked. He penciled it in, looking at it.

She asked, "And what does *self* want?"

"To play the game, where you can get away from all of the others. I mean, it's a complicated game, sure. But everything is pretty fundamental out there. That's always been the reason."

"For what?"

"That I've played."

"Most people wouldn't consider being carried off on a stretcher an escape."

"That's what you think it is?"

"I guess it depends on your point of view."

She turned the napkin around, pointing to the large circle in the middle. "So, who is this person?"

Brody looked at it for a few seconds. He hadn't thought about that, either. "I guess that's what others see."

She balanced the tip of the ballpoint on the new self circle. "Not necessarily related to this," she said.

When he didn't say anything, she said, "I can relate to that."

She folded the napkin over and scrawled something and handed it to him. Two words: Yes. No.

"Mine's pretty simple."

"I'm not sure I follow."

"You're doing good if you average one part every fifty auditions, presuming your agent even gets you into the casting call. So you spend a lot more time losing than winning."

"That's why I stayed away from baseball. Fail two out of three times at the plate, you're considered at the top of your game. I couldn't deal with those odds, let alone one in fifty."

"You just keep practicing, studying. And you work on various forms of self delusion. Telling yourself you're damn good, and it's just a matter of time."

"Winning solves everything."

"That's not what I'm saying. You can't keep going on the occasional yes. They're too few and far between. You've got to love the work." She laughed. "Listen to me."

Brody said, "And if that doesn't work?"

"There's always alcohol. I learned that one from my dad. But that hasn't been working for me lately. That's how I met Eric, in fact. We were in this program together."

There was an awkward moment of silence. She rose from the table. "Well, I've inconvenienced you enough. I've called a friend. She says I can stay with her until I get this situation under control."

"What did the police say?" Brody asked.

"You have to go in and make a report."

"They're not going to meet you at the apartment?"

She laughed. "Only in the movies. You make the report so you can get the insurance. That's all."

He thought about what he saw at the apartment. All that music, those videos. The Broadway show posters. Not the type of girl who would be hooked up with Molito. Brody eyed her across the table, getting beyond the hair, the body, the freckles on her nose. He saw something there and he hoped he had it right. He thought, sometimes you have to gamble.

"You know," he said. "I haven't been entirely honest with you."

She looked in his eyes for a couple of seconds, then she sat back down. "That makes two of us," she said.

★　★　★

After he told Shay about the police interview, she told him everything she could remember, except the document Eric gave her, that it even existed. She wasn't going to broadcast something she now believed may have gotten Eric killed.

Shay watched him walk outside to the balcony. He stood at the railing, his hands gripping and releasing an iron chair. For a second, Shay thought he was going to throw it over the side or through the screen. He had a look she'd seen on jocks when they hurled bats or helmets, or pushed over a table of Gatorade.

He turned around. "So, what Eric told you, you think that's why somebody broke into your apartment? What were they looking for?"

"I'm not sure." She joined him on the balcony.

"You write what he said down?"

"No."

"I don't get it. Why did he involve you—then me?"

"The guy was isolated," she said. "And he *was* messed up, but not in the way the papers say. You can't eat as many pills as he did and make sound choices. He was putting a lot of pressure on himself. I thought he was just being paranoid, but he must have seen it coming."

"Seen what?"

"He told me if anything happened, I was supposed to tell the commissioner."

"He wanted you to contact the league office?"

She nodded.

"You went over there?"

"No, I called. I couldn't get past the secretaries. They wanted me to talk to something called league security, but Eric said that I shouldn't do that."

"A guy named Bullard?"

"He didn't say a name. But up until then, some security guy was the only one he was dealing with. Except me, of course, and now, you."

"Jesus," Brody said.

"Exactly what do these security people do?"

"They're supposed to protect the integrity of the game."

"Eric said if I couldn't get it to the commissioner, I'm supposed to go to something called *NFL Magazine*. I guess it's a sports news show. I thought about the police, too."

"You go to them with this story and they're going to drag you—"

"I know," she said.

Brody gazed at the river, then back at her again. "If Smith was right, if these people are dangerous, you're going to have to be careful. If they found your place, they'll find you."

"That's what made me think of going back to Albany."

"You've been followed?"

Shay hesitated, then said, "There was this guy. I thought I was just upset after seeing the news about Eric." She paused. "Then, at the radio show, I thought I might have seen him again, standing at the bar when I went to the bathroom, talking to a girl. But maybe it was someone who looked like him. The guy the first day didn't have an accent. The guy at the bar did."

"You don't sound very sure."

"He sounded Hispanic. I do accents. I've got fifteen on my resume. You know, for voice-overs. The guy kind of sounded like that, but it was off. But as far as I know, he could have been from Chile. I don't know how they talk down there. I—" She stopped and looked at him. "That's what scared me. More than the apartment. That's why I wanted to go home with you."

"So the hysterics, that was acting?"

She half smiled. "I'd prefer to call it character development. The fear was there. I just fed it. But, yeah, ten years in this city, you're not a New Yorker until you've been burglarized."

He asked, "What if I wouldn't have bought the act?"

"I'd have developed the character further."

"So what does the poor, helpless girl do next?" He was being sarcastic, but she sensed a trace of meanness.

"Improvise."

He spun around, away from the railing, facing her. She could see the muscles in his jaw flexing.

He said, "You know how hard it is to get here?"

"Where?"

"Fucking *here*." He tapped his chest with his finger, hard, then motioned to the skyline. "There's only thirty-six in the world who get to do this on Sunday. Only a couple in this town."

"What, mislead police?"

"Start at my position in this league."

She said, "Now those odds, I can relate to. But I suggest you don't start feeling sorry for yourself. You can't afford to. Not here."

He looked stunned for a moment, as if he wasn't used to a woman talking to him that way. Then he laughed and grabbed his head with both hands, twisting it a little, as if he were trying to determine if it was properly connected. "I can't fucking believe this. This is bullshit. This team. Now *you*. What did you have to involve me for? You're fucked up, you know that? Actress. Broadway. What the fuck? How do I know that?"

She raised one eyebrow. "I could dance and sing."

He walked into the apartment, slamming the sliding screen behind him. When he didn't come back after a couple of minutes, she stepped inside. She walked to the guest room where she'd slept, picked up her purse and slung the overnight bag over her shoulder.

She found him in the living room, standing in front of a painting. She looked at the picture for a few seconds, then asked, "Who is that, anyway?"

He kept his eyes on the painting. "Y.A. Tittle. Giants quarterback."

"Was he good?"

"In his day. Now he's not even in the top twenty."

"So why do you have it?"

"It says a lot about the demands of the game."

She traced her fingertips along the frame. "You ever notice when you look at these vintage pictures, the athletes look older. I mean, they could be your father. They don't look like today's athletes."

He glanced at her. "You mean they look like men?"

"Nothing personal," she said.

He noticed her bag and purse. "Where you going?"

"You don't need any more circles on your napkin."

He shook his head, massaging his cheek near his scar. "No, that's not the way we're going to do it. You need to talk to my agent, my attorney. He's working on this. He's coming in for the game."

She said, "So find me after you conquer the world."

He gripped her shoulders gently. A softness had returned to his eyes.

"I want you to come to practice with me tomorrow," he said. "They have seats right near the field for friends and family. You'll be safe as long as you're connected to me."

"What makes you so sure?"

"They have a lot of money invested."

She frowned. "I have auditions. Work."

"I'll give you money."

"For what? I have a script I should be studying."

"We'll go get it, and anything else you want to bring."

"And I promised Eric. I'm thinking the TV show."

"You go to a producer with a story like this, and nothing to back it up with but a couple of hunches, they're going to put you in the waiting room with the people who think they've seen E.T." He hesitated, then added, "When the time comes, I'll go with you. You've got my word. But I need to buy some time, find out what's going on."

"And just how do you propose to do that?" she asked.

"That's why I offered to pay," he said. "And please don't take this wrong. You're good."

"Good for what?"

His eyes smirked. "If you're up for it, I've got a new role in mind."

★   ★   ★

Later, they hopped a cab to Times Square, Shay showing him the theater district. Shay already into it. She held his hand, rubbed his shoulder at the crosswalks. Kissed him a couple times on the cheek.

When he stopped in front of the Virgin Records megastore, she put her arms around him and kissed him on the lips, bending one leg up behind her, like they did in the Forties and Fifties flicks.

"How's that?" she said.

"That doesn't feel like acting."

"When you nail it, it shouldn't," she said.

He said, "Let's go in here."

She glanced up at the Virgin sign. "I hate these kind of places."

"It'll just take a second," he said.

Inside, there were a couple of floors of CDs, videos, books, interactive media. They saw a coffee shop and theaters on the basement level. *Virgin* everywhere. A Virgin travel agency. Virgin Atlantic Airlines. A soda machine with something called Virgin Cola. The logo everywhere you looked, in Virgin red.

Shay said, "See what I mean. This is everything that's gone wrong with this town. The ma-and-pa stores can't compete."

"People must want it," Brody said.

The store was jammed.

Shay said, "I liked the old peep shows better. At least they weren't trying to take over the world." She let go of his hand and crossed her arms. "Can we go now?"

He retrieved her hand and pulled her toward a row of CDs, the pop/rock section. "In the game, you get the best defense when the defense is rested. You do that by generating offense, that keeps the defense off the field."

She rolled her eyes. "Am I going to have to learn football cliches, too?"

"They're cliches because they're true. That's what I was telling you earlier. The game is very simple. It's the people who make it complicated. The wheels start to come off, you go back to basics."

He seemed to have switched gears, walking fast, up and down the aisles, his eyes scanning the racks. On a mission, Shay along for the ride.

She asked, "You on steroids?"

"I'm looking for a certain type of music. I've got this idea. Like I was saying, a little offense."

She halted, her arm extending, then pulling him back. "Let me help," she said.

"I'm not talking about show tunes."

"You think I fall asleep to Julie Andrews hitting a high C every night?" She drew him close to her, his arms in her hands, making it look like affection, but talking the other way. "What's with you jocks, anyway? Just like Eric. Your way or the highway."

"I thought you didn't know anything about sports."

"I know that in my high school, everyone kissed their asses. And they called that *building character*."

He blinked.

She leaned closer, whispering now in his ear. "Let's get one thing straight right now. I'm doing this with you because I don't have a lot of options right now. The way I figure, my butt could be on the line more than yours, and that means I'm not just another one of your troops. If that's the way you're thinking, I'll take my chances on my own."

She put him at arm's length, giving him her best loving smile. "Understand, *Brody*?"

"Jesus," he said, "I'm just looking for some music that doesn't set people off."

"That's what music does," she said.

"What I mean, something people couldn't say was black, or white. Or country. Or rock. Or pop. Or rap."

"Juilliard, remember?" she said. "It's a music school."

He sighed. "Okay, Juilliard."

She thought about what he wanted, then began, "Well, there's triphop. That's a slow hip hop beat with a white psychedelic sound. A lot of people like to listen to it while they have sex."

"That's not what I had in mind. It's for the team."

She started walking down the aisles now, pulling him along this time. She stopped in the Techno section, ran her fingers through the collection, then pulled out a CD. Saying, this is what he needed, a sub genre of techno. A hard hip hop beat, but with heavy metal guitar and synthesizer. Totally eclectic. Few words, but a definite bad-ass attitude. "They're from England, huge in Europe. You won't hear them on the radio. Though they got hot for a while on MTV."

She handed him the CD, the band the Prodigy, the title, *Music for a Jilted Generation*. He looked at the first few song titles: "Break & Enter," "Full Throttle," "Voodoo People."

"They got a name for this?"

"Jungle," she said.

He stared at her.

"A million people showed up in Berlin for a music festival, this band the headliner. But you have to play it loud. Very heavy bottom. They're—hypnotic."

He sliced open the CD with his fingernail and opened the book inside. He saw one of those epic air-brush paintings inside, the kind people put on the side of custom vans. A sunset over an oppressive city, a deep precipice in front of it. Cops and squad cars and paddy wagons on the city side. On the other, across a suspended bridge, a guy standing in a green pasture. He was giving the finger to the cops, ready to cut the bridge with a machete.

She asked, "You want to explain to me what this has to do with offense and defense?"

He pulled her toward the cashiers, saying, "First we've got to find a boom box. Something big."

CHAPTER

★ ★ ★ **20** ★ ★ ★

After she asked a half dozen questions about the 32-foot *Donzi*, the tender captain offered Dominique Goldman the wheel. They were well past the Circle Line cruises steaming to and from Pier 83. In deeper waters of the Hudson, she poured on the fuel.

Carl Montan was sitting on the bench seat on the port side, under the air spoiler. He watched her there for a while on the bridge, her hair fluttering in the wind. She was wearing Sperry's, black linen slacks and a black-and-white striped top, looking a little like an NFL zebra. He'd worn a white ribbon shirt and linen tweeds. She'd told him their host had insisted: Casual, please.

She put some air under the boat as she jumped the wake of a Staten Island ferry, the tender up to thirty knots now.

"Nicky, dear, I think you need a license to do this sort of thing," Montan said.

She blew the horn. Montan walked up to the bridge, struggling with the bumps. She was signaling a thirty-footer, approaching between the buoys.

"Asshole's on the wrong side," she snapped.

"You do know what you're doing."

"Comes with the Hamptons. I was in a boat before I was driving. I figured why should the boys have all the fun."

Montan looked at that haughty ass she had, those nipples pushing through the stripes. He wished he was dealing with her in a different situation, a different job. He'd love to slap her around a little before he fucked her. Ask her if that comes with the Hamptons, too.

He moved closer. "That's exactly why I should not be here," he said over the humming engine. "You would have done fine on your own."

"I want to show interest from the front office."

Montan ran his fingers through his hair. "But if Papa found out, Christ—"

Dominique said, "Leave Papa to me."

The tender captain said, "There's *Dorothy*." He pointed at a distant shape that hovered on the glare between the Statue of Liberty and the Jersey City shore. They were just past Liberty Island.

The captain said, "I'll take the wheel now."

Dominique backed off on the throttle and sat on the bench seat. Montan looked at her for a couple moments, her legs crossed, her eyes on something distant on the water.

Montan said, "I think the guy behind the wheel is hallucinating."

She looked at him, her eyes weary now. "Carl, what in Christ's name are you talking about?"

"Who's Dorothy?"

"Don't be silly," she said. "That's the name of the yacht."

The 200-foot Feadship was anchored, the vessel sparkling white on the murky water of Upper New York Bay. Three decks, each divided by long lines of black glass windows, a white sphere and the sleek shapes of other navigational equipment on the masthead. Montan had seen a feature on the boat in *Power and Motoryacht*, launched by its Holland manufacturer only four years ago, listed it as one of the hundred largest in the world.

A fiftyish man with salt-and-pepper hair and a blue sports jacket greeted Dominique at the top of the stern.

Dominique put out her hand. "David Harvey, I'm Dominique Goldman."

"I'm one of Mr. Harvey's aides," he said. "If you'll follow me, please."

They strolled the spotless gangway along the windows to a staircase to the upper deck at midship, then doubled back toward the stern. They passed at least a couple dozen boys, scattered in small groups around the ship. Four were playing ping-pong in a rec room near the stairway. Others were engrossed in laptop computers or games of Magic Cards in deck chairs. White. Hispanic. Blacks. They all were wearing nicely pressed khaki shorts and T-shirts with the Mecca logo, white on blue. Most of them in the ten-to-fourteen range. A few of them the later teens.

Dominique whispered, "Why do I find myself thinking about Michael Jackson?"

Montan said, "Say something. I dare you."

The upper gangway led back to a large sundeck. Two more boys were there, but left when they saw the aide. The aide showed Montan and Dominique to a sun-drenched table. There was Brie and Camembert. Oranges, kiwi and passion fruit were arranged on a bed of ice. Arrangements of newly-cut white lilies and blue larkspur lined the deck railing. A salty breeze from the Atlantic toyed with the petals.

"Can I get you a non-alcoholic beverage?" the aide asked. "Mr. Harvey will be right out."

"Ice tea," Montan said.

Dominique sat down on a couch. She smiled. A cold, perfunctory smile. "Diet Coke. With a twist of lime, and a splash of seltzer. In a glass, of course."

The aide went to a bar just inside the glass doors of a stern lounge. Montan leaned over to Dominique, saying, "You're starting already."

"I read in the *Times* once about Hollywood pitch meetings," she said. "These people size you up by what you ask for when they offer you a drink. The non-alcoholic, though. That kind of surprises me."

"It's a family oriented company."

She turned. "Carl, I don't want you to say anything. I just want you to look at him pensively. Let him try to figure out what your role is here."

"Consider it done," Montan said.

Dominique put her fingertips on her eyes momentarily, then pulled them away quickly, saying, "Fuck, I can't believe I did that."

"Asked for a glass?"

"No, mistook the toady for Harvey."

"There's not a lot of pictures around of the man."

"Two, actually," she said. "An old corporate portrait and a photo taken during the rap music hearings." She leaned closer. "They say he'd be another Hughes if he didn't conduct his business face to face. If you've seen him, you're in a pretty elite group. I figure that alone was worth the trip out here."

The aide brought the drinks.

David Harvey was a few seconds behind. He was wearing a white-and-blue striped Polo oxford, open at the collar, stone-washed jeans and topsiders, a blue blazer slung over his shoulder. He walked directly to Dominique, tossed the jacket aside and put his arms out. She stood. He grabbed her shoulders gingerly and kissed her on the cheek.

She appeared so taken by the gesture she forgot to introduce Montan. He held out his hand.

"Carl Montan," he said. He could see Harvey's eyes smiling.

"Sir?" the aide asked.

"I'll have what Mr. Montan is having," Harvey said. He sat down, gesturing toward the fruit. "Please, enjoy."

Montan snatched a kiwi. Dominique sat down, folding her hands in her lap.

Harvey's hands went to the table surface, unconsciously doing a little drum roll. "So, I'm sorry to keep you waiting. I was asking the captain to chart us a short course into the Lower Bay. The city looks much more manageable from out there, don't you think? Then I was delayed with a couple of the boys."

Dominique came straight at him, saying, "Who are they?"

Harvey smiled. "The program is called New Start. Something I started many years ago. I take boys from troubled homes, give them summer internships in my companies. At the end, they get to spend a week here on the *Dorothy* with me."

Dominique smiled back. "I'm surprised," she said.

Harvey looked a little miffed. "You have to give back something. That's my philosophy, Mecca's as well."

"No, I mean the boys," she said. "No girls. Considering your company's reputation for equal opportunity."

Harvey nodded thoughtfully. "We did try that the first year, but at that age, it proved to be too much of a distraction for these young men. A very close friend of mine does something very similar for the girls in the program. They're at my beach house in Malibu. It just works better that way."

The aide handed Harvey his tea, then left. Harvey leaned forward, touching her hand. "Actually, Dominique, I have to confess. I would be less than honest if I didn't say I had ulterior motives."

The yacht was moving now. Montan relaxed, taking a bite of the kiwi. He noticed Dominique's neck muscles constrict. She thought she was on to him, he decided, but she didn't know David Harvey like he did.

Harvey continued, "The lion's share of my business involves children. I pay a lot of money for the best research and market surveys, and you know what they tell me? Damn near nothing. By the time the R&D people detect something, it's already a trend. No, I learn from these young people. The two most popular attractions at our hotel in Las Vegas, the game design lab and the film clinic, were actually suggested by New Start kids. We've already sold nearly twenty million of the companion software in our computer stores."

Harvey let go of her hand and leaned back. "To be perfectly honest, Mecca owes these young people a great deal. They're our future, in more ways than one."

She seemed satisfied with the answer.

Harvey patted out another quick rhythm. "But, we're not here to talk about that, are we? We're here to talk about your football team. I've had my eye on the Stars for years, but my calls and letters have gone without a single response. Until yours, that is."

Dominique said, "My father is very stuck in his ways. But I do have some influence."

"Fathers and daughters," Harvey said, smiling. "I'm told it can be that way."

"I'm not talking about using the family car," she said coldly. "One day I will own this team." She stopped, setting the Coke down. "But let me ask you, Mr. Harvey—"

"David, please."

"Why your interest? With your assets, you could purchase a proven winner. Or lobby for a new franchise. And other teams that have become available in recent years."

Assets. Montan liked that, Dominique using the euphemism for money, showing him a little Harvard Business School.

Harvey said, "I'm a New Yorker at heart. Plus, I love the game." He explained he was born in Queens, a month before his parents moved to L.A., later Las Vegas. He said with Mecca, he split his time between California, Nevada and New York.

"Where do you stay?" she asked.

"Right here," he said, holding his palms skyward.

He paused, his eyes serious now. "I think a sports franchise should be owned by real people with real ties to the community, don't you? Take Sony and the Mariners, for example. There's just something sterile about that. It's a matter of accountability. Your father, actually, represents the best of that. He would be a very good partner. I've always admired him from afar. Our roots are not all that different."

Dominique smiled, but it disappeared as quickly as it came. "Then why not offer to buy the Stars outright?"

Harvey tapped his fingers together, pondering his answer. "To be perfectly honest, I'm not sure the other owners would approve it. But I do believe I have enough support for a minority ownership."

"I would think the NFL would welcome you."

Harvey shook his head. "The progressive owners know I have a lot to offer. If what my people tell me holds true, we will emerge next year as the largest media and entertainment company in the world."

"But nobody knows how large, being privately held. A half dozen stockholders, according to your incorporation papers. Quite a conglomerate in the hands of so few."

Harvey glanced at Montan, grinning. "This young woman does her research."

Montan sucked down another piece of kiwi, giving him his best bored look.

Harvey's eyes flitted back to Dominique. He held up his hands in surrender. "Please, don't say *that* word. 'Conglomerate.' It's like 'Hollywood.' It's used so disparagingly these days."

He sipped his tea and continued, "Mecca is what it is today because it has come to understand that diversity does not mean we can't all get along. We do much better as a people that way. It's the company's ruling philosophy. You'll find it not only in our corporate culture, but in many of our animated features and sitcoms as well."

Dominique said, "I'm not sure I'm following you."

Harvey said, "We believe in social responsibility. If one of our sitcoms charts new ground—teen pregnancy, for example—we break the story on our network news first. Then, the week the episode runs, our news magazines do segments, couching it in a wider discussion of the issue, of course. Half of America will be watching when the segment finally airs."

He gestured toward Manhattan. "Or, take publishing. Before our houses joined the Mecca group, imprints published an important book, then hoped other media noticed. Another company would purchase film rights. Everyone competing with one another, wasting resources. Today, Mecca not only publishes the book, it's reviewed in our newspapers, covered by our news magazine shows, adapted and produced by our film makers and airs as a miniseries on our network, preferably the week the book debuts. Nothing is left to chance, or the public's unpredictable taste."

"Some would say that's too much power," Dominique said.

"That's why we champion uplifting material," Harvey said. "That's why I testified before Congress about gangsta rap."

Dominique pushed a strand of hair from her eyes, doing her best to not look impressed. "You were saying about the league," she said.

Harvey laughed. "I'm sorry. I get very excited about our company." He paused. "There's another faction of NFL owners, most of them long-time interests, who are fiercely independent. They come from an entrepreneurial tradition that's not in step with today's climate."

"Like my father," Dominique said.

Harvey stood up, walking over to the stern railing, the flowers on both sides of him. Behind him the Statue of Liberty dwindled in the watery distance.

"It's more than that," Harvey said. "Unlike your father, a few have hidden agendas. Our network pays several hundred million dollars to the league in broadcast royalties a year. Everyone knows we lose a great deal of money broadcasting football. Officially, these owners would say my inclusion as a full owner would put the league at a disadvantage during negotiations. The idea is ridiculous, of course. I want the league to prosper. That's why our *NFL Magazine* has been so vigilant in trying to root out corrupting influences in the NFL."

He held out his hands, saying, "I've made enemies, obviously." He put both fingers to his lips. "Nonetheless, my people tell me I do have the votes for minority ownership, particularly in helping to rescue a team that by all appearances is in serious financial trouble."

Dominique glanced at Montan. He was giving David Harvey that pensive look she wanted.

Harvey walked over, standing over her. "That's why I'm prepared to offer your father a hundred million dollars for a forty-nine-percent interest in the New York Stars. Included with that will be a team jet, the development of a full-time practice facility on real estate I already hold near the Stardome—and an end to your stadium problems with the city."

"The city isn't budging," Dominique said.

"Your father doesn't have the influence I do."

Harvey popped a piece of passion fruit into his mouth and lifted his tea. "Now, before we talk any further, let's go up to the bridge. I'm told you're quite the seafarer. I'd like to see how you handle the *Dorothy*."

Dominique didn't move. She said, "Two things first."

"Of course."

"If I take this offer to my father, the first question he will ask is: What does David Harvey expect to get?"

Harvey dropped his head, shaking it, then coming up with a boyish grin. "Now I see why your father wants to leave you the team." He paused briefly. "But we can discuss that upstairs."

She still didn't move.

Harvey said, "I'm sorry. You said two things, didn't you?"

She stood up, picked up her glass and handed it to him.

"Yes I did, David," she said. "Would you fix me another drink?"

★　★　★

Brody introduced Shay Falan to the coterie of wives and girlfriends sitting along the rail at the Stardome, then walked across the turf to the tunnel, the new purchase from Best Buy dangling from his hand.

The locker room was noisy, the atmosphere urgent with opening day only a couple days away. Full pads practice, third down plays and strategies. Trainers wrapped tape thicker. The big men became bigger, piling the armor on. When the pads came out, demeanor always changed.

Brody walked straight to his locker, set the new boom box down on his stool and put on his pads and pants. He glanced around for Bobby Loeb. He spotted his fingers hanging over the edge of the stainless steel whirlpool, his head back and eyes closed, his nose and forehead barely visible in a layer of steam above the rim.

Brody slipped the red jersey over his head. He seated his pads with a couple hard thrusts into the locker. Then he picked up the boom box and his stool and set it in the center of the room.

He shouted, "Everybody, listen up."

He reached down and turned the player on. Loud, the track already cued.

The tune opened with the heavy hip-hop beat and a muted bass guitar line. The tune, "Their Law."

All the players stared.

Brody put his foot on the box to keep it from vibrating off of the stool.

Josaitus came running out of the training room, waving his hand like a coach protesting an official's call. "Hey, you can't play that shit in here. You know the rules."

Brody didn't move. "That's not shit, Squat. That's Jungle."

Josaitus walked quickly toward the box, the tool belt jangling under his stomach. He reached down for the switch. Brody's palms met his chest.

He shoved him back, hard.

Homer Cobb stepped forward first, saying, "Name like Jungle, Brody, let me fucking guess."

Brody tossed the CD to Cobb. "It's Prodigy. They're from Britain."

Cobb opened it, studied the jacket photo. Two blacks. Two whites.

A guitar riff joined the beat. Heavy metal. That's for the Metallica fans, like Cobb, Brody thought.

Everybody watching now, Squat trying to regroup.

He wagged his finger at Brody. "Whatever you call it, Carl's not going to be happy when he hears."

Brody spit the words. "Carl don't have to live out of no fucking cage."

He surveyed the other players, making eye contact.

Darius Wallace, in shoulder pads and a cup stretched over his long designer briefs, strutted across the carpet, a straight line for Brody, the box and Squat. Wallace stopped behind Josaitus. He lowered his arms slowly like a couple of fork lift booms. They landed on Squat's shoulders, the trainer's knees buckling.

"Carl finds out," Wallace said, "we gonna know who told him, Squat."

What happened next, Brody didn't expect. Four players in Glamour Boy's posse charged, Brody thinking maybe they were coming for him. Instead each grabbed one of Josaitus's limbs and flopped the trainer down on the floor, spread eagle.

"Tape that motherfucker up," somebody shouted.

A half dozen more converged, a low-contact pile up, some of the athletes hooting, others laughing. Somebody pulled the medical tape from Squat's belt. One player held Josaitus by the hair. Another wrapped the tape around his mouth.

Reggie Thompson was standing at his locker with his arms folded. He nodded at Brody, shot him an all-knowing grin.

Homer Cobb was nearby, still reading the CD's liner notes, ignoring the melee on the floor.

He looked up. "Any words in this shit, Rick? This ain't bad."

"Listen," Brody said. "Here they come."

There were only five words in the entire track. The vocalist snarled them in an English accent at a hard break.

One line: *"Fuck 'em and their law."*

Then the beat resumed.

Homer Cobb picked up the box and held it over his head. "Yeah, fuck 'em," he roared. "And the Pack, too."

CHAPTER

☆ ☆ ☆ **21** ☆ ☆ ☆

Montan listened to Johnny Josaitus rant for five minutes on the phone before he gave him some solid advice. "You forget it, for now. When they come to you pissing and moaning about injuries, looking for an excuse from practice, then you remember. That'll get them back in line."

Montan asked, "V.R. say anything?"

"V.R. doesn't give a shit."

"You realize I step in now, you'll be hanging from a chain in the weight room as a body bag."

"What about Brody?"

Montan said, "Leave Brody to me."

Montan spun his chair around, looking up Park Avenue. He took a draw on a Hoyo de Monterrey and exhaled. "How's Bobby?"

"He's comfortable," Squat said. "He likes the inhaler. A lot of players do."

Montan told him Clinton Lisle, the old backup quarterback, didn't look too sharp when he watched him in practice the day before. His passes floated and his spiral wasn't tight.

"Tendinitis in the right elbow," Squat said. "All the reps he's getting with Bobby out. He hasn't complained yet, but I can tell."

"I'm surprised he thought he could hide that when we picked him up."

"That age, they don't seek treatment, or have their own people. Too much maintenance, he knows he's gone."

Montan said, "Bottom line, I want Brody starting. The town expects a lot from this kid. Keep him healthy. Do whatever you have to do."

Montan hung up, dragged again on the Hoyo, then dialed the surveillance apartment across from the Lucerne. The Turk answered. Montan could hear music playing in the background. Montan began asking questions.

The Turk said, "He took Bimbolina to practice today. She sat with the girls."

"I heard," Montan said. "Anything else?"

"Surfer's got the scope on them now. Says he and the bim look like they're getting ready to go out."

"They make any calls?"

"She ordered dinner from the market. You know, that place ain't bad. Surfer and I been getting carry out, too."

Montan asked, "Either of you seen Brody actually do her?"

"We've got a clean shot at the balcony, the living room. So far, they've kept the bedroom blinds drawn. But in Times Square she couldn't keep her hands off of him." The line was quiet for a second. "Carl, you decide to do anything, I want it."

Montan thought, the Turk thinking with his dick again. "Maybe you. Maybe the Surfer. Maybe both. I don't think it will come to that."

"All the Surfer talks about is waves," the Turk said. "Keeps talking about Montauk out on Long Island. He's getting restless, saying shit like he's 'losing his stoke.' "

LA guy who can't put away childish things, Montan thought. The Turk had found the Surfer a couple years back, the Surfer working in Long Beach with people the Turk and Montan knew. The Turk had said that was why the Surfer joined a crew. Flexible hours. He wasn't punching a time card. When a swell hit, he was good to go.

Montan said, "Brody, the bim, go out, send the Surfer. You've been too close too often. I don't give a shit how good you think you are."

"They're clueless."

"Nevertheless, I don't want to risk it."

The Turk complained, "But this fucking Brody never goes anywhere

but fucking practice. This apartment's closing in on me. I need something to do."

"The scope's working, right?"

"Yeah," the Turk said.

Montan said, "I'm sure there's some other bedroom windows up
there without blinds."

He hung up and balanced the cigar in the ashtray, looking up Park
Avenue again. The girl didn't concern him greatly, even the idea she'd
hooked up with Brody. Maybe she was just another player bim. Maybe
she was more than that. But the bim, he could handle. He was more
concerned about Brody, the expectations he had for his number one
draft pick. Carl Montan expected Derek Brody to be the highlight of
his New York Stars career.

Montan plucked a key ring from his desk and walked across his
office. The door on the west wall appeared to be oak, but beneath
the paneling were two inches of high-tension steel. He slid a key into
the lock.

The file cabinet covered an entire wall of the ten-by-ten room. The
only other objects inside were a metal table, one chair and a fluorescent light overhead. He slipped another key into the cabinet's access
door and opened it. He pushed a red button. A motor droned, bringing up shelf after shelf of files, arriving like passengers on a Ferris
wheel. Most were in yellow jackets. There also were a couple dozen in
red. The system was no different from most firms and organizations.
The yellow jackets were official, material disclosed during discovery in
lawsuits and union disputes. The red ones were for Montan's eyes
only, or a shredder, if it ever came to that.

Officially, the red files did not exist.

Montan pulled one thick red jacket, locked the cabinet and returned to his desk. He put the smoldering cigar back in his mouth and
opened the folder, spreading the material out: IQ tests. A high school
counselor's notes. Interviews provided by the Stars' PI.

Montan found the page from the team psychologist. It was broken
down into four sections: Social. Coachability. Motivation. Summary.
He found the Motivation section, particularly designed for the coaches
and the director of player personnel. He'd given V.R. a copy, but V.R.
wasn't big on the shrink reports.

Montan read:

Derek needs to understand you believe he's capable of quickly assuming the starting quarterback's role. He will be very motivated to excel as a professional to please his dead father, particularly because he appears to harbor unrealistic guilt, believing he contributed to his father's death. He desires the material and social trappings of a pro, as further proof of fulfilling his potential for his dad. But his primary motivation is to secure a clean slate, particularly among those who've focused on his accident. He figures the world owes it to him, considering what he has had to overcome. Make him believe he can achieve it, and you will maximize his potential as a player.

Montan chuckled. The shrinks were good, but not that good. They didn't get everything.

But he did.

He found a State of Michigan car crash report called a UD10. Fastened to it were crash scene photographs, statements from individual police officers and paramedics and a white ten-by-twelve envelope. The return address on the envelope: CIA, LANSING, MICHIGAN. A clever acronym, Montan thought. Crash Investigation & Analysis. The private accident reconstruction agency was used almost exclusively by plaintiff's attorneys. It was staffed with former state police and other traffic experts who knew how to translate skid marks, mangled metal, injuries and witness reports into the last few seconds before a deadly crash.

Montan had commissioned the study a year before the NFL draft. CIA sent him twelve pages of numbers and analysis. There was one more new feature, which Montan thought made the $10,000 reconstruction worthwhile. Montan reached into the envelope and pulled out the CD-ROM and slid it into his desktop computer. The CIA logo came up, then a menu. Montan pointed and clicked the button labeled: VIDEO RECONSTRUCTION. He leaned back, drawing on the rest of the Hoyo as he watched the screen.

The computer animation was pretty realistic. The red pickup drove down the two-lane highway, evergreens on both sides gliding by, a crescent moon above the treetops, signifying it was night.

The Escort appeared first as a dot in the distance, then quickly grew in size, the camera view from the back window of the truck now, two people visible in the seat. When it crossed the center line, it clipped the corner of the Escort, sending it spinning into the trees. The truck rolling over now, two bodies ejecting, one cleanly through a shattering windshield, the other out the door, colliding into a tree, the truck finally coming to a rest in the pines.

Montan played it again, this time in slow motion, watching the driver and passenger's movement in the truck moments before the first impact. When the truck goes over the line, the passenger appears to reach for the wheel, but pulls the driver down on top of him.

Montan backed up the action, freezing the frame just before the accident begins. His own instincts had alerted him first, well before he'd ordered the reconstruction. He'd suspected when the UD10 noted that both the driver and passenger had been drinking. He was willing to lay money on his suspicions when his first background check showed Brody never touched alcohol at U-of-M.

Montan moved the mouse pointer to the figure behind the wheel and clicked. Type appeared:

DEREK BRODY.

Under it, his date of birth.

Montan reran the CD-ROM several times. The video version simply mirrored the written conclusions from CIA. Based on the forces of inertia, the injuries to father and son, Derek Brody's father could not have been driving. What threw off the county cops was the location of young Brody near his father when an ambulance arrived. The CIA report concluded the quarterback had crawled thirty feet to aid the old man. Brody had withheld that in his police statement later at the hospital, as well as the fact that he was the driver. Saying it was the old man, and getting only 18 months.

Shit, Carl Montan thought, for that alone the boy deserved major time.

Montan picked up the phone again. He punched up a familiar number.

"Bullard," the voice said. Answering in that cop way, just a last name.

"Raymond, Carl Montan over at the Stars." He played it official. FBI agents liked to run tape. Even retired, corrupt ones.

"Yes, Carl."

"Raymond, I've got a player I'm a little concerned about. He's had a history of run-ins with law enforcement. I thought you might want to check it out."

"Which player?"

Montan thought, Brody wants to play fucking games in the locker room, let's see how he does in the real world.

★   ★   ★

Shay directed him across the Queensboro Bridge, then out Long Island Boulevard to the expressway, interrupting her story to tell him where to turn. He had the top up on the Mercedes, but the air on. Almost the end of August, and the air still dirty, muggy and hot.

Shay said, "So I'm sitting there in the stands and these women, it's like their minds are divided right in half. Of course, first I get asked about fifty questions: Where I met you, how long we've been together, what are our plans, you know. Then it's, let me tell you this, honey let me tell you that. I mean, most were trying to be helpful, until this group of a half dozen others show up and sit down behind me."

Brody glanced in his mirror. The dark blue Crown Vic was still behind him, a couple of cars back.

"I'm sorry to interrupt," he said. "But did you ever see a movie called *Crimes of Passion?*"

She looked a little bemused, but answered. "Kathleen Turner is a designer by day and a whore by night, the movie she said she wished she never made."

"A bunch of us on the Michigan team rented it one night. Somebody had heard she dropped her top in the non-rated version."

Shay's face contorted with curiosity.

Brody said, "Remember how the guy is assigned to tail her."

"I think so."

"He waits for her to come out of her day job. She goes into the parking lot for her car after work. And he's sitting out there in a pickup truck. The only vehicle in the lot. Then he tails her home. Parks across from her apartment, the only truck on the street. Sits out there for a couple hours, then follows her in a cab when she leaves. And she never notices him. What are the odds of that?"

"I'd say pretty slim. But that's Hollywood."

Brody glanced in the mirror again. "Okay, how about if the truck starts following her in the city, makes a dozen turns, follows her across a bridge, then on to the freeway, then into Queens? Twenty-five minutes. Is that realistic?"

She stared at him, then realized.

He said, "Don't turn around."

She said, "What are you going to do?"

He said, "Exactly what we planned."

She cradled her hands between her legs, and breathed deeply. A half minute passed. Brody finally said, "You were saying something about divided minds."

She continued, a little slower this time. "Yeah, I mean, these women know the game. What you were doing out there."

"It was a scrimmage between the starting offense and defense." A good one, too, Brody thought. He'd connected well with receivers all afternoon.

"Whatever. What I'm saying is some of these women, they'd be talking one second about potty training a kid, then suddenly see something on the field, see their man do something, and start screaming. This one, shy, I thought. She's sitting there doing a needlepoint when suddenly she jumps to her feet screaming, 'C'mon Scotty, kick his fucking ass!' "

Brody laughed. "Welcome to football."

Shay said, "The car still behind us?"

Brody nodded. "You were also saying about this group that came in and sat down behind you."

Then Shay explained that was how she heard it, late in the scrimmage. He kept connecting with some white receiver, she said.

"Toby Headly," Brody said. Headly was still pumped from the gag at the Plaza.

"So one of the black girls, or maybe she was a wife, I don't know. She's sees you doing that, but she doesn't know who I am, because she arrived later. And this girl says, 'The only reason he's throwing to that motherfucker is because he's white. My man's been open, but he's been ignoring him all day.' "

Brody saw the entrance to the Long Island Expressway ahead. She pointed. He ran the Mercedes up to eighty on the merge, slid into traffic, then turned to her. She'd dressed very conservatively. Slacks, a cotton knit blouse with a high ring collar, sandals, a small silver crucifix hanging from her neck.

"So that's how you got me into this," Brody said.

"It reminded me of the sniping at Juilliard. That's one thing my father was right about."

"You had a problem with blacks?"

"No, from students whose idea of roughing it through college was a five-room condo on the Upper East Side."

"I don't see the connection."

Shay squeezed his arm, not acting now. "That's why I accepted the invitation. I figured with a cheering section like that, you need all the friends you can get."

★　★　★

Leonard and Jeneane Toysy's house was a handsome, red-brick colonial with white shutters in Manhasset. A Ford Explorer in the driveway and a Dodge van, about a half dozen other players' cars parked nearby. Brody figured the Toysys had to be the only black family on the street, but you'd think the big Pro Bowler would be welcome anywhere. Ordained minister, national FCA involvement, Long Island board member for the United Way. Every year he bought a block of two dozen seats at the Stardome for kids he mentored for charities over the years.

Brody found a parking spot a half block from the house. The Crown Vic had disappeared a couple miles back. Still, he came around and opened the door for Shay and held her hand as they walked.

Near the sidewalk, Toysy's neighbor was watering his lawn. He asked, "You Brody?"

Brody nodded.

"Leonard says he has big hopes for you. You ready for Sunday?"

Brody nodded. "I plan on giving 'em hell."

A minute later, they rang the doorbell.

Toysy's wife answered. She was a tiny woman, not even five foot tall, a size three max, Shay later said. Toysy, six-eight and 292. Later, Brody and Shay laughed about it, trying to imagine how they looked in bed.

"Welcome to my home," she said, saying it like it was definitely hers. She ran it, not him.

Toysy appeared right behind her, putting out his hand.

"Derek, welcome. And Shay, is it? We were just about to get started."

Toysy was beaming, a smile almost as wide as his massive neck. Other than his stature, he bore little resemblance to the saliva-spitting mad dog that had been crushing quarterbacks for nearly ten years, a spot in the Hall in Canton virtually assured.

The couple led them into a large family room, all the furniture pushed back toward the walls and replaced by six rows of polished wooden chairs. Brody saw the rest of the God Squad sitting there, and their wives or girlfriends. Except for the white girlfriend of the Stars' middle linebacker, Anthony Hotson, the chairs were filled with blacks.

"Everyone," Toysy boomed. "All of you know our brother, Derek. This is his beautiful friend, Shay." Toysy looked down at her and smiled, then turned back to the group. "I believe the Lord is working through Shay." Toysy, sounding like a southern preacher now. "It is Shay who brought Derek here tonight."

There was light applause. Brody heard a couple of "Amens." All of them beaming at him now. Shay smiling, soaking it all right up.

Jesus, Brody thought. She had charisma. He wondered how she looked on a stage.

They sat near the back, right behind Tony Hotson and his girl-friend. Hotson turned around, extending his hand to Brody, smiling huge, that kind of smile Brody had seen channel surfing when the *700 Club* flashed on the screen.

"Welcome, Derek," Hotson said, still shaking the hand. "Man, welcome." Then he leaned close and whispered. "We prayin' for you, man. But you watch your back, you understand what I'm saying? You watch Squat and Carl. Glamour Boy, too."

Brody wanted to pull him into another room, but Leonard and Jeneane Toysy took positions at the front of the group now. Toysy had an acoustic guitar over his shoulders, its neck dwarfed by his large hands. He banged out the chords to "Precious Lord." Everybody stood, singing.

Brody mouthed the words, more conscious of his voice than the content. But Shay was another story. She had her eyes on some point in space, her pupils beaming. Singing with a smile.

Jesus, he thought, she had a voice, too.

Toysy saw her, and heard her, too. He walked down the aisle toward her, singing, the guitar strung over his shoulder. Shay came out from the chair and stood next to him, belting it now, and walking with Toysy, waving one hand over her head, the way gospel singers do.

When it was over, the entire room applauded. Shay dropped her head, smiling bashfully, joining Brody back at the seat.

"What a performance," he whispered.

"I've always loved gospel," she said.

Toysy, in the full preacher cadence now, was saying, "Hallelujah."

The group responding, "Hallelujah," too.

Toysy stood at the front again, the guitar gone, his hands folded in front of him.

"I feel the need tonight for a special healing," he said.

"That's right," somebody in the audience said.

"I feel there is someone here in need of prayer."

"Oh, yes."

The whole prayer meeting breaking into a rhythm now.

"Who will come up and receive the healing?"

"Yes, Lord."

"Who will come up and take the power of prayer?"

"Hmm-hmm."

There was a moment of silence, then one of the wives stood. She walked slowly up the aisle to the front and stopped in front of Toysy, looking up.

"Yes, what is it?" Toysy asked.

"I have a demon."

"Praise God," Jeneane Toysy said.

Brody thought, nothing like an exorcism. That ought to pump everyone for the game.

"And what is this demon?"

"It says things to me. In my mind."

Toysy seemed concerned. "And what does it say, child?"

The woman's eyes blinked a couple of times, and then she spun toward the makeshift congregation and put her hand on her hip, her body language changing suddenly. She glared at Tony Hotson's white girlfriend.

She snapped, "The demon says we got to find a way to stop all these white ho's from stealing our good black men."

Toysy looked up at the ceiling. Then he began to pray.

★   ★   ★

When they returned to the Lucerne, he walked her to the bedroom door, resting his hand against the doorjamb. She studied his eyes a while, thinking for a second, who would look away first, but they lingered a couple of moments. The ride back had been serene, no one following them. Brody had said maybe he was imagining it. Maybe he was getting paranoid.

She said, "That prayer meeting, the girls in the seats, I think I've got an even better idea what you're up against. Was it that way for you at Michigan?"

"At Michigan people weren't dying." He squeezed her shoulder. "You did good. You even had me convinced. I'd love to see you in a show."

"You can't fake it. You learn to find a part of you that's that way. Then you go with it."

And she was starting to wonder about him. She couldn't have done this role of his so well, if something wasn't there.

He said, "The God Squad liked you. You know what that means?"

She shook her head, her face now with a girlish smile.

"We've got to go back. See if that demon is gone."

They both laughed.

Brody said, "Look, I'm going to have to figure out what I'm going to do with you this Saturday."

"I thought you didn't practice the day before a game."

"They put us all up in a hotel. Even when we're home. Curfew, all that. Then Sunday morning we're all together. Team breakfast. I'm interested to see if many keep it down in the pros."

"You get scared?"

"Don't tell anyone, but I've been terrified from the day I walked into camp."

"I've got a script stirring me up like that. I plan on working on it all day Saturday. I called my agent today. It looks like he's going to be able to get me a reading in LA next week."

"Maybe I can get my attorney here Saturday night. I'd feel more comfortable. Then both of you could head over to the game together."

She nodded. "I've never seen a pro game." She found herself playing with a lock of her hair. "It sounds exciting, especially when you know the back story."

"The script?"

"No, the game."

"Good," he said.

She added, "You know, I don't know who the bad guys are, and I know you've been in prison. But something tells me you're one of the good guys."

"I'm working on it," he said.

In bed, she found herself thinking. About his words, and more. She thought about what they talked about on the way back, prison, a little bit, then she started asking him about his family. He told her about the Upper Peninsula, how it was a lot like upstate New York. Evergreens and maples everywhere, and cold winters. People who talked a lot like Canadians, always putting "eh" at the end of a sentence, referring to everything as "she."

"She's blowing pretty cold out there, eh?"

They talked about his father, how he'd put everything he had into him. How football became their life after his mother died. Yeah, it was just a game, he said. It gave them something to do together. They just got carried away the night of the car crash. "Both of us," he said. "I couldn't believe the old man was buying me beers."

"And they served you?"

He said, "Up there, the number one leisure activity comes out of a bottle or a can."

"I noticed you don't," she said. "Is that because of what happened?"

"I just don't have time for it."

She asked, "What happened, anyway?"

He was silent a couple moments, then said, "I ran."

She hadn't pushed him for the details, but she guessed something was there. "But you must have come away with something. I mean, that sort of thing changes a person's life."

He never answered. And she let it go.

And now she found herself thinking about the way he touched her shoulder, and her touching his arm in the car, thinking she felt something. Not all the play acting they were doing. He was pretty good at it, too. But a soft squeeze, then another touch that lingered a little. And his eyes. Seeing something there, but not sure what it was. Maybe the kid before the world—before this town—grabbed him.

As the city's ambient light cut white lines through the blinds, she kept thinking he might just show up. Be standing there at the door.

He'd maybe say something stupid. But how else did you do it?

Like, "What you doing?"

Her saying, "Laying here."

"You sleeping?"

"No."

Idiotic, obvious things like that. Making a little verbal dance out of it. And then her doing the rest with her body. Sitting up in the bed, maybe just holding out her arms.

She turned the pillow over and wondered for a while if he was thinking the same thing in that room of his with the big timber bed. When he didn't show up at the door, she thought, this whole thing is crazy, and she had it wrong. This Derek Brody was self-obsessed, on a mission. He'd never even asked her about her movie. Then she realized, she hadn't thought about drinking for a week now.

It took her a half hour to drift off. Sleep came when she stopped peeking at the door.

Dominique Goldman pitched David Harvey's offer at the executive session Friday morning. Mecca would purchase the Stardome outright from the city, a cost of more than $200 million. It would be renamed the Mecca Dome. Harvey's minority share of the team itself would be individually held. For that, he was offering a hundred million, paid directly to her father. A limited partnership would be drawn up. Harvey would be responsible for half the team's operating costs. She capped off the presentation with Harvey's offer for a practice facility and a team plane.

Papa Goldman listened at the head of the conference table without interrupting. It was Jack Petrus who asked the question.

"I'm not sure what this Harvey gets out of the deal."

Dominique said, "A voice in the league and the promotional value of owning a sports team in America's biggest media market."

Papa finally spoke. "If you were not my daughter, you would be leaving today with your things in a cardboard box."

Dominique was standing now, at the opposite end of the long table. She slapped both her hands on the mahogany and said, "Papa, all I'm saying is what harm could it do to meet with the man?"

Goldman began packing his pipe. He looked at Montan, then Petrus, then back at his daughter. Carl Montan was a little surprised she made her move at the session. He thought, they must not have taught her that at Harvard. You line up your support before you go into a meeting. You don't lay it out for the first time in front of every-body, and risk somebody handing you your ass.

Papa said, "Nicky, you met with these people without my permission."

"I met with Harvey only."

"I'm surprised I haven't read about it already."

"It was private. On his yacht."

Goldman said to Petrus, "Jack, you know about this?"

Petrus shrugged. "I told the Mecca people we were not interested in offers. I sent them a one-sentence fax."

Papa glanced at Montan. "Carl, don't tell me you're part of this."

Dominique slapped her hand on the table again. "Papa, listen. This was my idea. Mine, alone." She turned to Petrus, glaring. "And you ought to be goddamn thankful somebody in this organization has the balls to do some independent thinking."

Petrus's face reddened. "I resent that. Your father and I have been together since—"

"Fuck you, Jack," she said. "That's exactly my point."

Papa Goldman held his hand up, pharaoh-like. "There's no call for personal attacks. This is a business, not Jerry Springer."

Dominique walked the length of the table, then sat down next to her father, shifting her chair toward him as if no one else in the room really mattered.

"Papa, all I'm saying is what stake do Jack and Carl really have here? Something happens, Jack's retiring anyway. Carl, he moves on to an-other job. Christ, open your eyes. *We are in trouble.* Our CPAs know it. City Hall knows it. The league knows it. That's why you have no lever-age there. And now, with these audit stories, the fans know it. Christ, what is it you don't understand about the numbers?"

Goldman lit the bulldog pipe.

"Christ," she finally said. "I fucking give up."

Goldman looked at Petrus. "Jack, what do sales look like for the opener?"

Petrus leafed through a legal pad. "They're up over last year. We're expecting about 45,000. There's a bit of a buzz about Brody. Not only the preseason appearance, but it seems a lot of people liked that pic-ture of him in the *Post.*"

Dominique said, "And I thank you all very much. That was another idea of mine that some of you fought."

Papa said to Montan, "Carl, why is V.R. starting the rookie? Why not Lisle? He's got experience."

"Brody's had one hell of a camp," Montan said. "And V.R.'s always been a gambling man."

Goldman set the pipe down, then stretched his arms out on the table. He was looking at Dominique, but she didn't see him. Her head was lowered, her forehead supported by her fingertips.

Goldman said, "Jack, no bullshit now. What do we have to do this year to pull us out of this?"

Petrus leafed through the pad again. He danced around the answer for a good minute, talking numbers and percentages. The price per ticket. The $2.50 the city took as a service fee. The $1 building bond tax. The Stardome's 72,000-seat capacity. The per-cap expenditures of fans at concessions, money they weren't getting anyway. The unpredictability of the Stars' share at away games.

"The bottom line," Goldman finally demanded.

Petrus sighed. "We would have to average at least in the low sixties at home."

"And just how do we do that?" Dominique asked.

"We'd have to get off to one hell of a start. Win Sunday, then pound the hell out of Detroit the following week. That's a Monday night game. The network exposure alone would get people excited. Then we'd have to sustain it at least into the bye week. Maybe be in the playoff hunt."

The table was silent.

Goldman stuck the pipe back between his teeth. "Carl, how realistic is that?"

Montan said, "You know what they say, on any Sunday any team is capable of anything. I signed on to get you above five hundred by this year."

"I said, realistically."

Montan could feel Dominique looking at him now.

"His growing popularity notwithstanding, Derek Brody is a rookie, Papa. It would be unprecedented. The only similar situation I can think was a Monday night game some years back. Eric Hipple, remember? He came off the bench for the Lions in his first pro start and carved Dallas into body parts. It was the highlight of his career. He didn't do much after that."

"But we've got Bobby Loeb."

Montan shook his head. "Brody's got to carry the next couple. It doesn't look good for Bobby. They're saying maybe three weeks now on injured reserve."

The owner rose, everyone's eyes on him now. He walked to the big window with the Park Avenue view, smoking his pipe with his back to them. When he turned around, he spoke from a cloud of smoke.

He pointed the pipe at Petrus. "Jack, call Harvey's people. Tell them I'm willing to discuss this further. I'll meet with Harvey, and Harvey only. Set it up for Sunday."

Dominique's eyes lit up.

Petrus said, "But we're playing the Packers Sunday."

Goldman exploded. "Goddamnit, Jack. I know the goddamn schedule."

Petrus's jaw flexed.

Goldman added, "Set it up for my suite at the dome. *During* the game."

Dominique interjected. "You don't understand, Papa. David Harvey is very private. He's a recluse."

"You've been saying that for years, you know that? Since you were a girl."

"I only just met the man."

"No, goddamnit. 'You *don't understand*.' You think I was born goddamn yesterday?"

"Those were different times."

"Business doesn't change."

"So you're saying?"

He pointed the bulldog at his daughter, punctuating his words with little jabs of the stem. "I'm saying if this goddamn cartoon king wants to talk about my football team, then he's going to have to come to my goddamn turf."

★   ★   ★

Friday and Saturday were not good days.

Everything began deteriorating at Randalls Island, practice moved to Downing Stadium because of the tractor pull at the dome. It was raining. The field was soft. The locker room was freezing, all that concrete still holding the chill from the night before. Some players forgot their natural turf cleats. V.R. was in a foul mood, wrapped in a rain slick, his golf cart back at the dome. Brody saw Shay sitting alone in the ancient stands under a big golf umbrella, shivering, trying to read her movie script.

It was a half day session. A half day to work on first and second down, a splash of nickel and red zone, two-minute offense, short yardage and goal line. They were in helmets, shorts and jerseys. No pads. They all lined up, offense against defense, for the first rep, a second down passing play. Brody dropped back five steps and let the ball go, the ball skipping off Reggie Thompson's hands.

That's when he heard this distant booing. Distant heckling and bursts of profanity that seemed to be floating in with the wet wind. He checked the stands, but they were still empty.

As they huddled, Brody asked, "Where's that jeering coming from?"

"Mentals," somebody said.

"Where?"

Homer Cobb pointed over the south rim of the tiny stadium. Beyond it, Brody could see a large, maybe twenty-story, building lined with row after row of windows. Many appeared open, but covered with bars.

"Manhattan Psychiatric Center," Cobb said. "Motherfuckers boo us every time we practice out here."

Brody thought, my God, there was no end to it.

When Brody came to the sideline so the Old Man could get his reps, Tommy Molito was standing on the sod, his hands stuffed in a black trench coat. His hair was so black and shiny it looked like he was wearing black shoe polish. Droplets of rain beaded on the strands.

He approached and lit a cigarette, unconsciously offering Brody one first. "You haven't taken me up on my invitation, shooter," he said. "My girls are anxious to meet you."

Brody didn't take his eyes off the field. "I've got a girlfriend," he said.

"That's what I hear."

Molito motioned to the stands. "Devoted, too. Coming out on a day like this. Shit, you can't find women like that anymore."

Brody pivoted, the Mole smiling with that shit-eating grin. Smoking a cigarette, and chewing gum, too. Brody said, "You stay away from her, you understand what I'm saying?"

Molito shrugged his shoulders, holding his hands out, casual about it. "Hey, forget about it. I got more pussy than old man Goldman's got players." He slapped Brody on the shoulder, grinning again. "Hey, shooter, I know you're a little nervous. Big start and all."

The whistle blew. Brody jogged back on the field. In the huddle he saw a Stadol inhaler come out, a guard pulling it from underneath his elbow protector, giving himself two blasts.

Brody pointed. "What the fuck is that?"

"Rain gets my allergies going."

Bullshit, Brody thought.

Two hours later, they found there was no hot water in the Downing Stadium showers. Some players said they were going back to the Stardome to change. Others just said they were going home.

Johnny Josaitus was looking at Brody as he pulled on his street clothes over his sweaty, grass-stained skin. Looking a little eager, that look valets and doormen got when they were looking for a tip.

All week, Brody had been spreading cash and gifts around. He'd walked around with a clip, tipping the equipment boys and assistant trainers with hundred-dollar bills. He'd sent the equipment manager a basket of single-malt scotch and cigars, and similar baskets for the media reps. Just thanking them for their help. His equipment was arriving spotless at his locker. He was spending less time waiting to be taped. The media reps were limiting reporters to ten minutes at his locker. But he hadn't taken care of Squat.

Brody motioned him over. He stuffed three hundreds into his tool belt. "That's for the trouble the other day," he said. "I never intended it to go that far."

Squat crossed his arms over his belly. "You think you can bring this team together with music?"

Brody said, "I'll try anything that works."

"You know, I was an assistant one season with the Lions years back. They got on a roll at home, started winning games. They adopt this Queen song, 'Another One Bites the Dust.' That fucking tune did them in. All it did was get the other teams riled up."

Squat reached into the belt, pulling the folded cash out, seeing the Franklins, or yards, as some players called them. He stuffed it into his pocket and said, "You know that league urine drop I was telling you about?"

Brody looked up, nodding, as he tied his shoes.

"They want you back at the dome at five. The lab people are coming."

"I thought I wasn't supposed to know the time."

Squat ignored the statement. "They're going to want two beakers, one for illegals, the other for steroids." Squat hesitated, then asked, "You going to have a problem?"

Brody glanced up again. He knew where the trainer was going. And he'd covered himself that morning with a drop at Scanlon's lab.

"I'm not sure," Brody said.

"You're not *sure?*"

Brody figured everything he said would get back to Montan. He saw an opportunity. A couple of them, in fact.

"This girl I've been hanging out with. She burns a lot of herb. Says she can't get off unless she's got a buzz. We've done an awful lot of heavy breathing together, if you know what I mean."

Squat nodded. "Meet me in the training room at quarter to five. I'll be right over."

Brody got up, grabbing his duffel bag.

"And Brody," Squat added. "It wouldn't hurt to bring another three yards with you, too."

★ ★ ★

That night, he didn't tell anybody about what happened. Not Shay, or Toby Headly and Jedi Conlin who came over to watch Green Bay's pass coverage films. Shay sat in the kitchen, reading her script between serving junk food and Lonestar to the two receivers. Brody didn't tell Scanlon, either, when he called him later, asking him to fly in on Saturday night.

Scanlon protested, saying he was busy.

"I've got a girl you need to meet," he said. "I want you to stay here."

Scanlon said he had something for him, too. He'd been doing some research.

Brody said, "We'll talk about it after the game."

He fell asleep with his playbook, then reported Saturday morning for a light workout and a series of meetings, first defense and offense separately, then the entire team together in the film room. It was when Brody saw the films for the last time that he noticed something odd about the helmets of the Pack's defensive backs. Sometimes when they lined up he saw the "G" on their temples showing. Sometimes he saw the strips coming down the middle of the helmets to the front. He made a note of it.

Afterwards, the offensive coordinator drilled him on hand signals, in case the radio went out again. He and Henderson did it rapid fire.

Henderson: "I give you this signal."

Brody: "Seventy-two left *left* flank."

Henderson: "This?"

Brody: "Slot."

Henderson: "Right. And I just do this?"

Brody: "That's your bleeder."

Henderson: "And this?"

Brody: "That's your snitch."

Henderson: "This."

Brody: "Pimp."

Henderson: "This."

Brody: "Zip out of Gotti . . ."

Afterwards, he called Shay Falan to see if she was okay. Then Brody walked out of the dome and jumped into the Mercedes. He pushed the car past a hundred on I-495, then darted south on the Meadowbrook Parkway. He took the bridge across South Oyster Bay and drove for miles along Ocean Parkway, through the JFK memorial Wildlife Sanctuary and the Gilgo Beach State Park.

He parked the car at a public beach and walked to the water. The ocean was glass, swells rolling in every five minutes or so in sets. He pulled a reed from the sand and stuck it in his mouth, then plopped down cross-legged on the beach. It reminded him of the north shore of Lake Michigan. In high school, everyone used to meet near the sand dunes there, fifteen miles out of town, beyond the jurisdiction of the city police. They'd park their cars out of sight in the trees, lug cases of beer down to the shoreline, build a bonfire and drink themselves into oblivion. Wake up the next morning on the beach with a headache and sand fleas in their hair.

But that's not the way it went that one night. He'd been out with the old man, the old man asking him to drive, the old man three sheets to the wind. One bad decision, he thought, by both of them. They should have just slept it off in the truck. Instead, fifteen minutes later he's crawling thirty feet across sand and pine needles, trying to talk to him, trying to save him. The old man all busted up. The old man making him promise. Saying he had too much of a future.

Once bad decision, and six years later he's sitting in a training room with this trainer, the trainer threading a catheter up his dick. Filling his bladder with cold urine. *His* urine. Holding it for fifteen minutes, feeling like he was going to bust, until the league lab came in. Just so he can learn how they did it. And for what? He didn't even know where any of this was going.

One bad decision, and a reprieve.

Looking now like some kind of curse.

★   ★   ★

At seven, he checked into the team hotel, a Marriott in Rockville Centre, drawing Bobby Loeb as his roommate. Loeb had insisted on staying at the hotel, despite his status on injured reserve. They didn't sit together at a brief orientation in the hotel banquet room, dessert and snacks for those who wanted it. Brody sat with the offensive line, vaguely aware of the chatter about cars and girlfriends and the talk shows a lot of players watched that week on the days practice ended by noon.

After the coaches had their say, players began drifting back to their rooms. Brody saw Reggie Thompson lingering alone at a table, his posse gone. He picked up his apple pie and walked over. Glamour Boy was slumped deeply into the chair, his right arm behind the chair's back, his eyes surveying the room as if he were checking out strangers in Grand Central.

"Whatup, Rick?" Thompson said. He grinned. "I see you like your pie."

"Apple," Brody said. "Want some?"

Thompson said, "I was referring to what I been seeing of yours up there in the stands."

Brody held his tongue.

"Sit down, Rick," Thompson said.

Brody sat side saddle.

"I heard about that shit you pulled at the Plaza," Thompson continued. "Maybe we let you hang with us one day. Maybe we got a few things in common, at least that's what I hear."

Squat telling him about the urine test, Brody figured.

Brody took a couple of bites of pie. Let him think it, he decided. It couldn't hurt him. Not on this team.

"Media guide says you grew up in Canton, Ohio," Brody finally said. "What's it like there?"

Thompson picked something from his teeth. "You got ball and the Hall. You got to drive to Cleveland if you want to get it on."

"What about the people?"

"It's got its share of white trash, ridge runners coming up from West Virginia, looking for that city welfare check."

"Not many blacks, then."

"A few."

"You got a big family?"

Thompson ran his tongue across his teeth, doing it with his mouth closed, staring at him now. He said, "I see where you going, Rick. Gonna ask that niggah a few questions. See if you can understand that niggah's sociological situation. Thinking, hey, maybe that niggah ain't all bad. That motherfucker bought his momma a house."

"I'm not saying the word," Brody said.

Glamour Boy smiled. "But you thinking it."

"That's bullshit."

Glamour Boy leaned forward. "See, what you have yet to learn, Rick, is you don't have to have color to be a niggah around here. Sooner or later, you're going to find that out."

Brody waited for an explanation.

Glamour Boy leaned back, a coy grin there now. "Think about it. The draft. You get in your time machine, bring back a big Mississippi landowner and take him to that. He sees all those negroes waiting to be picked . . . Shit, that motherfucker would be puttin' up his hand for the motherfucking auctioneer."

Thompson laughed, loud.

"They don't pay slaves," Brody said.

"Yeah, but then, you get on a team, the man tellin' you where you gonna live. What you gonna wear. What you gonna eat. Later, the man might decide to *trade* you. Shit, that's just another word for *sell*."

Brody set his fork down. "You weren't happy about being traded from the 49ers, were you?"

"Shit, man, they all plantations. Every fucking one."

Brody stood. The guy was hopeless. He started to walk.

"Hey, Rick," Thompson said.

Brody turned around.

"You all be lookin' for me tomorrow up the right side, you hear?"

Five minutes later, he walked into the room with two double beds and paintings bolted to the walls. He ducked into the bathroom for a burning piss, aiming between the band of white paper wrapped around the toilet seat.

Bobby Loeb was sprawled on the bed, head propped up, the TV on one of those pay channels with adult films, the hardcore shots cut out for the hotel crowd. The air conditioner was on high, the room roaring with white noise. Brody walked over and switched off the fan.

Bobby said, "Hey, leave that there."

"It's cold in here, Bobby."

Loeb reached into his shirt pocket and produced a joint, holding it up with a graceful gesture. "And make sure it's on exhaust, too," he said.

Brody folded his arms. "Why don't you take a walk, Bobby."

Loeb lit the joint anyway, took a deep hit, held it, then said in a restricted voice, "Glamour Boy says he might be droppin' in."

Loeb exhaled, coughing a couple times.

Brody walked back to the door, putting the chain on. When he returned he sat on his own bed and reached for his playbook from the table. He tried to study a couple of pages, but the smell and the moans on the TV kept distracting him. He looked up and saw a porn star on all fours, yelling at the guy behind her, "Fuck me."

Bobby said, "Man, I love this bitch. Ashlyn Gere. She's so fucking nasty."

Brody said, "A real girl next door."

There was a knock on the door, a hard one.

"Shit," Loeb said, a tinge of panic in his voice.

Loeb tried to leap to his feet, but was stopped by rib pain. An ash fell on the bed spread. He swept it off with one hand, then butted the joint in an ashtray and slid it into the nightstand drawer.

"The window, Rick, open it," he said.

Brody scampered over and opened the curtains, searching for a window latch. It was solid glass.

"Fuck, fuck, fuck," Loeb said, staccato-like. He pulled the covers over him, his clothes still on. "Answer that, man. But don't fucking let anyone in here."

"Maybe it's Glamour Boy." Brody said.

Bobby Loeb said, "Glamour Boy don't bang on the door like that."

★   ★   ★

Brody's heart was still pounding as he and Raymond Bullard walked down the hall. He told the NFL security man Bobby Loeb wasn't feeling well. Bullard suggested they talk in the lobby. Brody thought that would be a nice touch the night before the game. Players coming and going. They'd see him there with Bullard and figure he was in trouble or, worse, think he was turning snitch.

"My car, then," Bullard said.

Bullard followed Brody into a fire stairwell, the metal door swinging shut behind them. Brody jumped up on the landing railing, balancing.

"How about right here. I need to get back to my playbook."

Bullard peered down three floors of stairway. "I was hoping we could talk in private."

"This is private," Brody said. "Just don't start a fire."

Bullard scratched the back of his lacquered hair. "You never called me."

"I had no reason to."

"Eric Smith's a good reason. You think because you being there didn't make the papers, I wouldn't know?"

Brody shrugged. "Last I checked there was nothing in the league rules about talking, or have you guys come up with some kind of pissing test for that, too?"

Bullard said, "I saw your statement in the police report."

Brody thought, fuck this guy. "So you come here anyway and roust me the night before a game."

He dismounted the railing, but Bullard grabbed his arm.

Brody glared.

Bullard said, "I was working with Eric. We'd been talking for two or three weeks. He was about to come in."

"Come in?"

"With some material."

"What are you talking about?"

"You know I cannot discuss details. Unless, of course, you have some relevant information you'd like to provide on your own."

Brody said, "You're wasting my time here."

Bullard smirked. "You're starting to sound like a New Yorker."

Brody shook his arm free.

Bullard said, "He was going to provide me with some documents about your football team."

"I don't own the team," Brody said. "I only play with it on TV."

"Look, you were the last person to talk to him. That's my only real concern. But, frankly, I'm starting to have some misgivings about your honesty, particularly when you talk to police."

"That's bullshit." Brody reached for the doorknob.

Bullard said, "Small town police departments, particularly."

Brody let go of the handle.

Bullard, leaning against the railing now. "Twenty-five years in the FBI, you learn about these small town cops and prosecutors. Everybody knowing each other. The judge married to the prosecutor's sister. Deals made at the local coffee shop. Everybody in bed with everybody. Difficult to navigate in terms of background checks, but it can be done."

Brody said, "You've got something to say, say it."

"That's just the kind of thing we specialize in over at the league. There's always public records. Witness statements. Accident diagrams. My business, you get to know a lot of experts over the years. Crash specialists. Guys that can look at a scene and tell you exactly what happened."

Jesus, Brody thought. This guy *knew*.

"Don't worry," Bullard said, a smile hiding in his eyes. "Our records are confidential."

Brody said, "What do you want from me?"

"I want you to go over that night with Smith, everything you remember. Everything Eric said, everything he did."

Brody thought about it, then asked, "How long you been with the league?"

"Six years."

"Then you know I can't do this now."

Bullard nodded. "I was thinking next week. You comfortable with coming over to the offices on Park Avenue? Tuesday, ten o'clock."

"Can I bring my attorney?"

"Do you need one?" Bullard said.

CHAPTER

☆☆☆ **23** ☆☆☆

Thirteen hours later, Derek Brody watched the Green Bay Packers boot the opening kickoff. Reggie Thompson backpedaled, caught the ball and stood casually in the end zone until a horde of converging Packers reached the five-yard line. Only then did he drop to one knee and down the ball.

Stars first and ten on the twenty.

Brody jogged onto the field, his eyes on the waiting football, only vaguely aware of the world beyond the immediate confines of the game. He'd put himself there in stages, a state of mind nothing or no one could touch, even the turmoil of the week before.

He'd started in the hotel with an eight o'clock alarm, the first in a series of game-day habits. A half hour of cartoons while Bobby Loeb slept. A pre-game breakfast at nine a.m. There were meats and breakfast foods. He had two potatoes, pasta and one cup of coffee. One time, at Michigan, he'd had a link of sausage with the carbs, and lost. He'd lost on potatoes and pasta, too. But he never ate meat before a game again. They were required to report at least two hours before kickoff. Brody, driving, arrived at the dome at 10:15. He made that *his* report time, simply because the Michigan bus always arrived two hours and forty-five minutes before college games.

In the locker room, other habits ruled. He slid his pads into his freshly laundered pants first, hung them up, then scrawled his name on the taping list. Then he took a shower, a good half hour of hot spray. Getting loose. Washing the city off of him. Washing away all the events of the week. In curtains of water, he imagined pictures. He pictured the Pack's uniforms. Green pants, yellow jerseys, helmets with the stripe in the middle, the white "G" on the side. He pictured the game plan in motion, exactly what they were going to do. He pictured the Pack's coverage, its shifting defensive formations, its blitzing tendencies—everything he'd gleaned from the films. He tried to picture what their linemen would look like. Snot dripping down their lips. Elbow pads and jerseys stained with blood. Linebackers screaming obscenities. He always prepared himself for that, so he couldn't be shocked by it. Then, he saw himself playing the game he loved. He saw himself laughing in the sandlot game they used to play on that slope in his small town. Then he put the Stars and Packers there, the Stars sprinting downhill, the Packers struggling up.

After he was taped, the ritual continued. First he slipped on his tights and a T-shirt. He'd brought the shirt, the same one he'd worn in every game since high school, the school's faded name across the chest. He ate a Milky Way with a banana, then donned the full uniform. He found Toby Headly, the tight end, and played catch in the locker room. This loosened him up mentally, something playful about it, like throwing a Nerf ball around a house full of china. None of the others complained. He guessed—he hoped—they were also absorbed in their own game-day routines.

During the field warm-up, he'd allowed himself a look around the Stardome. He imagined the thousands filling the lower sections and part of the upper bowl. He checked the section where he saw the garbage man a week earlier, but he wasn't there. He scanned the fifteenth row below the press box, his guest seats. He saw Shay Falan's red hair first, then Scanlon. They were talking, empty seats around them. He looked away and started running intervals.

After the warm-up, they all returned to the locker room for a twelve-minute wait. Equipment was readjusted. Defensive linemen sprayed their jerseys, some with silicone, others with Pam. Here and there, a couple of players yelled out war cries, but mainly it was silent.

V.R. walked into the locker room and stood near the door, both hands on his hips, taking a moment to look over the team. He talked briefly about a new start for the Stars, then revisited familiar rhetoric.

"Three hours, gentlemen. You give me three fucking hours, we send these cheese balls home on a goddamn quiet airplane."

An official stuck his head in the door, shouting, "Two minutes."

Leonard Toysy put his hand out and lowered it, everyone dropping to one knee. They said the Lord's Prayer. It wasn't so much about victory. It was like taps and the invocation before the Indianapolis 500, or the priest's blessing before the running of the bulls. It was the moment many secretly admitted what they could not afford to think on the field.

The goddamn game could put you in a wheelchair.

Darius Wallace leaped to his feet, screaming something about dirt and blood and human entrails.

And the pads began to clash.

★   ★   ★

V.R. called the first play: A delayed hand-off to the halfback over the right side. They broke the huddle and lined up, Brody approaching the center now. He stopped just short of the center and checked the Packers' defensive alignment. Brody heard an opening salvo of trash talk from the right tackle in the pit.

"Yo, Homer, I'm going to beat you. Then when I'm done, I'm comin' to your house to fuck you. You follow what I'm saying, my man?"

Homer Cobb spit.

Brody put his hands under center.

"Yo, Homer. Who's the paperboy playing quarterback?"

His concentration broke as the ball hit his hands. Big players, coming at him in an explosion of noise. Grunts. Groans. Obscenities. He didn't see jerseys. He saw linebackers the size of college linemen and linemen the size of phone booths.

Brody backpedaled two steps and swung the football to his right, only to see running back Danny Davis sprint past him, two steps ahead of the play. His awareness of the snafu lasted only a second, five yards back, alone with the ball. The middle linebacker shot through the line. The last thing he saw was the glee in his eyes. The last thing he thought, hang onto the fucking ball.

When he got up, he could hear booing.

When Davis joined the forming huddle, he said, "Sorry, Rick."

Brody looked past Davis's face mask. His pupils were dilated, white foam in the corners of his mouth. Amphetamines, Brody thought. He pushed the thought from his mind.

"Just let it happen," he said. "Let the line do its fucking job."

The play crackled over Brody's headset. A quick out to Reggie Thompson.

Fifteen seconds later, Brody dropped back five with the snap, looking left, then right. Glamour Boy wide open at the first-down marker. Brody fired a bullet, watching it right into his numbers, until Thompson's jersey suddenly disappeared behind a green and gold blur. The Packers' right corner was in full stride. Seconds later he was holding the ball over his head with one hand, pointing back with the other at Glamour Boy, taunting him as he crossed into the end zone.

Packers 7–0.

Brody jogged toward Thompson as they headed to the sidelines. "My fault," Brody said.

Thompson spat. "You see the way that motherfucker was pointing? You get your shit together, Rick. No nigger gonna point at me like that."

It did not get worse, at least with turnovers. He spent the first quarter trying to find the rhythm in three down sets. It was the quickness that blurred his focus. Linebackers with the speed of college running backs. Defensive backs who could instantly close cushions. Three-hundred-pound tackles and ends who sprang back to their feet after being knocked down. Everything seemed twice as fast as the preseason. The audibles gave him trouble, not recalling them, but executing them in time. The defense stunted and shifted. He battled the play clock more than the opposing players. He had difficulty telling when the defensive backs were playing man-to-man or zone. Judging by the comments in his radio headset, so were the spotters upstairs.

But the Stars defense allowed only one touchdown in the first half, an impressive performance, or maybe the Green Bay quarterback was just having a bad day. Fans would be able to take their pick, depending on which sports columnist they chose to believe on Monday.

Late in the second quarter, Reggie Thompson ran the ball back 40 yards on a punt return, the Stars starting at their own forty-five, their best field position of the game. The last two sets of downs Brody found himself looking at the helmets on the defensive backs. He'd seen a dozen defensive formations. Some he saw the helmet stripes, some the side-profile "G."

He took a sack watching the coverage on the next play, testing a theory, a suspicion. On second down, he ignored the play V.R. called and looked for Toby Headly on a short pass underneath. Headly gained only two yards. The crowd booed. It wanted the bomb with less than two minutes left. But for Brody, it was the most significant play he'd called all day.

He'd suspected right. When the corners were playing zone, he could see the "G" on their helmets. They were watching the snap, concerned only with defending their zone. When they were playing man, they showed their stripes, their eyes riveted to the receivers in front of them on the line.

Brody made four first downs in eight plays, passes completed to Headly, Conlin and Glamour Boy. They were on the Packer twenty-five with nine seconds left in the half when V.R. took a time-out. They had time for two plays, an end zone throw and a field goal, if the TD attempt failed.

Brody walked over to V.R. The coach said, "You seeing something I'm not?"

Brody caught his breath. "I'm dialed in."

V.R. wanted a running play. The accuracy rating of the Stars kicker dropped dramatically beyond thirty-five yards. They would surprise the Pack with a run, he said. At worst, they'd improve the kicker's position for a field goal.

Jogging back out, Brody pondered the formation. The play put the two running backs toward the tight end and two receivers split on the opposite side. Davis would line up right behind Brody, the fullback behind the tight end.

He looked at them all before he broke the huddle. "Listen good now. Depending on what they show us, everything is subject to change."

When Brody reached the center, he saw the Pack in the four-five formation: Four defensive linemen over each guard and tackle, two linebackers over the middle and the outside linebacker lined up over the tight end. First he audibled the runner's direction, not wanting to run Davis into the defense's strong side, but the weak one. He wanted the guard pulling and back running up inside.

"Jersey auto switch! Jersey auto switch! Run check, 200, 200."

The defense shifted again, the strong safety suddenly showing blitz. Brody audibled the fullback to block the strong safety.

"Gotti! Gotti! Gotti!"

"Queens Ripper! Queens Ripper! Move it! Move it!"

Then the Packers shifted again, this time to a four-six defense. Eight Packers on the line of scrimmage now, juking forward, their hands opening and closing in anticipation. Brody thought, here it comes, a Green Bay Packer blitz.

"Two eighty. Two Gacy. Check ninety-five!" To the right side of the line, then to the left. "Two eighty. Two Gacy. Check ninety-five! Queens! Queens! Queens!"

The new play: a quick toss to Glamour Boy on a wide flare to the strong side.

"Hut! Hut!"

Bodies collided. The strong safety penetrated the line. Brody cocked his arm, looking for Thompson taking the cornerback to the right sideline; instead both of them were on an inside post, Glamour Boy taking the pattern the other way. Thompson's hand went up under the goal post, just as Brody juked right, the blitzing strong safety skidding past him on his belly.

Brody turned to see nothing but empty green turf ahead of him. He sprinted with the ball under his arm, past the line of scrimmage, twenty-five yards to the corner of the end zone. A linebacker exploded out of a tangle of jerseys to the left. A foot race to the cone, the linebacker having an angle, Brody with the speed.

Three yards out, Brody dove, the ball outstretched in his hands. He sensed the linebacker also was airborne, but he kept his eyes on the ball, kept his grip. He saw smudges on the laces. He saw the nose cross the white stripe.

Touchdown.

Then he saw the linebacker's helmet crash into the spot on the turf where his hands had once been. When he looked for his fingers he saw only blood.

★   ★   ★

Shay Falan thrust her hands over her head, unconsciously leaping to her feet with everyone else. She'd arrived at her first pro football game not knowing if she'd be bored or repulsed. Now she realized she was standing, her body alive with the kind of excitement she'd only known on stage.

Mike Scanlon was on his feet, too, his neck straining to see around the fans in front of them. They'd exchanged small talk about the entertainment business at the apartment the night before. But today he'd been very quiet. He seemed preoccupied.

She hit him in the arm. "Touchdown, isn't it?"

Scanlon turned. He had a sick look on his face.

She followed his finger as he pointed to the field. She saw players jogging to the bench, others coming out, the kicking team. Then she spotted Brody. He was on his feet, walking slowly toward the sidelines. He was holding his left arm straight up, gripping it at the elbow. The left hand was a claw, streams of red down his forearm.

A training crew ran out to meet him. A player jogged over and supported him under the left arm. Then another player showed up on his right side. His toes dragged along the turf as they pulled him off the field, the P.A. system belting "Start Me Up" by the Stones. Seconds later, she saw him in the back of a golf cart. It sped across the field and into the tunnel.

She turned to Scanlon. "My God, you see that hand?"

Scanlon nodded. "Thank God it's his left."

The attorney pushed his hand through his hair.

"Now what happens?" she asked.

"They've got to kick the extra point."

"I mean to Derek."

"We'll have to wait and see if he starts the second half. I think that player's helmet, maybe his face mask, cut him. Maybe it looks worse than it is."

She saw his jaw muscles flexing with anxiety.

"You look pretty worried," she said.

"You're perceptive."

"But you said it was probably nothing."

Scanlon turned, looking at her. "My worries have nothing to do with his hand."

★   ★   ★

Johnny Josaitus and an assistant trainer took him straight to the training room, the crowd roaring as they reached the tunnel, Brody knowing the extra point was good. He lay on the table, the left hand elevated as the assistant began sponging off the blood.

For the first few seconds after the TD Brody had felt nothing, but then the pain came, almost buckling his knees. Now it pulsated with every beat of his heart.

The team physician walked calmly to the table, taking the hand. When he moved it, his ring finger felt like it exploded into fire.

"Fuck," Brody snapped. He wanted to look.

The physician said, "Remain still. Turn your head the other way and hold it there, please."

He saw Toby Headly, Homer Cobb and Darius Wallace standing together at the doorway, watching. Squat stormed over, shooing them away.

The physician said, "I'm going to freeze this. You're going to need stitches."

He didn't feel the shots. He felt the burning turn into a dull ache when he laid the arm down.

"You can look if you want now, son," the physician said.

Brody elevated the hand. The skin was split open at the lower knuckle of the third finger, the ball at the end of the finger bone poking through, separated from its joint. The doctor had a mask and gloves on now. He was threading a surgical needle, forceps in each hand.

"You've got a compound dislocation here, perhaps some fractures in the adjacent fingers. I'll re-seat the finger joint right here."

V.R. walked in, saying, "How is he?"

"He's done for the day," the physician said.

V.R. approached the table and looked. "Jesus Christ," he said. He slapped Brody lightly on the cheek. "Nice run, asshole. But I'm betting you don't try that again in this league."

Five minutes later, Brody sat up. He laid his left hand on his pants, black and silver soiled with smears of blood. He opened and closed his fingers.

"Feels fine now," Brody said.

The physician said, "So does a guillotine, if you use enough Xylocaine."

Brody slid quickly off the table and rotated his left arm, flexed his fingers a couple more times and turned to Squat. "Can you tape these three fingers so I can bend them?"

Squat nodded.

Brody felt someone behind him. It was V.R. again, this time accompanied by Carl Montan, dressed in a charcoal suit, the jacket slung over his shoulder.

"He's all done," the physician said again.

Brody said, "Done running, he means."

The physician said, "That freeze is going to wear off. Before it does, you might injure it even more."

Brody said, "Then you freeze it again."

Brody said to the head coach, "I'm telling you, V.R., I've got the coverage wired. I can win this game."

"Tell the Old Man what you're seeing," V.R. said.

Brody said, "No fucking way."

V.R. rested his hands on his shoulders. "You check the uniforms out there, Brody? That's not Ohio State. Every foam-spitting fucking asshole is going to be looking for a piece of that hand you walk back out there."

"The line is solid."

V.R. looked at Montan, Montan on a nearby table now, his arms folded. Montan said, "He's an adult. He knows the risks." The doctor had his back to all of them, washing his hands. The coach shook a finger at Brody. "Three fucking downs, Brody. Presuming you last that long."

Brody saw Montan, the deadness in his eyes. At that moment, he *knew*. He knew everything that Eric Smith had said was correct. It wasn't V.R. or Jack Petrus or even Papa Goldman who ran the New York Stars. It was Carl Montan.

And Carl Montan wanted him in the football game.

★ ★ ★

When Montan returned to the owner's suite, he gave Dominique Goldman the news. She spun around from the skybox bar and clapped her hands a couple of times.

"He's okay, everyone. Just a finger. He'll start the second half."

Papa Goldman lifted a glass of scotch. "They're good boys. Good goddamn boys. Right, Carl?"

"Character matters," Montan said, toasting back.

David Harvey lifted a glass of ginger ale.

The Mecca chairman was Goldman's only outside guest. They'd sat side by side during the first half, watching, then talking about price of doing business in New York during the TV time-outs as Dominique fetched refreshments. Montan had made eye contact with Harvey only once, shaking his limp hand when he arrived. The rest of the time he'd been on the phone to the bench, checking field injuries, or sitting with Jack Petrus, a good twenty feet from both men.

Papa Goldman had said he'd wanted no distractions, but Dominique had defied him. Between the quarters, several of her contacts stopped by to say hello. The local head of the United Way. The general manager of a network affiliate. A gossip columnist from the New York *Daily News*. She'd introduced Harvey, who remained gracious. No doubt the visit would end up in the gossip column, and the speculation would begin from there. She'd planned a very public twist to her father's arm, Montan suspected. He saw it coming and had already cleared it with Harvey, Harvey saying, "At this point that sort of thing might do us some good."

Montan pulled Dominique aside after the columnist left. He whispered, "You're irrevocably shameless."

She whispered back, "Is there any other kind?"

As the teams jogged from the tunnel for the second half, Montan reclaimed his seat next to Petrus. Fans were cheering. It had been a long time since New Yorkers had greeted the Stars at the second half with anything other than the sound of spooked cattle. It had been a long time since a quarterback had run down the tunnel to cheers.

The sound irritated Montan. He wondered if the team psychologist had made a couple of miscalculations about Derek Brody. It wasn't an exact science.

"Brody seems okay," Petrus said.

"He took the needle," Montan said.

Petrus said, "Squat?"

"Doc did a little surgery. His hand looks like he ran into a band saw. Doc tried to bench him."

"V.R. wanted him playing?"

"No, I did. It's an acceptable risk."

"You mean, for *him*?"

"For us. That hand gets hit again he's gone for the season. I'm beginning to think Brody may not be our man."

Petrus's face flushed.

Montan looked again for Brody. He caught a glimpse of his number in the middle mob of Stars forming on the sidelines. Petrus swiveled in his chair, facing him, his back to the owner.

He pointed. "You know, that's what you'll never understand, Carl. You think you know players, but you don't. You can't. Because you never played the game."

Montan glanced over. "Three years of high school ball qualifies you?" He turned back toward the field below. "This is not the time or place to elevate your blood pressure, Jack. It's awfully goddamn hard to get an EMS crew up here."

Petrus didn't back off. "But the players know it. That's something they all understand."

Montan said, "The TD was a fluke."

"I'm not talking about the TD. I'm talking something you can't measure with those goddamn tests. If he finishes this game, the players will know it."

Montan was tired of Jack Petrus. Tired of his complaints, tired of his whining. He leaned close and discreetly grabbed the GM's tie, his breath in the fat man's face.

"And just what the fuck is *it*, Jack?"

He tugged the tie, but the clip-on snapped off.

Petrus said, "*Character*, Carl. Letting him play with that hand, you've just pinned Derek Brody with football's Purple Heart."

CHAPTER

★ ★ ★ **24** ★ ★ ★

He swallowed a Demerol, put the others from the team doctor in his locker, stepped into the shower again. New pictures in his mind, instant replays. Three touchdown passes in the second half. One to Toby Headly. One to Conlin. Glamour Boy dropped one in his numbers on the two, then came back and made a spectacular end zone grab on a seemingly uncatchable pass. He remembered the way the center exploded off the ball, the protection from the rest of the offensive line.

Stars 28, Packers 21. He stayed in the hot stream of water a long time, not wanting his mental picture of the scoreboard to fade.

There were at least twenty reporters waiting. Josaitus dressed the hand in the training room first, then Brody came out and answered questions until they stopped asking.

"You guys got enough now?" he asked.

"Plenty," somebody said.

Another, "Nice game, Derek."

Reporters calling him by his first name now.

The reporters wandered off, searching for other subjects. Brody faced his locker. "One more question," a voice said.

He turned around. Franky Carcaterra was standing there, a producer behind him with a tape unit over his shoulder, the talk jock with a mike at his side.

Carcaterra's microphone remained at his side. "What you say we talk later this week?" he asked.

"I'll be here at practice."

"No, I mean business. I'm wondering if you're interested in doing a weekly spot. Through the rest of the season."

"I'd have to think about it."

"The station pays. Twenty K, probably. You can have your agent—"

Brody interrupted. "It's not about money."

Carcaterra handed his microphone to his producer, saying, "Go get yourself a Coke or something. I'm done here."

Brody pulled on socks. He knew Shay and Scanlon were waiting for him in the tunnel.

"Brody," Carcaterra said.

"Yeah."

"I was wrong about you, okay?"

"After only one win?" He kept his eyes on his feet.

"No, I took a lot of cheap shots. You saved my ass the other night."

Brody stood up, studying the guy there with his hands in his pockets, eating crow. Brody said, "They were cheap, all right. But most of them were right."

★　★　★

They all left in a cab, Scanlon and Shay more hyped than he was, revisiting the key plays, heaping on the praise. Brody rolling the window down as they drove through a crowd gathered around the players' exit.

"Hey, Brody, you suck," somebody shouted. "You're just fucking setting us up."

He saw a fistfight break out as they pulled away.

Scanlon had asked them to accompany him to LaGuardia, saying the later flights to Detroit were all booked. He was leaving in two hours. They could grab a bite at the airport. Brody wasn't hungry. He'd been famished in the shower, but now the Demerol was killing his hunger and numbing the pain in his hand. Shay suggested they eat at the apartment later.

In the airport, Scanlon paused in front of a small concourse lounge. "I need a drink." A half dozen people were in the small bar, businessmen mainly, flying out the day before for Monday meetings, some noses in newspapers, others watching the four o'clock game. The Giants against LA.

"Fine," Brody said.

Scanlon ordered a double Jack Daniel's, Brody a Virgin Mary, Shay the same. As they waited, Scanlon reached into a small carry-on and produced a manila folder, sliding it to the corner of the small table. He glanced at Shay. She was sitting close to Brody, rubbing his shoulder, still in character. Then Scanlon looked back to Brody.

"I told you on the phone," Brody said. "She's okay."

Shay's back stiffened. "If you don't mind, I've also got a few things to say."

Scanlon looked at her a couple more seconds, then back to Brody. "I got this on Thursday," he said. "But I wanted to wait until after the game."

Brody put up his hand. "Before we start, NFL Security paid me a visit last night. Guy's name is Bullard. He says he was working on the Smith case. He says Smith was supposed to have some documents. I'm supposed to see him Tuesday. But Shay here says Eric didn't trust the guy."

Scanlon turned to Shay, but was interrupted when the bartender brought the drinks. Right behind him were a couple of patrons who'd been watching the game.

"You're Brody, right?" one of them asked.

Brody smiled. He tipped the bartender twenty, then made a couple of minutes of small talk with the fans. Both of them with their theories of what had been wrong with the Stars for years. He eventually signed two table napkins.

"Maybe we should find a private lounge," Scanlon said.

"People in my business say never make eye contact," Shay said. "Of course, that's the kind of problem I'd love to have."

"I don't mind," Brody said.

Brody turned to Scanlon. "Anyway, I've got a meeting with this security guy on Tuesday, but I'm not sure what to tell him."

"How about starting with the truth?"

Brody asked, "You sure you're a lawyer?" He paused. "Plus, I've got to tell you about the drug test. I—"

"Derek, later," Scanlon said. He waited for silence. "I need to show you something first."

Scanlon swigged the bourbon, opened up the folder and said, "Absolutely top secret. You may be the first active player in the game to see anything like this."

"See what?"

"*This*," Scanlon said. He tapped his finger hard on the folder. The small, square bar table tipped, the drinks sloshing over the rims.

"*You got change?*"

The voice was loud, with an accent.

They both looked up, a guy looming over them. Close, his legs an inch from the table. He was holding out a hundred-dollar bill, a self-conscious smile on his face, the kind some foreigners get when they're trying to fit in, but don't quite have it down.

"Airport stores say, no change," he said, loud again. "I say it's American money. They say, no change."

A couple of the suits in the lounge looked over their newspapers. The guy had a silk shirt, a small gold chain around his neck, three buttons undone, black chest hair poking out. He had a thick mustache. Brody guessed Arabic, kind of a sing-song accent, like from India, but with more of a bark to it.

The bartender yelled across the lounge. "Hey, man, I got change over here. But you need to buy a drink."

The Arab cocked his head. "You got wine? Red, my *buddy*, not white."

"Like I said—"

The Arab spun around, but his hip caught the corner of the table. Half the Virgin Mary hit Scanlon's shirt before both drinks crashed to the floor. The paperwork scattered everywhere.

The Arab on his knees instantly. "Sorry, my buddy. I pick it up."

Scanlon looked down, frozen, his sport shirt soaked with tomato juice. Shay rescued a couple of the documents that were soaking up bourbon, the bartender not far behind with towels.

They moved to another table. The Arab followed them over, the manila folder in his hand.

He handed it to Scanlon. "Anything I can do for you, my buddy. I do it."

Scanlon glared at him, then smiled. "Sure, *buddy*. You can start by buying me another drink." He added, "Then you can go up the concourse there and get me one of those I Love Fucking New York T-shirts for the flight home."

The Arab wandered over to the bar, perched on a stool and said loudly, "Drinks on me." Smiling. Clueless. The bartender tossed wet towels into the sink and took his money.

Brody looked at Scanlon and laughed. Hard. He was flying on the Demerol. Shay squinted at the Arab.

"You were saying," Brody said.

Scanlon handed him the folder. "Take 'em. Look at them later."

Brody slid the folder under his thigh.

Scanlon said, "What you've got there is research from another NFL team's player procurement system."

"What team?"

"The team doesn't matter." He paused. "What matters is these execs have you guys *wired*. They take no chances drafting and signing. I mean, *no chances*. The guy I got these from said, as far as he knew, every team has some kind of system. Some are better than others. Though not everyone goes to these lengths. A lot of teams just rely on NFL Security reports."

"What do you mean, *lengths?*"

"You'll see. Psychological reports. Psychological and motivational advisories for coaches. Stuff the shrinks put together trying to help coaches and front office people."

Brody said, "I took tests. But tests don't throw footballs."

The new drinks came, doubles. The bartender motioned with his head back at the Arab, who was smiling, lifting his glass of red wine. The bartender said quietly, "You believe that guy?"

Shay was looking at him again.

When the bartender left, Scanlon said, "Give me back that folder for a second." He thumbed through the papers, muttering, "Shit, these are all out of order." Finally he pulled a sheet out. "Listen to this. This is a report on a new linebacker they drafted this year."

Darien is articulate, confident and likes to trash talk on the field. Relationships are very important to him, largely because of the absence of his father, who is currently serving time in prison for rape. He can handle criticism from someone he respects and trusts. But do not dress him down in front of his teammates. Social acceptance is very important to him. If he needs to be reprimanded, do it privately, one-on-one.

"Anyway, you get the idea."

Brody said, "Coaches crawl into players' heads. This is just another way."

Scanlon swallowed more Jack, then said, "Think about it, Derek. You're a sales manager at a computer software company. You come in and tell your boss you'd like to add a couple new regional salesmen, he's got this kind of shit on *you* sitting in his desk. He's looking at you thinking, I'm not going to expand this guy's territory because he's compensating, because the company shrink is telling me the guy is insecure over the size of his dick."

Scanlon realized Shay was there, saying, "Sorry." She gave him a courteous smile.

Brody said, "What does this have to do with the Stars?"

Scanlon handed the folder back and lowered his voice. "By the way, this material is covered under labor and privacy laws. It's not supposed to be disseminated by employers. That's why I don't want to even get into who this guy is, his position."

"So how did you get it?"

Scanlon said, "I put him in the fifth row for Garth Brooks." He took another drink and continued, "What I'm saying is, some teams, they're very thorough. On *everything*. When you go through that stuff tonight, you'll see there's not only references to NFL Security reports, but references to additional material from a PI firm retained by the team. The PI stuff is where it gets really interesting. You'll see NFL Security didn't catch half of it."

"Half of what?"

Scanlon glanced back over his shoulder, the Arab toasting them again, smiling. He lowered his voice. "Those players you gave me. Well, my guy punches in their names in his computer, their reports come up. My guy didn't want a thing to do with any of them from the get-go."

"You're saying they have known problems."

"Fuck-ups—*if* somebody bothered to dig," Scanlon said, confident of it. "They came up clean in their NFL Security checks. The PI firm caught all the shit."

"Fuck-ups how?"

"Their summaries are in the folder."

"Tell me."

"Drug problems, mainly. Drinking. Bar fights. There's a rape in there. Booster money. Illegal payments from agents. You name it. One of the picks was rolling dope on a street corner between college and camp. Needless to say, when the draft came, he wasn't on my guy's wish list."

"You think the Stars check that deep?"

Scanlon paused, then said, "That's what got my attention. When you get home, take a look at the lineman who dropped dead on the field a couple years ago."

"The Iowa nose tackle, the heart attack."

"Right. But it wasn't exactly. It was an aortic embolism, a hereditary thing. A medical time bomb. My guy picked it up when they did a check with the Insurance Bureau. It's like a credit reporting service used by medical carriers. The bureau compiles medical reports from personal physicians and hospitals. My guy says it's more reliable than college physicians or the Combine."

"So, that means the Stars didn't check. They can't be very thorough."

"Well, that's my point. According to my guy, they told the internist at the Combine to check it out, and he confirmed it. That meant at least four teams *did* know. I guess some teams share physicians during the physicals to avoid repetition."

"You're telling me one of them was the Stars," Brody said.

Scanlon nodded. "My guy said it was the talk of the Combine. Everyone figured the Stars were just rolling the dice."

"So where does that put this Carl Montan?" Brody asked.

"He's got a reputation," Scanlon said. "The most incompetent director of player personnel in the league, my guy says. And, shit, he says, who's going to tell old man Goldman that? Shit, everybody likes kicking the shit out of the Stars."

"But Montan put together that expansion team."

"They figure he got lucky."

Brody motioned for the folder with his right hand. "My NFL Security report in there?" Scanlon fished out the document, and Brody scanned it. There was a reference to the car crash. The report called him a passenger. Raymond Bullard was lying. Montan had probably dug up the truth, and passed it on to Bullard.

"And Montan?" Brody asked.

"My PI says there's nothing before football. It's like he came out of the federal witness protection program or something."

"What about Vegas, what Smith said?"

"We do a lot of shows with people out of Vegas," Scanlon said. "I've made some calls. But nobody seems to have ever heard of the guy."

"Maybe you need to ask Wayne Newton," Brody said.

"Or dig up Howard Hughes."

"I was serious," Brody said.

"So was I," Scanlon said. "Hughes owned quite a few Vegas hotels about the time your guy supposedly was out there. The Desert Inn. The Sands. Smith tell you where he worked?"

Brody shook his head.

"That might help. But maybe not. All those Hughes people have pretty much disappeared from the Vegas scene. Hughes tried to take over the town, you know. Then he got into that germ thing. Did you know that nobody saw Hughes for years?"

"Your people told you that?"

"No," Scanlon said. "I saw it on A&E."

Shay said, "There's a guy out there now like that. His company does business on Broadway."

Scanlon glanced at his watch. "We're getting off the track. My point is, I think we may have a problem. I'm not saying the Smith matter is related, not until I see some evidence. But the Stars do have serious money problems. And what kind of future is there for you, especially with this idiot Montan?"

Brody thought about it. He said, "Montan's not an idiot. Montan runs the team. Just like Smith said. It's not just those picks, it's everything. The race shit. The factions. He's put it all together. I've got a hunch this team isn't supposed to win. That's where maybe this guy Tommy Molito comes in."

Scanlon leaned forward. "You realize what you're saying?"

Brody looked at him. The Demerol had taken away his anxiety, but not his reason.

Scanlon answered for him, emphatic in a restricted voice. "They started *you*. If what you're saying is true, you were picked to lose football games."

Brody thought, yeah, in the first round. He said, "But now they have to start me. I've proven I can play injured."

Shay asked, "What if they don't?"

Scanlon said, "That crowd outside the dome will burn it down."

Scanlon finished the bourbon, rattling the rocks a little as he tipped it, getting the last of it. He said, "I need another drink."

"Maybe your buddy will spring for another one," Brody said.

They turned and looked, but the Arab was gone. Scanlon caught the bartender's attention and pointed at his glass.

Scanlon said, "I could kick myself in the ass. Maybe I should have insisted you go with IMG or Proserve. Maybe their agents would have picked stuff like this up."

"Only if a shoe deal was involved," Brody said.

Scanlon spun his glass on the tabletop. "I still can't figure it. We've got some circumstantial evidence here, and nothing else. I mean, I should probably take your deposition about everything. Start a record." He looked at Shay. "You, too. What Smith told you." He turned back to Brody. "But we don't have anything concrete. Nothing we could take public."

Scanlon slumped a little, the bourbon hitting him now. "Besides, why would they want to field a losing football team. We'd have to explain it."

"To move it?" Brody offered.

"*Major League*," Shay said. "Charlie Sheen with a mohawk. My agent had me reading for one of the bimbo parts."

Scanlon shook his head. "These owners have court precedents. They want to leave town. They just cut a deal and go." Scanlon slammed the glass down. "More theories."

"Maybe we should set up a meeting with Goldman," Brody said. "He seems straight up."

"I get it for you, *my buddy*."

It was the Arab. He was grinning, coming through the door with an I ❤ NEW YORK T-shirt stretched between his hands.

★   ★   ★

As the Arab left, Shay's eyes followed him out the door and down the concourse. She turned back to the men. Brody looked depressed, his game high gone. Scanlon draped the shirt around his neck like a scarf, slumping deeper into his chair.

Shay sipped the Virgin Mary, straightened her posture and said, "Can I throw my two cents in now?"

Scanlon glanced over, humoring her. She eyed Brody again. He had this look, and she knew. She'd been there many times. They tell you great work. Tell you that you've been cast. Then you find out they have a different part in mind.

Shay said, "There *is* some evidence. Eric Smith gave it to me."

Brody hesitated, then said, "You said there was nothing. You said he didn't give you shit."

She half smiled. "I didn't know you. Now, I do."

Scanlon pulled the shirt from his neck, starting to say something. She lifted her hand. "There's one more thing." She hesitated, then said confidently, "I do know makeup. I do know spirit gum when I see it. It glistens, behind the hair."

Brody and Scanlon looked at each other, Scanlon with a miffed frown. Shay gestured with her head toward the door.

"Your *buddy* here," she said. "Well, I'm pretty sure that's the guy who's been following me around."

CHAPTER

☆ ☆ ☆ **25** ☆ ☆ ☆

Montan met the Turk in the Shea Stadium lot first thing Monday, the Turk sitting in Montan's sedan, telling his story. In the distance, workers were cleaning up the lot from a Mets game the day before. A seagull poked at a crumpled bag of Doritos on the pavement in front of the Mercedes.

"I see you bought one for yourself," Montan said. The Turk was wearing the I ❤ New York T-shirt.

"The guy gave it back. Near the gate."

"I wouldn't wear it, either," Montan said.

The Turk was finishing a smoke, chuckling as he exhaled. He lowered the passenger window and aimed the butt at the seagull. The bird winged its way toward the stadium.

"There he goes," the Turk said.

"Who?"

"The bird."

Montan shook his head, thinking, so fucking what? He rested his chin in his hand for a couple moments, then turned to the Turk.

He said, "You sure those background reports were not ours?"

The Turk nodded. "I saw names. Glamour Boy, some of his posse. Couple of clean players, too. All Stars. But it was a different system. It was on that wide computer paper, but a reduced copy. No team letterhead or anything. But it was definitely player background material, some kind of scouting system."

"You ever think of just grabbing a newspaper at a nearby table and just listening? Trying not to be so creative?"

The Turk looked over. "It wasn't a good set-up. Three fucking TVs going, them talking low. That's why I went over. At least I'd get a look at the paperwork. It all sounded pretty serious."

"You said you couldn't hear them."

"The way they were looking at each other, talking a lot with their hands. Except Bimbolina. She hardly said shit."

Montan glanced out the window. Now there were a half dozen gulls in front of the car, poking at the debris.

"They're something, aren't they?" the Turk said.

"Brody's got his agent doing some homework," Montan said. "That's all."

The Turk pointed. "No, those gulls. Surfer was telling me all about 'em. That bird here earlier, he's the scout. He finds something he likes and he gets the others. Like ants in Vegas. You got to kill the first one you see, or the next thing you know they're crawling all over your fucking kitchen."

Montan thought, fuck the birds, and the ants.

"So where is he?" Montan asked.

"Practice."

"No, the agent."

"Agent made his plane."

Montan looked at the clock in the Mercedes. He had a meeting at Papa Goldman's home in the Hamptons in less than an hour. "The bim is still at the apartment?" he asked.

"No wives or girlfriends at the dome on Monday. Brody's got to meet with—"

"I know what he does on goddamn Mondays," Montan snapped.

The Turk shook his head. "Brody takes a cab to the dome. Can you fucking believe that? Leaves that nice ride in the fucking lot all night."

"He's a player," Montan said. "Players are spoiled children."

"Surfer called me on the cellular. Says she's out on the balcony again. Reading the newspapers."

"I'm surprised you're here."

"It's still early. Sun gets high in the sky, temp hits eighty, her top goes down. I'll be there."

Montan glanced at the clock again, considering the options. Players he could handle. The attorney, *that* was a problem. And the bim. She wouldn't have been there at the airport if she wasn't in the middle of it. Smith probably spilled his guts to her. Then she decides to hook up with Brody, trying to be clever. Now all of them, trying to figure it out, getting close to it, but not there yet. If they had it nailed, the agent would never have boarded the flight. He'd stay in New York and pull his boy out.

Montan slid the Mercedes in drive. "I've got an important meeting."

The Turk opened the door, but he lingered to light another smoke. The gulls were stepping nervously around the Doritos bag. The Turk climbed out, then spoke through the open door. "Carl, I say we take out the bim. I don't like the way this shit looks."

"And what would you do with this attorney?"

"You let me do Bimbolina, I'll do two for the price of one."

"Now is no time to panic," Montan said. He told himself that, too.

He floored the sedan, the tires squealing. The gulls scattered in front of him. When he checked the mirror, he saw a crippled bird flopping on the pavement. The Turk standing there with his cigarette, watching it.

The guy smoked too much, he thought.

★   ★   ★

The thirty-six-room house was an English revival Tudor at the end of a winding blacktop drive, the front gate with a silver star bolted to its iron arch. Red brick, parapet gables, a crenellated tower. A deck off the great hall in the back overlooked a pool, the beach and the Atlantic beyond that.

Inside, furnishings and house staff provided the only company. Papa Goldman had lived alone since Dominique left for Harvard. He filled it for the annual player party and some charity functions Dominique fought to stage there. But largely, he'd progressed in isolation after his bitter divorce. Papa Goldman despised the society crowd his ex-wife cultivated in the Hamptons and on Park Avenue. He used to entertain politicians and community leaders, but made the effort only for his football team. But as the losing continued, Goldman had become increasingly removed. He commuted with his chopper to the mansion, or spent more uneventful nights alone in his apartment off Third Avenue. The last people he'd shunned were the other owners and executives in the NFL. He'd attended the spring meeting, but made none of the cocktail parties or other unofficial functions. It was no surprise to Montan that the new, insurgent owners wanted him out of the league.

Carl Montan followed the brick path that wound around the house. It ended at the pool and the stairs to the beach. He could see the *Donzi* tender anchored just offshore, two boys in blue shirts sitting in the stern.

Papa Goldman was in the pool, naked but for swim goggles and an unflattering Speedo squeezing his sagging skin. He was jogging in place in chest-high water, his body bobbing with each step, a two-pound dumbbell in each hand. The team physician had suggested the routine, saying the buoyancy would cushion his brittle joints. But it didn't look healthy. His face contorted, Papa Goldman looked like a tired old man trying to escape a nightmare in a slow motion run.

Montan turned to a wrought iron table, its glass top covered with coffee, tea, juice, bagels, smoked trout and cheese. There was a bowl of fresh fruit and a stack of Monday papers. Montan nodded to the man sitting across from Jack Petrus.

"Sorry I'm late. I had a player problem."

David Harvey lifted his coffee cup, "Nothing you can't solve, Carl, I'm sure."

"Carl," Goldman called.

Montan pretended he didn't hear. Harvey looked relaxed, his legs crossed.

"Carl, goddamnit."

Montan walked to the side of the pool, Goldman still bobbing. "Yes, Papa."

"There's one or two goddamn concerns I have here."

David Harvey said, "That's what we're here for, Papa. That's exactly why we're here."

Goldman glared at Montan. "Not least among them is Nicky. You had no reason to involve her."

"She's an insistent young woman," Montan said.

"She insist you bed her as well?"

"As a matter of fact—"

Harvey interrupted. "That sort of nonsense is irrelevant." He picked up the *Newsday* sports page.

Goldman's glare shifted to Harvey. "You never told me you were going to use my own daughter in this goddamn charade."

Harvey opened the paper. "For the record, I haven't told you anything. Yesterday was the first time we've ever spoken, Papa. You don't mind me calling you that, do you?"

Montan said, "She'll get the credit, Papa. She'll be delirious with the coverage. Savvy female exec saves the Stars, keeps the team in New York by finding white knight. That sort of thing."

Goldman jogged five feet closer, the swim goggles steamed up. "You've goddamn led her to believe I'll be retaining the majority interest. She won't be satisfied with a token share of the team."

"Perhaps we can find something for her in the studios," Harvey said. "They appreciate her kind of ruthlessness out there."

Harvey held up the sports page. "I presume everyone has gotten a good look at today's papers."

No one answered.

Harvey looked at Petrus and said, "I also presume you've seen some activity in ticket sales."

Petrus's eyes went to Montan for support.

Montan poured himself a cup of coffee. "Go ahead, Jack," he said.

Petrus cleared his throat. "We had lines at the ticket office after the game. We'll see a bump this week. Maybe twenty or thirty percent."

Harvey tossed the section to Montan. "Some of these sports columnists occasionally show bursts of insight."

Montan opened the page, the headline: DEREK BRODY—SALVATION OR SHOOTING STAR? He scanned the copy.

"Read us the last line, Carl," Harvey said.

Montan knew something like this was coming. He stayed calm. "Fans are asking questions," he read. "Is Derek Brody for real? Are the Stars for real? No doubt, they will get their answers next week when the team plays Detroit with the entire country watching."

Harvey put his fingertips to his lips, then opened his hands. "That pretty much sums it up." He looked at all of them. "I hope none of you have made a major miscalculation here."

Montan looked back at the paper, but he could feel Harvey's eyes on him. He set the paper down. "We could always start our backup," he said. "Put Brody on injured reserve."

Petrus said, "That will only drive ticket sales higher, Carl. Everybody will be anticipating Brody's return."

"That's simply not acceptable," Harvey said.

Goldman jogged a little closer, only a few feet from the pool's edge now. "You told me yesterday you expected league approval."

"I told you that at the beginning of the game," Harvey said. He paused. "I have friends among the new owners, but it's a fluid situation among the others. They will fight the transfer of ownership if this organization begins to show signs of life."

Goldman half smiled and said, "You may have a problem. This kid looks good."

"You mean we've got a problem," Harvey said.

"I may be on my ass, but I'm still the owner of this goddamn football team."

Harvey laughed, then took a sip of juice. He set the glass down and motioned toward the ocean. "Yes, and a beautiful home in the Hamptons. A nice apartment in the city. Name recognition. Two fortunes in two different enterprises. It's all very impressive. But none of it would be possible for you had the company not carried your marker at the Sands."

"Christ, it's been years," Goldman snapped.

Harvey glanced at Montan. "Carl tells me you were quite a whale in your day. What was it, Carl?"

"Three million in one weekend."

"No, the total."

"Thirteen million. Most of it on cards."

"I was unlucky," Goldman said. "And foolish."

"I disagree. You were very lucky that you chose to play at a casino owned by Mr. Hughes. The others, they buried their mistakes in the desert. Instead, the company allowed you to not only recoup, but prosper. You think without a Teamsters strike against your competitor, all that beer would have found its way into your cans?"

"The company gave me no choice."

"You made your choices at the tables," Harvey said. "Now, all the company asks is that you honor your long-standing obligations to Mr. Hughes."

"Goddamn Howard Hughes is dead."

"But his money lives on," Harvey said.

Petrus interjected, "Papa hasn't placed a bet in years."

Harvey toasted the GM with his orange juice. "I'm happy for his recovery. Did you know Mecca contributes millions each year to programs for chronic gamblers?"

"That's awfully white of you," Goldman said.

Montan tried to play the peacemaker. "Papa, you knew three years ago this is where we were all headed. You insisted on including Jack, and we've honored that. Both of you will be well compensated. A hundred million is a lot of money, not to mention the twenty percent share you retain of the team. That will only grow in value. Long term, it will be quite a nest egg for Dominique."

Goldman dropped the barbells on the pool bottom and waded slowly toward the ladder, sweat dripping from his red splotched face.

He pulled off the goggles. "For years I've lived with this over my head," he said. "I'll be goddamned if I'm going to pass it on to my daughter."

Harvey said, "You simply have no choice."

"I was thinking more along the lines of an offer. The entire team. No minority interest."

"In return for what?"

"Another fifty million and you put those obligations in the grave with Hughes," Goldman said. "You get the entire team."

"And your daughter?"

"That's *my* concern."

Harvey thought about it. He finally said, "That's reasonable and perfectly acceptable." Harvey, smiling, motioned to Goldman's robe, folded over a chair. Not such a bad day after all, Montan thought. He picked up the terrycloth and held it open above the ladder. Goldman struggled up to the top, his trembling hands clutching the chrome.

"Think of it this way, Papa," Montan said. "You're finally going to be able to give Nicky what she's always wanted."

He draped the robe over Goldman's shoulders.

Goldman said, "And what the goddamn hell is that?"

David Harvey said, "The fortune you never had."

CHAPTER

★ ★ ★ **26** ★ ★ ★

They walked together early Monday to buy the newspapers. He explained she couldn't come to practice. Mondays he met with the coaches and the other quarterbacks to study films of the Sunday game. She told him she was feeling restless. She'd canceled dance classes and vocal sessions. She told him she'd be hearing from her agent any day. She needed work.

"Good players hardly see their girls for six months," Brody said. "Good coaches don't have wives, they have widows."

Shay said, "I'm not a girl, and aren't you getting a little ahead of yourself?"

"Just a manner of speech," he said.

They lingered in front of the Lucerne. Brody held his hand up, the elbow at a right angle.

"You'll never catch a cab that way," she said.

"I'm just elevating the hand. It hurts."

She moved closer and ran her hands through his hair, looking in his eyes, playing the role again, but tired of doing it that way now. "What they gave you isn't working?"

"I'm sticking with Advil. I was pretty out of it last night."

"I'll say," she said.

She'd listened to Brody and Scanlon argue in the airport lounge about Eric Smith's log. Scanlon wanted to pull him from the team and start filing lawsuits. Brody suggested they see the documents first. Give it a couple of days, then do it. Scanlon countered by saying he was going to remain in New York, but Brody insisted he fly back to Detroit. If he stayed, if they were being watched, he'd only set off alarms, he said.

Now Brody was saying he'd return with his car after practice. Then, they would go to the safety deposit box and pick up the document. Make a copy, FedEx the original to Scanlon, plus fax him the copy. Then they would conference with Scanlon by phone from the Lucerne.

Brody looked up First Avenue, then turned to her. "Promise me you'll stay in the apartment."

She nodded.

"And don't worry if I'm not back by noon. I have to spend some time in the training room. It's always packed the day after a game."

"You can lift weights with that hand?"

"That's the weight room."

"What's the training room?"

"That's where they heal you as quickly as possible so you can get back on the field and kick the shit out of yourself all over again."

"Who runs that?"

"The trainer. Guy named Josaitus."

She asked him to spell it.

"I think I remember seeing that," she said. "I thought it was a funny name."

"In the game program?"

"No, the papers Eric gave me."

He released her and walked about five yards down the sidewalk, circling in frustration, flexing his bandaged hand. "Shit, I need to heal this," he said. "Detroit's no pushover."

She glared at him in disbelief. "My God, you are planning on playing next Sunday."

"It's *Monday Night Football*," he said. "National TV."

"You're completely delusional, you know that?"

"I like to think of it as confidence."

"With all this going on?"

"At this point, my game is the only thing I'm confident about."

He watched her for a while, that arm propped up, looking a little like a scarecrow on the sidewalk. He waited until the anger left, then walked slowly toward her, stopping with his chest nearly touching her breasts.

"Now kiss me," he said. "In case someone's watching."

She'd never met anyone like him. He made one part of her feel strong, another part helpless. She wrapped one hand around the back of his neck and pulled him close. Tightly. Derek Brody groaned a little in pain, but Shay Falan didn't let go.

★   ★   ★

There were two Sonys in the meeting room: A large screen against the wall and a small TV on the desk where the offensive coordinator, Hadley Henderson, sat jotting notes on a legal pad. Bobby Loeb was riding a folding chair backwards, Clinton Lisle in another one against the cinder block. Loeb and the Old Man were playing catch with a Nerf ball. The arena quarterback was sitting on the floor, reactivated while Loeb was on injured reserve. He was studying a playbook.

Brody walked in. Loeb, clear-eyed for a change, stuck the ball in his crotch and started clapping. Slowly. Brody took an empty chair next to Lisle.

"Better get a tape," Loeb said. "Measure his head. I think my old paper boy's gone up a helmet size."

Brody sat side saddle. He rested his elbow on the back of his chair. He let the left hand dangle, the finger throbbing. He was determined to downplay the injury and hang on to the starting spot.

V.R. walked into the room, Tommy Molito trailing behind him. Molito's head was bobbing as if he were keeping time to a rock station he'd tuned in through the fillings in his teeth.

Molito lifted a hand. "Nice fucking game, shooter."

Brody slapped his palm.

"The club. Where the fuck you been, man?"

Brody shrugged. "A lot of late nights."

"Forget about it," Molito said, drawing out the phrase. "You know we're open for lunch, too."

Brody nodded, not saying he'd be there, not saying he wouldn't. Molito positioned himself by the door, folding his arms.

V.R. walked closer and said, "How's that hand?"

Brody said, "I'll be okay."

"You've got be ready Wednesday. And I mean practice. I don't want to see you staggering around the field on that shit Squat keeps in his big black bag."

Brody said, "Give me a football."

The Nerf suddenly sailed over. Brody reached up and clutched it with the bandaged hand, thankful for foam.

V.R. faced Loeb. "Bobby?"

"Bobby, what?" Loeb snarled.

"Bobby with the fucked-up ribs. Squat tells me you're not making much progress."

"You've got to get me off this injured reserve, V.R. Give me a fucking flak jacket, that's all."

V.R. walked over to Loeb. "Let me see your hands."

Loeb glanced up, a look of curiosity on his face.

V.R. repeated, "Your fucking hands, Bobby."

Loeb held them out, palms up. V.R. took one in each of his own hands, examining them like he was doing some kind of double palm reading, then suddenly lifted them high over Loeb's head.

"Fuck," Loeb screamed, contorting in pain.

"I guess Squat was right," V.R. said.

Molito said, "See you tonight, Vinnie?"

"Maybe," V.R. said.

Molito slid a stick of gum into his mouth and pointed at Brody. "Like I said, shooter, nice game."

Right, Brody thought, time to go now, Tommy. Meet somebody in Little Italy maybe. Give them your Stars injury report.

Loeb shook his head as Molito's leather heels faded down the hall. Loeb looked up at V.R. "Coach, why do you let that jukey motherfucker in here. I mean, shit, man, you think we don't know what's going on?"

Brody hung his head a little, but listened. He didn't hear an answer. When he glanced up, V.R. was lifting the small Sony off the desk.

"Let it go, V.R.," coach Henderson said calmly.

V.R. carried the TV over to Loeb, stopping when the slack in the cable ran out, Henderson already reaching for the deck so the wires didn't jerk it off the desk.

V.R. showed the TV to Loeb. "You here to watch film, Bobby?" His voice controlled.

"Let it go, V.R.," Henderson said again, but louder.

V.R. throttled the TV, doing it as if he had to shake it so Loeb could really see it. "Well, are you, goddamnit?"

"Why, sure, V.R.," Loeb said.

V.R. hesitated.

"Let it go, V.R."

V.R. said, "The hell you fucking are."

The head coach spun around and threw the TV into the cinder block wall, the cables snapping free. Glass shattered and scattered across the cement floor.

Henderson jumped to his feet. "V.R., let it go!"

V.R. made a fist at Loeb, shouting now, "If you spent half the fucking time working on your game instead of everybody else's fucking business, you'd be in the fucking Pro Bowl, you sorry sonovabitch."

V.R.'s hand came back, as if he was about to strike the injured quarterback. Brody stood up. Everyone did, even the Old Man.

"V.R., Jesus," Henderson pleaded.

Breathing hard now, V.R. dropped his hand and said, "Just get the fuck out of here."

Loeb didn't move. "This *is* the quarterback meeting," he said. "And last I checked, I'm still a fucking quarterback on this team."

V.R. lunged forward, Henderson pushing the table aside. The head coach reached Loeb first. He grabbed a handful of his T-shirt with his left hand, and the back of his belt with his right. He pulled Loeb to his feet, the chair beneath him falling away as he dragged Loeb toward the door. Loeb's legs scrambled for footing, but he was too off balance, his hands clutching his injured ribs.

Henderson froze, saying, "Aw shit, V.R."

At the door, Read grabbed two handfuls of shirt and stood Loeb up. He shook him once. "You go see Squat now, Bobby," he said. "I think I like you better fucked up."

V.R. pushed him into the hall and slammed the door. For a moment he composed himself, his back to all of them. Then he spun around.

"What the fuck are you all looking at?" he barked.

A few seconds later, Clinton Lisle whispered to Brody, "If this is winning, someone remind me to call in sick when we lose."

★   ★   ★

Four hours later, Brody and Shay were sitting at a table in the safety deposit vault at Citibank on Broadway, Brody reading six typewritten pages. The log was in the form of an affidavit, beginning, "I, Eric Smith, if sworn and called to testify, do hereby affirm . . ." Brody leafed through the paperwork looking for the name of a law firm, but found only a notary's stamp and signature.

He asked Shay, "Smith say anything about having an attorney?"

She shook her head. "He said he was spending a lot of time at the library. I think he had a lot of time on his hands."

The pages had dates, locations and names of players. It detailed player misconduct over three seasons, Smith in the middle of most of it, but other players involved as well. Drug and steroid use. Bar fights. Concealed weapons. Gambling on NFL teams, Smith placing bets with Tommy Molito. Police were called to a couple of the bar fights. There were identical entries after those: "Montan called. No charges." Johnny Josaitus was running a pharmacy, indiscriminately dispensing prescriptions and anabolic steroids. Smith listed them: Percodan, Percocet, Stadol, Soma, Ultram. Smith made entries about rigged urine tests and Squat's catheter. There was a reference to a street pusher called "the slinger," who provided players with heroine, cocaine and weed.

Brody found the names most disturbing. But he was surprised Reggie Thompson had only two entries: A urine substitution last season. And an arrest with Eric Smith and a third player picked up by vice near Grand Central, propositioning an undercover cop. "Montan called. No charges."

Twelve players in all, all still playing with the Stars on both sides of the ball: Antoine Lense, Darius Wallace, Homer Cobb and others. They get in trouble, Carl Montan rides to the rescue. The party goes on. More than half of the names matched the background reports Scanlon had obtained.

Brody thought, Montan's dirty dozen. Only one name surprised him, the third player in the vice bust with Smith and Thompson.

It was Bobby Loeb.

Brody folded the document and stuck it in his pocket. They walked out of the vault, Brody saying he saw a Federal Express office down the block. Shay stopped at a black marble counter stocked with deposit slips, pens attached by chains. She began writing on a slip.

"You're out of ink," Brody said.

She glanced at him, then back at the paper. "There's a guy standing out on the sidewalk. Blond guy with the backwards hat. It says Billabong above the brim."

Brody stole a glance. "What about him?"

"Listen to what I'm saying. That guy was at the hot dog stand outside the structure where we parked."

"I saw him," Brody said. "He followed us here. I didn't want you to worry. But I noticed the hat."

"The way he was wearing it?"

"No, the name. Billabong's an Australian surfboard outfit. They pay a lot of money in surfer endorsements so kids nowhere near the ocean will wear their stuff. He seemed a little old for it."

Brody looked again, then past the guy when their eyes almost met. He grasped Shay's hand and started walking across the lobby. Walking casually, studying the CD rates posted near the business office.

"You thinking there's a back way out of here?" she asked.

Brody said, "I'm thinking maybe it's time I open an account."

★   ★   ★

The way she watched Derek do it, he'd asked to see the bank manager, the secretary saying the bank manager was busy, but Derek saying, "Tell him Derek Brody is here from the New York Stars, and that I'm considering doing some business with his bank."

In two minutes they were both sitting in the manager's office, the manager talking football between segments of his pitch about the bank. They talked for ten minutes, Derek finally wondering out loud if he could have his Michigan bank wire transfer $500,000 to the branch.

"Why of course. I'll have my secretary give you the routing numbers as you leave."

Derek stood, then sat back down. "Your secretary wouldn't be able to do me a big favor, would she? I'm pretty pressed for time."

"Anything," the manager said.

Two minutes later, the secretary brought back copies of Eric Smith's log, the FedEx envelope he'd also asked for on top. Brody tucked one copy in his pocket, put the original in the FedEx pack. The bank's return address was on the mailing slip. He wrote in Scanlon's address on the label and handed it to the secretary.

"This needs to go out today," he said.

The manager motioned for it. "Let me take care of it personally," he said.

As they walked out of the bank's door, Shay was thinking some things had to change now. The charade had to end. She'd talked to her agent that morning. A film director wanted her in LA at the end of the week to read for the movie part. She was just about to tell Brody when she saw the guy with the hat again. He was standing with a newspaper a half block down.

Brody had already spotted him. Later, he would tell her that the Smith log probably was the last straw, that and the aching hand and a tense meeting he'd had at the Stardome.

Or, maybe, he said, he just didn't like the guy's hat.

He dropped her hand and sprinted. The guy watched for the first five yards, then ditched the paper and bolted. Brody dodged pedestrians, his body cutting at sharp angles, briefly touching people he passed, as if that helped his balance. Keeping his center of gravity low. Shay gave chase. She saw them take the corner of Broadway and 34th, the hat guy close to the building. Brody only five or ten yards behind.

Ten seconds later she was there, around the building. She saw a vendor shaking an umbrella, shouting in a foreign language, Arabic maybe. The vendor's display was tipped over, umbrellas scattered everywhere.

The hat guy was on his back on the pavement, moaning, skin missing from his hands and elbows.

Brody had him by his collar.

"Who the fuck are you?"

The guy hesitated.

Brody pounded his head into the pavement. "Who the fuck are you and why are you following me?"

The guy's eyes blinked.

"You Brody?" he mumbled.

Brody pounded the head again. "That wasn't an answer. That was a question."

"Derek," she shouted.

The guy spread his hands in surrender. "I just wanted your auto-graph, man," he said, whining. "But I don't think I want it anymore."

Brody let go and stood up.

The guy scrambled to his feet and jogged away, shouting over his shoulder, "Asshole."

Brody stared at her, his chest heaving, a look of shock on his face. He clutched his injured hand at the wrist.

She asked, "Still feeling confident about your game?"

CHAPTER

★ ★ ★ **27** ★ ★ ★

A dog walking service had tied a dozen toys and miniatures in front of the high-rise across from the Lucerne. Montan waded through yapping poodles, pugs and schnauzers and entered the lobby. The doorman stopped him, telling him he'd have to call the tenant before going up.

Montan produced a key. "I am the tenant," he said.

Alone in the elevator, Montan thought about what he was going to do when it was over. Resigning might be the way to go. He'd lived well in New York on the million-dollar deposit David Harvey wired to his account in the Caymans four years ago. But New York ate money. Another three million, when the Stars deal closed, wouldn't last long. He was thinking Europe, the Mediterranean, maybe Monte Carlo, getting back into the gambling game. Carlo's casinos had style. No brats and credit cards and cellulite like Vegas, no blue hairs feeding quarters into slots like Atlantic City, soaking up that gaudy Graceland decor.

When he stepped off, he walked a hundred feet and slid the key into the apartment door. He didn't tell the Turk and the Surfer he was coming over. He wanted it that way.

He opened to manic surf music and the smell of weed, both intensifying as he moved down the hall. He hesitated at the edge of the living room, waiting for them to turn around. They were facing the window, enveloped in smoke. The Turk slouched in an overstuffed chair, his semi-auto Llama on the armrest. The Surfer was next to him in a recliner. The place was a sty. A six-foot-high pile of empty Pizza boxes stood in the corner. Empties everywhere. Dirty ashtrays. A waxed surfboard in another corner. Against the wall, a stereo and 19-inch TV on milk crates. Montan saw the Radio Shack scanner on another crate, a cassette deck wired to it. The receiver was on, crackling, but inaudible under the music.

The Turk handed a half burnt joint to the Surfer, the ash falling, the Surfer oblivious to the burn marks in the chair. Both of them deep in conversation, bitching about something. And nobody on the telescope at the window.

Montan said, "Kill that fucking music."

The Turk spun around, reaching for the Llama. His hand relaxed when he saw Montan. He rose. "Carl, I was waiting for you to call back."

Montan strolled over to the Surfer. He saw bandages on his elbows and a mindless look, the Surfer exhaling now, holding the joint between his thumb and forefinger only a couple inches from his face.

Montan kicked the joint out of the Surfer's hand. Then he put his Bruno Magli on the Surfer's face and pushed, the recliner falling until the Surfer was horizontal.

"You think I'm paying ten bills a month for this dump so you can pretend you're in fucking Malibu?" Montan punctuated his words with heel jabs.

The music stopped, the Turk over at the stereo now. "Carl, listen."

Montan rested an elbow on his elevated knee. "Listen to what?"

The Turk had his hands up. "You have no fucking idea what happened. I tried to tell you, but you hung up."

"All I see is a couple of fuckups not doing their jobs."

Montan looked back at the Surfer, the guy frozen. He lifted his foot off his face and kicked his bandaged elbow, saying, "You got a skateboard, too?"

The Turk was on his knees near the crate with the scanner, fumbling with something. Saying, "Carl, listen to me. Brody made the Surfer, then fucked him up, but the Surfer got away."

The Turk told him the story.

The Surfer said, "You should have seen the look on the dude's face when I ran away."

Montan walked over to the telescope and squinted into the eye-piece. He could see Brody's balcony, the chairs empty. Nothing happening inside.

The Turk said, "It's over, Carl. They've got the paper from Smith. The original. That's why they went to the bank. Bimbolina had it in her box. I told you that you should have let me take her out."

Montan glared at the Turk and said, "So they got some paper. You think that makes it over?"

The Turk reached into his shirt pocket and pulled out a cassette tape. "No, this does," he said. "You better sit down, Carl, and listen to the fucking call they made."

★ ★ ★

Brody thought Scanlon's plan would be like designing an offensive game scheme without studying the game film. You didn't devise a game plan until you saw a defensive formation that didn't match up. Scanlon had laid it out during their phone call from the Lucerne. He wanted to deliver copies of the log to the New York Police Department, another set to the Commissioner of the National Football League, another to a half dozen hand-picked reporters, then call a news conference in Manhattan, preferably on Wednesday, two days away.

He'd said, "It will take that long to get it set up. We announce we are unilaterally voiding your contract with the New York Stars on grounds of fraud and bad faith. We keep the money. Put it in escrow in lieu of damages we'll be seeking against the team in court." Scanlon took a breath. "This isn't going to be pretty. But if we break the story, we can control it. I can't see any criminal repercussions."

"You're forgetting two things," Brody said.

"Okay," Scanlon said.

"We still don't know why the Stars would acquire flawed players."

"Well, to lose."

"But why?"

"I think that will come out once authorities get involved. What's the second?"

"I'll be out of work."

"Jesus, tell me you're not serious."

Brody answered with silence. The idea of walking was unthinkable, especially now that he'd won the starting job.

Scanlon said, "Okay then, I have one more thing. I was going to wait until later, but since nothing seems to budge you, what the hell."

Scanlon said the family of the college kid in the car crash had filed a motion. He'd just been served. They were seeking further damages and asking the court to attach his Stars bonus. "We put your money in escrow in New York," Scanlon explained, "that makes it difficult for the Detroit lawyers to grab."

Shay was on the extension. She announced she was leaving for LA.

Scanlon argued that he needed to take her deposition to establish a chain of possession. "I need you to say on the record that Eric Smith provided you with the document. I can get a flight tomorrow morning, hire a court reporter in New York."

"I'm leaving Thursday," Shay said. She added she could be back by Sunday.

And then Brody rearranged Scanlon's plans. "You don't need to come to New York until Monday," he said. "We can deal with everything then."

"What's Monday?" Scanlon asked.

Brody said, "A football game."

Two hours later he was on the balcony, back from a long hike through Central Park as the sun went down. He wasn't looking at the skyline and the lights anymore. He was hearing the noises below. Angry car horns. Speeding cabs rushing fares at fatal speeds up First Avenue.

He heard Shay behind him. She'd been in the bedroom, the door closed, when he returned from the walk.

"What's the movie you're up for?" he asked.

She hesitated, then said, "They're remaking *The Pitfall*. Noir is making a comeback, and they're looking for a fresh face. The original had Lizabeth Scott. I get it, I'll have to dye my hair, maybe cut it, too."

"I'm sure you'll look great," he said.

She stepped from the doorway and sat down. He saw her travel bag sitting in the doorway. "I thought you were leaving on Thursday," he said.

"I've done what I set out to do. I've got other options now. Apparently, you seem to think you don't."

Brody waited a few moments to answer. "I'd be hurting the team."

"If I understand those papers of Eric's, your team has other priorities."

"Not last Sunday they didn't."

"Or, maybe you're trying to prove those columnists wrong. One game wonder, all that."

He'd thought about it. "Somebody tells you that you can't do something, can't go somewhere, that only motivates you more. That's football. That's a lot of things. You keep going, don't you? Seems to me you've been there."

He'd been listening to her war stories more than she probably realized.

Brody leaned forward. "Look, I bring down Montan with that log, a lot of players are going to sink with him. I cannot do that. My guess is, that's what held back Smith, too." He paused again, then added, "Besides, that's changed now."

"What's changed?"

"The players. You should have seen that locker room Sunday. That's the way it happens. One game can do it."

She stared at him for a couple of seconds, then said, "Listen to yourself. You're no different than he is."

"Who?"

"Montan."

"That's cold."

"Think about it. He wants to lose. You want to win. But both of you are manipulating the team. Christ, Derek, somebody's been *murdered.* And you're just going to ignore that, and God knows what else? And for what? For a two-hour high afterwards?" She laughed. "Shit, I thought I had a problem. You're more of an addict than I am."

She got up, looking as if she wanted to leave. Instead, she gripped the railing and looked out at the city.

Shay said, "You know, I like you. I don't know why. You're cocky. Delusional. Self-obsessed. Moody. But you don't fold, and I guess that's it." She paused, watching him closely. "I want to help you. But you keep too many secrets, Derek Brody."

"You seem sure about that," he said.

"The way I figure, that's why this guy Montan picked you."

More angry horns below, then silence.

Finally, he asked, "What secrets do you want to know?"

★   ★   ★

Shay listened quietly while he told her.

She said, "But you were really the driver?"

He nodded slowly. "When I crossed the line, I thought the old man was trying to grab the wheel, but actually he was pulling me down, trying to cover me."

"And he's been doing that ever since," she said.

He looked in her eyes and asked, "How did you know?"

"I knew it when I saw you play. The way you're handling all this only confirmed it. You're possessed. That usually doesn't come naturally. It requires motivation."

"You sound like a shrink."

No, she thought, an actor. Every character has its center.

He spoke quietly. The city drowned his words. She told him.

"I said, *I let everybody down.* My old man. The team. The town." His eyes glistened. "Twenty-four hours earlier, after the state final, you should have seen it. Five hundred cars behind the team bus, crossing that bridge to the Upper Peninsula. After we hit town, the cars kept driving up and down main street. For *hours.* When I fell asleep that night, I could hear them honking."

She asked, "You haven't been back there, have you?"

"I promised myself I'd go back when I win the Super Bowl."

"You think winning is going to change that?"

"I really don't know anything else to do," he said.

She walked toward the door, but stopped and turned behind him. She massaged his shoulders for a while, both of them silent.

"Sometimes I wonder," he finally said. "I know the old man was trying to help me, but I shouldn't have listened. I should have taken responsibility. Gone to prison for a long time."

She palmed his cheeks. His face was warm and flushed. She pulled him close to her and said, "But you have, Derek. You've built one for yourself right out there on that football field."

★   ★   ★

Later that night, he spent an hour in bed thinking about what she'd said, unable to sleep. He was glad the girl didn't leave. Not a girl, really. Girls asked him to sign their hats and bras and panties. Girls took everything he said at face value. She was a woman. That's what he liked about her. And that's why he wanted her to stay.

His hand began to hurt. He thought about the log sheet, the leverage Montan had on the players. Maybe that's why V.R. had blown a gasket in the quarterback meeting. Maybe Montan had leverage on the head coach, too, the leverage being Tommy Molito. But if Molito was the leverage, maybe he wasn't working with Montan. He'd only assumed so because Eric Smith had learned about Carl Montan's history from Molito, that they were somehow hooked up. And maybe they were, but in a different way.

He had some time tomorrow, his day off. He also had to report to the NFL offices on Park Avenue at mid-afternoon, his interview with Raymond Bullard.

He climbed out of bed and went to the bathroom. He popped four Advil.

When he stepped back into the hall he noticed the light from a small bed lamp casting a glow in the open doorway of the guest room. He walked to the living room and sat down.

He looked at the painting of Y.A. Tittle for a while. He couldn't see the blood running down his face in the dim light, the helmet on the grass, but he knew they were there. The thought of them made him pull out the Time-Life book with the original photograph. He flipped on a table lamp. He hadn't read the description under the photo in years.

> With the stunned look of a gladiator who realizes his competitive days are numbered, veteran New York Giant Y.A. Tittle kneels on the turf after a crushing tackle in 1964 by a 270-pound Pittsburgh Steeler. Tittle gamely played out the rest of the season, but it was his last.

As he walked back toward his bedroom he saw the light still on in the guest room. He moved quietly down the hall and halted at the threshold.

He expected to see her shape under the blankets, Shay asleep. Maybe the script on her nightstand, or in her lap. She'd been taking it to bed with her, like he did the playbook.

She was sitting against the headboard, her eyes closed, the sheet pulled up just over her bare breasts. The blinds were open, a cool breeze blowing in through the window.

"You sleeping?" he asked.

She didn't open her eyes, but said, "No."

He didn't see the script. "What are you doing?"

"Lying here. Or sitting, I guess."

She opened her eyes. "Actually, neither," she said. She put her arms out, the sheet falling away, her nipples the color of her hair.

She said, "I've been waiting for you."

"I can't use my hand much," he said.

She smiled and said, "You don't need a hand."

When he kissed her all of it left his mind. The team, the coach, the game, the league, Bullard, Montan, Y.A. Tittle—and the move he'd make on Tommy Molito tomorrow at noon.

CHAPTER

★ ★ ★ **28** ★ ★ ★

The Mole wasn't sitting in the big circular booth when Brody arrived at Tommy's Place just before noon. Head coach Vincent Read was. Brody slid into the seat, V.R. spreading cards face up on the table, setting up an odd version of solitaire.

V.R. said, "Tommy told me you were dropping by."

Brody didn't care the coach was there. It didn't matter. Little did. Not now.

V.R. picked up one of the cards, showing him its face. "Okay, what do you see?"

"One-eyed jack."

V.R. put the card back down, placing it the pattern of cards. "No, look. I've been thinking. This is the Lions defense in the 4–3. Normally, defensive ends opposite offensive tackles, tackles opposite guards." He picked up the jack again. "This is the fucking right tackle."

Brody could see it now.

V.R. continued, "This year, though, they've shown a tendency to move the tackle in the gap between center and guard." He placed the card there.

"Okay, on running plays."

"Right, but not always." V.R. paused. "But when they do, you don't want to zip it. You want to audible and snitch it up. Goddamn line rookies were animals Sunday, weren't they? I mean, they play like that again, they'll clear the right side right out of there and Danny Davis can snitch it right up Detroit's ass. All he has to do is hang onto the ball."

"I can see it," Brody said.

"It may work on a bleeder, too."

"Or, you could pimp it with Bundy. If Reggie can take out the left corner and the slot blow out the strong safety, Danny could break it big."

"Yeah, that, too. I'll get Hadley on it. Fax it over to you tonight."

The head coach began arranging the cards again.

"V.R.," Brody said.

"Yeah."

Brody waited for his eyes.

"You know what Bobby was talking about yesterday? Pissed you off? Me, I don't give a shit, as long you call winning plays."

V.R. hesitated, then said, "You don't know Bobby. But I do."

But Brody had been thinking about Bobby Loeb, too. The bad advice in camp. The paper boy comment from the Packer linebacker. He'd seen Loeb talking to Green Bay players on the sideline last Sunday.

Brody said, "What I'm saying, this Tommy, what's your story with this guy?"

V.R. dealt himself a couple more cards, saying, "Don't make trouble for yourself, kid."

Brody plunged ahead anyway. He was going to take a gamble with Tommy Molito, but now he decided to lay it on V.R. He told him that he was with Smith the night he was killed. "And he told me a few things. I thought at first he was just whacked out, but funny thing, a lot of what he said has come true."

Brody leaned closer, continuing, "Tommy told Eric Smith some things about Carl. So I'm figuring, if he told Smith, that means he also told you."

V.R. looked up. "You don't want to go there."

"I already am," Brody said.

V.R. reached for an El Producto and motioned for a box of matches from the waitress. She lit the cigar for him. Brody waited until she left, then continued.

"Look, I'm the one that's taking a risk here, coach. I'm sitting with you. But as far as I know, I could be talking to Carl right now."

V.R., his head back, puffed until he had an ash, looking at Brody down the length of the cigar. Finally, he took it out of his mouth and pointed the tip at him.

"I've spent thirty fucking years in this league. That's worth something, not all of it on a goddamn chalk board, but *worth* something. You don't think I realize I'm in the triangle?"

"Triangle?" Brody wondered.

"The league's Bermuda fucking triangle. The Stars. The Cards. The Bucks. You get in any three, you can only get a job with the others. You get in, but you can't get out."

"Unless you win."

V.R. shook his head. "Not going to happen."

"That's exactly what I'm saying," Brody said.

V.R. drew on the cigar again, studying him. "You think I don't realize the hand they've dealt? But I guess they fucked up with you." He leaned close. "I want you to know, Brody, I would have started you."

"You did start me."

"The word came down first."

"From who?"

V.R. said, "I think you already know the answer."

Brody tapped his finger on the cards, "You know, Montan's got shit on a dozen players. But I haven't seen your name on any lists."

"I don't bet football."

"That's what Eric said, but what about Tommy? What about league security?"

"This is a legitimate establishment. What they going to do, bust me for looking at some T&A?"

"But Eric Smith told me Molito is connected."

V.R. didn't answer. He raked in the cards, stacked them into a pile.

Brody said, "I see. So nobody says a thing. And you get the golf cart."

V.R. slapped the deck down. "Look, I figure I've got one year left on this team. Long as I'm in the triangle, I might as well drive."

"But you were picked to lose, just like the others. Can't you see it? And you want me to run your plays?"

"They don't call the plays. They're smarter than that."

"*They?*" Brody asked.

V.R. dropped the cigar in an ashtray. "Like I was saying, don't make trouble for yourself. We do three hours on Sunday. Let the rest take care of itself."

V.R. slid out of the booth and stood up. He surveyed the club: two topless girls ground in the laps of two businessmen at a nearby table, then two dancers working the brass poles on the stage.

Finally, he turned to Brody. "You need a ride somewhere, or you still want to wait for Tommy?"

Brody said he was staying.

V.R. nodded, resigned about it. "I'll tell him you're out here. In fact, I'll tell him to answer all your questions. But as far as today is concerned, our talk, I was never here."

He started walking.

"You didn't answer my question," Brody shouted. "Why's he glued to you, V.R.?"

Vincent Read shouted back over his shoulder. "Call it protection."

★   ★   ★

Ten minutes later, Tommy Molito came out of the dancers' dressing room, a girl on each side, his cellular at his ear. He walked straight to the booth. Brody rose. Molito flipped the phone shut and hugged Brody, patting him on the back.

The Mole stepped back and said, "Which will it be, shooter, the blonde or the brunette?"

"Neither," Brody said.

The smile disappeared. Molito made a motion with his fingers. The girls left, disappearing into the dimly lit booths lining the topless club.

Molito lit a cigarette. "Vinnie told me to take care of you."

Brody slid back into the booth. "V.R. told me not to ask."

"Vinnie is a smart man," Molito said.

Molito didn't sit down. He took another drag on the smoke, leaving it between his lips. He bent over, resting his weight on his knuckles. "So, you still curious?"

Brody nodded.

Molito gestured toward the bar. A guy in his thirties, wearing a dark suit, came out of the shadows, the driver who'd picked him up his first day in camp. Molito whispered in his ear. He nodded his head, then turned and walked away.

Molito checked his watch. "You got to be somewhere?"

"Not until three. Why?"

Molito said, "You want answers, we're gonna have to take a ride."

A black Chrysler town car was waiting at the canopy outside, the guy from the bar behind the wheel. Molito opened the door for him and they both sat in the back. Molito sat side saddle, his back against the door.

Molito told the driver, "Jump on the Queens, Joey."

Soon they were on the freeway, heading south. Molito said, "So, I hear the line is four points in Detroit. That'll move. How's the hand?"

"I'll play," Brody said. In fact, the hand was feeling much better, but he avoided details.

Molito said, "Some people are saying you may be the best thing this town's seen since Broadway Joe. You know, they give him a lot of shit, too. Said he was hanging with the wrong kind of people. He didn't give a fuck. And neither did anybody else, especially after he made geldings out of the Colts."

They talked football for a few minutes, Molito critiquing players around the league. He knew football. He knew the strengths and weaknesses of teams. He knew which Lions were injured and who was likely not to recover for the Monday game.

Brody saw the Brooklyn Bridge out his window, the Manhattan skyline. He said, "Where we going, anyway?"

Molito said, "Just a few more miles, shooter." He glanced out the back window. "You know, you do good in this town you make a lot of friends, some you don't even know you have. Some of them are good, some of them are not so good. This man I'm taking you to see, he's good. He says bring you over anytime. I mean, that just don't happen to anybody."

Molito looked at the driver, "Little faster, Joey."

The Chrysler accelerated.

Brody thought: Vinnie. Tommy. Joey. He remembered that Scorsese movie *Goodfellas*, nobody Tom or Vincent or Joe. All of them calling each other schoolyard nicknames, but playing with real guns.

It suddenly dawned on Brody: He'd gotten into the car with them and had no way out. Tommy and Joey. Where were they taking him, to the fucking godfather? That's the way Scorsese showed it. They say they're taking you to a meeting, then . . .

"A little more gas, Joey."

The Chrysler rocked back and forth gently as the driver switched lanes, speeding past a cluster of cars.

"Carl Montan," Brody said, blurting it out.

Molito looked over. "Slime fuck. Forget about it. What else you want to know?"

"Eric Smith told me he worked in Las Vegas."

"Eric was right, dead fucking right."

Tommy Molito reached behind his belt. Brody expected to see a wallet. Instead, he saw a stainless semi-automatic, Ruger written on the side. Molito smiling.

Brody's mouth went dry.

Molito glanced forward, saying, "You seeing what I'm seeing, Joey?"

"I see," the driver said, his head nodding.

Molito gestured with the gun, as if it was an extension of his hand. "Carl Montan, think about it. I mean, what kind of fucking name is that? Sounds like a perfume. In LA, everybody knew him as Charlie Montemarano. But the man had no respect for his heritage. At least that's what the old timers say."

Brody thought if he was going to die, he might as well die knowing. "He was in a *family*?"

"Shit," Molito said, drawing out the word. "He did some lifting with a Fratiano, nothing heavy, but he never got made. Even fucking LA didn't want anything to do with him. Then he falls in with that crowd at the Sands, and suddenly he's too fucking good for everybody. Again, at least that's what the old timers say."

"The Sands. That's not there anymore, right?"

"They blew it up. Made a big party out of it. In its hey day, Montan beached the whales."

"Whales?"

"High rollers. You keep 'em at the casino. Get 'em booze. Get 'em broads. Get 'em young boys, whatever it takes, as long as they stay and keep spending money at the games."

"So how does he go from there to football?"

"They say he started hanging around the sports book. Somebody picks up the phone to the university. Reminds the football program of all the money old man Hughes gave the college. Somebody says we got a guy for your scouting operation. Teach him the ropes." Molito paused, then added, "But now you're getting into an area where I can't help you."

Molito looked out the back window again, then racked the slide on the Ruger. He rested the piece on the top of the bench seat, Brody staring down the muzzle.

The Mole leaned forward. "Take Sixth, Joey." Almost shouting it. The Chrysler swerved across three lanes, its tires screeching. The back tire hit the corner of the exit ramp, Brody lurching forward, out of the gun's line of sight.

When the car slowed Molito was looking at him, bemused. He laughed.

"Joey, I think shooter here thought we were going to do him."

The driver turned around, grinning. "No fucking way"

Molito tucked the gun back in his waistband, then slapped his knee. "You thought that. Don't fucking tell me you didn't think that."

"You pull a gun, what am I supposed to think?"

Molito shrugged. "I thought we had a tail. A Crown Vic back there. You can't be too careful."

Brody spun around. He saw nothing but pavement.

"Forget about it," Molito said. "We lost him."

Brody said, "I want to know where the fuck we're going."

Molito smiled. "Bensonhurst. You'll like it, shooter. It's a colorful neighborhood."

★   ★   ★

They were the first streets in New York that Brody didn't see cruising taxis. He saw intersections without traffic lights. He saw duplexes with aluminum siding and wrought iron gates painted white. Most porches had metal awnings. He saw tiny front lawns with little shrines to the Virgin Mary. It was as if somebody had transplanted a small town from the Forties in Brooklyn.

They cornered a street marked with two signs: The top 18TH AVE-NUE, underneath, CRISTOFORO COLOMBO BOULEVARD. The street was lined with delicatessens and bakeries and food markets and pizza parlors and espresso bars. Most of their signs were in Italian.

Molito said it was the real Little Italy. "This is a neighborhood. You want Italian, you come here, not that fucking tourist trap downtown with all those fucking slants up the street in Chinatown."

They stepped out of the Chrysler at a storefront, the driver parking in a no-parking zone, but not worried about it. There was a small door and a peephole, something scripted in Italian across the top.

Molito rang the buzzer and turned to Brody, "The man I'm taking you to see, he's agreed to talk to you, but I will not give you his last name."

"Okay."

"You wouldn't know it to look at him, but he's got the cancer. He's come back to the old neighborhood to finish his life. So you must not only show him the proper respect, but I'm asking you, as a friend, to be kind."

The door swung open to the smell of dark roasted coffee and cooking sausage. There were maybe ten people inside, all older men. Most sat at tables, a couple at a bar, nobody speaking English. They walked the length of a dull hardwood floor to the back of the club.

The man was sitting alone at a round table with a demitasse cup of espresso and a couple of newspapers. Maybe seventy, Brody guessed. He had silver hair and a high hairline, coal black pupils wide open in the dim light. He was wearing nicely pressed gray slacks and a solid brandy shirt, buttoned at the collar.

He ignored Brody at first, standing up to hug Tommy Molito. Then he patted Joey, patting him on the shoulder, saying something in Italian. The driver walked to the front of the club.

Molito introduced Brody. "Uncle Sal, this is Derek Brody. Derek, this is my Uncle Salvatore. We all call him Sal around here."

The man rested his hands on his hips, his eyes traveling from Brody's feet to his face. He reached out and gently grabbed Brody's chin, angling his face sideways, examining his scar.

"They do this to you in prison?" he asked.

Brody said, "No, that got me there."

"Good," he said, nodding. "You did your time like a man."

Then the uncle stretched his arms out. Brody walked into his embrace, not knowing what else to do. He smelled like an old barber shop back in Michigan, where his father took him for his first clip. Brody hugged back, thinking, if only his dad could see him now.

The uncle gripped his shoulders, then put him at arm's length, shaking him a little.

"Young man, you made me a lot of money Sunday. I said to myself, these writers, these people on the radio, they don't know. They don't see what I see."

Brody felt like he was outside of himself, watching the entire scene.

"Sit," the uncle said. "I have cannoli and coffee coming. Or, perhaps you'd like some lunch."

"I'm fine," Brody said.

Molito sat next to his uncle and talked for a good minute in Italian, the uncle listening, nodding, his eyes occasionally glancing at Brody.

When Molito was done, the uncle said, "So, my nephew tells me you've found yourself in a situation."

"You could call it that," Brody said.

"Apparently you have some concerns about Charlie Montemarano. Excuse my language, but he always was a no good sonovabitch."

Molito said, "Uncle Sal worked the best hotels. In the good old days, right Sal?"

The uncle raised his eyebrows. "Tough, yes. But *good*." He shrugged. "People, they're going to gamble. It's in their nature. For some it becomes a problem. For others, they can come or go. But we never went after the children. Not like these people they've got running things from Harvard and Cornell."

"Children?" Brody said.

He nodded. "They'll tell you they're creating a family atmosphere. No more mobsters. 'We have pirate ships and circuses and movies. Good family entertainment.' " He turned to Tommy Molito, asking, "What's that word?"

"They call it imagineering," Molito said.

He nodded again. "These people are very smart. They're simply getting the children attached to going at a very young age."

A waiter brought the cannoli and a pot of espresso.

"Eat," the uncle said.

Brody bit into the cannoli. It was good, not too sweet, like other cannoli he'd had.

The uncle said, "We no longer try to fight them. They have too many resources. Everybody sold to the big chains. We had the Teamsters pension fund. But they have junk bonds. Some old interests are still there, but they run limo companies, ancillary businesses. The big hotels want to keep a few of us around for more of this *imagineering*. They figure it wouldn't be Vegas if you didn't see a few gangsters around." Molito was nodding, satisfied with what his uncle was saying, satisfied he'd delivered a starting NFL quarterback for his uncle's amusement, Brody thought.

Brody said, "I'm not sure what this has to do with my problem."

The uncle took a sip of the espresso, set down the cup and held up one finger. "Montemarano, he worked for Hughes at the Sands. But nobody really worked *for* the old man. They worked for the people around him. Hell, nobody *saw* the old man."

"I know about Hughes," Brody said.

"What you may not know, is that the old man had this new venture, Sports Network Incorporated. He was looking for a piece of football. In 1970, he offers ten million to Rozelle for a broadcast package, but Rozelle goes with ABC. That's how we got Monday night games. But these people around Hughes, they saw the future."

"I'm not sure I see the connection," Brody said.

"Years later, they find Hughes on that boat in the Bahamas with needle tracks all over his arms. You think that's some kind of accident? Then this new company shows up, Mecca, buying everything in sight. It's privately held. No annual report. But you check the names of the stockholders. Every one worked for Hughes one time or another. This guy David Harvey, he's their boy out front."

Brody glanced at Molito. "Mecca, don't they make some kid movies?"

The uncle answered, "Children, like I was saying. You won't find their product in my house."

"'You're saying Montan worked for Hughes and now he works for Mecca."

"'Independent contractor. That's the way it's done."

"And Papa Goldman just happens to hire him."

"Papa Goldman lost a lot of money at the Sands. We all knew about it. Hell, we were all trying to beach him, too."

"You're saying this Harvey is after the Stars?" Brody said.

"He's got football broadcasts. He's got friends inside besides Goldman. He's got that TV magazine, making it look like they're cleaning up the league."

"So."

The uncle raised his voice, his eyes darkening. "People in this country, they have no fucking idea what's going on. Twenty years ago you had Vegas, then Atlantic City. Now you've got games in half the states. You think that's another accident? They got the politicians, who want the tax. They've got the newspapers and advertising, selling good wholesome fun. But listen to me, *I know*. Average guy loses his house, his children's education, that's no trip to Disney World."

The uncle coughed, his face flushing red. He held up his hand, asking for a moment.

Brody asked Molito, "What's he trying to tell me?"

Molito said, "He's saying these new people are nationwide, except in one area. They don't have football, shooter. A hundred billion a year. Illegal books. Office pools, you name it."

The uncle added, "And this Mecca's got satellites. They got broadcasts. Pay-per-view. They got everything to bring it right into your home. Use your Visa card if you have to. Only one thing they *don't* have."

Brody said, "A football team."

The uncle smiled at Molito. "I told you, didn't I? He's a smart one." He looked back at Brody. "The league has its rules. That kind of thing, you got to change from the inside."

Brody mulled it over a couple of moments. He asked, "If what you say is true, why don't your people stop it?"

The uncle nodded to Molito. "I like this young man even better now that I've met him. Tommy, I want you to take good care of him, make sure he gets anything he needs."

His smile gone now, the uncle said to Brody, "What would you have us do, call a news conference? Besides, it's not the way it used to be. Our young people, our families, they spit on our traditions. All they want to do is raise hell."

He squeezed Molito's shoulder, adding, "Except for the son of my sister, of course."

Brody wondering if Molito and this uncle of his were engaging in a little imagineering of their own. "You're forgetting one thing," he said. "Papa Goldman says he'll never leave New York."

"The team doesn't have to leave," the uncle said.

"But he says it's not for sale."

The two Italians eyed each other. Molito said, "You shouldn't spend so much time with the sports pages."

The uncle opened the *Daily News* and pushed it across the table. Brody focused on a gossip column, the names of Goldman and Harvey in bold face type. He stared at it for a while, the other-worldly feeling leaving him now, replaced with something else.

He pushed the paper back. The uncle grabbed his hand, then motioned for the other. He turned them palms up and held them, the left still bandaged.

"You need to take care of these," he said. "It would be a shame to see them go to waste."

Brody smelled the old barber shop again.

"I've got two pieces of advice for you. First, stay away from this man Bullard. He was dirty in the desert. That doesn't change."

"I figured that," Brody said.

Brody waited. When the man didn't say anything, he asked, "And the second?"

The uncle released his hands and leaned back. "Just an observation," he said, waving. "But who am I to say?"

"Go ahead," Brody said. He picked up the cannoli.

The uncle wagged his finger like a scolding parent. "Don't run the fucking ball so much. It's a good way to get hurt in the pros."

CHAPTER

★ ★ ★ **29** ★ ★ ★

A light rain was falling when Carl Montan boarded the *Donzi* on Tuesday afternoon at Pier 83. The tender captain handed him a rain slick. Montan slid it on and took refuge under the canopy as the boat sped into the harbor. He thought, the man should do business on land, like everybody. At this point, he was sick of the goddamn yacht.

As they neared the *Dorothy*, he saw someone in a yellow slick at the stern. The slick appeared again as Montan climbed the boarding stairway. Closer, he recognized.

The goddamn Surfer.

At the top, the Surfer said, "He's waiting for you in the main salon."

Montan stopped and glared, momentarily studying the raindrops migrating across the bruises on the Surfer's cheek. He had a few words in mind, but decided to move on. A minute later, he was standing in the yacht's salon, David Harvey there in a leather and chrome director's chair, his legs crossed.

"Sit down, Carl," Harvey said.

Montan sank into a leather couch, trying to look casual.

Harvey said, "I trust you were greeted."

Montan nodded.

Harvey said, "One of the things we try to teach in New Start is proper manners. That's something that carries over well into adult-hood for most of my boys. That and loyalty."

Montan thought, the Surfer, one of Harvey's old butt boys.

Harvey tossed a cassette tape, Montan catching it high in his ribs. He didn't have to look at it to know it was a copy of Derek Brody's conversation with his attorney.

Harvey said, "You think I would have turned you loose for three years without some checks and balances?"

"I presume you've heard this?" Montan finally said.

Harvey nodded.

"Then you know that Brody hasn't decided. Odds are he'll do nothing. He goes public, he'll have a lot of explaining to police. He values his career too much." Montan paused. "Besides, Brody's my problem. There's no connection to Mecca here."

Harvey remained silent. Under other circumstances, Montan might have found his appearance humorous. He was wearing tight jeans and a sweat shirt, one of those ridiculous captain's hats.

Montan said, "Am I sensing a problem here?"

"Only if you make it one," Harvey said.

Montan had this urge now. Pull out a nice Hoyo and light it right there, wait for Harvey to ask him to put it out, saying smoking was offensive. Then tell him this was fucking America, that the right not to be offended was nowhere in the Constitution. On the job for three years. Making it all happen for the man.

Instead, Montan said, "You wanted a loser. I gave you one. And they were clean losses. Every one."

"Sunday excluded, of course," Harvey said.

"They got lucky."

Harvey rose and walked to the bar, offering Montan a drink. Montan told him it was too late for orange juice and too miserable outside for iced tea. Harvey worked a couple moments behind the bar anyway and emerged with a snifter.

He handed it to Montan. "Remy Martin, Louis XIII, isn't it?"

Harvey sat on the other end of the couch. "Your methods haven't changed that much through the years, have they Carl?"

Montan lifted the glass. "I thought we were never to discuss details."

Harvey smiled. "We'll make an exception this once."

Montan crossed his legs, leaning back a little. "It's a game of mistakes. The team that makes the fewest wins. It's like playing against the house odds."

Harvey said, "Go on."

"The players who can make a difference are like the whales. They have a need to put it all on the line, go down gambling. But to play like that, you better have some focus. All I did was take off the guard rails, enable the distractions. Just like the casinos. Soon, the house odds come into play."

Harvey pondered the analogy for a while, then said, "I'm not a gambler, Carl. I leave that to fools like Goldman and a public that seems to have nothing better to do with their lives. I believe in certainties. And one thing I'm certain of is that I will make a very public, successful offer to buy the New York Stars outright next week."

Montan nodded, agreeing. "The Stars can't beat Detroit. Brody's going to play injured."

Harvey shrugged. "The team wins, the team loses. It doesn't matter now."

"I thought you were concerned about the league vote."

"I am," Harvey said. He smiled. "And you've laid some very nice groundwork."

Harvey uncrossed his legs and tilted his hat. "Losing isn't the only way to discredit an organization. There are other ways to create the public demand it be sold."

"I'm not sure I understand," Montan said.

"Flagrant and persistent violation of league rules and policy. Dirty players. That's quite a scandal. This quarterback of yours could start it rolling. If he doesn't, there's other ways."

Montan saw where he was going, but wasn't sure he liked it.

Harvey continued, "A lot of players would lose their jobs, of course. As well as a team executive, a key executive whose hiring practices would reflect badly upon the owner's watch. Of course, that executive would have to be someone I could absolutely trust to remain discreet in face of the humiliation. There might be some criminal charges, but nothing serious."

Montan finished the cognac in a gulp. "You mean someone to take the fall," he said.

Harvey smiled. "And there would be another million in it for you, of course."

★   ★   ★

It wasn't until his cab found gridlock traffic on 34th Street that Carl Montan realized. He remembered the old adult bookstores and peep shows there, the hawkers on the sidewalk, luring customers inside. The place all family fun now. He remembered how Mecca had come in with the proposal, the city helping with the condemnations and the vice busts, everyone working together to replace the sin strip near the Garden with that good, clean fun.

That's when he realized he'd been set up.

He thought, if the Surfer told Harvey about the log and Brody's attorney, he told him about Eric Smith. Surfer walks into New York homicide, lays it all out. Takes a deal for immunity. *That* was a scandal and a clean motive, the Surfer swearing Montan had ordered Smith killed to protect his executive position on the team. Most likely, they'd bring in Raymond Bullard. Flip him, too. Have two witnesses against him, Bullard knowing nothing about the Mecca deal. Maybe a third witness: Squat, once the shit started hitting the fan.

And what was his defense? Only Goldman and Petrus could connect him to Harvey. They were bought off and had their own secrets. The only other witness who'd seen him within a hundred feet of David Harvey was Dominique Goldman. But *she* had asked him to accompany her to the yacht, and he'd pretended not to know the man. Once the prosecution started digging, they'd find his sheet in LA, his connection there. They'd find out about the Turk. They wouldn't flip the Turk, because they never flipped the shooter. Carl Montan could see a five-day trial and a lot of photographs and stories they both could read while filing appeals on death row.

He gave the hack a new destination.

Twenty minutes later the cab dropped him off at the stakeout apartment across from the Lucerne. He found the Turk getting up from the couch. He switched the TV off with the remote, a hard-on poking at the zipper in his jeans.

He started to report. "The bim's booked a flight to LA. Then Brody picked her up."

Montan walked to the window, looking out at nothing in particular, but thinking. He asked, "That whore back at Stony Brook, the Surfer get dirty on that?"

"I thought you didn't want to know the details."

Montan turned. "I do now."

The Turk sat down and lit a cigarette. "It was fucked up, really. We put the equipment locker with the ho in the back of the Vic and start driving. I'm thinking what am I going to do? Haven't told the Surfer what's gone down yet, but I'm figuring, what the fuck, he don't need to know anyway. Pretty soon the bitch is banging inside the locker, needing fucking air. But the Surfer can't hear it, because he's got earphones on. So I figure, shit, let the locker do it. Be nice and clean."

The Turk hit the cigarette again. "Then I get thinking, well, shit, I'm not going to lug this bitch around myself. So I tell the Surfer we got something to get rid of in the back seat and wonder if he's got any suggestions. 'Cause he knows Long Island pretty well."

"Did you tell him it was the whore?"

"I said *something*. That's all. Surfer says we can go to Montauk Point where he surfs, saying at night there's nobody out there."

"So you dumped her from the beach?"

"No, get this. Surfer wants to stop at this shack he's got out there and get his fucking board. I say what the fuck you need that for? And he says, maybe the surf's up. And I say, what about the sharks? You told me once they feed at night. And the crazy fucker, he says he doesn't care. So we stop and get the board, and it's pitch black by the time we get there, nobody around. We drive right to the beach. I start to open the trunk, but when I turn around, he's already heading for the water with the fucking board. Last I see him, he's paddling out, yelling something about the tide."

The Turk dragged the cigarette again. "So I pull the bitch out myself. I mean, what if somebody pulls up? So I wade out there in water up to my chest, and almost fucking drown turning the ho loose in the tide past the shore break."

"Surfer's gone?"

"Fucking disappeared. I go back to the beach, and all I can hear is waves, and now I'm figuring, the stupid motherfucker has drowned, or he's shark food with the ho."

The Turk chuckled. "I'm just about to leave and the guy walks out of the water with his board, dripping wet. I say, where the fuck were you? I'm all over his ass. And you know what he says?"

Montan shook his head.

"He says, 'night patrol.' That's what he calls surfing when it's dark."

More distance, no direct involvement, Montan thought, just like Smith's apartment.

The Turk butted the smoke. "By the way, you heard from the Surfer?"

"I just saw him," Montan said. "He's traded in his board for a big boat."

Montan told the Turk the whole story, told him how he saw the setup coming with Harvey, the Surfer at Montauk confirming it.

"But I told the Surfer what went down on the way back in the car," the Turk said. "I was pissed."

"But the Surfer didn't see it. You telling him only makes it better. He can say he was scared to come forward, his conscience eating at him. His lawyer will run with that."

The Turk said, "You think this Brody can beat Detroit?"

"No," Montan said. "But the entire team can."

Montan sprawled in the recliner, angling it back a little.

The Turk rose, scratched his hair with his fingertips. He said, "You want my opinion?"

Montan didn't answer.

The Turk reached down behind the overstuffed chair, retrieving the remote in one hand, and the Llama .22 in the other. "The way I see it," he said. "You want somebody to do something, you get something they want, then you put a fucking gun to their head and politely ask."

"That's out of the question."

"Not when you're out of answers. Brody and the team win, we're going away, one way or the other."

Montan had been thinking about that. Destroy the files tonight, leave them nothing. Go on the run. He wondered how long he'd last before they found him. Not the cops, but Harvey's personal security force.

Montan looked up. "Brody doesn't give a shit about anything but football."

The Turk hit the remote, then motioned to the TV, saying "We can look at film, too."

Montan glanced at the screen, expecting to see game footage. Instead, he saw poor video quality, dark images. A woman on top, her head pulsating in time with her hips.

He faced the Turk. "I'm not interested in your fuck films."

The Turk grinned. "This kind you can't buy in a store."

Montan looked again. Saw the corner of the window now, the low lighting. It was a telephoto shot, but he couldn't make out the faces.

He asked, "That's not Brody and the girl?"

"Got it last night."

Montan brought the recliner forward. "Based on what I heard on the phone tape, I thought what they had going was an act."

The Turk's eyes were glued on the screen. "Yeah, but tell me, Carl," he said, pointing the Llama at the screen. "That look like acting to you?"

CHAPTER
☆ ☆ ☆ **30** ☆ ☆ ☆

He blew off the meeting with Raymond Bullard at league head-quarters. Didn't even show. If Bullard wants him, he decided, let him find him. With a Monday game, he had two days off. They drove up the Hudson River in the Mercedes. They were like a couple of tourists, checking out the small rail towns, seeing West Point. They stayed in a motel near the academy. They made love and fell asleep watching old movies she brought, then drove back at sunset as dawn painted the cliffs along the Hudson with amber light.

When they arrived back at the apartment, V.R.'s game plan rolling off the fax machine. He'd designed a complex running attack, adding two dozen new audibles Brody had to memorize. By Thursday, the day his hand no longer felt pain, those circles he liked to draw on paper started collapsing on Derek Brody. For the first time since he'd arrived in New York, he was starting to feel like there was little he could control.

The team was amped, players knowing their agents and families would be watching on national TV. Pads were cracking; receivers were making diving catches. V.R. was barking at everybody. The Prodigy song was now elevated to ritual. Wallace and Cobb had come up with a dance for the tune, a cross between a line dance and a mash pit. There was talk of not only going 2-0, but straight to the playoffs. On Thursday, Brody stood on his stool in the locker room, telling everyone not to get too high, not to peak early. Everybody listened, nodding. Then they turned the music back on again.

Back at his apartment, the phone was ringing constantly. Somehow, his unlisted number had gotten out. Calls from stockbrokers and financial advisors and insurance salesmen filled his answering machine. Franky Carcaterra called several times, too, wanting to meet about the show. *Hard Copy* left a message, saying they wanted to interview him about the accident, the producer running a line, saying he'd talked to MADD and was offering him a chance to end years of criticism. Brody called Dominique Goldman. She claimed she hadn't given the number out.

He suspected Carl Montan.

He called Mike Scanlon from practice, at a dome pay phone. He told him about the meeting with Molito's uncle, the entire story. Scanlon wanted to know the uncle's full name. When he said he didn't know, Scanlon said, "Jesus, do you have any idea what this could do to you?" Brody didn't want to know. He wanted to know about this David Harvey and Mecca, was the scenario feasible?

"He does business in Hollywood; anything's possible," Scanlon said. "You know how that town started don't you?"

"They needed good weather."

"No, they wanted to be as far from the East as possible. They were trying to screw Edison out of the patent royalties for his motion picture camera. It's in the culture, only place in America where a signed contract doesn't mean a goddamn thing."

Brody said he didn't care who owned the team.

"Then bail, damn it," Scanlon said.

Not yet, Brody said, it was personal now.

On late Thursday afternoon, after practice, he put Shay Falan on an airplane to LA. He gave her three thousand dollars and told her to take her time booking the return. She tried to refuse. He slid the money into her blazer. He suggested she take the weekend to drive up the coastline to Malibu and beyond. She deserved the break, he said.

"I don't do well on solo vacations," she said.

"Then look at real estate," he said. "I'm convinced you're going to need a place up there one day."

She told him she wanted to return on Monday. After all, Scanlon wanted the deposition. He told her Scanlon planned to spend next week in New York, considering what was coming down. He'd given Scanlon permission to go public on Tuesday, adding, "unless I can find another way."

"You don't want me there, do you?" she said.

"Yes, I do," he said. "But these Monday games, I'm told they get pretty rowdy." He lied about the second part. He had to eliminate one of those circles for now.

Shay said there were sitcoms she could pursue. She added, "Maybe Tuesday, then, or Wednesday. I'll see how it goes."

He gave her the phone number to the team hotel and told her to call him there on Sunday night.

They kissed.

"Break a leg," he said.

"You, too."

"We don't say that," he said.

He lingered for a couple minutes, watching the 737 pull away from the gate. But when the jet disappeared down the tarmac, he pushed Shay Falan out of his mind. As he left Kennedy, he was starting to feel reckless, like a ten-yard run into the end zone with the seconds ticking off on the clock on the last play of the last game. You didn't worry what they were going to do to your body. There was nothing ahead to save it for.

He picked up the car phone, made a call. An hour later, he was sitting under a stuffed bison head with Frank Carcaterra at the Cowboy Bar.

Carcaterra made his pitch how they'd do it. An hour slot the day after each game. Brody would review the team's play, take questions from callers, then discuss the upcoming game.

"You've got the skin for it," Carcaterra said. "These fans can be brutal."

"Not to mention the host," he said.

Carcaterra shrugged. "Listen to the show for a month before you judge it. It's not so much about players. It's about fans. And it's about us, the people with the pens and the mikes."

The talk jock lowered his voice. "Look, I'm just trying to introduce some equal time. All this bullshit can only fly so long. Jordan puts a ball through a round fucking metal hoop fifteen times a night, bags eighty million in one year, signs some autographs and he's everybody's hero. I mean, think about it."

"You're saying he's overpaid?"

"You're not hearing what I'm saying here. Me, I'll go with the transit driver on midnights in the fucking Bronx. Guy making 35K a year and trying to get his kid to school every day without him getting shot. His old lady rags him into buying the new shoes the kid's seen Jordan wearing. The driver's old man is fucking dying of lung cancer in North Central, and he goes to see him one morning instead of taking the kid to school. The driver comes home, and his kid has been wasted by some homie for his Jordan Nikes. A month later, the midnight driver is in court, watching the homie plead out in juvie and he just fucking *stands* there. He doesn't sky the wood railing and kill the motherfucker, 'cause he's got another boy graduating and he's trying to set an example. He doesn't even get a paragraph in the *Post*'s crime roundup. But that's a fucking hero, man. And ain't nobody paying him a motherfucking thing, except to drive that fucking train."

Carcaterra took a breath.

Brody said, "Somebody you know?"

Carcaterra nodded slowly. "My old man. Ten years ago."

"So it's personal?"

"No, it's truth."

"Sometimes they're intertwined," Brody said.

Brody let a couple moments pass. "I'd like to do the show," he finally said. "But I need to know something first."

"Shoot," Carcaterra said. He sipped a Bud longneck.

"You ever play the game?"

"They wouldn't even let me carry towels."

"You study it much?"

Carcaterra leaned forward and raised his eyebrows. "Before I started doing sports rap, I was doing late-night advice in Cleveland. That answer your question?"

"You seem to know a lot about the mechanics of the passing game."

Carcaterra sat back, sensing where he was going now.

"Let me ask it this way," Brody said. "Front office ever give you a little background?"

"The Stars? Shit, no. They're talking to shadows, except Goldman's daughter. But she's always on the hustle."

"So players talk?"

"You get phone calls. That's another thing wrong with the Stars. Awful lot of dissing going on."

"Reggie."

"What?"

"Reggie Thompson, he's been messing with me since I arrived."

Carcaterra looked a little confused. "Shit, Reggie's too busy chasing the next party. At least that's what they say. I hardly know the man."

"Then who?" Brody demanded.

"I can't give you a name. You do a little homework, you can put it together."

"I don't have time for that."

"You've got all season."

Brody said, "You want me on the show, I need some kind of answer. Otherwise, as far as I know, you're just setting me up."

Carcaterra slammed the half-finished beer down. "Look, I don't give a shit. I thought I was doing you a favor."

Brody was saving something, now he went with it. He leaned forward. "Franky, you want to know what really happened back in Michigan?" Carcaterra curved both hands around the tall neck. "For the record?"

"Off for now, but you've got my word. We'll talk about it on the first show."

Brody wanted it out. Wanted it no longer over his head, if there ever would be a first show.

Brody said, "Agreed?"

Carcaterra nodded.

"Say it."

"Agreed," Carcaterra said.

He told him the whole story, Carcaterra listening, never asking a question. Brody expected some kind of commentary afterwards, but Carcaterra silently sipped his beer for a few moments.

Finally, Carcaterra said, "I'll give you a question. You give me the answer. Let's do it that way."

"Okay."

He lowered his voice. "Before you got here, who was supposed to be the man?"

"Bobby."

"That's a good answer."

No way, Brody thought. "But he got injured," he said.

"That he did."

"Bobby Loeb was the only one who'd talk to me."

Carcaterra took a last pull on the long neck. "Think about it."

"And he's been helping me along," Brody added.

Carcaterra raised his eyebrows and said, "From fucking day one."

★   ★   ★

The next day, Brody had his worst practice. He couldn't hit receivers. He couldn't remember audibles. Toby Headly tried to give him a lecture in the huddle, but stuttered out only a couple of consonants. Afterwards, V.R. called Brody to his office.

"Distracted?" he asked.

"I'm not used to throwing without pain."

V.R. chuckled, then his eyes darkened. "Like I told you, three hours on Sunday. That's all you can count on here."

"I'll hold you to that, too," Brody said.

And he walked out.

On Friday night, for the first time, they all came to his strategy session. Jedi Conlin, Toby Headly, the second string receivers. Brody dispensed with what was left of the Lonestar and filled the coffee table with snacks from the deli.

Fifteen minutes after they were supposed to start, Glamour Boy showed. He strutted past Brody without saying a word, four cans of Colt .45 dangling from his fingertips.

Brody thought, at least he's here. He wanted him at the apartment, but not only for the meeting. He'd been thinking about Bobby Loeb and Glamour Boy all day.

They watched film for two hours, looking at the coverage styles of players in the defensive backfield. Loeb kept focusing on the left Detroit corner, his defender. He was a rookie. Detroit felt obligated to start him because they'd paid him $6 million, the rook getting the money because he'd held out the entire training camp. It showed in the film, the new Lion unsure of himself in last Sunday's game, receivers giving him the slip with pro moves he'd never seen at field level.

"He's mine," Thompson said. "You just get the ball to me, Rick. That's all."

It was the only thing Glamour Boy said, but he kept repeating it. He had one Colt left when the meeting broke up. As the players drifted to the door, Brody motioned Glamour Boy aside. He asked him to stay after.

Thompson snickered. "You want me, or you want Uncle Tom?"

"I want the guy who plans to keep playing," Brody said.

He found Thompson slumped in the leather couch after the room cleared. When Brody sat, Thompson popped the top on his can and said, "You got this Colt to say what you gotta say. I drink fast, too."

Brody hesitated, then said, "Reggie, let me ask you something. You make circus catches all day long, but by my count, every time I've put it in your numbers, you drop the fucking ball."

Thompson said it like it was a rule. "Told you early on, Rick. I don't like it there."

"Why?"

"You never asked."

"I'm asking now."

Thompson stuck the malt liquor in his crotch and rubbed his bald dome. "All you need to know is that's what got me here."

"Where?"

"The fucking Stars."

Brody waited.

Thompson continued. "Fucking post over the middle, in the seam four years ago. San Francisco, sixth game. Motherfuckers hit me high and low. I was out for ten minutes, they said. Done it a dozen a times before. But that one, I couldn't forget it. Funny thing, I don't even remember the second half. Saw it later on film. Maybe that's why I couldn't forget it. And when they traded me, the coaches knew I couldn't forget it, too."

"I appreciate you telling me that," Brody said.

"Shit, ain't no secret. Everybody in the league who matters knows it now."

Thompson's face suddenly looked combative. "What the fuck you saying? Last I checked, coach decides who rides the lumber. Or you thinking you have a couple good games here, you can get me shipped out of here now?"

Brody stood, walked over to his desk and returned. He sat an arm's length away from Thompson on the couch.

"You're not getting traded, Reggie. That would involve another pay check. Suspended, no doubt. Run out of the league, maybe. At the very least, a whole lot of union mediation you don't need at your age."

The receiver started to get up, trying to look casual about it. "I don't have to sit here and listen to this bullshit."

Brody held out Eric Smith's log. "You don't need to listen. You need to read."

Thompson hesitated, staring at the document as if it were a subpoena he didn't want to touch. Finally he snatched it.

Brody said, "Eric Smith left that. He was planning on going to the commissioner."

Thompson's eyes focused, staying with the paper as he sat back down, tucking the beer between his legs. He appeared to read it all. When he finished he said, "Where the fuck you get this?"

"That's not important. What's important is where the original is."

"League's got this?"

"No. But I know somebody who is begging me to use it. Call a press conference. Send copies to the commissioner, another half dozen to the police."

Thompson scanned the room, eyeing the nouveau western decor. "This like one of those old cowboy movies, Rick? I got until noon to get out of town?"

Brody made his move. He'd been working it out while throwing all those bad passes earlier in the day.

"There's one name on there more than any other, and he isn't a player. I'm figuring you can tell me something I might be able to use."

"Carl?"

Brody nodded.

"No way."

"No way you can tell me something, or no way you just want to stay Carl and Bobby's house boy."

Thompson glared.

Brody said, "Way I figure, they got you jumpin' for them night and day."

"Way I figure," Thompson said. "You better be able to back up what you say."

Brody said, "Glamour Boy don't get the money he wants, he gets a call from Bobby, Bobby telling him it's because of the new rookie's deal. Rookie gets to camp, Bobby has another chat with the main brother, gets him all worked up about that dead kid back in Michigan. Shit, he knows all the brothers listen to Glamour Boy. Meanwhile, Bobby is telling the rookie that Glamour Boy is NWA, Nigger With an Attitude. Glamour Boy comes over and wants a song, Bobby says earlier to the rookie, they come for you, you tell them to fuck off. Rookie doesn't know the score. Walks into it. Pretty soon, Bobby can just lay back and watch, rookie versus Glamour Boy."

Brody knew by Glamour Boy's eyes he was on target.

Thompson said, "You said Carl, too."

"Carl's playing Bobby, or he's got something on him. Carl's playing you, and me. Carl put me in that red 600, knowing it would piss you all off. I'm figuring Carl told Bobby your million went to me. He's playing everybody, you see."

Thompson's head tilted the other way. "Playing for what?"

Brody said, "Money. Who the fuck knows? The better question is why. Carl came here to run the Stars into the ground, Reggie. So Papa will sell the team."

"How do you know?"

"You don't want to know."

Thompson half chuckled, then swigged the Colt. "Then why should I believe you?"

"Because you know everything else I've shown you and told you tonight is true."

Brody inched closer. "Reggie, listen to me. They wasted Eric. They wasted him because he was going to go to the league with that list."

"You reading minds now?"

"I was at his place in Soho, an hour before."

"That wasn't in the papers."

"Carl kept it out. That's how he works it. But you gotta know it's in his files. And I believe once the team's sold, they're going to clean house. You, I and everybody on that list are going to be chucking the ball in the arena league."

Thompson picked up the paper again, studying it over momentarily. He flicked it aside and walked over to the picture of Y.A. Tittle, his back to Brody.

He turned around. "So what you figure I can do for you, Rick?"

"I'm figuring you get around. I'm figuring Bobby's been talking to you. I'm figuring you might be able to tell me something that isn't on that list. Something I can use to take down Carl, maybe do it without involving half the team."

Thompson slugged down the Colt, his eyes never leaving Brody. He walked over and set the can down on the coffee table.

Hard.

"Nice party," he said.

He started walking toward the door.

"You're going down, Glamour Boy," Brody said. "We all fucking are."

Reggie Thompson didn't even turn around.

★ ★ ★

Five minutes later, the phone rang. It was nearly midnight. He figured it was Shay, her watch set to Pacific time.

"Hey, Bro."

He recognized the voice. They hadn't talked in nearly a year. It was Johnny Cheeseman, his high school halfback, and he sounded drunk.

"Bro, tonight some fuckin' Indian was running you down in the State Bar, so I fuckin' kicked his ass on your behalf."

"You tell him that?" Brody asked.

"Damn straight. I told him it was you and me. Red 235 remember?"

"I remember. How'd you get my phone number?"

"Before it wasn't. But now it is."

"What do you mean, *it?*"

"Is listed now, man."

Brody could hear voices, the clatter of glasses and Bob Seger and "Night Moves" in the background. Cheeseman probably still at the State.

Cheeseman suddenly screamed away from the mouthpiece.

"Tailgate!"

Doing it in that guttural roar.

He heard a couple responses, the same word, bellowing from the bar's background. Then, the voices closer, screaming it into the receiver.

"Tailgate!"

Cheeseman came back on and said, "Tailgate, man. We're fucking going. We need tickets. That's why I'm calling."

"I can't help you with other teams."

"Detroit fucking Lions versus New York Stars, Bro. We got this motor home lined up. We're leaving tomorrow. We'll be rolling into New York fucking City the day of the game."

"Who's we?"

"Me and about a half dozen guys from the team, that's who. Maybe ten. Maybe more."

Shit, Brody thought.

He told him he could leave a dozen tickets under Cheeseman's name at the will call. Now, he'd have to find the seats through channels. He received only four. They weren't going to be easy to come by for the Monday game.

Cheeseman said, "Hey, Red 235, remember?"

"I remember."

"Tell me."

"Tailback through a trap on the right side."

Cheeseman burped loudly.

Brody carried the phone to his bedroom, Cheeseman babbling, reliving old games, but always going back to the state final. The highlight of his life, carrying the ball into the end zone to win the game. Brody switched off the light, closed the blinds and fell on his back onto the bed, holding it on his ear. In the darkness, alone with the phone.

When Brody didn't say anything for a while, Cheeseman grew maudlin, the way drunks do when they run out of gas.

"Hey, Bro. Do me a favor, man. Call Red 235."

Brody closed his eyes. "It's just off center."

"No, in the game, okay. Red 235."

"Okay."

"I hate the fucking Lions."

"I hate 'em, too."

"So call it Monday. Red 235. Against the Lions. We'll all be watching. Looking for it."

One circle gone, another one takes its place. Brody wanted to drift off, or away.

CHAPTER

★ ★ ★ **31** ★ ★ ★

L ate Saturday afternoon, Carl Montan was leafing through the
paperwork with the room assignments at the Marriott. "I'm making some changes," he said.

Vincent Read rolled his eyes. "You had me come all the way to fucking Midtown for this?"

Montan nodded slowly. "I've been looking at my personnel reports.
I've come to believe certain players bring out the worst in each other.
It's high time we did something about it."

V.R. said he had a Saturday night date, tickets to the revival of *1776*,
his first night out in months. He didn't have time to pore over the
roommate pairings. "Besides, if it ain't broke, why fix it?" he added.
"We fucking won last week."

Montan smiled and said, "Finally get a date with a dancer, V.R.?"
Montan asked. "Better watch those ladies at Tommy's. They've got
the dry hustle down to a science."

V.R. stared across the table, his eyes dead.

"This will only take a few minutes," Montan said.

He jotted a couple dozen changes, lining out names, writing new
ones in. He worked quickly. He'd been thinking about it all afternoon.
He moved white players in with blacks. He assigned offensive linemen
with defensive tackles. He put God Squaders with Thompson's posse,
and sedate kickers with flamboyant cornerbacks. Darius Wallace with

Homer Cobb. Antoine Lense with Leonard Toysy. Toby Headly with Anthony Hotson.

He slid the list back across his desk to the head coach.

"This isn't like you, Carl," V.R. said.

Montan laced his hands together, resting them on the pecan desk top. "I got to thinking: I've been using the carrot for the past three years, giving them nothing but the best. But, frankly, it hasn't worked. I'm thinking maybe it's time to use the stick."

V.R. looked at him a few moments. Montan thought, he has no say here, and he knows it.

The coach's eyes shifted to the list. "You've put Glamour Boy with Brody?"

Montan nodded.

"They don't get along. Everybody knows that."

"They'll learn."

Montan added, "And everyone reports to the hotel by seven."

"No, it's nine."

"It's seven now. Sign in, but no sign out. No incoming calls, either. No cellular phones. No pagers. Hotel bar is off limits. Everybody stays in their assigned rooms."

V.R. tried to reason with him. A lot of players had friends and family in town for the game, he said. Some had planned gatherings at their homes for the afternoon and evening before. The players already had to sit around the hotel all day Monday. "These players are going to be mighty pissed," he concluded.

Montan smiled. "Isn't that how you want them, V.R.?"

For a moment, the head coach looked as if he was going to say something. Instead, he snatched the papers off the desk and headed for the door.

Montan said, "Enjoy the show."

A half hour later, a cab dropped Montan off in front of the Disney store on Fifth Avenue, bronze sculptures of Mickey Mouse and other characters above the entrance. Below the awning, the Turk was waiting.

Montan walked straight to the store window, looking in. He saw coffee mugs and watches and stuffed animals and action figures from a new animated feature just hitting screens from coast to coast. The Turk walked closer, looking inside, too.

"You set?" Montan asked, not looking.

"All right so far," the Turk said.

"Glamour Boy bit?"

"Big. He's meeting the slinger at five tomorrow in the Village."

"Good."

Montan glanced over briefly. "Brody has to report to the hotel by seven tomorrow. After he leaves, I want you to take a good look around his apartment. Make sure he doesn't have any more surprises for us."

The Turk lit a cigarette, nodding.

Montan looked down Fifth, then asked, "Got a line on your girl-friend?"

"Bimbolina checked into a hotel in Century City. I heard her make the reservation."

"Just take care of it, that's all."

"I wouldn't miss it."

Montan turned, looking at him now. The Turk had his eyes on something in the window, a Pocahontas doll.

"Turk, look at me," Montan said.

The Turk pivoted, the smoke hanging out of the corner of his mouth.

Montan said, "Remember, business first."

★ ★ ★

Dominique Goldman told Brody to meet her in the Stardome press room after Saturday practice, saying the top players had to do background interviews with the *Monday Night* crew, most of it off camera. She was waiting outside the conference room, the door closed, an interview in progress inside.

While they waited, she spouted broadcast numbers, saying *Monday Night Football* had been one of the top ten TV shows in the country for years. The Stars had not had a Monday game for three years. "This is a big opportunity for you," she said, pushing her hair behind her ears.

"I need a favor," he said.

"Within reason," she said.

He handed her a copy of the Prodigy CD, pointing out the song they'd be playing in the locker room. "Team gets down with this," he said. "Maybe the PA people could pipe in the opening lines before big plays. But not the lyric, unless you want the crowd shouting, 'Fuck 'em.' "

She didn't laugh, or even grin. "The PA and scoreboard program is already set," she said.

He said, "That's where the favor comes in."

"Only if you buy me dinner."

Brody nodded. "Next week," he said.

Inside the conference room, the Monday crew asked him football questions, how they planned to block the Lions, the coverages he expected, what to look for in the Stars game plan. He told them he didn't think they could run the ball against Detroit, figuring anything said was bound to get back to the opponents in the form of questions they'd ask the Lions.

They asked him about his background, his father's influence on his game. They didn't ask him about prison. One of them asked, "Tell us what you like to do at night in New York."

Brody said, "What does that have to do with football?"

The play-by-play man said, "We need something to talk about if the game goes into the tank."

That Saturday night in New York, he did what he always did two days before the game. More film. More playbook study. He worked on memorizing the audibles again.

The next evening, at least a dozen players were standing around the hotel conference room, all bitching, when Brody arrived at the Marriott just before seven. At the sign-in table, Brody saw a foot-high pile of cellular phones and pagers, all of them marked with tape and the uniform numbers of players. Johnny Josaitus was slumped in a chair behind the table, his arms folded across his belly, displaying a certain smug satisfaction.

Brody asked Squat what was going on.

Antoine Lense answered for him. "Rick, these motherfuckers are locking us down."

Somebody added, "They changed the rooms, too."

Brody looked back at Squat. The trainer explained the new rules, then handed Brody his room key. "You're bunking with Glamour Boy tonight," he said. "Good luck."

"What you gonna do, Rick?" somebody asked.

Brody faced the players. He liked what he was seeing, the team wanting him to deal with it. If they were doing that here, they'd do it on the field.

He saw Leonard Toysy, the FCA preacher, standing off by himself with his arms folded. "Leonard," he said, "don't we have Bible study tonight? Or, is it a prayer meeting?"

The big man walked slowly over to the table and stopped. He glanced at Squat, then Brody. "That's right," he said.

Squat said, "Front office wants everybody in their rooms."

Brody shrugged. "But I don't think they can do that, Squat. The league recognizes the Bill of Rights, freedom of worship, not to mention the players association."

Toysy turned to the team. "The man is right. We're going to gather in both study and prayer at ten o'clock. Right here. Lock down or no lock down."

Squat said, "But the coach says—"

A voice interrupted, "The coach speaks for himself."

It was V.R.. He walked through the crowd of players up to the table and turned around, his back to the trainer. The number of players had grown now to nearly three dozen.

He said, "I'm expecting all of you at the prayer meeting."

Everyone saw V.R. wink.

★   ★   ★

Shay Falan hung up the phone after the call from the casting director, ran out the double doors to the hotel balcony and let out a gleeful scream. Beyond Century City toward Santa Monica, she saw the ocean and LA's hazy sky. But her eyes focused on Wilshire Boulevard. The Napa Valley wine outlet store might as well have been talking to her for the past two days.

After the Friday reading, the store had compelled her to call an AA hotline she found in the phone book. The woman who answered directed her to a meeting in a church basement near Venice Beach. She remembered what a guy had said at her table, after she complained she drank because of inactivity and repeated failures. Not just a guy, but a well-known film actor. He'd said, "The most dangerous time is when you think you got it licked. There's nothing that'll get you back in the bag quicker than a little success."

Shay Falan knew what he was saying now. She walked back into the room and picked up the phone. First, she called the airline reservation line. Five minutes later she punched up Derek Brody's phone number at the Lucerne. The answering machine beeped.

"Derek, pick up, it's Shay."

She said it twice, then the machine hung up. She glanced at her watch, four o'clock Pacific. He said he didn't have to be at the hotel until nine. She dialed again, and this time left a message.

"Derek, I got the part. I *got the part!* Principal photography starts in two weeks. I've got to meet with the costume people to be measured and . . . What I mean, there's no reason for me to stay here now, so I've booked a flight tomorrow. I'll be arriving at Kennedy by eight, so that gives me time to get to the game. So, leave me a ticket at the stadium. Maybe you can put me with your agent again. I'll call the hotel later to make sure you got this."

Then she dialed the AA hotline again.

★   ★   ★

Three hours later, a couple of assistant coaches pulled the room divider across the conference room at the Marriott, letting the team split itself into two groups. On one side, Leonard Toysy led the God Squad in scripture readings and prayer. On the other, the games were under way.

Brody was leaning against the divider, watching V.R. go up five hundred in a game of seven-card stud. Reggie Thompson's posse was playing dominoes at another table, but Glamour Boy was missing. Brody had found his clothes hanging in the closet when he checked in, but he hadn't seen the receiver all night. He wanted to try talking to Thompson again. He'd brought the background reports Scanlon had obtained from another NFL team in one last effort to convince him of the front office conspiracy.

Brody noticed Jedi Conlin slide through the conference room door and whisper something to the posse's table. All of them stood. He caught them at the elevator. He wedged his hand in the closing door and stepped on. Their eyes looking away.

He looked at Conlin, asking, "Glamour Boy?"

Conlin's eyes were glazed. Brody grabbed him by the shirt, slamming him into the elevator wall. "I asked you a fucking question."

Conlin's head lowered, a sick look on his face. "Shit, Rick."

"Shit what?"

"He wanted to use my room. I went back upstairs get some more money for the domino game. But he won't come out of the john."

A minute later, Brody was knocking on the bathroom door, three players behind him.

"Glamour Boy."

He knocked again.

"Glamour Boy, it's Rick. Open up."

"I tried that," Conlin said.

Brody stepped back. "Help me kick it in."

"I ain't going to fuck up my leg," somebody said.

Brody rammed it open with the first blow, the trim flying off and sliding across the tile floor.

Reggie Thompson was sprawled in the bathtub, clear snot dripping from his nose, his right arm hanging over the edge. Brody saw an empty dope seal a few inches from the receiver's fingertips, and a rolled hundred-dollar bill.

"Got to be scag," somebody said. "Coke don't lay you out like that."

Brody slapped Thompson. Hard. He glanced over his shoulder. They were all looking like they were gawking at a car accident.

Somebody said, "We better get Squat up here."

Brody spun around. "He's fucking breathing, ain't he?"

"Then we better get Carl. He'll know what to do."

Brody glared as he flushed the paraphernalia down the toilet. "Fuck Carl. Carl is not your friend."

He stood up. "Let's get him to my room before the room checks. He's not supposed to be here."

"How we gonna do that?" Conlin asked.

Brody reached for the shower fixture and twisted it. Thompson collapsed into a half fetal position when the water hit him.

"We'll walk him down the fire stairs," Brody said.

"Then what?" Conlin asked.

Brody turned the shower to its coldest setting. "Then we'll walk him some fucking more."

★　★　★

It was nearly two a.m. when the other players left, Glamour Boy propped up in the bed now, conscious but not talking much, the light from ESPN flashing across his face. Brody was sitting against the other headboard, the playbook in his lap. Between play study, he'd listened to the Sunday scores. Watched the Sunday highlights. Everyone in their division was 1-1. They won tomorrow, they'd be in first place. Sure, early in the season, but if they won, at least he'd be going out on top.

Thompson mumbled something.

Brody closed the playbook and looked over at Thompson. "What's that, Glamour Boy?"

"I said you didn't have to save my ass," Thompson said.

Brody laughed. "If I could have, I would have cut off your fucking hands, saved them, and left the rest of you there. Now, I'm not so sure."

"What you mean, Rick?"

"I'm saying I think I finally don't give a shit."

"How you figure?"

"Girl told me something once. Said I was no different than Montan. Tonight, I believe I've proved her right."

Brody kept his eyes on the TV.

Thompson said, "All I did was fuck her."

"Don't push me," Brody snapped. "Not tonight."

"Not your girl, man. The ho. All I did was fuck her and give her a couple of perks."

Brody lowered the volume. "What ho? And why should I give a shit?"

"The ho I picked up. You wanted it. Now I'm giving it to you."

Brody shook his head. "Glamour Boy, you're not making any sense."

He hit the power button on the remote and sank his head into the pillow. From the corner of his eye, he could see Thompson brace his hand against the headboard and rotate his body slowly, his legs falling over the edge of the bed. He centered his feet on the floor, and rested his forearms on his knees.

"It was Bobby," he said. "I *paid* for it, that's all."

Brody closed his eyes and said, "That's why they call them whores, Reggie."

"But see, Bobby didn't pay. And it was Bobby who went fucking nuts. He starts grabbing her hair, slapping her around and shit. Pretty soon, a couple of other guys are all over her. Out at Stony. Right there in the dorm."

Brody opened his eyes.

Thompson said, "They're gone now. I figured that's why Carl cut them."

"You're telling me you picked up a whore and some of the players trained her? Bobby started it?"

Thompson nodded. "Now you with me, Rick."

Brody switched on the bed lamp and swung his feet onto the floor. Stress lines covered Reggie Thompson's bald head. He hesitated.

"Go on," Brody said.

"You remember that shark shit in the paper? Those pieces that washed up?"

Brody nodded.

"Bobby dumped the girl?"

"No, Bobby split. And everybody else. Left her in my fucking room, so I call Squat. I want Squat to get her back on her feet. Next thing I know, Carl's fucking there with his people."

"What people?"

"Guy he calls the Turk. He's supposed to be a scout, but you only see him when shit comes down."

"Kind of dark complected? Foreign looking?"

"You met him?"

"I've seen him."

"So, I come back an hour later, the ho is gone. Then I see the paper, put two-and-two together."

"They dumped her?"

"Carl told the Turk to take her away in an equipment locker."

Brody picked up the telephone.

"Who you calling?"

"My lawyer."

Glamour Boy pressed the receiver button down. Brody touched his hand, trying to move it, but Thompson held firm. Thompson looked in his eyes. "You go somewhere with this, your man's got to help me get a deal. Like I say, I just fucked her. That's all."

Brody nodded, letting go of his hand. When Thompson pulled his away, he punched up Scanlon's home number.

He heard only a dial tone. He slammed it down.

"Shit, they've got it blocked," he said.

★   ★   ★

A couple minutes later, he was alone in the dark conference room, talking with Mike Scanlon at the pay phone, Scanlon droning in a low sleepy voice, Brody explaining.

Scanlon asked, "Where's Thompson?"

"He's here."

"Will he talk to me?"

"He wants to, but he's upstairs. I'm at a pay phone. They've restricted our calls."

The line crackled a little.

Scanlon said, "I say we stick with the original plan. I've got the news releases and copies of the log ready to go. I'll be bringing them with me tomorrow."

Angry now, Brody spoke in an urgent whisper. "Jesus, you've got the whore, Montan and this thug the last people with her. What the fuck do you want?"

"Thompson will talk to the police?"

"You've got to get him a deal."

"That's not the problem. Hearsay is the problem. That's why I need to talk to him. Right now, you've got only hearsay, and that's not admissible in any court."

"I'm not talking gossip."

"Listen to me, Derek. Thompson says when he last saw the woman she was on the floor, Montan there. He leaves, comes back and she's gone. Says Montan told this Turk to take her away."

"In a locker."

"Exactly." Scanlon paused. "So, how does he know that?"

Brody hesitated, thinking about it. Shit, Glamour Boy didn't say. "I don't know," he said.

Scanlon continued, "So, if he wasn't in the room, he couldn't have heard it or seen it. This Turk tell him later? If he did, that's hearsay. The cops would have to flip the Turk, get him to testify. And that poses its own set of legal problems."

Brody told Scanlon he'd call him back. He'd run upstairs and get more details from Thompson. Maybe bring him to the phone.

He walked the length of the hall quickly and reached for the door. It was locked. He rapped gently. When Glamour Boy didn't open, he dug into the pocket of his sweat pants and found his key.

A cool breeze greeted him. Inside, the drapes were pulled back, the glow from the parking lot drawing his eyes to the window. The window open, the screen punched out. The bed was empty. He ran back and checked the bathroom.

But Reggie Thompson was gone.

CHAPTER

★ ★ ★ **32** ★ ★ ★

Shay tried calling Brody at the Marriott, but the hotel operator said he wasn't registered, then denied the Stars even stayed there. At LAX, she called the Stars front office and punched her way down three blind alleys of automated options before finally reaching the Stardome box office. Yes, the clerk said, a ticket was waiting under her name at the will-call.

The flight touched down at Kennedy at 8 o'clock. She had an hour to get to the Stardome. She checked her bag in a locker and bought the *Times* after she saw the headline at the newsstand. She read it in the cab. David Harvey was negotiating to buy the New York Stars, the story reported. There was no comment from Mecca or the team. There was a quote from the mayor, who revealed Mecca had also made an offer to buy the Stardome.

The scene in the parking lot was more animated than Shay remembered from the previous Sunday. The cab crunched empties under its tires. Fans mingled among the cars. A couple of hooting guys in their early twenties pounded on her window, asking her to drop her top. She saw an idiot run a pass pattern in the crowd, the guy knocking over a teenage girl as he tried to haul in the pass. She saw a fight break out.

The cab stopped outside the south gate. One line led to the will-call, another to a check-point where fans were being frisked for projectiles. Two barrels were spilling over with beer cans and liquor bottles.

She reached for the door. "Be careful out there," said the driver, an elderly man. "A lot of these people have been drinking since they got off work."

"Just good old wholesome family entertainment," she said.

She tipped him five. She was thankful she'd be sitting with Scanlon inside.

★ ★ ★

Brody had told V.R. that morning about Reggie Thompson, leaving the drug overdose part out. When Glamour Boy failed to show for the team dinner, the news quickly spread among the players—that and the *Times* story about the team being sold.

Brody stuck to his routines. He drove the Mercedes to the dome three hours before the game. He noticed two people in a black Buick following him. The car did a U-turn and left when he pulled into the player parking lot.

They were all dressing when V.R. came out and made it official, his eyes full of fury, two assistants behind him.

"I'm not going to ask what happened to Glamour Boy," he said. "And I don't give a shit what's being reported in the paper today. There'll be plenty of time later for both. I only give a shit about the game plan. I only give a shit about smash mouth and Detroit bodies left to rot on the field. Remember, three hours on Sunday."

It was Monday. But nobody was eager to point that out.

Brody summoned the mental game pictures during the pre-game shower, then added one more: The image of his teammates livid, not over room assignments, but something more.

When the team returned from pre-game warm-up, Brody glanced at Thompson's locker, the receiver's pads, polished helmet and spotless uniform untouched. No Glamour Boy. He decided to proceed with a plan he'd hatched after Thompson disappeared. Brody walked into V.R.'s office, and told him he was calling a team meeting. That meant there wouldn't be time for a final talk from the coach.

V.R. listened with a blank look, then said, "I don't know what you're up to, Brody. And you know what? I don't want to know."

They closed the doors to the locker room. Players only. The team meeting was a sacrosanct NFL tradition. No coaches or trainers or other team personnel. Brody didn't see Bobby Loeb. The last time he saw Loeb he was on the sidelines in a suit.

Brody was dressed and taped, his helmet under his arm. He stood on his stool, waiting until the locker room stilled. "Some of you might have seen the paper today," he said. "Word is Papa might be selling the team."

There was a murmur. He waited again for quiet.

He continued, "What the papers aren't telling you, and what the reporters don't know, is that that's the way the front office wants it. None of this would be going down without all the games the team has lost."

"What you telling us, Rick?" somebody shouted.

"I'm telling you, we're not supposed to win. We've all been set up. They've been trying to tank this team for years."

"Bullshit," another voice said from the back.

The room filled with chatter.

Brody banged his helmet against his locker, shouting, "I'm not done here." He reached into his helmet and pulled out the folded sheets of the background checks Scanlon had obtained. He unfolded the papers and held them at arm's length.

"This is a list," he said. "A lot of your names are on it, including mine. The front office has one just like it. In player personnel. It's got every fuck-up every one of us made before we got here. I'm not naming names, but you know who you are."

He had their full attention now.

"Way I figure, we lose the team gets sold. First thing the new owner does is clean house. That'll mean a lot of us won't be picked up by other franchises. And it won't stop there. There's another list floating around, too. One with everything you've pulled here. All this time you thought the front office was helping you, you were just going deeper into the pocket of Carl Montan."

"Who made that list?" Leonard Toysy asked.

"Eric Smith," Brody said. "That's what got him killed."

It took a good fifteen seconds to still them all again.

Brody finally resumed, "Way I figure, we have a choice. We win and work this out together. Maybe go public. Or, we lose and get picked off one at a time."

Antoine Lense shouted, "That's no fucking choice."

The chatter began once more.

Leonard Toysy stepped forward. He snatched the paperwork out of

Brody's hand. He looked at the top page, then handed it back. He walked five feet, stopped in front of Lense and in one fluid motion picked the free safety up and slammed him into the locker. Brody figured Toysy didn't like Lense's sins in black and white.

The room fell silent again.

"Leonard," Brody said, staying calm. "What are you doing?"

Toysy had the safety at arm's length. "First I'm going to say a prayer, then I'm gonna kick his ass in Jesus's name."

The jerseys came from all directions, some players charging, some trying to restrain teammates, some scrambling out of the way. Jedi Conlin leaped on Toysy's back, applying a choke hold. Darius Wallace tried to pry Toysy's taped hands from Lense's neck.

Brody sank to his stool.

He sat until a football sailed across the room and slammed into the equipment cage. Someone shouted, "Listen up!" Brody turned to the locker room door, expecting to see a furious Vincent Read.

It was Glamour Boy, in street clothes, his dark Oakleys over his eyes.

The melee dissipated in seconds.

Thompson boomed, "You all got to forgive White Boy Rick, here. He's just a rookie. The man's got his priorities wrong, getting ahead of himself and all."

A game official stuck his head in the door behind him, saying, two minutes. Thompson ignored him. Nobody moved but Leonard Toysy. He pushed Lense aside and took a couple slow steps toward Thompson.

"*Priorities?* Where you been, Glamour Boy?"

Thompson slid off his sunglasses. "Right here, preacher. Listening."

Thompson surveyed the entire room, waiting for someone else to challenge him.

No one did.

"What you saying, Reggie?" Lense asked.

Thompson's voice rose. "I'm saying first things first. First we win, just like Rick says. Then we worry about sticking it to the man downtown."

★   ★   ★

Four minutes later, Brody stood at the end of the column of offensive starters in the tunnel, his helmet under his arm. They'd be introduced one at a time. As names were called, they'd run out through the goal posts and be greeted by a line of teammates stretching from the end zone to the fifty-yard line.

When it started, the noise—the shouting crowd and the riffs from "Their Law"—swelled into the tunnel like a flash flood. Brody felt a pair of hands massaging the base of his neck. He half looked back.

Carl Montan, in a double-breasted dark suit, a silver handkerchief poking out of its pocket.

Brody shook his arms, walking forward, staying loose. He said two words. "Why me?"

Montan said, "Because when it really matters, you'll take the easy way out. Character doesn't change."

Brody spit, then tugged on his helmet. "You telling me to toss it, Carl?"

They stared at one another for a couple of seconds. When he turned toward the tunnel, he felt Montan's warm breath through the helmet's ear hole.

"I'm telling you where your girlfriend is sitting," Montan said. "Your end zone, first half. Five rows up, right corner. I figured you'd want to stay close."

Brody spun around, but Montan already was walking away.

★   ★   ★

Shay thought at first she was in the wrong seat. The spot, low in the end zone. No armrests like the week before. Bleacher benches, molded a little for the butt, the numbers painted on the seat. She checked the ticket again, then sat down, her seat the second one from the aisle, the aisle seat empty. Scanlon caught in traffic, she guessed.

She spent five minutes reading a program and dodging the sharp points of a star around a guy's head next to her, his face painted silver, his breath two hundred proof. Drunks all around her, in fact.

She stood during the introductions, cheering, Number Fourteen running out last. She lingered on her feet for a few moments as the team massed around Derek when he reached the bench.

Scanlon sat down in the aisle seat.

"You see that?" she said, turning.

But it wasn't Scanlon.

It was the guy in the Village, the guy at the sports bar, the guy at the airport lounge. He was wearing a silk shirt, open halfway to his belly. Chest hair and gold chain. Disco king with cold eyes.

"Like my souvenir, Bimbolina?" he said.

Her eyes followed his to his lap. He had an official Stars stadium blanket there, his hand in it. She could see the tip of a gun poking out between the folds.

"You do like it," he said, smirking. "I thought it might come in handy later on."

★ ★ ★

They started from their twenty. As Brody ran out to form the huddle, his eyes scanned the right corner seats past the goal post. He found Shay's red hair, then he saw the guy sitting next to her, the guy from the airport. Everybody around them animated, the two of them very still. He looked to the sidelines for Montan, but didn't see him. He wanted to drag Montan onto the field, right across the yard stripes by the collar of that suit. Do it right there in front of eighty thousand. Beat him until he couldn't walk.

The coach's voice filled Brody's helmet. "Mug up, Brody. What the fuck you waiting for?"

The offense formed the huddle. Everybody focused. He and Glamour Boy had fired them up. Now there was no way to cool them down.

He saw only one choice. Keep it close, he told himself. Play all out. You don't play all out, you get injured. Keep it close, let the team walk off the field with their heads up. Let the key moment present itself.

Then toss the game.

V.R. called a running play in his helmet.

Brody told himself, let V.R. call the plays. Keep it simple.

He told the huddle, "Black Jersey Pimp 25 on two."

Ten seconds later, he handed off the ball to Danny Davis, a simple slant. Brody dropped back, miming a pass. The offensive line blew a gaping hole in the defensive line, and Davis cut back, exploding into the secondary. The middle linebacker missed his ankles. Davis made a move on the strong safety.

Hands on his hips, Brody watched the muscles expand and contract in the back of Danny Davis's thighs. The white rubber soles of his shoes coming up, flashing like strobes. Two Lions were still chasing him as Davis crossed mid-field and found a lane along the sideline.

Davis sprinted past the players on the bench, all on their feet now, past V.R. scampering along the sidelines, waving his hands, Tommy Molito trailing him with the cable for the headphones.

He stood on the twenty until his helmet crackled, "Brody, extra point. Get the fuck off the field."

When the gun ended the first half, it was Lions 21–17.

★   ★   ★

Dominique Goldman charged into the owner's suite while the marching band from Syracuse was on the field. Papa Goldman was sitting next to Jack Petrus. Montan was sipping a drink at the bar. Petrus started to get up.

"Sit down, Jack," she said.

Petrus slunk back into his chair. She looked down at her father, who was nursing his favorite pipe.

She said, "The buzz in the press box is you're selling the team."

Goldman looked up. "It was in the _Times_, didn't you see it?"

"The _Times_ said a share. They're saying in the press box you're selling it all."

Goldman set the pipe down. "I'm broke, Nicky," he said. "And more than that, I'm tired."

She pointed a finger. "But you said you'd run the team into the ground first."

Goldman looked up and said, "That's right, my dear. And I have."

★   ★   ★

The way Shay Falan thought she'd do it, was just get up. Get up and start walking right up the staircase, then run. What was Disco King going to do about that? Shoot her in front of everyone? When everybody jumped up at the first touchdown, she'd looked over her shoulder, her eyes following fifty rows up to the top of the stairway, the concourse there.

That's when she saw two more men, looking down at her. They had Stars starter jackets, their hands in the front pockets. Probably guns in there, she decided. It made sense.

Disco King was not alone.

At the half, Disco King switched hands under the blanket, and started feeling her thigh with his right. He asked her if she had freckles there.

"You'll never know," she snapped.

He asked, "How about farther up?"

She pushed his hand away, then got this idea she could just stand up. Start screaming rape. She glanced at the fans choking the stairway aisle, then studied the faces around her. Everyone a little drunker now. She decided, yes, she could yell rape, even murder.

And all they'd do was cheer.

★　　★　　★

Brody spent the half-time on his stool, his head down, listening to V.R. talk about Lions tendencies on both sides of the ball, but not really hearing it. He was hoping the Stars had played themselves out. Make it easy for him.

Glamour Boy strolled over after V.R. was done. He said he wanted to talk, but over by the equipment cage. Brody followed.

"What the fuck is wrong with you, Rick?" he said. "I'm eating this guy up on the right side."

Brody asked back, "Where'd you go last night, Reggie?"

"I'll tell you after. Something for your attorney."

"You're running a little late," Brody said. Thompson gripped the collar of his shoulder pads. "This the second half, man. The team is with you, you understand what I'm saying? You got us out here, now you got to take us home."

The third quarter was scoreless. They started shouting at him in the huddle during the fourth.

"Rick, you forget how to fucking audible?"

"Rick, I own this motherfucker on the right."

"Rick, throw me the fucking ball."

When they regained possession of the football well into the quarter, he lined up behind center, watching the opposite end zone now. Shay there, eighty yards away. But he couldn't keep up the charade anymore. They drove to the Lions' thirty. He felt like he was driving them to her funeral. On third and nine, he backpedaled five steps, saw Conlin open at the down marker on the left, but hesitated. Deliberately. He took a painful sack.

They attempted a field goal, but missed.

He stood on the sidelines as the Lions ate up the rest of the fourth. The Lions on the Stars forty now, less than a minute left. The offense was on its feet on the sidelines, screaming at the defense to get the ball back. V.R. called defensive time-outs, stopping the clock twice. The fans remained in their seats, only a few walking up the stairways, eager to beat the traffic home.

Brody's eyes looked across the empty green turf to the end zone. He thought, move another ten yards to his right. The game gun fires, sprint forty yards. He could do that in under five seconds. Climb the barrier in one. Six seconds total. Six seconds to get Shay. He figured he could cover thirty yards before the guy realized what was going on.

He was looking for her hair when he saw the bleachers leap to their feet, then roar. Brody glanced back at the field. Leonard Toysy scooping up a fumble. Lumbering toward the end zone, surrounded by a linebacker and a defensive back. To the fifty. The forty. The thirty.

And then somebody caught him from behind.

Stars ball, first and ten on the twenty-five. Brody eyed the game clock. There were thirty seconds left. They were out of time-outs.

V.R. snatched Brody's helmet from his hands and slid it over his head, then grabbed him by the face mask. The coach had to shout over the crowd. "Jersey white hitman, fake Felon left, then look for Glamour Boy across the middle from the right end zone, or run the fucker in yourself."

Brody froze.

The play clock started. They had thirty seconds.

"Got it?"

Brody pushed V.R.'s hands off his mask. Ten seconds later, he called the play in the huddle.

"I'm with you, Rick," Glamour Boy said. "Just get me the fucking ball where I like it."

Later, he would remember coming up behind center, forcing himself not to look in the bleachers. He couldn't hear the crowd anymore as he fell back, faked the sweep handoff to the left, then rolled right.

Fifteen yards of clear turf in front of him, but a linebacker charging toward him now, his receiver leaving his zone.

Then, Glamour Boy with three steps on the right corner, sprinting in a hard post toward the goal post. The free safety heading right at Reggie Thompson from the left.

Glamour Boy.

Brody thinking: Throw it right at him. In his numbers, and he'll drop it.

He stepped into the pass hard. He let the ball go, a rocket at only twenty-five yards. As hard as he could throw.

He saw the ball hit Thompson's numbers, just before the Honolulu blue jersey filled his face mask.

On the way down, he heard the crowd explode.

★ ★ ★

Disco King grabbed Shay Falan's hand and began pulling her up the aisle. Nobody moving from their seats. Everybody on their feet, cheering. She looked over her shoulder and saw Derek flat on his back, alone on the field, the training crew running out.

When she didn't see the guys in the starter jackets, she made her move, halfway up the stairs. She gave him a dancer's high leg kick, her toe landing deep between his legs. Disco King clutched his stomach, and she sprinted. She glanced back. He was coming already.

She was two feet from the concourse when the two starter jackets converged from both sides of the aisle. One enveloped her in a bear hug, then Disco King caught up. The other starter jacket clutched Disco King by the biceps, saying something in his ear. The two walked away into the crowd.

Shay Falan screamed.

A girl somewhere in the crowd screamed back.

"Stars!" other voices shouted.

She screamed again.

The guy in the jacket grabbed her shoulders and spun her around. "Forget about it, lady," he said. "You're going to make me fucking deaf."

★ ★ ★

Brody saw the ceiling of the tunnel first, then Squat's back just beyond his feet. Squat and an assistant trainer were wheeling him on a chrome stretcher toward the locker room.

Now past the locker room. Toward the loading dock. Brody saw its accordion door rolling up.

"Where you taking me?"

Squat glanced back. "To the hospital. You need an MRI."

Brody saw Squat's black bag dangling from his right hand. He tried to sit up, but he was strapped.

Outside, he could see the ambulance waiting in the dimly lit loading zone, its parking lights on. Behind it, he saw the black Buick that had followed him to the Stardome.

Nothing else around.

The stretcher stopped behind the ambulance doors. The assistant trainer headed back into the dome, the loading door whirring down. Squat disappeared around the ambulance. Brody's fingertips strained for the strap buckles.

Brody didn't see two guys in starter jackets emerge from the shadows. The first he saw them, they were undoing the stretcher straps. He tried to run when his feet hit the pavement, but he collapsed. They picked him up under the armpits and dragged him.

The back door to the Buick opened. They shoveled him inside.

Shay Falan was pressed against the opposite door, a shocked look on her face. "Derek," she said, "these people say they're friends of yours."

The driver turned around. "Nice game."

Brody spun toward the open door.

Outside, twenty yards away, he saw Squat on his knees on the pavement. Tommy Molito was standing over him, his cellular in one hand, his Ruger in the other, deep in the trainer's mouth.

The Mole said, "Your call, shooter." He casually flipped the cell phone shut. "Does this fuck stay or does he go?"

CHAPTER

☆ ☆ ☆ **33** ☆ ☆ ☆

arl Montan saw uniformed cops talking to two ambulance atten-
dants near the service entrance. He saw Johnny Josaitus surrounded by reporters. Montan pulled the trainer away, asking
what happened.

Squat was shaking. "I'm shipping Brody to the MRI like you said,
and the next thing I know this car pulls up, dinos everywhere. And
Tommy's there, wanting to take Brody. Next thing I know I'm sucking
on Tommy's gun."

"You call the police?"

"The ambulance crew did. They ran."

Five minutes later, Montan was stuck in traffic choking the stadium
lot. He paged the Turk three times, punching in his car phone number, but the Turk didn't call back. He turned on the radio, listening
to the game recap. When the broadcast crew named Reggie Thompson player of the game, he switched it off. He bolted from the column of cars inching toward the gate, nearly running over a traffic cop
charged with maintaining two lanes. Out the exit, he drove straight to
Midtown.

He spent most the night at MetLife, a good part of it in the file
room, the shredder grinding coded player files. He filled two garbage
bags with the paper spaghetti, then walked the bags out of the office
and dumped them two floors down. He spent an hour deleting records

in the computer. He finished with a Hoyo de Monterrey and the last of the Remy Martin Louis XIII, half a bottle.

Thinking about Europe again.

He liked the idea even more now. Tour the Bordeaux district. Get the Beaujolais Nouveau right there in France. Fuck waiting for it to come over on the Concorde. Maybe run into Princess Stephanie in Monaco. He always thought she was hot, a little like Dominique, in that aloof sort of way. He decided, watch the entire Stars situation from there, tune in CNN International. Sale goes through, send David Harvey a bill. See if the man paid. If not, forget about it. Move on. When the money runs out, hire into a sports book, or create a new one. The way those soccer fans trampled each other to death in Europe, shit, there had to be some serious action in that game.

He took only three things from the MetLife office. His appointment book, forty thousand in cash and his humidor of prized Hoyos. He'd drive straight to Kennedy and grab the first international flight he could book.

On his way on the empty streets of pre-dawn Manhattan, he turned on the radio again, the sports wrap. He couldn't help but admire how the media was on it already, without any help from him. The host was reading from the morning edition of the *Post*. The paper had gone with an organized crime angle, reporting Derek Brody had sped away from the Stardome with reputed mob figures. The story mentioned V.R., saying the head coach had brought Tommy Molito into the Stars inner circle. It reported both V.R. and Brody frequented Molito's topless club. V.R. had done a brief post-game interview about the game, then left the stadium. The host was speculating, comparing Derek Brody to Art Schlichter, the Baltimore Colts rookie quarterback who'd admitted in 1983 to associating with gamblers and losing more than $700,000 in NFL bets.

As WFAN cut to a commercial, Montan's pager went off. He looked at the number, but didn't recognize it.

The Turk, he thought.

He dialed the number on his cellular.

David Harvey didn't say hello. He said, "Congratulations, Carl, you really pulled it off. I particularly liked the wise guys. How'd you manage to hook that up?"

Montan tried to sound natural. "These people find their own trouble."

Harvey sounded like he was in a bathroom, water running in the background, shaving maybe, but all business. "Look, I'm facing a full schedule this morning, but I want to close this. I can ride this underworld angle right into league approval. I just woke up old man Goldman. He tells me my offer-to-purchase is approved by team counsel. All I need is his signature, and the team president's."

He wanted Montan to personally deliver both Goldman and Petrus at half past noon.

"Goldman's not going to get on that *Donzi*," Montan said.

"The *Dorothy* has a pad for Goldman's chopper. Soon as they sign, I'll move the first half of your payment to the Caymans. The rest, you'll have to wait until the league signs off on the sale. In fact, my instincts tell me I should wait for that before I wire you anything. But I presume you're going to need it soon."

Harvey paused. Montan could hear his razor cutting through his beard.

"Carl, a little advice. This is going to get very ugly. I'd suggest you don't stick around."

"You've got a point."

Montan was on 24th Street now. He could see the Midtown Tunnel ahead, the start of the freeway to Kennedy.

"After that, of course, you and I shall never talk again," Harvey said. "In fact, we never did."

David Harvey hung up.

Montan turned on Second Avenue before the tunnel. He reached into the humidor and bit off the end of another Hoyo. The Cuban would sober him up, he thought. It was a good day for the Canali, or maybe he'd go with the ribbon shirt and the Vestimenta jacket.

Those packed afternoon flights, a suit didn't travel well.

★   ★   ★

Mike Scanlon arrived at the room in the Hampton Inn near La-Guardia just after eight a.m. He was talking as he came through the door, almost shouting. "You ought to hear the news. They're saying you were last seen with underworld types. Why didn't you let me know where you were earlier? Where have you been? Why are you here? What do you plan on doing? What the fuck is going on?"

Scanlon stopped when he saw Tommy Molito sitting on the bed. Brody was propped up on the other, still in his game pants and his old high school T-shirt, the pads off. Shay was at the small room desk. Molito's driver, who let Scanlon in, walked past the attorney. Scanlon's eyes went to the semi-automatic poking out of his waistband.

Scanlon looked at Brody. "I guess these are the underworld types," he said.

Brody made the introductions. Tommy. Joey.

Brody said, "You took a couple of cabs like I told you? Nobody followed?"

Scanlon took a deep breath and nodded. He exhaled and said, "You okay?"

Brody pushed himself higher on the headboard. "Bad headache. Never did like to roll out." He turned to Molito. "I need to be alone with my lawyer for a few minutes."

Molito said they'd be right outside.

Brody explained how it all went down, how Molito told him they'd been keeping an eye on him at the request of his uncle. How his crew picked up on this guy called the Turk when he broke into his apartment at the Lucerne, then followed him for a day, saw him move in on Shay at the Stardome.

"So this *Turk*—Jesus, I can't believe this shit—what happened to him?" Scanlon asked.

Brody said, "Tommy didn't go into that."

Shay said, "Hopefully, he went the way of disco."

Scanlon blinked a couple times.

"You could ask Tommy," Brody added. "But I don't think we really want to know."

"*Tommy?* You're calling him *Tommy* now? And what does he fucking call you?"

"You don't want to know that either," Brody said.

Scanlon sank to the other bed, trying to deal with it, but looking overwhelmed. He turned. "Ambulance attendant says on the news this morning somebody pulled a gun."

"Tommy," Brody said.

"There's another report saying you and Vincent Read have been frequenting this club. That's—"

"Tommy's club."

Scanlon said, "Okay. And what else did Tommy do?"

"It was V.R., really. V.R. told Tommy to grab me. The trainer was taking me for an MRI. Squat didn't want to give me up at the loading dock. I guess Tommy had to persuade him."

"It's a high-tech X-ray, so what?"

"Usually the team physician orders an MRI, not the trainer."

Scanlon looked over at Shay Falan. She smiled sarcastically and said, "Quite a game. They all this way?"

Brody said, "That's another thing, I tried to toss the game. But the team had other plans."

"Tommy told you?"

"No, Montan."

Scanlon stared at Brody.

"I suppose you're going to tell me I've blown my chance at a shoe deal," Brody said.

Mike Scanlon lowered his head a few moments, then came up laughing. He laughed for a good ten seconds. When he was done, he took a deep breath and put his hands out, as if he were trying to stop an invisible moving wall.

His demeanor suddenly changed. "All right, nobody panic. I've got everything under control."

He told them the rest on his feet, pacing a little. They would hold a noon news conference. Hold it right there at team headquarters at MetLife, right where they all work and breathe. "It's going to be good, just the look on their faces. Show 'em how we practice law in Detroit."

Shay looked up, curious.

Scanlon continued, "We say you've got a major announcement to make. Of course, the league and every law enforcement agency that comes out of the woodwork when you mention the mob and football in the same breath will be there, taking notes. Your friend *Tommy* might take some heat, but he can handle it. And the mob thing will cease to be the issue, anyway."

"The Mecca deal will," Brody said.

Scanlon shook his head. "You've got nothing but a theory and the word of some old gangster. You can't take down a conglomerate like that with innuendo. You do it with evidence. So, you hope the authorities can flip Montan and unravel the rest from there."

"You're saying the Smith log?" Brody said.

Scanlon stopped pacing. "No, the news conference, we go with Reggie Thompson."

"You talked to Glamour Boy?"

Scanlon nodded. "When I couldn't find you in the locker room, he pulled me aside. We had a long talk in his car. Montan and this Turk? He's got them dead nuts on that prostitute at Stony Brook."

"You said that was hearsay . . ."

"That's right."

". . . if he wasn't there."

"That's right, too."

"So Glamour Boy's saying now he *was* there?

"No, he didn't say that," Scanlon said. He reached into his coat pocket. Scanlon grinned as he produced the cassette, saying, "But his camcorder was."

Scanlon's other hand came out with a second tape. He held them both up. "Can you believe that guy? He calls it his *instant replay*. Told me he hides the camera in his high school helmet, his good luck piece. Says he forgot the cam was on in all the excitement." He tossed Brody one of the tapes. "It's all on there, including Montan ordering the prostitute taken out. He even made copies. He said he figured he might need them one day."

That's why Glamour Boy left the hotel Sunday night, Brody thought.

"I've already made arrangements to drop one of these off this morning to Suffolk County Police, put the investigation into motion. The second tape we release at the news conference. The wise guys will be old news. Down the road, of course, you're going to have to do some explaining."

Scanlon paused, holding out his open hands. "Am I earning my four percent yet?"

Brody asked, "What about Thompson?"

"I've already talked to the district attorney. They'll need him to establish the video. Reggie's also filing a request with the NFL first thing this morning to enter the league drug treatment program. League-player contract says they can't dump him after he does that. But I won't be able to do anything for Bobby Loeb. I've seen the tape. He's clearly the instigator. Christ, it's brutal."

Shay asked what Brody already was thinking. "And Derek?"

Scanlon looked first at her, then Brody. "You're going to have to come clean. On everything. Lying to NYPD on Smith. That's where the Smith log will come in. After the news conference, we go to the detective with it. Help them tie the Smith murder to Montan. Of course, Stars can dump your contract under the good character clause. We could fight that. Or, depending how you handle it, maybe I can sign you with another team next spring."

"So you're saying?"

Scanlon took a breath. "I'm saying the way it stands, no, I don't think there's a shoe deal in this anywhere for you."

★   ★   ★

A couple of news crews tried to ambush him as the cab dropped the three of them off outside MetLife. The cameras followed them inside to the elevator. Scanlon held them at bay there, then slid in between the closing doors.

YOU WANT TO OWN THIS TOWN? JUST WIN.

They walked past the mural and Dominique Goldman, who was standing next to the receptionist. She caught up in the hall, grabbing Brody's arm.

"My father wants to talk to you," she said. "He's in the board room." She pointed to the double doors.

They could hear the chatter of reporters through the open door ahead.

Brody looked at Scanlon.

Dominique said, "He wants you alone."

Brody nodded to Scanlon.

Scanlon pointed a finger at Dominique Goldman. "Anything happens to my client, it'll be raining lawyers in here." He turned to Brody. "We'll be inside setting up."

Papa Goldman was at the head of the long table, Jack Petrus off to one side. Petrus appeared to be sweating. He wouldn't look Brody in the eye. Goldman didn't have his sterling-banded bulldog. He looked older, and tired. So did the city behind him outside.

"Sit down, young man," he said.

Brody didn't head for a chair. If he stood, he thought, they'd get right to it. Simple curiosity had brought him inside. When he didn't sit, Goldman stood up.

The owner began, "You told me when you first got here you were here to play football, but apparently you've gotten a little off track. That's easy to do in this business. It was easy for me, as well."

Goldman turned and looked up Park Avenue. He continued with his back to him. "Carl told me this morning you've somehow come into possession of some material regarding one of our former quarterbacks."

The owner paused, then turned around. "I've made mistakes. I know that. But I'm hoping my daughter will not have to pay for them. I want you to know, she has had nothing to do with any of this."

Brody waited, half expecting Goldman to make him an offer, or a threat. But none came. Goldman turned back to the window.

Outside, Brody could see the owner's helicopter floating toward them above the rooftops. Brody lingered, watching the chopper, trying to read the owner's mind. The Long Ranger disappeared overhead, heading for the MetLife roof.

Goldman turned to Petrus. "Let's get this over with."

He looked at Brody and added, "That was a nice throw last night."

Brody said, "But it was a better catch."

★   ★   ★

Frank Carcaterra was in the back row, the rest of the chairs filled with press. He expected that. What he didn't expect were the players lining the walls. Both sides of the ball, nearly the entire squad, even special teams. He didn't see Reggie Thompson, but Scanlon had told him not to expect the receiver. Scanlon had said, "I advised him, they're already going to see enough of him on the tape."

Brody sat in a chair near the lectern and looked for Shay Falan. He spotted her near the door, Bobby Loeb standing next to her, a smirk on his face, no idea what was coming.

Scanlon already up now, hushing everyone. He started with a statement. It sounded very formal, Scanlon saying his client, during his brief tenure with the Stars, had come into possession of material that seriously called into question the integrity of certain executives of the New York Stars.

"This material was turned over to the appropriate law enforcement

officials this morning," Scanlon continued. "And while my client has not been directly involved in these matters, any questionable associations that have already been reported need to be judged in this context."

The reporters grew restless.

Scanlon quickly moved on to the facts, then turned on the video. He'd excerpted three parts from the tape: The assault, using less-than-revealing footage suitable for television news. Montan ordering the prostitute taken away. Montan and the Turk putting the whore in the equipment locker, the team's silver star shining on the trunk. The crowd was transfixed. Nobody noticed Bobby Loeb slip out the door.

Brody did. He also saw the two Suffolk police officers and a detective cuff him in the hall, then lead him away.

Scanlon turned to Brody. "And now I believe my client would like to make a statement."

It didn't dawn on Brody until he reached the lectern that he hadn't prepared. He thought, this is the part where you make the big speech. He was looking for a place to start.

The room grew silent, waiting.

He heard it in the distance at first. Then the thumping grew louder, the turbulence buffeting the windows. A sound guy with a TV crew pulled off his headphones, saying, "What the hell is that?"

"Dummy up," Carcaterra said from the back row. "It's just Goldman's chopper."

What came next, everyone heard.

Later, the experts would say everyone was lucky the helicopter was a hundred feet higher than the tower. A quick-thinking cameraman spun around and got the only video shot. That night's exclusive: Goldman and Petrus and Montan as passengers to an unknown destination. The Bell Long Ranger as a golden fireball.

Plummeting more than forty stories to the street.

CHAPTER

⭐ ⭐ ⭐ **34** ⭐ ⭐ ⭐

The place they found was called the Inn at Millrace Pond. There was a historic grist mill, millrace house and stone cottage rooms. The town was called Hope, which is why Brody took the exit off of I-80, the freeway starting to wind through some hilly terrain.

That afternoon, they sat down on a bench near the pond, the hint of fall in the air now, that smell of earth and dying leaves. Football weather.

Brody said, "You sure we're in New Jersey? The sky's blue."

"Absolutely sure," Shay said.

The National Football League had suspended him for two weeks, maybe more, pending a preliminary investigation. The next game had been canceled, automatically forfeited. Raymond Bullard was not con-ducting the probe. He was missing. Vincent Read had resigned. Bobby Loeb had been arraigned on rape charges. A half dozen players had filed for admittance into drug rehab.

The day after the chopper went down, Scanlon had shuttled Brody through three interviews: New York detectives, Suffolk police and the league. He started to get into the Mecca angle with one of the New York detectives. The detective wanted to know if he had a source, somebody he could talk to about that.

"Just a theory," he said. He figured The Mole already had his hands full.

"Anybody who had contact with Harvey was probably in that chopper," Scanlon later said.

The New York news media was on a feeding frenzy, speculation ranging from a mob hit on the helicopter to a short in the fuel tank. The news about Mecca and David Harvey was that Dominique Goldman wasn't selling. Her father had a ten-million-dollar insurance policy. The New York Stars were liquid through at least the bye. She called Brody as he and Shay were packing.

"I expect you back," she said.

Brody didn't commit. After he hung up, he gave the Lucerne notice. He didn't know where he was moving. But he decided he wanted something a little closer to the ground.

He figured he had to start with the family of the dead student in Detroit. Walk up to the door and ask to come in. Tell the mother that he was driving, not his father. Not say he was sorry. Saying sorry seemed meaningless. Instead, tell the mother he wished he'd handled it all differently. Tell her he would if it happened now. Then tell Scanlon to settle the case, whatever it took.

From Detroit, he planned to drive three hundred miles north to Evergreen Shores. See Johnny Cheeseman and the guys who came to the game. Show Shay his hometown. That's the way it should be, he figured. Go back in the middle of a big controversy. Go back the way he'd left.

He was glad about the league suspension, actually. He was glad to be out of New York, on the road. They'd left the interstate to explore the old roads, see people and houses and small businesses rather than mile markers. Shay had spotted the inn as they pulled into Hope. He thought it was a good idea.

He was watching a falling elm seed spin into the pond when Shay reached for his hand. She asked, "You think they'll get this all sorted out?"

"The reporters and the fans will have the last say."

"You think so?"

"They're the experts. Just ask them," he said.

He changed the subject. He wanted to know all about the movie she'd landed, the noir revival of *Pitfall*. She said the 1948 version had a married insurance executive as the hero, played by Dick Powell. The

Powell character has an affair with a seductive blonde. But a dirty cop, played by Raymond Burr, also has the hots for the girl. He incites the girl's ex-con boyfriend to murder him. Confronted, Powell shoots him in self defense, but then covers up the crime so his wife doesn't find out about the affair.

"I'm playing the girlfriend, the Lizabeth Scott part," she said. "But it goes downhill from there."

Brody wanted to know how.

"The producers ordered the writer to involve the wife in the murder plot against her husband, so the hero would be more morally acceptable. That's not in the original. So I wouldn't call this remake noir. You should feel a little morally compromised rooting for the hero in noir. But the Lizabeth Scott part is still a great role, so what the hell."

Brody asked, "You're saying it's all too tidy?"

She nodded. "You need to leave some loose ends. Characters disappearing from the story. Conflicts left unresolved. But if the characters are good, the people should be able to carry on the story in their heads, figure out what might happen."

"Such as?"

"This."

"This what?"

"You still haven't told me whether you're going to play if they lift the suspension."

He paused for a moment. "Well you said it."

"Said what?"

Brody grinned. "I guess it depends on my character," he said.

★   ★   ★

They didn't make love that night. They lay in bed in each other's arms, the window half open in the cottage. They talked a little. They heard a screech owl out there somewhere in the dark treetops. They listened to the wind rustling the leaves.

He slept good. Better than he had in weeks.

When he woke, she had coffee and bagels and cream cheese on the small table there. She said she'd gone into the village.

"That's some car," she said. "I felt like I was in a fighter jet."

He rubbed his eyes. "Remind me to call the dealership," he said. "I'm sure they want it back."

They took a walking tour around Hope, stretching a little before hitting the road. They read a plaque that said the village was founded in 1774 by Moravians from Bethlehem, Pennsylvania. The town got its name from a legend, somebody jumping off the mountain over the village to escape a band of Indians, surviving the fall.

Shay said, "I guess that's why they call it Hope."

By noon, it had turned into one of those Indian summer days. A lot of people liked them in Michigan, but Brody always thought something didn't feel right about the temperature hitting eighty when the colors were starting to show on the trees.

They put the top down on the Mercedes and drove up Hope Mountain, looking for a view. There was a roadside park. Shay walked to the edge of a drop-off there and started singing. All that time together, he'd never heard her solo. He didn't know the name of the song, or even listen to the words. But he could hear that voice, like nothing he'd ever heard.

Whatever his plans, he decided, he wanted to make them with her.

A minute later, they were headed back to the interstate, following a narrow two-lane winding road. Brody pushed the car up to fifty, showing Shay how the car handled the turns.

A half mile later, he pushed it to sixty.

"You're going awfully fast," Shay said.

"I know."

"So slow down."

Brody glanced in the mirror, then looked at her momentarily. "You know those missing characters you were talking about last night?"

"Jesus, just watch where you're driving."

He looked in the mirror again. "Well, we've just found one," he said. "Or, I should say, he's found us."

Shay Falan spun around. It was the blue Crown Vic, only five yards from their bumper now. Brody could see the Turk, his face swollen and bruised, a smoke hanging from his lip. Brody caught the glare of metal, a handgun pressed between the Turk's hand and the top of the steering wheel.

"LoJack," Brody said.

"No, it's that guy," she insisted.

"No, he must have located us with the LoJack."

"What the hell is that?" she said, her voice increasing in volume now.

"Anti-theft device to recover stolen cars. Haven't you heard the commercials?"

"I'm a New Yorker," she said. "I hardly drive."

The Crown Vic made a move around him on the left, but Brody cut him off. The Turk tried the move on the right, Brody swerved over, cutting the Vic off again. The Mercedes barely swayed, solid in the turns.

Brody saw a sweeping downhill curve ahead, a small guardrail on the left, a scenic lookout beyond.

He didn't look at Shay now. "Hold on."

He pushed the accelerator another inch, taking the Benz up to seventy into the turn, then seventy-five.

The Turk made his move again on the left.

This time, Brody let him have the lane, then pressed the accelerator to the floor. Holding it there.

Shay shouted, "Christ, he's coming, and he's got a gun."

"He'll never make it."

She screamed, "How the hell do you know?"

Brody said, "I've got ESP."

When the Vic's right wheels left the ground, the Ford achieved some serious hang time. It looked like a big blue glider trying to get airborne for about fifty yards, then it spun over.

Brody hit the brakes just before the Vic tumbled into the guardrail, then over, down the mountainside. He stopped the car on the berm.

"Nothing but the best for the best," Brody said.

"What?" Shay demanded.

"Electronic Stability Program," he said.

Shay Falan bolted out of the passenger door, shouting some serious profanity into the picturesque countryside.

He let her walk it off.

A couple minutes later she poked her head into his window. She started to say something, but he reached up and touched a finger to her lips.

He offered her the car phone. "You want to report this?" he asked. "Or, should we wait a while and get a little morally compromised."

She tossed the phone away into the interior and grabbed him by the shoulders. First she kissed him. Then she shook him like an angry schoolteacher.

"You're playing football," she said. "Or, we are finished."

"Why's that?" he asked.

Shay Falan said, "Because you're one hell of a lot safer on the field."

· A NOTE ON THE TYPE ·

The typeface used in this book, Transitional, is a digitized version of Fairfield, which was designed in 1937–40 by artist Rudolph Ruzicka (1883–1978), on a commission from Linotype. The assignment was the occasion for a well-known essay in the form of a letter from W. A. Dwiggins to Ruzicka, in response to the latter's request for advice. Dwiggins, who had recently designed Electra and Caledonia, relates that he would start by making very large-scale drawings (10 and 64 times the size you are reading) and having test cuttings made, which were used to print on a variety of papers. "By looking at all these for two or three days I get an idea of how to go forward—or, if the result is a dud, how to start over again." At this stage he took parts of letters that satisfied him and made cardboard cutouts, which he then used to assemble other letters. This "template" method anticipated one that many contemporary computer type designers use.

Animal Habitats

The Crab on the Seashore

Text by Jennifer Coldrey

Photographs by
Oxford Scientific Films

Gareth Stevens Publishing
Milwaukee

Where crabs live

Crabs can be found on rocky, sandy, or muddy seashores all over the world. It is not always easy to see them during the day, because they come out to feed and move around mainly at night. Crabs have many enemies on the seashore, both in the sea and on the land. During daylight hours, and especially when the tide goes out, they need to hide for safety. The seashore is a difficult place to live because the plants and animals get battered about by the wind and waves as the tide comes in and out. But, in spite of all the dangers, crabs survive quite well in this *habitat*, as we shall see.

A rocky shore, like the one above, is a good place to look for crabs when the tide is out. Here are plenty of craggy rocks and boulders, some covered with large bunches of seaweed, all ideal places for crabs to hide. Other crabs shelter in rock pools — these may be small and shallow and carpeted with green and pink seaweeds. Or they may be deep, with steep, rocky sides and large masses of kelp and other brown seaweeds growing up from the bottom.

Here is a pool on the lower part of the shore with the tide about to turn. At low tide the sea washes in and out of it continually. Rock pools higher up on the shore get completely cut off from the sea at low tide.

This Common Shore Crab is resting in a shallow rock pool at low tide. Its green coloring makes it look like seaweed.

Many of the shore crabs spend most of their lives in the sea. If they are out of water for too long they cannot breathe properly. So, when the tide goes out and they are left behind on the shore, they hide under stones, in damp crevices in the rocks, or underneath seaweeds. Some find a safe home in rock pools.

This Edible Crab, larger than a Common Shore Crab, hides beneath a stone in a deeper pool.

This Circular Crab is digging itself down backwards into the sand for safety. You can see its body slowly disappearing.

Crabs living on open sandy stretches of the beach have nowhere to hide. So, when the tide goes out, they burrow down into the sand and disappear from view. Only their eyes and the tips of their feelers are left peeping out at the surface.

Burrowing into the wet sand helps a crab to keep its body moist which is important for breathing. It is also a good way to hide from enemies and to escape the battering waves as the tide goes in and out.

Tropical land crabs

On the shores of many tropical countries are crabs which live mainly on the land. They are able to breathe in air and only occasionally venture into the water, although they must return to the sea to lay their eggs.

Red Rock Crabs are found on rocky shores where they shelter in cracks and crevices in the rocks. They are often called "Sally Lightfoot" crabs because they are very nimble on their feet and can cling onto the slippery, wave-washed rocks with amazing skill.

Ghost Crab.

Nimble "Sally Lightfoot" crabs.

This is a male fiddler crab, with one pincer claw much larger than the other.

Ghost Crabs, like this one from Bermuda, live on sandy shores. They dig large burrows in the sand, high up on the beach. They come out at low tide, mainly at night, to search for food on the lower part of the shore.

Fiddler crabs are another sort of land crab, found on muddy shores, bays, estuaries, and in mangrove swamps. They live in burrows between the tides, and come out only at low tide to feed and look for a mate. When the tide comes in, they rush back into their burrows and plug the entrance hole with mud or sand.

The Common Shore Crab has an oval body which can be anything from 1-4" (2.5-10cm) across.

The crab's body

Most crabs have a wide, flat body, covered with a thick, hard shell. The tail end is tucked underneath and the body is divided into segments. Female crabs have a broader and more rounded tail flap than the males do. Sticking out from the sides of the body are five pairs of jointed legs. The front pair of legs is usually much larger than the rest, with pincer-like claws at the ends. These are useful for grasping food as well as attacking enemies. Male crabs are generally bigger and have larger claws than females.

If you look closely at the head of a crab you will see it has two large eyes on the end of stalks. Between the eyes are two pairs of feelers or *antennae*. These are used by the crab to feel things around it, as well as to smell for food in the water and to pick up the scent of other animals nearby. Special hairs on the tips of the legs and on parts of the mouth are also able to smell and taste food.

Just below the mouth are three pairs of small limbs which the crab uses to hold and tear up its food, and to push it into the mouth. These limbs are also used by the crab to clean its eyes and antennae.

Crabs have quite good eyesight, but they have no ears and cannot hear, although they may be able to feel vibrations in the water. They also have a pair of special balancing organs, one at the bottom of each small antenna, which tells them which way up they are.

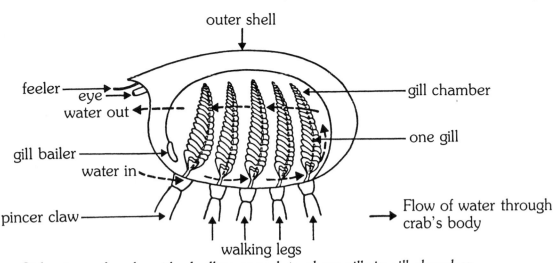

outer shell

feeler

eye

water out

gill bailer

water in

pincer claw

gill chamber

one gill

Flow of water through crab's body

walking legs

Side view of crab, with shell removed, to show gills in gill chamber.

Breathing

Hidden under the shell in a special chamber on each side of the body, are rows of *gills*. Crabs, like fish, breathe by pumping water over their gills, where the oxygen is absorbed and passed into the blood stream. Water is drawn into each gill chamber through a hole near the bottom of the crab's front legs. A special paddle-like limb then drives a current of water round, up and forwards over the gills, until it finally comes out through an opening near the mouth. Special "fringed" hairs around the entrance and also inside the gill chamber filter off sand and other particles so that the gills are kept clean.

This close-up of a Common Shore Crab shows what the head and underside are like.

7

Burrowing crabs circulate the water through their bodies in exactly the opposite direction when they are buried in the sand. They draw in water through an opening near the mouth, which is just above or very close to the surface. This prevents them from sucking in a mass of sand which would soon clog up their gills. Once back on the surface the current is reversed and water is drawn in again through the sides of the body.

The Masked Crab is a burrowing crab which you can find on sandy beaches at very low tide. It is quite small, with a body about 1 inch (2.5cm) across and 1½ inches (4cms) long. It has a very special way of breathing when it is buried. Its second pair of antennae are extremely long; and, as the crab digs itself straight down backwards into the sand, these antennae come together to form a breathing tube (above and left). The rows of hairs on the inside edge of each feeler interlock and keep the tube tightly shut. When the crab is finally buried, only the tip of the tube is left sticking out of the sand. The crab can breathe by drawing in a clear supply of water down the tube and into its mouth, where a fine comb of hairs catches any stray sand grains before the water passes into the gill chambers.

As the Masked Crab (above and left) digs down, backwards, into the sand, its two long antennae lock together to form a breathing tube.

Molting

Crabs are well protected inside their heavy coats of armor, but in order to grow they have to cast off their old outer shell and grow a new one. This is called *molting*. When it is time to molt, the crab takes in a lot of water and its body starts to swell. The old shell splits open across the back and the soft crab underneath hurriedly pulls itself out backwards. It leaves behind the complete empty case, including the transparent eye stalks. A freshly-molted crab has a new and very soft shell and is in great danger of being attacked and eaten by *predators*. It hides for several days while its new shell gradually hardens. Crabs sometimes eat their old shell after they have molted; it contains a lot of lime which is useful for the re-building of a strong new shell. Young crabs molt several times a year, but as they get older crabs molt less often, not usually more than once a year. Some crabs stop molting when they reach a certain size, but others go on growing and molting throughout their lives.

You can sometimes find empty crab cases when you walk along a beach. Here is one left on the rocks of a seashore in Bermuda.

Hermit crabs

Hermit crabs are found in pools or under stones on the lower part of the shore. Unlike other crabs, the back end of their body has a soft outer skin and needs protection, so they find shelter by moving into an empty snail's shell. Small hermit crabs live in periwinkle shells (left), while larger hermits are usually found in whelk shells. The soft body of a hermit crab curves round to one side (usually to the right), and fits well inside the spirally-coiled shell of a sea snail. Two tiny limbs at the tail-end of the body fasten onto the central column inside the shell and this holds the crab firmly in place. Once attached, it is almost impossible to get a hermit crab out of its borrowed home.

Behind its heavily-armored pincers, a hermit crab has two pairs of strong walking legs which it uses to drag itself and its heavy shell along. The final two pairs of walking legs are very small and remain hidden inside the shell, where they help to hold the crab in place.

The heavy, ridged shell of a Common Whelk provides a sturdy home for larger hermit crabs like this one.

Here we see a hermit crab moving from its old shell (behind) to a larger whelk shell (in front). The tail-end of its soft pink body is about to tuck itself into its new home.

A hermit crab can grow and molt inside its shell, but sooner or later, it becomes too big for its home and needs to move. It looks around for a larger shell to move into and, having found one, explores it carefully with its feelers and pincers before deciding to move in. Then it quickly changes shells, moving into the new one tail first.

Hermit crabs are well protected inside their snail shells and often come out to feed in the daytime. If danger threatens, they quickly withdraw into their shells, like turtles, using one of their large pincers to block the entrance. Safe inside their homes, hermit crabs can survive the beating of the waves and being rolled around among the pebbles on a rocky shore.

A Common Shore Crab walking in a pool.

Movement

Most crabs use their long, jointed legs for walking, crawling, or running across the seashore. The heavy pincers are held up off the ground while the crab scuttles along sideways, using its pointed toes to help it grip. Crabs sometimes move backwards, but very rarely forwards.

The last joint on the back legs of the Common Shore Crab is rather flattened, which allows it to swim a little by paddling through the water. Many crabs cannot swim. Large crabs like the Edible Crab and also the hermit crabs crawl around very slowly on the bottom. They cannot chase after fast-moving *prey*, but they are well protected by their heavy armor and do not need to move quickly to escape from danger. Spider crabs have extremely long, spindly legs which are very fragile. They move slowly across the weeds and stones on the bottom of the sea or in rock pools. Larger spider crabs live out at sea and can sometimes be found washed up on the shore.

A small spider crab moves across a stone in a rock pool.

12

The lightly-built swimming crabs (above) move gracefully through the water. Their back legs are flattened and rounded like oars or paddles. As they swim, the hair-fringed paddles move in a figure eight and this propels the crab sideways through the water. Swimming crabs can move extremely fast; they can even catch fish by darting up from the bottom to grab their prey in their pincers. Swimming crabs also use their paddles for digging down into the sand to escape from danger.

Ghost Crabs, like the one below, are among the fastest crabs. They dart across the beach on tip-toe at tremendous speed, their bodies held above the ground. Suddenly they stop, their pale bodies merging with the color of the sand so that they seem to disappear like ghosts.

A Common Shore Crab feeding on another dead crab.

Feeding

Most crabs are *scavengers* and will eat the dead or dying remains of almost any other animal they can find. This may be anything from an injured starfish in a rock pool to a dead seabird lying on the beach — it may even be another crab! Crabs feed in other ways too. Some are predators and will catch and eat small living animals, such as worms, fish, shrimps, barnacles and various types of shellfish. Others, like the spider crabs, eat seaweed and other small creatures which they pluck off the rocks and out of crevices with their long, thin pincers.

This crab is scooping out the tasty insides of a mussel after breaking open its shell.

A Common Shore Crab pokes its pincer inside a brown periwinkle shell to investigate.

Crabs like the Common Shore Crab, the Edible Crab, and the swimming crabs have powerful gripping pincers for catching prey. They break open hard-shelled creatures such as periwinkles, mussels, and limpets. One claw holds on to their prey while the other scoops out the soft body and passes it to the mouth.

Periwinkles are good to eat. This crab crushes the shell of a yellow periwinkle before picking out the soft body and pushing it into its mouth.

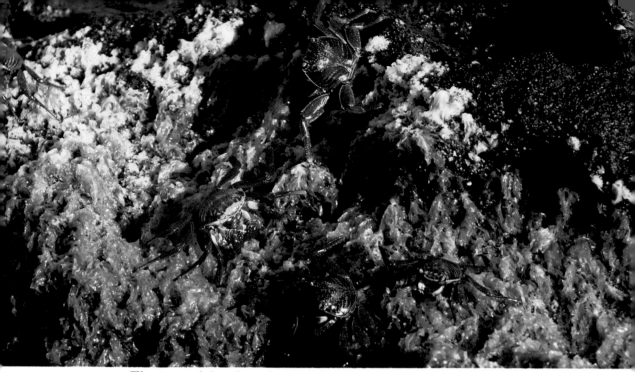

These red land crabs are feeding on seaweed which they scrape off the rocks with their spoon-shaped claws.

Some crabs, including hermits and fiddler crabs, feed by scooping up the mud, sand, or any other bits and pieces lying around them. They pass this up to their mouths where special finger-like feeding-limbs, fringed with hairs, sieve off tiny particles of food. Anything not worth eating is spat out as small round pellets into the sea. This is called filter-feeding.

Fiddler crabs filter food from the muddy shore. Males take twice as long as females to feed, because they can only use their small pincer to scoop up the mud. The larger pincer, which is used in courtship and to defend the crab against other male crabs, is far too heavy to be of any use in feeding.

A male fiddler crab feeding on a muddy shore in Iran.

This Broad-clawed Porcelain Crab catches food from the water with its hairy mouth parts.

Many burrowing crabs are filter-feeders, straining off tiny food particles (including microscopic animals and plants) from the water as it passes into their mouths.

The tiny porcelain crabs are also filter-feeders, but instead of using their broad, spiny pincers to scoop up food, they throw out a sort of hairy net from their mouths into the water. Small pieces of food get trapped in the comb of fine hairs and these are pulled back into the mouth.

A close-up of this Australian porcelain crab shows the hairy comb-like nets fishing for tiny bits of food in the water.

Courtship and mating

Crabs usually live separately, but when it is time to mate, the males and females come together in pairs. In crabs that live in the sea, the females give out a special scent which attracts the males to them. A male often carries a female around beneath him for several days before they mate. As they lie close together, the male passes his *sperm* into the female's body to fertilize her eggs. Mating usually takes place just after the female has molted, when her body is soft. The male may then stay with her for a few more days to protect her while her shell hardens. Some crabs lay their eggs very soon after mating, but others do not do so for several months.

Female crabs lay enormous numbers of eggs which they carry around beneath their bodies in a large round mass. The many thousands of tiny eggs — often bright orange — are held together by a special sticky substance. They become attached to special limbs beneath the mother's body and they are also held in place under the broad flap of her tail. A female crab carrying eggs is said to be "in berry."

A female Common Shore Crab "in berry."

This handsome male fiddler crab from Kenya uses his large pincer to court a female.

Land crabs mate on land, often down their burrows. Before this happens the male crabs court the females with all sorts of wonderful dances and displays. Male fiddler crabs put on an amazing show. They come out onto the shore and wave their enormous, colorful pincer claw (which is about half the weight of their whole body) in the air, while dancing about on the mud. At other times they tap out noises on the ground with their large pincer to attract a female over to their burrow. Although they live on land, female land crabs go into the water occasionally to keep their eggs moist. They also return to the sea when the eggs are ready to hatch.

A female land crab scatters her eggs into the warm shallow water off the Solomon Islands.

Eggs and larvae

Females carry their eggs around for several weeks — sometimes months — before it is time for them to hatch. The mother then releases them into the sea where they hatch almost immediately into tiny crab *larvae*. The larvae, no more than ½mm across, float away into the sea and mingle with the many other tiny free-floating creatures in the *plankton*.

The tiny larvae don't look anything like a crab at first. They have no walking legs, but only two pairs of limbs, with feathery hairs at the tip, which they use for paddling in the water. They have a long, jointed tail, a pair of very large eyes, and several long, sharp spines sticking out from the body. These spines help to keep the larvae afloat in the water, and may also be useful in protecting them from hungry predators.

The crab larvae float about near the surface of the sea, where they feed on other tiny animals and plants in the water. They grow in stages and shed their skins several times as they gradually become more crab-like. At right is a larva 2-3 weeks old, at the last stage of growth before it becomes a crab.

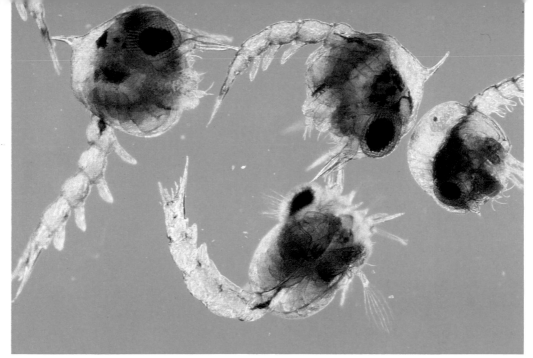

These young crab larvae are only 1mm long. At this early stage they don't look much like their parents.

Approximately ⅛ inch (3-4mm) long, it now has a pair of pincers and four pairs of walking legs, but it still has a tail with paddles underneath to help it swim. After the next molt, a fully-formed but tiny crab appears. Its tail is now tucked under its body and it can no longer swim. It slowly sinks to the bottom of the sea. Very few of the many thousands of larvae manage to survive to become crabs, and most are eaten by fish, jellyfish, and other animals in the sea. Many of the tiny young crabs are eaten too. After sinking to the seabed, they hide for safety under anything they can find.

Now about ⅛ inch (3mm) long, this older larva will soon become a tiny crab.

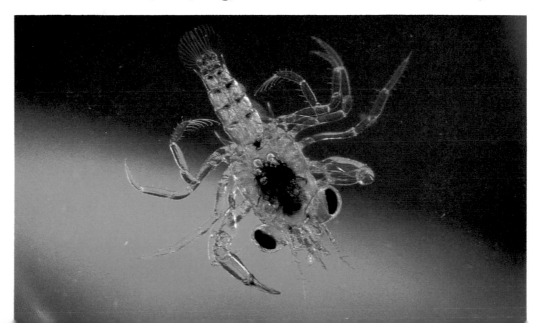

21

This large seagull has caught a crab which was left stranded on the beach.

Predators

Adult crabs have many enemies too. On the seashore they are specially at risk during the day or when the tide is out. Here they may be eaten by shore birds such as the Oystercatcher and various types of seagull. Cormorants and shags dive for them in the shallows around rocky coasts, while herons catch them on mudflats and in estuaries. If you look carefully on a beach you will sometimes find the scattered remains of a crab and the tracks in the sand which tell the story of what happened.

The body of a Red Rock Crab pulled to pieces on a beach in Bermuda.

The footprints in the sand give a clue about the fate of this poor crab.

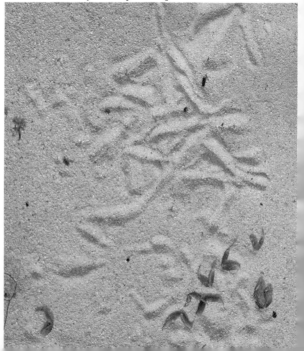

Other enemies may be lurking in the larger rock pools — a small octopus or cuttlefish, perhaps, or even a larger crab. For crabs *do* eat each other and a small or recently-molted crab — or one that is injured — is always in danger of being attacked and eaten by larger crabs. The incoming tide brings other predators: large fishes such as eels, sharks, rays and dogfish, larger octopus, and squid, all of which hunt for crabs in the sea around the coast.

Here a Lesser Octopus is about to pounce on a crab. Octopuses prey on crabs by catching them with their tentacles. They grip the crab with their suckers and pass it down to the mouth, which chews the crab's body with its horny beak.

Crab pots on the seashore.

Human enemies

People also are enemies of the crab. Some of the larger crabs are good to eat and fishermen catch them in special basket-like cages which they lower onto the seabed. A piece of bait tempts the crabs to come into the cages but they cannot climb out again. Fishermen also hunt and collect small shore crabs on the beach to use as bait for catching sea-fish.

Human beings cause further harm to crabs and indeed to all the plants and animals of the seashore when they *pollute* the sea. Oil *pollution* is one of the worst problems. When large amounts of oil, spilled from tankers at sea, get washed ashore on an incoming tide, many plants and animals are smothered and killed (below). Unfortunately, the detergent often used to break up the oil is even more poisonous to sea creatures. Many other harmful things are pumped into the sea by man, including human sewage, radioactive waste, the warm water from power stations, and various chemicals from mines and factories. All of these, if not properly controlled, can damage and kill the wildlife on the seashore.

An oiled beach in southwest England.

Many of these chemicals are taken in by the smaller animals, including some crabs, which filter their food from the sea. The poisons gradually build up inside their bodies, so that larger animals which eat them get a much bigger dose and often die.

Escaping from danger

Life is full of danger for crabs living on the seashore, but there are many ways in which they can protect themselves. Their thick, heavy shells cover them like a suit of armor and they use their strong pincer claws to frighten and attack their enemies. The pincers of a crab have a very powerful grip, as you will know if you have ever been caught by the fingers or toes! Crabs often fight each other and some can be extremely fierce. If threatened, they rear up on their back legs, waving and snapping their pincers as a warning. Other crabs are not so bold. Many small crabs will stop moving when disturbed and lie completely still on their backs until the danger is past. Small Edible Crabs often draw their legs up tightly when this happens, while Common Shore Crabs usually stick them out stiffly.

The Velvet Swimming Crab is very ferocious. This female, carrying eggs, has been disturbed and is waving her pincers to frighten off her attacker.

This Broad-clawed or Hairy Porcelain Crab is hiding upside down in a rock crevice. It is wonderfully camouflaged, and has a thick fringe of hairs around its claws and legs which often gets buried under mud and sand. This helps to hide the crab, as well as holding it firmly.

Many crabs can burrow into the sand to escape from danger and this can be useful when the tide comes in, bringing predators like octopus and squid, or fish like rays which cruise along the bottom looking for food. Some crabs hide under stones, in rock crevices or among seaweed, their flat bodies making it easy for them to creep into narrow spaces. Porcelain crabs are small and flat and ideally suited to living on rocky shores. Their sharply-pointed and spiny legs help them to cling to the rocks when the tide washes over them.

It is hard to recognize this spider crab under its covering of seaweeds.

Most crabs are fairly well *camouflaged*, their colors blending with their surroundings so that they are hard to see. Some are able to change the color of their shells to match the background, and you can find Common Shore Crabs ranging from mottled greenish-brown to pink or yellow. Spider crabs are well known for dressing up in bits and pieces of seaweed, which they stick onto the spiny hairs of their body to disguise themselves.

Crabs have another very unusual way of escaping from danger. If one of their legs is caught by a bird or fish, or even in a battle with another crab, they are able to shed the leg — just like a lizard sheds its tail. This is also useful when crabs get their legs trapped under stones or boulders, which can easily happen when waves crash in on a stony beach or into rock pools. The leg comes off automatically at a special breaking point near the base, and the wound quickly heals over, leaving a small stump. The amazing thing is that the crab later grows another leg to replace the lost one. This starts to form as a small leg-bud, and at the next molt it becomes a complete new leg. It is still smaller than the other legs, but reaches full size after a few more molts. This ability to grow a new part of the body is called *regeneration*.

One of this crab's walking legs has been broken off near the base. Another leg will eventually grow in its place.

Many animals and plants live in this rock pool. Here we can see two sea-anemones, two prawns, a blenny, and some periwinkles, as well as many different kinds of seaweed.

Neighbors and partners

Crabs share their lives with many other animals and plants on the seashore. On rocky shores there are many different types of seaweed, as well as a large variety of animals. Sponges, barnacles, limpets, periwinkles, and many other creatures cling to the rocks and seaweed, while in rock pools we find animals such as starfish, sea-urchins, sea-anemones, small fish like gobies and blennies, as well as prawns and lobsters. On sandy or muddy shores, the close neighbors of crabs include many burrowing worms and shellfish, as well as starfish, shrimps, and various fish.

Many of these animals and plants are food for crabs, as we have seen. Crabs also use the seaweeds for shelter, while some use other animals, like sea-anemones, for their protection. Sea-anemones have stinging tentacles which they use to kill small fish and other prey. Many larger fish and other animals keep well away from them, but some crabs take advantage of this by hiding underneath them. The anemones don't seem to do these crabs any harm. In fact there are some tiny crabs which choose to live among the stinging tentacles of sea-anemones.

A small porcelain crab protects itself by hiding under a green sea-anemone.

Hermit crabs go one stage further and often have one or more sea-anemones living on their shell. This is a very special partnership, as the crab is protected by the anemone, and in return the anemone gets carried around in the water where it finds fresh food and oxygen supplies. It also feeds on many of the crab's leftovers, as hermit crabs are messy eaters when they tear up food with their pincers.

When the hermit crab moves into a new shell the anemone usually goes with it, either moving itself or sometimes being stroked and coaxed by the crab. Sometimes a pink ragworm lives inside the whelk-shell home of the crab where it is safe from enemies. The worm sticks its head out now and again to pick up scraps of food left by the crab. It doesn't seem to be of much use to the hermit, although it does it no harm.

Apart from anemones, crabs often carry other lodgers around with them on their shells, including barnacles, tube-worms, and sponges.

This hermit crab has several animals living on its shell, including a sea-anemone and several white tube-worms.

Life on the seashore

Many of the plants and animals on the seashore are closely linked to each other because of what they eat. We can see this more clearly if we draw a diagram showing exactly what eats what. This is called a food chain. Here is a food chain for the crab on the seashore. Crabs feed on many different things, both animals and plants. The animals feed on even smaller creatures. At the other end of the chain, larger animals like birds and fish eat the crabs.

Some chains are longer than others and some animals are linked to each other by a very complicated pathway. Perhaps you can add some more links to the chain.

Food chain

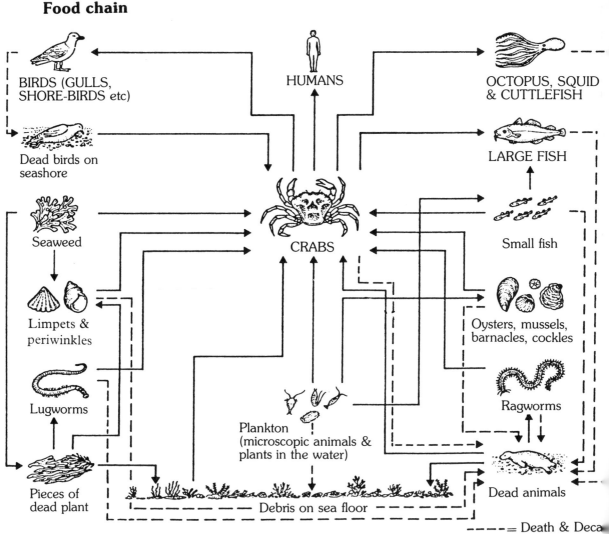

BIRDS (GULLS, SHORE-BIRDS etc)

HUMANS

OCTOPUS, SQUID & CUTTLEFISH

Dead birds on seashore

LARGE FISH

Seaweed

CRABS

Small fish

Limpets & periwinkles

Oysters, mussels, barnacles, cockles

Lugworms

Ragworms

Plankton (microscopic animals & plants in the water)

Pieces of dead plant

Debris on sea floor

Dead animals

---- = Death & Decay

A fiddler crab comes out to feed as the sun goes down.

On the seashore, as in any other habitat, many of the plants and animals depend on each other for survival. Living between the tides is especially difficult and dangerous, as the habitat is constantly changing. The sea comes in and out twice every day and the plants and animals are forever being disturbed as the water surges around them, often churning up the sand and pebbles. They no sooner get used to being covered with seawater for several hours when things change again and they find themselves left high and dry on the beach. Here they are exposed to the weather. In winter it may be much colder out of the water than in, while in summer it may be very hot and sunny and then the animals are in danger of drying out and dying.

Crabs, like many other creatures on the seashore, manage to survive because their lives have become adapted to all these changes and their bodies are well suited to this way of life. Although many of them move out into deeper water during the winter, they are able to live successfully on the seashore during the warmer months of the year.

Glossary

These new words about crabs appear in the text in italics, just as they appear here.

antennae . . . . . . feelers on the crab's head, used for touching, tasting, and smelling.
camouflage . . . . animal disguise; how an animal hides by looking like its surroundings.
gills . . . . special structures on either side of the crab's body, used for breathing (see drawing on page 7).
habitat . . . . the natural home of any plant or animal.
larvae . . . . young forms of certain animals, which hatch from the eggs and are totally unlike their parents. A larva has to change its body several times before it becomes an adult.
molting . . . . shedding an old shell or skin.
plankton . . . . . . small animals and plants which float and drift on the sea.
pollute . . . . to make dirty and therefore damage and spoil.
pollution . . . . . . damage caused to plants, animals, and places, from dirt, rubbish, and poisons left by people.
predators . . . . . . animals that kill and eat other animals.
prey . . . . animal that is hunted and killed by another animal for food.
regeneration . . . growing new parts of the body to replace lost or damaged parts.
scavengers . . . . . animals that feed on the dead or dying remains of other animals.
sperm . . . . (short for spermatozoa) male sex cells.

Reading level analysis: SPACHE 4+, FRY 7, FLESCH 79 (fairly easy), RAYGOR 6, FOG 8, SMOG 3

Library of Congress Cataloging-in-Publication Data

Coldrey, Jennifer.
  The crab on the seashore.

  (Animal habitats)
  Summary: Describes, in text and photographs, the lives of crabs in their natural habitat explaining how they feed, defend themselves, and breed.
  1. Crabs — Juvenile literature. [1. Crabs] I. Oxford Scientific Films. II. Title. III. Series.
  QL444.M33C649   1986   595.3'842   85-30293

ISBN 1-55532-085-6
ISBN 1-55532-060-0 (lib. bdg.)

North American edition first published in 1986 by

Gareth Stevens, Inc.
7221 West Green Tree Road   Milwaukee, Wisconsin 53223, USA

Text copyright © 1986 by Oxford Scientific Films
Photographs copyright © 1986 by Oxford Scientific Films

Conceived, designed, and produced by Belitha Press Ltd., London.

Typeset by Ries Graphics ltd.
Printed in Hong Kong
U.S. Editors: MaryLee Knowlton and Mark J. Sachner
Design: Treld Bicknell
Line Drawings: Lorna Turpin
Scientific Consultants: Gwynne Vevers and David Saintsing

The publishers wish to thank the following for permission to reproduce copyright material: **Oxford Scientific Films Ltd.** for pages 1, 2 *below*, 3 *below*, 4 *above* and *below*, 6, 7, 8 *above* and *below*, 10 *above* and *below*, 11, 12 *above* and *below*, 13 *above*, 14 *above* and *below*, 15 *above*, *below middle* and *right*, 17 *above*, 18, 22 *below right*, 23, 25, 26 *above*, 27, 28 *above* and *below* and 29 (photographer G. I. Bernard), pages 2 *above*, 5 *above right*, and 13 *below* (photographer David Thompson), page 3 *above* (photographer Barrie E. Watts), pages 5 *above left*, 9, 21 *above* and *below* and 22 *below left* (photographer Peter Parks), page 5 *below*, 16 *below*, 26 and 31 (photographer J. A. L. Cooke), page 16 *above* (photographer Godfrey Merlen), page 17 *below* (photographer Rudie H. Kuiter), page 19 (photographer P. & W. Ward), page 20 (photographer Waina Cheng), page 22 *above* (photographer Ronald Templeton), page 24 *above* (photographer R. P. Coldrey), and page 24 *below* (photographer C. M. Perrins). Front and back cover photographer: G. I. Bernard.